The Promise Land

The Promise Land

Dane Bagley

ISBN 978-0-9979576-1-7 (eBook)
ISBN 978-0-9979576-0-0 (paperback)

Cover Design by Ronnell Porter
http://www.wix.com/ronnelldporter/design

Author Photo by Karen Bagley
http://www.karenbagley.com/

For Thomas, Kaylyn, Tyler, and Katie,

with whom I have shared my love and my life's adventure.

Table of Contents

Chapter 1

The people who called themselves, *of Dargaer*, had enjoyed the past five years of peace and prosperity. Never in their lifetime, nor throughout their known history, had this people lived so long without an episode. Their ruler, Drashmaer, was deservedly credited. He had established the sentinels and perfected the weaponry. He had organized the people and had empowered them. Their confidence in him, and in his ways, were no longer bounded.

Drashmaer too began to be swollen with confidence and pride. His people were happy, contented, and safe, and most importantly, completely loyal to him.

It was planned by no one, but rather it came about through the circumstances. Never had their harvest been so abundant. Never had they enjoyed the resources of time, of grain, or of leisure. So, they brewed by the barrelful and had more kegs than any had ever seen before. The work of the harvest was completed and the food was stored—more food than they ever had for the long winter that lie ahead. It may have been carried on the wind through a chain of whispers. Perhaps it was sensed more than heard; but that night many barrels would be cracked, and the contents would be drunk, and temperance would not be known.

Friendliness and good feelings abounded. A wink or a smile, or a cheerful expression emanated from all corners. The people of Dargaer had no concept of a holiday or celebration. It was a luxury to which they had never been permitted, for they had faced nothing but fear over their many years. Finally, they had hope, and they had drink, and they had time, and nothing would be needed for them to do on the morrow. They had no word for it, no clear way to express it verbally to one another, but tonight they would party like no other time in their known history. Everyone felt it and knew it, and twilight was approaching.

"Aye, she's a lovely lass, but she pays ye no never-mind," said Jashion, a handsome young man of seventeen with fair skin and light brown hair.

"Aye, 'tis true, that 'tis. But her pa's got him fourteen kegs and I'd make my way, that-a-way, even though she weren't there, I would" said his freckled red-headed companion, Jarem.

"'That so, eh. Ye ain't even got a mug to drink with," said Jashion.

"I'll cup me hands and drink it like that if I had to. Your comin' with me, ye are ye know."

"Suppose so."

"What we waitin' for, come on."

As they made their way they passed the home of old man Frairmore. He was in his early fifties; he was the oldest man of Dargaer. He was outside his small shack; he smiled brightly as he saw the boys. Frairmore had thinning, straight, grayish-brown hair, and was rather short. If anyone was looking for the wisdom of age, there was no point in stopping here. Frairmore was kind and sociable, but as dim as a mud puddle. How he'd survived the years was anyone's guess.

"Where ye off, me lads?" asked old man Frairmore.

Jashion sunk from the question, but not Jarem. "To Turney's, old man."

"Aye, to Turney's. Aye, good that 'tis. Aye, to Turney's 'tis, good luck to ye lads," he said with a wink and a smile. Frairmore turned in to his shack and the boys continued on.

As they meandered the sun set and outdoor fires began to speckle the ground, while the stars began to speckle the sky. The smell of roasted goose and roasted pig permeated the air as the spits dripped with their juices. Several companions had joined the boys as they made their way to Turney's. The echoes of talk and of laughter grew as the night grew dimmer. First mugs, then bellies were filled with brew.

The boys, six in all, felt starving and thirsty, though they were neither. But the scents, and the sounds, and the mirth were contagious. Their anticipation waxed as they approached.

"I hear it's a whole side o' beef, he's roastin'," said Bagen.

"Lamb, too," said Darron.

"Fourteen kegs!" said Jarem.

"Aye," muttered the throng.

As they approached Turney's their hearts didn't sink and they weren't disappointed. Meat and brew aplenty was there for the taking. Siccly Turney approached them, a long blond and fair skin beauty of seventeen. Even the food and drink were momentarily forgotten as they gazed upon her.

"Where's ye mugs, ye sillies?" she said to no one of the group in particular.

Jarem, the bravest, spoke up, "I'm just cuppin' it with me hands, me will."

"Nay, but ye'll keep ye filthy paws out of the brew, ye will," she said with pleasant sternness. "I'll fetch ye a couple of mugs, I will, but ye'll share, I say," she said turning and moving toward her home. These boy's expectations were already far surpassed.

Singing and dancing began as the hunger and thirst abated. From some distance the guards could hear the echoes of the gaiety. Stalwart had been the guards, never loosing focus of the task at hand. They kept their eyes trained on the sky with their weapons close and ready. Each of the guards, surrounding and protecting the people, had witnessed the death of family, friends, and loved ones. They knew the danger and they kept their eyes focused; but this night they were distracted. The sounds and the aromas led to an acute awareness of the festivities. Though they were well fed before they took their post, they too felt a hunger and a thirst gnaw at them. To a man they felt it, but to a man they kept their guard.

It may have been wives or daughters, girlfriends or chums, but slowly people made their way out to the boundaries—to their favored sentinel, and brought with them the excesses of food and drink. Perhaps they felt their absence, or perhaps they knew that the guard's presence allowed for the celebration, but the sentinels were on their minds.

So the man, eyes steady on the sky, would hear footsteps approaching, and the smell of pork would make his mouth water. Then a loved one, with breath stinking of the brew and eyes wild with delight and drunkenness, would stand next to him.

"Here, ye must have some. It's so very good, and there is so much. Just take a minute, I'll watch the sky with ye. Ye see, all's well, and the sky is quiet. Take some, I'll help ye."

The temptation was too much; so each man slowly lowered his weapon and took his plate. He kept his eye on the sky, but his weapon was down, and his mouth was full, and his stomach began to be satisfied; but then he was thirstier than ever. With time, barrels were rolled out and mugs were brought.

"Nay, I shan't have a drink," they would each say.

"Nay, but ye must have one—just one, now. Ye must wash down the meat. It'll do ye good—keep ye alert. There now, just a mug full, that's it. It's very good, isn't it?"

So, in the wee hours of the night the festivities roared in Dargaer, the guards having lost sight of the sky and forgotten where their weapons lay. Never before had the people of Dargaer celebrated as such.

Off in the distance a creature lay sleeping. With senses of smell and hearing far in excess of the most impressive blood hound, this creature snapped open its fiery red eyes and breathed in deeply and knowingly the odor of Dargaer.

"Ye hadn't e'en a pint, had ye," said Siccly to Jashion.

She had been dancing and frolicking around all night. Yes, she'd been drinking the brew some, but more so she had been drinking in all of the admiration from the many young men milling around her home that night. With most of them sleeping or senseless, she made her way over to Jashion. He'd had his eye on her from afar, but was shy by nature.

"Nay, but Jarem's been hoggin' the mug all night," Jashion replied.

"Aye, 'tis true, that is," she said as she looked over at him to the left.

Jarem was sitting down with a mug full and singing at the top of his lungs. Earlier some music had been playing, but at this point the only sound was a drunken a cappella, for which Jarem had the lead part. They both laughed as they watched him for a few moments. Jashion knew that Jarem would be pleased that Siccly knew of his existence, and that she was paying him some attention. She turned back, smiled brightly, and then began to sway into dancing. Jashion felt a spark of delight as he saw that he had Siccly Turney to himself, and that she seemed to be enjoying herself. He had watched her flit around all night, from one boy to the next, and could see the look in each boy's eye when it was his turn. With most of the boys past the point of conversation, or even standing, it was his turn.

Yes, he may have been the last one standing, but the look in her eyes told him that it was more than just that.

"I's watchin' ye all night, I was," said Siccly sweetly. "I knew that ye'd outlast all these other sillies, I did. I figured once they was out, then I'd have ye to me-self, I did. S'now look, we's dancin' alone, we is."

Jashion's heart began to melt. Jashion was tall and handsome, with just enough bashfulness to be attractive. Siccly had her pick, and she was indicating that she was picking Jashion. What she said to him at this moment was completely true; she felt the conviction of it as she spoke to him. That is how he sensed the sincerity and why his heart began to flutter. But, it was equally true when she had said similar things to the other boys throughout the night. Siccly's emotions and infatuations were a bottomless pit; she had fallen in love over and over again throughout that night—madly, but not deeply in love.

Here she was feeling it for Jashion and, in reality, these feelings had been building for some time. He was not stinking and stumbling with the brew, as the other boys, and this piqued her interest. He was quiet and bashful, but not awkward. He was tall and handsome, and though shy, still, he was self-assured. She had noticed that he was paying attention to her from a distance that night. She had also noticed that he had paid attention to other girls as well. This played well in his favor, for she liked to have all of the attention, and at this moment she had it all.

Was Jashion in love with Siccly? Sure, who wasn't? Siccly knew how to stir the pot such that all of the boys had feelings for her that were simmering, but none were boiling or burnt. He, like the other boys, admired her beauty and was enthralled by her attention, but was not so overcome that he hoped that it would turn into anything real. She was in her own league compared to all of the other girls, but also compared to all of the boys; so, no one considered themselves a match for her. Instead, all of the boys took pleasure in watching any one of them receiving of her flirtations. She was a prize to be sure, but a prize far beyond any of their reach.

So Jashion indulged in allowing his heart to beat faster as he gazed at her beauty at close range, and over a prolonged duration. He could stare because she was watching him stare, and her eyes told him that it was okay—it was what she wanted.

The instrumental music had started back up and her swaying began to take up the rhythm of the song. She reached for Jashion's hand and took it encouragingly. She helped him lead her into a twirl. When their eyes met again she smiled excitedly. Jashion became aware that he was smiling widely. He was experiencing exuberant pleasure in her company, and was expressing it without latent caution.

"Ye'd really hadn't e'en a brew, had ye? Not e'en one?" she said pleasantly trying to start some conversation.

"Nay, not e'en one," he said matter-of-factly.

At this point he would have been happy to take a brew, if that was what she desired. He was not likely to do anything that could have jeopardized his companionship that evening.

Instead she replied, "Aye, well it's for the better, it is. Ye smell better, and ye're not so silly as the rest of 'em. I'm havin' a good time with ye, I am. And your fun e'en without the brew, ye is."

"Aye," he said.

He felt relieved. He had planned on drinking with the boys that night, but every time he had come to that point, he shrank away. He hadn't sworn it off, but he also didn't really want to partake. It may have been because of his father. His father had taken to drinking when his mother was killed in the last attack, five years earlier. On a stormy night, two winters past, his father had been out late. Word was that he had drunk a mighty bit. He had decided to brave the storm, and mounted his horse. Jashion had become accustomed to being left alone at night with his father coming in late and drunk. But the storm was fierce and he was not able to sleep. When the lightning struck and the thunder sounded simultaneously he shot up and looked out the door. He saw his father's horse rise up, but his father was not mounted. The horse was spooked and kept prancing up and down. Jashion ran and saw his father on the ground trampled. The horse took off; he knelt by his father's side. His father tried to speak but was unable to utter any words. The smell of the brew on his breath was his last memory of his living father.

His father died that night and was buried the next day. Jashion was alone, but he worked in the fields and earned his keep. It was not so unusual for a person to be an orphan in the land of Dargaer. It was lucky if the child were old enough to earn their keep. Times were good and Jashion was fine. He was well fed, happy, and no worse off than most anyone he knew.

"I like ye, ye know," said Siccly. They'd been dancing for a little while without speaking. She'd stopped and had leaned in close as she said it. He could smell the brew on her breath, but it was milder than he expected.

"I like ye, too," said Jashion bravely.

"Course ye does, ye silly. All the boys like me, they do. It's only who me likes that counts," she said mirthfully.

She smiled flirtatiously and Jashion blushed. She may have said it in jest, but truer words could not have been spoken. *That silly boy may have noticed the other girls, but I'll have any boy I like*, she thought. *Now, he only has eyes for me, and I'll keep it that way for as long as it pleases me.* Perhaps she would have liked that for some time. The more time she spent with Jashion, the more she liked him. There was something different about him, and he was handsomer than the rest. He required a little effort on her part, and that stood for something too. *Plus, what could a girl do with a silly boy passed out on the ground.*

Speaking of passed out on the ground, that was the state of the sentinels surrounding Dargaer. A large dark silhouette could have been seen crossing the starlit night sky if anyone had been looking—but they were not. The large dark creature with scorching red eyes flew over the barrier of the guards and looked down on the scene it had expected. There would be no warning and the creature would not be in danger. Dromreign would consume, devour, and destroy the fools of Dargaer. Most were so wasted that they wouldn't know what was happening to them.

Dromreign, the fierce black dragon turned its eyes from the guards and then turned its attention to the heart of Dargaer.

Human flesh was a delicacy and the dragon had not feasted like it would that night in quite some time. As Dromreign looked over Dargaer it noticed that each little residence had the after effects of a fire— perhaps some embers, or a little flame. The real fire had not yet begun.

A woman screamed, and it knew that it had been spotted. No matter, the screams were a delight to its ear. Human flesh tasted better when laced with adrenaline. Dromreign roared and belched out a ferocious flame. Already shacks were alight and more screams rung through the air. A larger bon fire caught its eyes; the dragon turned towards it. Dromreign lit up the meager homes that were in its path and headed towards a larger home, with more humans, and a larger fire.

"What's that sound 'n' smell?" ask Siccly scrunching up her nose.

Something was going on but Jashion was in such a trance that it took him a moment to awaken from it. They separated mechanically from each other and began to look around, listening attentively. Another roar shot through the air and Jashion caught the look on Siccly's face. She was stone white and petrified. He looked in the direction that Siccly was looking and caught his first sight of Dromreign. A little fire was still in the dragon's nostrils, and those red eyes penetrated into his soul. With no time to react Siccly was in Dromreign's talons. Dromreign roared in delight and fury as it ignited the Turney's home. Siccly had no ability to scream as her lungs were crushed in its grasp. Siccly would become Dromreign's first meal, with Jashion powerless to oppose the gigantic creature.

The first pass of Dromreign over the Turney's would not be its last. In the next pass, only moments later, it provided an ignominious death to a large group of drunken and passed out partiers, Jarem among that group. Jashion watched in horror and then began to run.

Dromreign saw him running, but elected to ignore him, choosing mass destruction over the chase.

Jashion was filled with horror, disgust, and fright. He ran and hid behind a boulder. He could see and hear some others screaming and running, but it seemed that most were too wasted to move. They, the people of Dargaer, were like sitting ducks. *Where had been the guard? Were they drunk, too?* Jashion was as powerless as Dromreign was powerful. There was nothing he could do to stop the bloodshed and destruction. Dargaer was going up in flames, his people were dying and being devoured. The sounds and smells of horror and violence were all about him, but he could not shake the memory of the worst smell of all. It was smell of Dromreign as the dragon flew right past him and captured Siccly. It was rank, and putrefying, and vulgar. He, unlike anyone else it seemed, had his wits about him, but he regretted it then. He wished that he had the brew to dampen this experience. He had no desire to take in what his eyes, ears, and nose beheld.

Dromreign had devoured his fill of human flesh. But, its appetite for cataclysmic destruction was unquenchable. Jashion collected his thoughts, and saw that the dragon was systematically destroying the homes and the people in its way. It was heading away from Jashion, but at some point, it would be back his way. Jashion had never set foot out of Dargaer, but soon there would be no Dargaer left. He began to run southeasterly out of Dargaer. As he ran past burning homes, and burning flesh, and heard the shrieks and cries, a particular sound caught his ear.

It was someone crying. Though he heard this sound all around, this one was different. It was a little child, and she didn't sound hurt, but rather scared. He couldn't tell where it came from at first, and he was afraid to stop his course. Still, this child was alive and perhaps he could save her. He dared not yell out, but stopped and listened. A small and burning shack behind him and to his right seemed to be the origin of the sound. The roof looked to be on the verge of collapsing. He ran to the shack and ripped opened the door. A little girl, about six years of age, was crouched and huddled on the ground. He could not see any others inside. The child was wearing nothing but a white night gown, and held a little doll. She looked his way as he opened the door. Tears were streaming down her cheeks.

"Is ye alone?" he shouted.

She nodded, and continued to cry.

"Shush and get ye here," said Jashion.

The child did not move, but continued to sniffle and gaze up at him. Jashion ran towards her, and she shrieked in fear. He picked her up; she did not resist. The roof would collapse at any moment. He took her and ran towards the door. As they exited the door, the roof did collapse, and he felt the heat on his backside. The child cuddled up to him then, as stiff as could be. In the distance, he could hear Dromreign shriek. The dragon was heading his way. He looked to his right and his left, but did not see anything that could hide him and provide him shelter. He ran on, hoping to find his way out of the city before Dromreign was upon them.

Again, a boulder emerged, and again Jashion hid behind it. The backside of the boulder provided a small caved-in area and Jashion place the girl on the ground in the cavity. She looked up at him with fright, but he shushed her again, and looked up to catch a view. Dromreign could not be far from them.

Indeed, it was not. The beast's red eyes could be seen in the dark, and the dragon was heading his way. He ducked behind the boulder and pushed into the cavity as best he could, pinning the child between him and the rock. His head was down, so that he could not see the dragon fly directly overhead, mere feet from the top of the boulder. But what he did not see he could smell. It was even fowler this time as the scent wafted down upon them. The little girl couldn't take anymore. Between the fear, and the terror she was experiencing, that scent sent her over the edge and she vomited on the spot. Jashion backed away, in part from the vomiting, but also because he wanted to see if Dromreign was returning to where they hid. They would not be protected from its gaze if it came at them from the other direction.

The dragon was nowhere to be seen, but that was even less comforting. The smell of the vomit could not penetrate the foulness of Dromreign. The little girl was finished heaving, and looked at him as though he would punish her.

"Come ye here, is ye done?" he said gently.

She looked at him carefully, and nodded slightly. As she approached he wiped her mouth with the bottom of his shirt. He picked her up and after scanning the area again, took off running. The dragon's screech could be heard some ways off in the distance. He felt a hint of hope that they may make it to the edge of Dargaer.

They reached the edge of the dwellings and began to make the climb up the rocks to where the guards should have been. Sure enough, the guards were there sleeping in a drunken slumber.

"Wake ye, ye fools!" he said as he kicked a guard in the back. His arm muscles were burning with the weight of the girl, and his anger knew no bounds. He continued to scream and kick the bodies that he saw, but there was no hope of arousal.

"Can ye walk, me arms tired?" he asked the girl.

She nodded and he began to lighten her to the ground when he noticed her feet—they were bare.

"Aye, ye got no shoes, do ye. Ye can't walk bare-shodden, can ye?"

The brave little girl nodded and he let her go. They walked away in the darkness towards the east. Jashion had no understanding of the land, nor did he have any plan except that he was heading away from Dargaer.

They walked as fast as the little girl's legs could carry her. As they walked she began to sniffle again.

"Ye feet hurtin', isn't they?" he asked kindly.

She shook her head and kept walking ahead. It was true, there was plenty to cry about that night, even without one's feet hurting. Jashion reached his hand down and grabbed hers. She held her doll in her left hand and Jashion's hand in her right.

"Ye a name, don't ye?"

She nodded, but did not offer any words. Jashion had not realized that he hadn't told her his name either. The pair walked for some time in silence. The ground was soft, but occasionally she would step on a stone and he could see her wince. Dawn was slowly approaching; they could see quite a way in front of them. Jashion did not know what he was looking for, but he knew that whatever it was he could not see it. As far as he could see there was nothing ahead.

"I'll carry ye s'more now."

The pretty little girl with long, dark-blond hair looked up at him. Her tear stained cheeks and her bloodshot eyes only began to tell the tale of her night. Her little legs were tired and her feet did hurt. She had never stayed awake through the night and she was exhausted. Jashion lifted her up and cradled her in his arms. His arms and legs were tired too, but seeing that the child fell to slumbering quickly in his arms, he was pleased that he was carrying her.

Off in the distance a wooded area was spotted to his right. In every other direction all he could see were rocks and dirt interspersed with weeds. He hadn't remembered passing a tree. The wooded area broke up the scenery, and provided a destination of sorts. Perhaps it was the burning of his arm muscles or the hope of a spring of water, but somehow he lengthened his stride as he walked towards the trees.

It was dawn, and though still very early, it appeared to him that he walked in daylight. His mind was on what lay ahead, temporarily suppressing what lie behind. If he had considered it, he would have known that Dromreign did not stay out in the daylight, but rather only appeared with the cloak of darkness.

But perhaps he would not have realized that the path he had chosen was precisely the path that Dromreign would take back to its lair. It wasn't until he heard the fierce shriek of the dragon in the distance, far behind him, that he realized their predicament. He and the child were in the open and unprotected. They would be spotted easily from the air. The only hope of a place to hide were the woods ahead.

With the sound of the shriek he began to run towards the woods. The second shriek, heard only moments later, indicated the speed of Dromreign—it was gaining on them quickly. Had they been seen? If so, even the woods could provide no protection. Dromreign would turn them into a heap of ashes in no time. Jashion's only hope would be to reach the woods before they were noticed. But they were alone, and Dromreign could track them by their scent. *Was he following that scent now? Would he follow it to the woods, and then scorch it anyway?* Jashion's heart pounded with his exertion, fatigue, adrenaline, and fear.

Further screeches from the dragon were louder than ever. It was fast approaching. The woods were closer too, but perhaps not close enough. The child's eyes opened with a penetrating scream from Dromreign. Jashion felt that they had been seen, but with nothing else to hope for he raced for the woods. The girl began to tremble in his arms and her body tightened. She did not make a sound; she was petrified. The next shriek brought chills to his spine and the hair on the back of his neck stood up. He was so close to the woods; was it any use? He passed the first outlying tree, and headed towards the more densely wooded area further in. He did not stop nor look around, but kept going towards the darkness ahead. Fallen tree limbs began to crack under his footsteps, and his running slowed. He dared a look over his shoulder, but saw nothing. The screech told him that Dromreign was nearly to the woods.

As Jashion turned his head to look ahead, a sharp burning began on his right leg. He had scraped it on the sharp edge of a rock. It forced him to slow to a stop. The pain was intense and his already exhausted body wanted to just collapse in a heap. But the child was in his arms, so he forced himself to drop to his knees slowly. He laid the girl in front of him and then going to a sitting position, reached for his right leg. Already his pant leg was soaked in blood, and the warm and sticky sensation of blood on his hands unnerved him. The girl had not noticed his leg as she was looking up and to the northwest, the direction where she heard the shrieks.

A shadow approached the ground near them. Jashion looked away from his leg and over at the girl. Her widened eyes told him what she beheld. Dromreign was nearly above them and she had a clear image. He had seen this same expression, just hours earlier, on the face of Siccly. The reminder sickened him and his heart sank. Not wanting to look, but not able to keep himself from doing so, he gazed up at the sky. Though hidden somewhat through the foliage, Dromreign was passing overhead. Jashion looked down at the child and put his blood-stained finger to his lips.

She would have screamed, and if she had they would have been finished. Dromreign's eyes were burning in the sunlight, and its dark-adapted eyes saw poorly in the day, anyway. If it had been tracking them, it could have followed their scent. But its nostrils were so full of the scent of human from its recent conquest that the trickle of scent from these two had not triggered an arousal. Dromreign's belly was full, and its only desire was to return to its cave and sleep contently. Still, its keen ears would have heard her scream, and it would not have let them be. The dragon would have burned down this section of the forest, rather than let them live.

As the dragon passed by, its vulgar scent permeated the air. The two companions had been holding their breath. When the immediacy of their vulnerability was past they both let out their breath and panted heavily. Fear, fatigue, and for Jashion, pain, mingled with the rotten scent of Dromreign made it impossible for them to feel safe, secure, and pleased for having escaped. The little child, sleep deprived, hungry, cold, aching feet, began to sniffle again. She did not have the strength to turn it into a full cry. Jashion winced in pain. He worried that his escape from Dromreign may only lead to his bleeding to death.

The little child looked over at Jashion's leg.

"Ye's bleedin'," she said.

"Aye," he said, feeling faint and lying down.

She stood and walked over to his other side to have a better look. She crouched down and looked for a few moments.

"Ye need a bandage, ye does."

The cut was about mid-cafe on the right side of his right leg. The pants kept them from having a good look at it.

Jashion began to think. He did need to do something about his leg. He tried to roll up his pant leg, but it was so blood soaked that he could not. A sharp edge rock was in sight.

"Fetch me the rock, will ye," he said to the girl.

She hopped over quickly and brought it to him. It took some time as he worked at cutting the pant leg off just below the knee. The girl watched him for a bit, and then stood up and walked around the area some. She then came back and crouched near him again, and watched.

"Me's Jemma," she said.

Jashion stopped for a moment and looked at her with a smile.

"Glad to know ye, Jemma," he said kindly and then went back to work.

"Who's ye?" she asked.

"Oh, Me's Jashion."

She nodded, and then sat down beside him. He stole another look at her face, and saw the sheer exhaustion. She needed sleep, food, better clothing or a blanket, and shoes. He had none, and needed to take care of himself. But she sat patiently and did not complain.

Finally, he was able to get through the material, and after removing his right shoe, he gently pulled down the lower pant leg and removed it, exposing the wound. Jemma pulled up to her knees and leaned over for a good look. It was a deep gash, but bled less than would have been typical owing to his extreme sympathetic response to all of the trauma. Warriors often survive deep cuts because of their blood being brought deeper into their tissues because of their bodies autonomic response to excitement or danger.

Jemma grabbed the pant leg and began to wander off.

"Where ye goin' wi' that?" he asked.

"Me's goin' to wash it."

Jashion had been so preoccupied that he had not noticed the stream nearby. Jemma was gone for some time. He began to be concerned, but he was in no position to get up. He thought of calling to her, but worried about making too much noise. He lay back, filled with fatigue, and closed his eyes.

The next thing he knew, he felt moist coolness on his aching leg. He opened his eyes and realized that he had drifted into sleep. Jemma was by his side and was attempting to clean his wound with the washed pant leg. He watched her for a few minutes. It was painful, and she was so little, but he let her to her work. Again, he closed his eyes, and again he was awoken by the same sensation. This time he did not open his eyes, but rather drifted off again.

In reality, Jemma cleaned and washed the pant leg over ten times in the stream. The bleeding had not stopped, but it had slowed. Finally, she sat next to him and just held the makeshift bandage on his leg. He snored peacefully. She saw that the bandage was not being filled with blood, and so she let it stay there. Jemma was glad to help this young man, who she knew had saved her life. She was, however, famished. She was also cold. Her feet had spent a lot of time in the cool stream. It felt good on her feet at first, but then she was having a hard time staying warm. Food, a fire, and a place to lay her head were all that she wanted. She saw her doll, and tried to turn the dolls belly into a pillow. It was uncomfortable, and she was so cold. So, she walked back over to Jashion. Jemma could feel his body heat on her feet as she stood next to him. She lay down close and rested her head on his shoulder. Jashion did not move, but rather snored deeply. It was only a matter of moments and Jemma was snoring softly as well.

This wooded area was indeed the only place on the path from Dargaer to the lair of Dromreign that was safe from the attack of the dragon. If they had not made it to the woods they would not have survived. This wooded area, however, was not a place of safety—far from it.

Chapter 2

Aiden's arrival was never inconsequential. The maidens could not help but steal a look as he walked by. He was tall, with thick, dark hair that came down just past his shoulders. His muscular build was accentuated when he came home from the hunt—he was shirtless and the sweat made his upper body glisten in the waning sunlight. Though just eighteen, Aiden had begun to lead the hunting expeditions. He arrived first and strode in confidently caring prized game behind his back. The other men followed in the pecking order, each carrying the spoils of the hunt. No one was hurt, everyone was happy, and meat there was aplenty.

Aiden's mother heard the calls, recognized his voice, but did not leave the hut. She was preparing the meal as Aiden entered the home. He walked in silently and secreted himself towards his mother whose back was towards him. He dropped his game and put his hands around his mother's head covering her eyes with his hands, all in one motion. She knew that was coming, but still it startled her. *How does he do that?* she thought.

"They never see it coming!" he said, smiling confidently. His mother turned around and embraced him warmly but quickly.

"It went well, I see," she said. "Now, hurry and bath. You stink."

"The young ladies don't seem to think so," replied Aiden.

She turned back to her preparations and said, "bath—and get a shirt on."

Aiden's father entered the hut as Aiden turned to leave. He and Aiden nodded respectfully as they walked past each other.

"Sit down, you look tired," she said to her husband. He was tired and thoroughly ready to get off of his feet. He made his way towards a chair near where she was cooking. "It's time that he takes a wife," she said as he sat down.

The man, sitting in the chair that faced the door of the hut, looked out without replying.

"He is the man of the hunt. Who's ever heard of the man of the hunt coming in to his own home and having his mother there to greet him? He must be married and in his own hut." She paused momentarily, but still no reply from her husband. "There are plenty that would marry him. He'd have no trouble at all. He can pick whomever he chooses. I know he's young—too young yet to marry—but he leads all men. I can't see him going on another hunt and returning to sleep in the same hut with his mother and father." She was emphatic as she ended the statement.

Neither she nor her husband had looked at each other. She stared at her preparations and he looked out the door. The man leaned back some in his chair. This time the pause in the conversation lasted several minutes. The stir fry that she was cooking was beginning to sizzle, and the aroma brought on the man's hunger.

"I believe you're right," he finally said. "That boy will not return from another hunt and sleep here."

She appeared vindicated as he turned his head to look at his wife. She was not a woman who wore her emotions superficially. He gazed at her for a moment, but she did not look back at him. He could see other emotions begin to emerge...subtly. Aiden was the youngest of five children, four of which were boys. They were all in huts of their own, and had families. Aiden's departure would mean that an era was over. Her stiff upper lip prevailed.

"You've spoken with him, then?" she said.

"I've spoken with him much over the days of the hunt. I've also listen as he has spoken with others. He is ready to move on. I think that this hunt is his last," he said reflectively.

Again, a pause.

"His last while living here?" she asked.

"Yes."

Another pause.

"Perhaps his last with us at all," he said finally.

The wife looked over at her husband and studied his eyes. He looked back at her unaffected. She turned back to her stir fry, and they left off speaking for some time.

"He has not found one who suits him?" she asked.

"He has not found a hunt that suits him," he said. "He is restless. He seeks game that is not to be found here. He listens at night to the wind in hopes that something bigger may be found. There are bigger things to hunt than can be found here."

A scent of burning entered the air. The man looked over at his wife again. She was staring in front of her, forgetting to stir.

⌘⌘⌘

Jashion and Jemma awoke to the dimmer light of the early evening. The heat of the day had warmed them, but in nearly every other way they were uncomfortable. Jashion was stiff, his leg ached, he was weak with hunger and thirst, and his head was cloudy. When he stirred Jemma had awoken and moved a few feet away from him reflexively. She was in better shape than Jashion, but still not well. She was warm then and she had drunk water in the stream before going to sleep. Still, her feet hurt and she was starving—twenty-four hours with no food was not compatible with her metabolism and the degree of energy she had exerted over the past day.

They spent some minutes sitting on the ground across from each other without looking at one other. Jashion was stretching his right leg, testing it before making any attempt to arise. Independent of the gash, his legs, arms, and back were sore from the events of the night. He had lost some blood and that, combined with his hunger and thirst, kept his mental state in a daze. There were perhaps two hours left of daylight by the looks of it. The forest was nearly quiet, but some sounds were heard. Not the least was the sound of the nearby stream.

"Ye found a stream, didn't ye?" he said, breaking the silence.

"Aye. It's not far, can ye walk?"

"Nay, but I must, I had."

Jashion shifted to a kneeling position and then put his left foot on the ground. The movements sent sharp pains from his gash. He stayed in that position for a few seconds bowing his head down. Jemma hopped up on her tender bare feet and walked over to offer what help she could. With some effort, and in obvious discomfort, Jashion made it to his feet. The stretching sent more pain; as he shifted his weight to the right leg he wondered if he shouldn't just sit back down. But he had no choice. Both he and Jemma would starve right there if he didn't move.

Jemma reached up and grabbed his right hand. She would lead him to the stream and thought that by holding his hand she was taking some of his weight. The two made it slowly toward the stream, stopping frequently. The stream was down a small incline. Jemma could make it up and down easily, but the extra burden was very difficult for Jashion. Finally, he sat down and scooted himself down to the stream. The water was cold and very refreshing. He knelt over the stream and cupped his hands, drinking in as much as he could. Once his thirst was partially abated he sat back and removed his shoe from his right foot. He gently put his right leg into the stream up to his knee. Once the gash was submerged he felt an exceedingly sharp sting. He sat back, closed his eyes, and waited it out. Eventually the stinging stopped and the coolness of the water helped it to feel better.

When he opened his eyes again Jemma was nowhere in sight. Sitting there with his leg in the stream he began to look around. It was getting darker and very shadowy, yet the visibility was still tolerable. As he listened intently he heard occasional rustling of leaves and he would turn his head to look. He did not see anything move. After several minutes, he decided to call out.

"Jemma. Where is ye?"

For several minutes it was still. It felt calm and peaceful. The sound of the rushing water of the stream combined with an occasional bird call contrasted beautifully to the night before. He became psychologically settled enough that he could begin to reflect upon what had happened. Everyone was gone. He had no home. A chill ran up his back as he visualized Siccly being taken. He recalled the fire and the fury. He had watched his friends and companions burn. Currently his life was spared, but he was in a precarious position himself. His only companion was a little child whom he would have to protect and care for. He was injured and had never been away from food, from shelter, and fire.

Jashion's heart was heavy, but his physical hunger began to gnaw at him and awaken him from this dread. His head was finally clear, and he felt some renewal to his strength.

"Jemma. Jemma," he called out again.

This time, from across the stream, he heard more significant rustling of the leaves, and Jemma shortly appeared. She had something in her hands. A large shadow was over the area from which she appeared, and he could not get a good look at her. She began to walk into the stream and over towards him. In her hands was a sprig of red berries.

"Ye hadn't any, had ye?" he called out once he saw what she was carrying.

Jemma stopped in the middle of the stream and looked as though she was about to get a scolding.

"Aye, me's eaten a bunch. These is for ye. There's more, there is." She continued on towards him. She arrived in front of him and looked at him pleadingly.

Jashion beckoned her to come and sit next to him. He was worried that the berries were poisonous. However, explaining that to her didn't make much sense. She had eaten them by the bunches, he could see from the stains on her face, hands, and nightgown. All he would do is frighten her at this point. She handed him the sprig full of berries.

"Thanks. I'll hav'm in a bit. I'm not hungry just yet."

She looked at him in disbelief. *What? Had he eaten while I was gone*, she thought. *And why hadn't he saved any for me?*

Jashion was starving, and they looked good. But if they were both sick what good would that do. He decided to give it a few more minutes to see if they had any ill effect upon her.

"I'll fetch us s'more before it gets dark."

"Nay, but ye'll stay here, ye will. I'll go with ye and we'll fetch 'um together, we will; in just a moment."

Jemma sat obediently but she was very confused. Jashion began to wonder more about her. She seemed to be holding up very well for a youngin' that had just lost everything. He considered asking her about her family and home, but then thought better of it. Like telling her that the berries could be poisonous, what good would come from bringing up all that she had lost? At least she had her personal discomforts to focus her mind away from the tragedy that she had just survived.

After several minutes, some tears began to well up in her eyes. She was looking down at the ground and her arms were around her shins.

"How's ye tummy, Jemma? Is ye tummy hurtin'?" he asked, getting concerned.

She shook her head and then wiped the tears.

"Ye tummy's fine, is it?"

"Aye, me tummy is fine. Me's still hungry, though."

"I'm famished," he said smiling, and she looked at him quizzically again. He began popping the berries in his mouth. They were sweet with just a slight bitterness. The sprig was cleaned off in a moment, not touching his hunger but rather igniting it.

He began to explain to Jemma that sometimes berries can be poisonous and that he was worried about her, that he had to watch her to see if she was fine.

"Me knows that these is not badens. Me saw birds at 'em, Me did. Birds don't go at the badens. Me had these'ns before. These is good, they is," she explained emphatically. In her mind, she could not understand how he thought that she might have brought to him poisonous berries—he was her friend. *Didn't he know that me was taking care of him*, she wondered.

Jashion began to remove his left shoe and to roll up his left pant-leg. He grabbed both shoes in his right hand and put his left leg in the shallow stream. He stood up and reached for Jemma's hand. She hopped up quickly and grabbed his. They made their way across the stream and over towards the berries. It was more shadowy on the other side, as the forest was getting deeper and the sun was setting quickly. The darkness was approaching faster than he liked.

Jemma was pleased when she found the berries and pulled Jashion towards them. Jashion was disappointed at the quantity when he arrived. If he ate every last berry he would only begin to satisfy his hunger, and she was still hungry.

Jemma was not shy as she confronted the bush. She picked and popped the berries ambidextrously. Jashion soon joined in. After just a few minutes they were spending more time searching than eating. He had found more than he had expected but was still hungry. It was rather dark then, and he wasn't sure what to make of their circumstances.

"Did ye find any more berries?" he asked when the bush was picked clean.

She shook her head and said, "Nay." Her upbraided expression concerned Jashion. He was not chiding her; he was just asking. He could tell that she must have been scolded regularly. *She constantly aims to please, and feels so bad if I am not pleased,* he thought.

"Ye did very good Jemma, ye did. I'm so full now, how about ye?"

Her beaming expression and the nodding of her head made him smile. Neither of them could have been full, but they were better than they were and she knew, finally, that she had done right, and that he was pleased.

The moment was broken by a distant howl. They had rested, and felt at peace since early that morning. It was clear that danger still lurked. They were not safe as the night approached. It would not have been far to travel back the way that they had come. They could have easily retraced their steps across the stream and back to where they had slept. They could have left the wooded area and gone back to the path that they had been following out of Dargaer. But Dromreign was still the most pressing danger in their minds. The deeper and denser the forest, the less likely that they could be spotted by the dragon and the safer it seemed to them. They pressed southeast and into the density of the darkening forest.

Twigs snapped and leaves crackled under the weight of their footsteps. Theirs was a symphonic sound contrasted to the silence of the forest. Everything within earshot knew exactly where they were and where they were headed. Jemma winced with pain at times as she stepped. Jashion, more focused on his whereabouts and the direction of his travel than on his companion, finally noticed the discomfort of his fellow traveler.

"Wear ye me shoes, Jemma," he said kindly.

"Nay, but they's too big for me, ye keep 'em," she said. "Me's fine, me is."

Darkness had been creeping in since they had awoken, by then it was enveloping them. The trees were nothing more than darker vertical shadows against the overall darkness. They walked slowly with their hands outstretched in front of them, trying to avoid running into anything in the blackness of the night. Their footsteps and the sound of their own breathing, mingled with an occasional scurrying of a small animal, was all that they had heard for some time. The second wolf howl of the night stopped them in their steps. It was louder and closer than it had been before. They both stood there silently and listened for several minutes.

Again, no sound could be heard and they silently rejoined their journey. The darkness became impenetrable to their eyes. Jashion turned his head and looked around instinctively, trying to glimpse what lie ahead with his peripheral vision. Even that was to no avail. His fingers felt the bark of a large tree in front of him. He stopped and felt around the tree and decided to rest up against it. He sat with his back against the tree as Jemma sat against the same tree on his right.

Neither of the travelers were sleepy, so they sat there with their eyes open and stared into the darkness. In the silence and in the darkness, they searched and listened intensely. After many minutes the sounds of the forest became apparent. Slowly their dark-adapted eyes perceived bits of light. One small patch of the sky was visible and some stars were making their way onto the evening's imagery. In time, they both stared up at this and another smaller patch of visible starlight. Danger did not seem very near. Only the scurrying of small animals could be heard and no longer did wolf howls pierce the silence.

They, however, could not have picked a worse spot to stop for the night. High above them, in the branches of the very tree with which they were resting against the trunk, was an enormous anaconda. The snake, too, was wide awake and silently listening in the dark. It had heard their approach and had sensed their presence as they stopped up against the trunk of its tree. Slowly and silently it was unraveling itself. Its head and tail, both loose, were dangling downward. Inch by inch it moved toward its prey, our travelers unaware.

This beast was well known to the other creatures lurking in the forest. Nothing was so deadly and as dangerous as this giant anaconda. Even the wolves would not enter into its domain. As the snake's extremities neared the ground, it sensed its prey— one small and one large. If it acted carefully it could have both. If one got away it would prefer to have the large one. But the small one would be the easiest to capture.

Jashion felt his leg near the gash. It was very warm— almost hot—swollen and tender. He, very gently, rubbed around the injured area. Since soaking it in the stream it had been tolerable to walk on. Sitting for a while it was becoming painful and he wondered how it would feel to try to walk again. He glanced toward Jemma, though he could scarcely see her outline, and wondered how her feet were holding up. She was indeed rubbing each of her feet with her hands. Jashion heard a branch snap up above him, and the two looked up. Nothing could be seen, and it became instantly quiet again. Then Jemma made a tiny shriek. A rather large insect had begun to crawl up her leg. She began to slap and push at her leg frantically.

"What's it ye're screamin' at?" Jashion asked as he turned and leaned towards her.

"A bug's crawlin' up me leg," she said in a forced quietness.

She was still fussing with her leg, though the insect was gone, as the anaconda's tail began to wrap around her trunk. She assumed that it was Jashion's arm coming around her to comfort her, so she did not turn from it—being glad for the comfort, and of having him close to her. She would have liked to have sat on his lap, and have both of his arms around her at this moment. But the embrace that she was about to receive was much more that she had bargained for. In mere moments, the anaconda had wrapped around her sufficiently to begin to squeeze and to pull her up. She shrieked again, this time violently.

Jashion could tell that she moved, and thought momentarily that the bug was back. He reached towards her, but her body was not there.

"Jemma," he called. There was no reply. The beast had her tight then, such that she had almost no function in her lungs. Jashion felt towards her again and called out more loudly. He stood up slowly such that upon hitting his head on the tree branch above him it did not smart too much.

"Ouch," he said and began to rub his head. He started to walk forward until his nose touched the coiled body of the anaconda wrapped around Jemma. It took him a moment to realize what his face was up against. He could feel that it was scaly and then he felt it move and the muscles tense. He began to beat upon the body of the snake with his fists. He swung again and again, but his blows couldn't break the snakes grip on Jemma. He bent down looking for a stick to jab into the body of the snake.

The snake was pleased, the large one didn't run; it would have both the large and the small prey to feast upon. While Jashion shuffled his hands around on the ground looking for a stick, the snake circled head first around his left leg. A stick was found just as the snake tightened around his leg. The stick and the beatings would be for the part of the snake attacking him, rather than the portion of the anaconda crushing Jemma.

Jashion and his blows were no match for the strength of the anaconda. In short order Jashion was wrapped up in the snake's coil. He fought with whatever limb had movement for as long as he could, but he could not break the grip of the snake, and the pressure was getting tighter. Soon he was having trouble breathing and each breath became shorter. The tightness evolved from pressure to pain, and he felt that his bones would snap in two. His fingers began to scratch and dig into the body of the snake near his hands—it was useless but he was going to give the fight every bit that he could. He began to feel faint from the lack of oxygen and slowly his consciousness began to fade.

Out of the dark another pair of eyes beheld the scene. This traveler had not made a sound and the anaconda had not so much as caught a whiff of his scent. Slowly, silently, ever so carefully an arrow was placed on the bow and the string pulled back. A silent exhale, a pause, and the string was released. For just an instant the anaconda heard the sound before this fierce beast heard no more. The arrow pierced the snake's head from underneath and went straight through its brain. It died instantly, but its massive coiled body was still crushing Jemma and Jashion.

The keen hunter reached behind his head and drew his sword from the scabbard he wore on his back. If he had had a companion, his companion would not have known where Aiden had aimed, or what he had struck—the night black with darkness. But Aiden saw in the blackness what others could not, owing to his synesthesia. He saw the anaconda's head drop, and he knew that it was killed. He raced toward the dead, yet still deadly, beast. Quick, powerful, and sure were the strikes he struck upon the body. He continued to work in near silence until the sound of two coiled heaps hit the ground.

A thud, but no other sound was heard. He went to the larger and unwound the coils. A man, unconscious, injured and weak, but alive, lay in front of him. This man would live, he would save him. Next, he turned his attention to the smaller heap and removed the smaller, tighter coils, revealing the delicate body of a child, a little girl.

Chapter 3

Jashion awoke but did not open his eyes. It was daylight, the sun directly overhead tried to penetrate through his closed eyelids. His head ached something fierce and his body felt bruised, beaten, and swollen all over. He could hear a fire crackling as a slight breeze wafted the scent of smoke to his nostrils. He was alive, he knew not how.

Slowly he opened his eyes and beheld the unfamiliar surroundings. A strikingly handsome, muscularly built young man crouched near the fire with a knife in his hand cutting or carving. The man was positioned with his side facing Jashion and did not show any sign that he was aware of Jashion's arousal. If Jashion had mused that the episode with the anaconda was the fit of a terrible night's dream (perhaps the berries were bad after all), the idea soon left him. For on the ground, skillfully carved in various piles, were the remains of the forty-foot monster. Its skin was beautiful, black with some green and orange in triangular patterns. Jashion stared for some time, his mind recalling the last moments of his consciousness.

Without looking over or pausing in his task the chiseled and dark haired man asked, "Have you decided to join us then?"

Jashion didn't think the man was talking to him. He scanned around as best as he could, in his prostate position, his surroundings, expecting to see someone else being spoken to. There was no one to be seen. The young man worked at his knife and did not turn towards Jashion or show any other awareness of his being. *Is Jemma alright?* He had not yet thought on her. He scanned for the child but saw nothing to indicate her.

"Ye know where's the lil' lass, does ye?"

Aiden continued in his task without acknowledging his voice in either reply or body language for some seconds.

"Where are you from?" Aiden finally returned.

"I's of Dargaer, I is."

Finally, a nod, but still he did not look away from his carving. Silence again, and still no sign of Jemma. He was starting to feel concerned.

"Those from Dargaer talk funny."

Jashion had no idea how to reply. In the brief moments of his acquaintance with this stranger, and in the few words shared, he too had had the same thought; except that he thought it was this stranger who spoke oddly. He pondered for a moment in self-consciousness whether it was *he* that *talked funny.* He talked just like anyone else that he had ever met—he had never met someone from anywhere other than Dargaer.

"Jashion! Ye's waked, ye is," Jemma cried from behind him.

He bent his head back to look in the direction of the voice and smiled brightly. Jemma ran nimbly towards him and crouched beside him. Jemma was still wrapped up in the anaconda. She wore an outfit made of snakeskin including moccasin-like booties, beautifully crafted.

"Is ye hungry? We's eatin' the snake that was eatin' us, we is. It's good, it is." She stood up. "Me got me clothes now. I shan't be so cold," she said as she twirled slightly showing off her beautiful adornment. She seemed rather well for all that she had been through, and considering the condition that Jashion was in.

Jashion tried to sit up, but did so with extreme stiffness and discomfort.

"Careful there, you're not well."

He stayed there in a half sitting position propped up on his elbows. Aiden made his way over to him with a portion of the snake on a stick, piping hot from the fire.

"Give it a moment to cool, or you'll burn your hands and mouth," he said as he jabbed the other end of the stick into the ground near Jashion, dangling the meat within easy grasp of his hands. "Your leg is bad. I've dressed it this morning, but it needs more attention. I've not yet found just the right herbs for it. I'll take a better look shortly."

"Jemma is well, she is. I's worried she mightn't made it, I was."

Aiden looked him in the eyes for the first time. What a presence. Aiden's glance was both terrifying and comforting—being filled with power and confidence. "Is she your little sister?"

"Nay, but I knowest not her kin. We escaped together from Dargaer—from the terror of Dromreign, we did."

Aiden didn't seem impressed. He put the back of his hand onto Jashion's forehead. "You've a fever. It's getting worse." He took another look at Jashion's gash. "Some food will do you good."

Jashion realized that the aching he felt over his body was not entirely due to the squeezing he had received. He was sick and his body was experiencing malaise. Still, the fever didn't account for all his body's ache.

"The little one was wrapped up in the tail end of the snake. It had all of its attention on you. It was just holding her—saving her for later. She was unconscious, but awakened just a few moments after I cut her free. She's tough, that little one is."

Aiden sat beside Jashion and reached for the meat. He broke off a bit and handed it to Jashion. Jashion, strangely, did not feel particularly hungry, but he knew that his body was weak and famished. The snake tasted surprisingly good. He took small bites at first. As he ate he began to feel the sensation of hunger. In time the piece of snake was gone, he hoped that more would be forthcoming. Aiden sat beside him as he ate without saying a word. Jashion had been preoccupied with his meal, but then he looked again at Aiden.

"Did you actually see the dragon?" Aiden asked.

"Aye. It's the wickedest, foulest creature me's seen."

"That's saying something considering what I just rescued you from."

"Aye. But I never saw'st this'n until it were dead just now. It had me before I knew what to think."

"The legend of that dragon has been carried far and wide. I admit, I did not believe it to be true. There are beasts in this part of the world unlike anything where I'm from."

Aiden stood up and walked back to the fire. He brought back another piece of meat. "Don't eat more than this for now. I'm not sure if you'll be able to keep even this much down. I'll be back as soon as I can. You need treatment; I'll see what I can find."

Aiden disappeared silently into the forest, and for some time Jashion was alone. He finished his food and then lay back down. He tried to move his position to comfort himself, but it was no use. He began to feel nausea and worried that he may lose his meal. He could feel the fever burning his temples. He moved his forearm to block the brightness of the sun. Discomfort, sickness, and aching were all he was aware of for some time. After a while Jemma reappeared. She chattered pleasantly for what seemed like hours. He was unable to listen or even acknowledge her. He heard and understood almost nothing. She didn't seem to mind or even be aware of his state. She was happy to be alive, to be clothed, to be fed, and she was glad to have someone to talk to. Jashion looked in her general direction—the most that he could contribute to the conversation.

"Ye's really sick, ye is," she said looking directly at him. Jashion nodded as best he could. "That man'll fix ye, he will."

Jashion tried to nod again, but was startled by the figure towering over him. Jemma turned around, looked up, and jumped.

"Ye scared me, ye did," she said to Aiden.

Aiden sat down by Jashion's gash and began to chew the leaves of some herbs in his hand. Slowly he placed the masticated green mush onto Jashion's wound. It stung, but Jashion didn't argue. After dressing the wound, he left again returning a few minutes later. This time he brought a whittled cup filled with water. He placed the cup on the ground and took some bark and began to scrape the back of it into a fine whitish powder. He placed the powder into the cup and stirred it with his finger.

"Drink this," he said handing him the cup.

Jashion sat up some, feeling much worse being supine. The water was cloudy. He took a small sip and wrinkled up his face. "Ugh...'tis nasty, it is. It's bitter—really bitter."

"Drink it up. Drink all of it," Aiden said and got up.

About half an hour later Jashion felt much better, the bitter taste still lingered in his mouth.

"I will take my sleep now while it is still light. I've not sleep since the night before last. Neither my body nor my mind will be worth much tonight against whatever beasts come our way, if I don't get some sleep. Call out if there is a problem."

"What'd we call ye," asked Jemma.

"Aiden."

"Aye, Aiden it is."

With that he lay down near the fire and seemed to be in sound sleep instantly. Jashion ventured to arise and walk around a little. The gash hurt more than anything, but his back was also very sore. His neck had a crick and his arms were bruised. Jemma had wandered off again; he missed her chatter. The forest was very dense where they camped. He looked at the sky and figured that it was mid-afternoon. It was a beautiful day—sunny, blue sky with a few wispy clouds and a temperature around 67 degrees Fahrenheit. As his eyes wandered to the southeast he noticed that the sky was broken with the face of a cliff towering high above the trees. It was very far away, yet seemed ominous once he had noticed it. For some time, he stared at what he could see of it through the density of the foliage of the forest.

Aiden slept peacefully until dusk when he seemed to waken and arise instantly. Jashion and Jemma were sitting near him and the fire. The safety of the day was disappearing and subconsciously they both wondered what hideous beast lay waiting to cause this night's terror. Aiden was their only protection; though he had been sleeping they huddled as closely to him as they could, trying not to disturb his slumber. His arousal brought comfort to them.

Without saying a word, he cut several pieces of meat and placed them on a large stone he had put into the fire pit. Jemma had ensured that the fire continued to be strong. Aiden felt Jashion's forehead. "The fever's returning."

He retrieved the cup and began to prepare the potion again. This Jashion both welcomed and dreaded. While Jashion choked it down and while the meat cooked, Aiden re-dressed his wound with the same herbs. It did feel less tender this time. The three then shared the meal in silence as the darkness began to cover them. The howling of wolves unnerved Jashion as it pierced the silence. Aiden was fully alert. This sound was the first thing that seemed to call his mind to attention.

"They are closer tonight," Aiden said.

They were closer. The trio had survived the anaconda. They set up camp in its lair and burned and devoured its flesh. They stayed in this forest that was not meant to have mankind within it. The wolves knew that this was not right. But their primal instincts suggested who the hunter was, and who the prey. There was a mighty hunter in these woods, and they were not sure if they were as mighty as he. Yet still, they howled and drew in closer. Even a mighty hunter had weaknesses. He must sleep. He couldn't see as well in the dark as they could, could he? He could be spooked, and they had the advantage of numbers. But the mighty anaconda, the one that even they feared, lay dead at his feet, and filled his stomach. The whole of the night both they, the wolves, and he, the hunter, would not see each other; but neither thought of anything else. A battle was brewing, yet it was quiet and no fighting had begun.

Jashion and Jemma drifted to sleep as soon as their hearts were settled. They slept the whole of the night peacefully. Aiden barely blinked. At dawn, more meat was cooking when the two awoke. They ate in silence again. Aiden again dressed Jashion's wound and declared that he was fever free.

"It is not safe here, and you need medicine that I cannot provide you. We need to leave today, but I must sleep some hours this morning. We will eat lunch and leave. I think that you can travel now." Aiden lay down and was instantly asleep.

Jashion and Jemma felt better physically after a full night's sleep, but they were discomforted internally. Aiden, who was a pillar of power and strength, seemed concerned. The look in his eyes and the sounds of his words were different than they had been the day before. They looked at him sleep and then looked at each other. Jemma arose first and put as large of a log as she could carry on the fire, sending embers and smoke into the air. The fire cracked and then they heard another crack, this time in the woods.

They both turned and looked. Standing in full view, no more than twenty yards away, was a large grey-brown wolf. It stared at them, but did not move.

"Aiden," shrieked Jemma instinctively.

Aiden was up, knife in hand, standing near Jemma before she could finish his name. He stared at the beautiful but daunting creature in front of him. Neither he nor the wolf blinked. Aiden listened and watched. The wolf appeared to be alone. Why had it waited for daylight to approach? It looked old and majestic. Perhaps it had a death wish, and preferred to be taken down by a mighty hunter rather than die of natural causes. Perhaps this wolf had something to prove—could it take down the mighty hunter alone? Perhaps it was scouting the camp and the circumstances. It began to look around and fixed its eyes on the anaconda in heaps upon the ground. The wolf turned its stare back onto Aiden. It looked him up and down and then slowly turned away and disappeared back into the forest. Perhaps, and most likely, the wolf came to deliver a warning. These campers would not stay another night here without the wolves upon them. The humans might prevail, the wolves may prevail, but one way or another if they stayed longer there would be a battle.

The three continued to watch where the wolf disappeared. Aiden's eyes and ears keenly scanned the forest. He heard no further sound.

"We must leave now," Aiden told them. Sleep would have to wait for another day.

They packed a little food and Aiden gathered his things, and they were off. They did not return the way that Jashion and Jemma had entered. For a little while the forest became denser, but then it began to clear. Jashion and Jemma were happy to follow Aiden's lead. Periodically they would stop and Aiden would listen. Then they would start up again. There was almost nothing spoken amongst them. Occasionally, Aiden would quietly whisper that they needed to watch their step, to not crackle the leaves, or snap the twigs. If they did make a sound, he would shoot them a glance. Both Jashion and Jemma were much more conscious of the sounds that they made as they traveled this time.

A stream came into view and they all stopped for a drink. Aiden looked around and then stooped down by Jashion. He unpacked the herbs and dressed Jashion's wound again.

"How's it feel?" he asked quietly.

"Better, it is—still achin' it is, though."

All of a sudden, Aiden was at attention. He looked across the stream and slowly pulled his bow into position. Jashion and Jemma froze with their hearts pounding. Aiden fit an arrow and slowly drew the string. Neither Jashion nor Jemma could see or hear anything. Aiden was as still as a statue. Then they heard a noise across the stream and the arrow released simultaneously. It struck and something squealed. Aiden took off and splashed across the stream. He disappeared where the arrow had gone.

Jashion and Jemma, still hearts pounding, looked over at each other in awe. Moments later Aiden was visible again. He was smiling and carrying an animal over his shoulder. He made his way to the other side and dropped a small wild hog onto the ground near the feet of Jemma. She looked at it and then back up at Aiden.

"This is good meat—better than snake. The wolves know which direction we're heading, but they stopped pursuing us some time ago. I think that we can stop and eat now. We will be safely out of the forest soon."

This news brought comfort to his fellow travelers. Aiden had a fire roaring in no time; the pig was butchered with more than enough meat roasting.

"How's it ye know how to do so much, ye isn't much older than meself, ye isn't?"

Aiden seemed to ignore the question as he made his way to the stream. He washed his hands and his knife and then walked over toward Jashion and the fire. Jashion looked up at him just as Aiden threw his knife towards him. Jashion jumped as the knife stuck, six inches from his thigh, in the ground where Jashion was sitting.

"I choose, and then I do," said Aiden. "We have plenty of meat for now, but you carve some up. Have you butchered meat before?"

"Nay, but I haven't. Why'd ye threw it at me?"

"Go ahead, give it a go."

"Nay, ye know how, and I knowest not how to do it."

"That is how I know how to do so much. I choose and then I do. I see the skills that men have, and then I do them until I equal their skill, or surpass them. I always choose to learn and then to do. I have a strong mind, a strong body, and keen senses. But I would not be as I am, except that I choose to do well at everything. A man can choose comfort, pleasure, relaxation, or laziness. He may enjoy his life in this way. But if he wants to be skilled, to be honored, to be feared, to be respected, then he must choose to do, and do well. This is my secret."

Jashion looked away, pondering.

"Have I just satisfied your curiosity, or do you too wish to become a man of skill and renown?"

"I'd like to acquire these skills, I would. But I shan't never be like ye."

"Pick up the knife and carve. You saw me do it. You were paying attention. You know the secret: you chose and then you do. Most men never do. They prefer to wish for things they do not have, but do nothing about them."

Jashion reluctantly pulled the knife from the ground and attempted some cutting—hacking really. Aiden ignored him, and walked off with Jemma. They returned shortly with some berries. Jemma's face was beaming.

"Me's the one that found these. Aiden say's that Me's great at findin' berries." She looked up at Aiden and he smiled and nodded reassuringly.

Jashion gave up carving as the food was ready, and the three ate and were on their way. Soon after they crossed the stream they could see the edge of the forest. It was flat and barren beyond the forest's edge; similar to the way when they had traveled to the forest from Dargaer.

As they passed the final tree, Aiden spoke, "We are heading to the land of the medicine people, the Tengeer's. They will provide you with the herbs you need for a complete healing. This may be a place to your liking. You may choose to live among them. Either way, we should find a home for Jemma. She is not your kin. She needs a mother to look after her."

Jashion nodded. He was still thinking about the things that Aiden had told him before—Aiden's secret. They walked in silence for a long while. In front of them was nothing but a barren land.

"Look behind you," Aiden said.

They all stopped and looked. The tree tops looked much shorter then. High above them was the cliff top. It reached up to the clouds. Jashion and Jemma looked up in awe.

"It is said that a promise land is on the other side of that mountain. If you follow the mountains to the right, and you see where it ends, it actually heads back further. You can't see it from here. If you follow that side of the mountain for some time you reach where I am from."

Jashion had many questions, but he would wait. He was tired, his leg hurt, and he was still pondering other matters. They turned and carried on in their journey, not stopping until they reached a little oasis in the early evening. At the oasis they stopped for the night. There was some water to quench their extreme thirst. They ate the left-over meat that they had brought, and Jashion's wound was re-dressed. Aiden, exhausted, lay down and slept before the sun had gone down. Jashion and Jemma followed shortly thereafter. They sensed no danger from Aiden's expressions. Jashion was tired, but he was not sleepy. He kept wondering about the powerful secret that Aiden had shared. The power was within him to be who, what, or how he would choose to be. He simply had to choose and then do. But making the right choices and then following through was no easy matter. Still, his life had been spared—why waste it?

The sound of sniffles drew his attention back to where he was. Jemma was softly crying. The poor child had been either fleeing or fearing for her life since he met her. Tonight, she was safe—truly safe, and she had time herself to reflect. She heard Aiden mention that she needed a mother—a caretaker for her.

Reality must be setting in. She had lost what family she had for good. She had escaped and survived. Soon, she would be turned over to who knows who. Jashion felt the pang himself and made his way over to the child.

"Now then, I's here," he said as he put his hand on her shoulder. She looked up at him and tried to stifle her tears. This only made her breath uneasily and lessened her control. "Nay, but ye let it out, ye will. I'm here with ye. Ye've earned a good cry, ye have."

With that Jashion lay down near her and she put her head on his shoulder, showering his shoulder with tears until they were both sound asleep.

The morning brought another journey. They had no food left over, so Aiden caught some fish and they breakfasted upon that. It was just after noon when they neared the village of Tengeer. For some time, there was a scent—a sweet but burning scent—that grew stronger as they approached. Slowly the ground had become less barren once they left the oasis. By the time they had arrived they were used to seeing trees, and bushes, and weeds. The ground had become blacker and softer. Tengeer was a rich land of growth.

"I want to use ye secret, I do. I do want to choose and do, but I don't know what to choose. It seems as there is so many things to choose, and where do I begin?"

Aiden did not answer immediately, but Jashion was used to this by then; he waited patiently for his reply.

"I'd start with your speech. It makes you sound stupid. I know that it is how you and your people speak. I have traveled far and wide, and most people don't speak as you do. You don't want to have everyone's first impression be that you are stupid and ignorant. I don't think these things of you. Quite the contrary; I'm as impressed with you as I am anyone I have ever met. I mean it for your own good."

This suggestion hurt Jashion some. The compliment, however, softened the blow. "How do I know what to say—what am I sayin' that's wrong?"

"Listen carefully to everyone. I'll help ye, I will," Aiden said sarcastically and with a smile. Jashion thought for a moment and then he understood his first lesson. Even Jemma smiled as she looked up at her two protectors.

Jashion was surprised to see the homes and the people so unprotected. There were no sentinels standing guard. The homes were in plain view. They must be so exposed to an attack of Dromreign. The dragon could see them from the sky and could destroy them so easily.

As they walked toward the village the people were calm and peaceful. Children scurried about and the women were pleasantly engaged doing chores. The men were sitting outside their adobe homes and rather enjoying this beautiful afternoon. For a while they had been spotted by several of the men. The women and children were either oblivious, or just ignoring them. One older man stood up, and the travelers made their way in his direction. As they came into view the women no longer ignored them—Aiden was being given a thorough looking over, like he was accustomed to.

The older man was smoking a pipe; the scent was strong and strange to the visitors approaching. "Now here's a rag-tag bunch of travelers, if ever I've seen. What brings you to Tengeer, lads?" His gaze was on Aiden.

A dark-skinned woman with medium length, dark brown, lightly curled hair approached. She was short and lightly built; she was not pretty, but neither was she homely. Her large dark eyes, her nicest feature, looked down and away from the men. Her body language showed timidity towards the men, but her attention was on Jemma. As Aiden and the man spoke the woman crouched down in front of Jemma. She spoke softly to her, and Jashion noticed Jemma smile. Jashion turned his attention back to Aiden and the older man. Soon Jemma was off and playing with some other dark skinned children, presumably the woman's, more or less Jemma's age.

"...well, let's have a look at that gash, young man. Ah, yes, it needs some attention for sure. You've done well, see," he said indicating Aiden. "The wound is making progress. You've done right, coming here. Survived the dark forest, the whole lot of you. I'm impressed. Doesn't look like that legendary monstrous snake fared so well. Did the little lass take care of the anaconda herself, or is she just carrying the trophy?"

Jashion was yet to speak. Aiden never answered a question immediately. Before anyone else could speak, the man, Tollybrit, indicated that he would get some medicine and he had Jashion sit in his seat.

The herbs stung as the wound was dressed. Jashion flinched, but tried to be brave.

"Yes, these'll hurt. It's a good hurt though...means this'll be on the mend."

Tollybrit continued to smoke his pipe as he dressed Jashion's wound. The smoke filled the air that Jashion breathed. He began to feel nausea and was getting very light headed. Aiden was bent down, watching everything that Tollybrit did. They spoke, as Aiden queried him about the herbs and the techniques in healing. Tollybrit was only too happy to divulge every bit of knowledge he had to Aiden. Aiden had impressed him right from the start, and he was only the more impressed with Aiden as they talked and dressed the wound. Jashion was too sick and light-headed to take in any of the conversation—the intensity of the pain was finally lessening, though.

"We'll do it just like this again in the morning, and he will be on the mend in no time." Aiden didn't reply, but both men got up and looked over Jashion, who looked rather green in the face.

"You alright, young man," said Tollybrit cheerfully.

"I don't think that he was prepared for the smoke of your weed," said Aiden with a smile, and both men laughed hardily.

Tengeer was used to playing the host, especially to the sick and injured. Tollybrit and others there were expert in herbs and in healing. People came from far and wide to employ them in their healing arts, and they rarely left disappointed. The Tengeer's were not wealthy as some, but neither were they left wanting of anything. They had plentiful and veritable food, comfortable shelter, clothing, a beautiful and, apparently safe, environment, medical expertise, and a pleasant affable society.

The three travelers were given accommodations, changes of apparel, and were invited to a large community dinner. The dinner had only been planned upon their arrival. Visitors were always treated kindly—though, typically, not this kindly. Aiden had attracted the attention of Tengeer, and on his account a community feast was prepared. Darkness began to cover Tengeer as the feast was finishing. A large bonfire was roaring. Aiden was the center of attention throughout the meal, to which he appeared comfortably in his element. He was not so slow to talk and reply when surrounded by so many jovial hosts, and in particular the women. The comfort and ease with which he spoke astounded Jashion. He, too, was receiving attention, though much more peripherally, and found the situation much more uncomfortable. Jemma was very happy, siting amongst many children, she too was a center of attention.

Three young men, all blond and blue eyed, had made their way to Jashion. They were all hard to tell apart, but only two were brothers. Daxton, sixteen, who was a cousin to the two brothers, was the most gregarious. The brothers, Marcus, seventeen and Terence, sixteen, were all smiles and less chatty. Daxton interrogated Jashion about Dromreign, the dark forest, and the anaconda. They also wanted to know everything about Aiden. They would have loved to have had Aiden's attention, but there was way too much competition for Aiden at the moment. Jashion, very conscious of his speech, gave short replies at first. The boys showed no signs of being nonplused; Daxton continued to question while Marcus and Terence smiled and nodded with eyes wide open. In time Jashion relaxed and began to speak at ease. With the boys showing no sign of offense at his speech he soon forgot himself.

The tale was terrific and terrible. Jashion became animated as he spun the action, the triumph, and the horror. Tollybrit soon disengaged from the conversation surrounding Aiden, and listened intently. Slowly all eyes and ears turned to Jashion and his story. No longer was he fielding questions. Instead, he was reliving his past few days. Chills went up his spine; the scenes and the horror at times overcame him. Sickness engulfed him as he described his friends and the girl devoured by the dragon. The tale ended as he described the enormous wolf staring he and his new friends down.

Everyone, including Aiden, was listening and had their eyes upon Jashion. The mood was tense. Nothing but the crackling of the fire could be heard. A child dared the question—"Could that frightful dragon come here?"

Tollybrit explained, "Na, the dragon doesn't like Tengeer. It's been since I was a child that Dromreign has come this way. The incense we burn seems to keep the beast away. I don't know if the scent is fowl to the dragon, or if it just disguises the smell of human flesh, but either way it has never come this way since we began to burn it."

Everyone was a little calmer once that was told. But many reflected that the dragon had been to Tengeer before. It became silent for several minutes. Tollybrit had something on his mind. He smoked at his pipe reflectively. He looked over at Jashion. Jashion was staring out into space. Jashion shuddered, and Tollybrit spoke.

"Young man, I've seen some of what you have seen. I've seen the destruction of that filthy beast." Jashion looked at him along with the multitude. "At one time I determined to escape this land and all of its evils. You've had a bigger dose of these evils, I dare say, but I had seen enough myself. I learned of a land, the promise land, where one can escape it all. A beautiful land with all of the amenities, and none of the evils. It is surrounded by a barrier that cannot be breached by the dragon. There are no wolves, no man-eating snakes, and hardly any sickness. The people are peaceful, loving, and kind. There is a land of tranquility and peace, a land where a man could live out the remainder of his days with nothing to fear. I say, I determined to go there myself—and I did. At least, I made it to the entrance. I could have gone in, but instead I turned and came back here. I dare say, it has been a good life for me. Still, I wonder what it would have been like for me if I was on the other side."

"What could have made ye turn," asked Jashion aghast.

Tollybrit let out a puff of smoke, and smiled deeply. "It's not easy, getting to the entrance. It's not easy going in. The entrance is at the base of the mountain through the depths of the dark forest. Many a person has fallen as they have tried to approach. The wolves will stop at nothing to keep a man from the entrance. Even if you make it, you have to determine if it is really what you want. It looks like nothing but a stream and a pool. You have to strip yourself of everything. You will not make it if you are sick or injured, or not in fit shape. You must fight the current and swim between two rocks in a narrow entrance. After you navigate the darkness of the underwater cavern, you emerge on the other side into a calm pool. It is impossible to take anything with you. You must leave everything of this land behind, no knife or sword, no seed, no trinket. It is you, and you alone that emerges into the promise land, if you make it at all. Everything you need is there, but many things that you may want are not. Many of the delights of this land are left behind forever.

"That is why I turned. There was something that I was not ready to leave behind. I stripped myself of everything and lay it down beside me. I took a hundred deep breaths, and almost jumped a dozen times. But something kept me from going. I looked down at my things, there was only one thing that I didn't want to say goodbye to. I heard the wolves howl. It was now or never. I either jumped in and said goodbye to this land forever, or I turned back and try to escape the black forest. It was the weed I smoke. Every witness bore the same, no weed to smoke on the other side. I brought a pack of seeds. I would carry the seed forth, and bring weed to the other side. But, I was told that I would not make it if I tried to carry anything. I thought about it: should I try with my pack? What if I failed? I might parish. What if I went without it? I considered what was on the other side, and what I was so pleased to leave behind. But ultimately, I couldn't image my life without my weed to smoke. I left the entrance, escaped with my life, and am here to tell the tale. I kept this land for this weed, and as you've seen, it is my constant companion"

The people of Tengeer laughed heartily, and Jashion looked on in amazement. Aiden looked at Jashion with a fixed stare.

Chapter 4

There are all sorts in this world—short, tall; fat, skinny; black hair, brown hair, blond hair, long hair, short hair, curly hair, straight hair, thick hair, thin hair, no hair. There are those who are muscular and those who are weak. Straight teeth, crooked teeth, white teeth, yellow teeth, missing teeth—there are even those who are toothless. Some bodies are perfectly proportioned, yet many have odd proportions—some subtle and some extreme. Some have blue eyes, brown eyes, green eyes and more—inset eyes, bulging eyes, and those in the middle. There are eyes that look gentle and eyes that look cruel; eyes that look fearful, and those that are frightful. Eyes that are fixed, and those that wander. People have big noses, long noses, those that point up and those that point down, and those that are round. We have black skin, white skin, and every tone of brown—from greyish, to yellowish, to reddish. Some skin is wrinkled and other is smooth, some is flawless and others have scars and marks galore. The vast variety of appearance of humankind is staggering. Some are beautiful and others are not. Some are ugly or even hideous.

Despite these varieties and differences, most people find a companion—someone who loves them and is attracted to them as they are. Even people that are not beautiful have a companion that is attracted to them.

"But wait," someone may say, "I have two points to make concerning this. The first is a cliché: beauty is in the eye of the beholder. And the second point is that attraction has to do with many of a person's attributes, not simply external features. Indeed, a person may be attracted to another for many reasons besides how the person looks."

To which I say, I am in entire agreement with the second point. But the first point, cliché or not, is simply not true. Beauty is beauty, no matter who is doing the beholding. Lack of beauty is also not subjective, and neither is ugliness. Each of these are attributes, and are apparent to all.

"Now hold on, you have described the various shapes, sizes, colors, and differences of many different people, and you have said that in most cases someone is attracted to them. How can beauty not be in the eye of the beholder?"

Ah, we have mixed two things and treated them as one. Attraction and beauty are not synonymous. Beauty is absolute and attraction is relative. This is so easy to confuse because attraction and beauty do go hand in hand so often. Beauty is something that attracts, but beauty is not attraction. Most people like the taste of sweet, but to say that something tastes sweet and that it tastes good is not the same thing. Some things that are not sweet taste good. Not all things that are sweet taste good to all people, yet everyone would agree that all things that are sweet are in fact sweet. Beauty is of great worth and it is attractive, but it is not equally attractive or of the same value to all people. The value we place—how attractive beauty is—*is* in the mind of the beholder.

Perhaps another illustration would be helpful. It has been wondered whether two individuals may perceive the same color differently from one another. In all likelihood, color blindness or color deficiencies have contributed to this query. Certainly, a person with normal color vision and a person with a color deficiency may call the same color by different names. One may call something brown, and another may call it green. Does this mean that they looked at the same thing and perceived it differently? The answer is yes. To one it looked brown and to the other it looked green. Because of the difference of their opsin's, each persons' retinas send different responses to their brains, and so in one the brain perceived brown, and in the other brain green was perceived. But the real question is about perception, and not about faulty signals. If both individuals—both brains— received an identical signal from their retinas, both brains would have perceived the same color. Two individuals with normal color vision will send their brains the same signal when looking at the same color and both will perceive it identically. The same shade of blue is perceived identically to both individuals, just as salt tastes the same to everyone with normal taste function.

So, a particular shade of blue causes the normal eyes to both send the identical signal to the brain. Then the brain perceives a sensation of color. Both people have been told that when they perceive that color that it is called blue, so both people say that it is blue. But how do we know that they both internally perceive an identical perception? Is it not possible that two individuals see the world in different colors, yet describe them identically because they have both been taught that this is blue, or this is red? Does blue or red look to you the way that blue and red look to me? The answer is yes, because blue is not subjective. Blue is blue, meaning the perception in our minds. It is real, it exists, blue is a real thing. All human minds, and perhaps all minds, that have eyes capable of sending the signal for blue will perceive blue. If we could correct the opsin's in a color deficient individual and their eyes sent the correct signals to the brain, then their brain would perceive the exact same colors as anyone else's.

But, and this is the important part, just because two individuals see blue the same, doesn't mean that they value it identically. For one, blue may be their favorite color, for the other it may be very unappealing. They look the same, but they are not appreciated identically. Foods taste the same to individuals, assuming correct taste and olfactory sensors, yet what is liked and what is not liked varies tremendously between individuals. One person may feast upon it, and the other is disgusted by it. A song sounds the same to both people, but one may love the song and another hates it.

Beauty is perceived the same from one individual to another, but its value or attractiveness is what can vary tremendously. In fact, people can be attracted to ugliness. Foods that have strong, unpleasant flavors many people have an acquired taste for. Music that may be repugnant to most may be pleasurable to some. Art that is clearly ugly is attractive to some. They may mistakenly say that, "it is beautiful to me," by which they mean it is pleasing or attractive. Yet, if it is ugly it cannot be beautiful. Variety or some of that which would be considered ugly, if lightly contrasted to beauty can enhance the attractiveness. A dark mole on a beautiful woman's face may actually enhance her appeal. A blemish is not beautiful but it may be very attractive. Music in minor contains discord, yet it can be so appealing. Bitter is not sweet, yet bitter may enhance the desirability of a particular food. The bottom line is that beauty is real, it is absolute, it is not subjective, but its value can vary from one observer to another tremendously.

Be that as it may be, I want to cast the readers mind upon a scene of exquisite beauty. In this view, there is a pleasant home. There is green grass, flowers along the side of the home, and trees surrounding. In the distance, there is a gorgeous view of a mountain top climbing so high it looks as though it will pierce the sky. The sky is blue, with some fluffy white clouds gently moving. It is late afternoon, or early evening, and as such the shadows are beginning to lengthen. There is a very gentle breeze that is moving the smaller branches lightly. Near the home there is an extended porch, and upon the porch is a young girl of about fifteen. She has on a blue, full-length dress. If she were standing it would come to her ankles. But she is sitting, and to our view we see her profile. Her feet are toward the house and are bare. At this moment, her face is towards this perspective and the breeze is gently blowing through her shoulder-length, straight, blond hair.

Our perspective is quite distant, allowing us to take in the whole home, the landscape and the scenery, so that we cannot see clearly the features of the girl. After beholding this beautiful scene, we zoom in our perspective to the young lady. We can see her features now plainly, if only momentarily as she turns her head and looks down towards her feet. She has lived with an unusual characteristic in appearance: she is without beauty. Yet, she is also devoid of ugliness. Her features contain nothing of the beautiful and nothing of the ugly. She is plain, completely and entirely plain. There is nothing in her that would cause someone to smirk or to be unkind. There is nothing to make fun of, or to tease because of exaggeration. She may not be called beautiful, but neither could she be called homely. There is nothing homely about her. She is just plain—boring, uneventful, uninteresting, forgettable, and up to this point in her life she has not been attractive to anyone. She is not unattractive, as this would require something of the ugly which she does not possess, but rather she just is not attractive rather than unattractive.

She has lived this way her entire life, so it is not uncomfortable to her. She has never been mistreated. She has friends, though not a close or best friend. She is liked by her peers, though not adored. She is not the person that is looked for when she is present, nor missed when she is absent. She does not know what it would be like to be the center of attention for she has never experienced it before. She is loved by her parents, and has a good relationship with them as well as her extended family. She is content in life; she does not feel anything is amiss. She does not long for attention, or to be attractive to others. She is not unattractive, nor is she ignored, shunned, or mistreated.

Hers is a fine simple life, and she is not wanting. Her name is Sarah Peningham.

When Sarah looked toward her feet she began to play with her left toes with her left hand. Though her gaze was in this direction, she was not really watching her fingers play with her toes. She was daydreaming. This was not willful daydreaming, and she was not fantasizing, rather her mind was wandering—seemingly uneventfully. She was not asleep, but this daydream took on some of the unusualness of a nocturnal dream. What she saw before her, playing on the porch, were three babies. In her daydream, she understood them to be her children. None of the three looked similar enough to be siblings, however. The other oddity was their ages. One was an infant sitting in a carriage cooing and wiggling his fingers and toes. Another was a six-month old baby struggling to sit up and playing with his toes. The final was a one-year-old baby, attempting to stand. Sometimes it would succeed and clap for a moment, only to then promptly loose his balance and fall on his backside.

The babies were each cute, happy, and full of life. Sarah smiled pleasantly at the scene before her mind's eye. It did not occur to her the strangeness that these three babies could all be hers, and yet were each only six months apart in age. The babies ignored each other, as young children often do, and Sarah's attention went from one child to the next, enjoying each of them in their own way. This was her first maternal daydream. Something was changing—awakening within her. She was growing up, maturing, and becoming a woman. She was entirely unconscious of this change.

Along with this change, something else was happening. For the first time in her life she had crossed a threshold. At this exact moment, her physical appearance took on a trace of beauty. Her development into womanhood showed promise of being kind to her looks. Interrupting her daydream, her mother called to her from within her home. She got up slowly and walked into her home.

"Sarah, honey, it's time to get you ready for the dance."

A big annual youth dance was this evening, and Sarah's mother, remembering fondly her own experiences many years earlier at this annual event, was feeling excited for her daughter. Sarah bathed and put on a lovely light pink, knee-length dress. She walked into her mother's room with her wet hair dripping; she sat down on a stool in front of the mirrors and began brushing through her hair.

Her mother joined her and took over the beautification, as it were. Sarah's hair was so straight and short that there was not much her mother could do with it. She tried bows, ribbons, and barrettes of various sizes and colors. Her mother chatted pleasantly throughout the primping, about the dance. Sometimes it was historical in nature and sometimes it was current events. Sarah hardly spoke but listened with delight. She did not have any particular expectations for the evening. She would be asked to dance, she was sure, but she did not expect anyone to take any particular interest in her; they never had before. Eventually her mother found a bow that suited her. Sarah was putty in her hands. Her mother made her up on occasions, such as this, as she saw fit and Sarah appreciated every minute of it. Mrs. Peningham never sought Sarah's opinion and Sarah never even considered giving one. The white bow selected suited Sarah fine.

Next the make-up was applied. She took her time and had Sarah turn for various profiles in the mirror. They were both chatting and laughing pleasantly. When her work was completed her mother asked her to arise to take a good look at her. She looked her up and down and then stared at her in her face. The gaze lasted longer than expected and Sarah dropped her eyes.

"Look at me, honey," said her mother pleasantly.

Sarah looked her mother in the eyes and smiled softly.

"You're beautiful," she said softly and significantly.

The words did not resonate immediately. Sarah had heard these words before, but not once had they, or anything like them, been directed at her before. After a moment they began to sink in and she blushed slightly. Her heart began to warm and beat more rapidly. The excitement she began to feel lifted her spirits and her countenance took on even more beauty as her blush was replaced with a smile.

"Really?" she asked.

Her mother looked upon her with a surprised but pleased expression. She had never seen physical beauty in her daughter before, as it had never been there, and she was unable to take her eyes off of her. Understand, she was only slightly beautiful, yet this beauty, enhanced by the carefully modeled make-up and hair, and then magnified by her brightened countenance, was breathtaking to her mother.

"Sarah, honey, you really are beautiful. You look so pretty. I hope you have a wonderful evening tonight."

Joy filled Sarah's heart, and she looked at herself in the mirror for nearly a quarter of an hour. She was pleased with the make-up, her dress, and her hair. Still, she didn't look so different to herself. The words, 'you're beautiful,' continued to sound in her ears, and gave her mood a delightful delirium.

She could not recall what happened from this time to the start of the dance. But there she was at the dance. It had been going for some time. Her spirits were still elevated and her face beamed brightly, however, so far, she had not been given any particular attention. Friends, and some of the boys, extended the usual courtesies, but no one seemed to notice anything special or different about her. The dance had been going for about an hour, and still no one had asked her to dance. The band struck up a favorite and popular slow song. It seemed that all of the boys were getting up to ask for a dance. Jimmy Smithy began to head towards her. He seemed to be looking at her, and she prepared herself to accept his invitation. He was a nice boy that she had known since they were children. He had grown taller this year and looked a bit gangly, but was handsome enough.

As he approached she smiled sweetly, but he did not acknowledge her at all. He walked right past her, even brushing against her shoulder, and then asked Maryanne, a perky red-head, for the dance. Sarah turned instinctively, and in seeing the happy pair felt her heart sink. Whatever joy and brightness she had been feeling began to dissipate. She turned around, red in the face again, and saw that the floor was filling up and she, all by herself, would soon be in the way. No other potential partners seemed to be looking at her, nor making their way towards her. Her head dropped and she made her way towards the punch bowl. She was not thirsty, but she had to occupy herself with something during this song. She would be one of the few sitting this one out.

"Who is she?" John asked his buddy Kevin.

"Who?"

"Her," he said pointing to the girl in the light pink dress heading over to the punch bowl.

"I don' know," he said turning his attention away and looking around the room. John and Kevin were both seventeen, handsome, tall, and muscular. John was the better looking of the two, but they were both very handsome young men. They had both just walked in, fashionably late. Kevin was frustrated that most of the girls had already been taken for this dance.

"Seriously, she looks familiar. Who is she?"

"Oh," said Kevin, somewhat annoyed by having to take a closer look, "um...that's just Sarah Peningham."

"Sarah Peningham? Do I know her? Wait...Sarah, *that's* Sarah."

Kevin wasn't paying any attention. John looked at her for a moment across the room with a surprised look on his face. He then turned his gaze and looked over the dance; the room was full of dancing couples then. His thoughts began to move on, but something made him look back. She was standing looking over the dance, all alone, holding a cup of red punch that she was entirely uninterested in. There was something in her eyes that caught his attention. Sarah Peningham was not in *his* league, but somehow the girl standing over there was. He hesitated for a moment longer and then made his way towards the punch bowl.

Sarah noticed that John was walking towards her, but not for one moment did she think he was heading to her. She continued to look on at the dance until he was directly in front of her.

"If you don't mind being away from your punch that you haven't touched, I would love to have this dance."

She looked up curiously and into his eyes. *He* was addressing *her*? John Bennett was asking *her* to dance? His eyes told her that he was in earnest, so she put her cup on the table and gave him her hand. Just that simple touch and she could tell how strong he was. She had never been asked to dance, or even been addressed, by someone like John Bennett. Soon his arm was around her waist and they were moving to the beat. Her heart was fluttering, not out of any infatuation—rather out of pure discomfort. Was she glad that she had been asked to dance? —and by John Bennett no less? She did not know, but what she did know was that her head was spinning with confusion.

John was speaking to her, and though she could hear him, she did not comprehend a word of what he was saying to her. She smiled and nodded throughout the dance in reply, but she was only reacting instinctively to his inflections and facial expressions. The song was already half-way over when their dance began, but it seemed as though the dance would never end. She wanted to flee as soon as the song was over, and hide herself, perhaps for the remainder of the night. Though her mind did not think these thoughts, or any other thoughts clearly, she felt inside as though she were the brunt of a cruel joke, or that perhaps he had lost some bet. Somewhere, though she had not seen it, boys must be pointing and laughing at her. John, too, would enjoy a hearty laugh afterwards. Whether any of this was true or not, at the very least she felt that she did not belong in his arms for even one dance.

The song ended and she removed her left hand from his right shoulder, muttered a, "thank you for the dance," and started to turn away. He did not let go of her right hand that was in his left. She turned back and looked up at him fearfully. He smiled and looked at her curiously.

The music had already begun for the next song; it also was a slow one. "I thought that you nodded when I asked you for the next dance, too? This one was so short, and we've hardly gotten to talk. Do you mind dancing with me again?"

She understood the words this time, but there was such a disconnect between what she was experiencing and what she was feeling. He looked at her reassuringly, still not returning her hand. Sarah's rapid heart rate actually began to slow and her breathing eased. Never had any boy wanted to stay and dance a second song with her before. Never had any boy looked her in the eyes as John did at this time. A rush of emotion washed over her insecurities and left her with a warm and joyful feeling. John Bennett was showing an interest in her; he saw something in her that he liked; he wanted to be with her; he was attracted to her. This sensation she had never so much as imagined before.

Sarah returned her hand to his shoulder and they began to dance again. Her heart began to race again, but this time the emotion was different—this time it was pleasant.

"You look very pretty this evening," he said and she blushed. "You've grown up so much, I hardly knew who you were when I saw you tonight. Actually, truth be known, I had to ask my friend Kevin what your name was."

"Kevin knows my name?" she said out loud, but not really to John. Sarah was stunned. *John and Kevin actually know who I am.*

"Sure he knows your name. I do too. I guess I just took one look at you and lost my mind."

The self-deprecating compliment was lost on Sarah. But what she did notice was that she was enjoying herself. She liked how strong and secure he felt. She liked being the center of his attention. She mustered the courage to gaze into his eyes while he gazed into hers. He was so handsome—powder blue eyes, light brown, short but styled hair, mildly cleft prominent chin, and a perfect smile.

Sarah's glow was back, and then some. She ventured a smile that was thoroughly appreciated—she could tell by the expression in his eyes. What did John see in Sarah? Her beauty was subtle at best, though she was made up very nicely. Her glow about her had been impressive, but her countenance had dropped by the time John had seen her. What John saw when he looked across the room at her, as she looked over the dance, was something he had never seen to that extent before. He saw goodness; he saw purity and innocence. He saw *her* permeating through her external shell. He caught a glimpse of the real Sarah, the eternal Sarah, who she had always been and who she would always be. Her external beauty did not compare with her internal, but neither did it distract from it. She was in possession of some external beauty and she had no features to repel or to diminish. Her simple beauty was sufficient when mingled with the glimpse John had of who she truly was. John was attracted to Sarah—more attracted to her than he had ever been to another young lady before. In such a short space of time he could no longer picture his world without her in it.

Sarah's attraction to John was not so singular or pure. He was tall, strong, handsome, popular, clever, and though all this she had known before, most importantly he was showing an interest in her. More than an interest, he seemed to be captivated by her, and that felt overwhelmingly good to her. Her attraction was building as she felt powerless to withstand the feelings emerging within her. Her rationality had not abated entirely, however, and she still couldn't believe what she was feeling and experiencing. It was getting harder to deny or disbelieve what was happening to her as they danced. They chatted pleasantly. They were both unaware of anyone or anything else around them. They each held the other in their world with an unblinking gaze.

This time the songs end was bitter and disconcerting to Sarah. She didn't want to run away. She didn't want to leave his presence, nor turn her gaze from his handsome face. She didn't want him to return her hand, nor release her waist. She lingered with one hand on his shoulder and the other in his hand. She did not back away, nor drop her gaze. She *had something then* and did not want to lose it.

John loosened her hand, but not her waist. His left arm went around to her back and he drew her in closer to him. Sarah's heart leaped as she entered into the embrace. She no longer wondered whether this was really happening as the much shorter Sarah embraced him with her ear against his chest. She could feel the rapid, full beat of his heart. John Bennett had given his heart to Sarah Peningham.

Chapter 5

The long morning shadows of the mountains were disappearing, revealing a beautiful, sunny, fall day. Kevin sat on the moist grass carelessly strumming his acoustic guitar. John had his back to an apple tree with a bright red apple in hand. He kept tossing it up, higher and higher. He enjoyed watching the contrast of the bright red against the blue sky. Two apple cores had been tossed recently and he wasn't thinking about eating this one.

"So, Amanda's great," Kevin said, "I want to go do something cool with her."

"Nice."

"Yeah, we really hit it off. Totally in the zone with her, you know—dancin', talkin', chillin'...her friend Janice was way cool too. I wanted to introduce you—hook you up, you know. You were pretty occupied, but anyway, she checked you out. She was likin' what she saw. Janice is gorgeous, and Amanda is super pretty too, and she was diggin' me, so it all just went from there."

"You two are already an item, or just hoping to seal the deal?"

"No, were cool, she's my girl. I didn't kiss her at the dance, but we were never alone, you know. Janice was brushin' off all the guys. I think she was waiting for you; but you never materialized. So, I didn't have any space with Amanda; but hangin' with both Amanda and Janice wasn't bad, you know. I was feelin' like the king," he said, giving John a knowing smile. His strumming had sped up and increased in volume, a little adrenaline was pumping as he talked.

"Nice," said John only halfway listening, he was reveling in his own recent memories.

"What do you think? Go to the falls, picnic lunch, maybe go swimin'? There's some nice hikin' up there too. Are you in?"

"When?"

"I don' know, couple of days—whenever they can."

"Oh. That soon."

"Sure, why not?"

John shrugged. "She's not even sixteen yet."

"Who?"

"Sarah."

"Sarah Peningham?" Kevin said in an ironic tone.

"Yeah, I've got to wait six more weeks before she's even sixteen," John responded, not noticing Kevin's tone.

"Really, I'm surprised."

"I know."

"I would have thought it would be at least a year before she was sixteen."

John caught his apple and looked over at his friend with a mild offence in his expression. Kevin stopped strumming and looked back pleasantly. "She's young, man. She looks really young."

"Really?"

Kevin chortled. "Oh yeah. It's cool, I mean six weeks isn't too bad. If you're still interested by then, you don't have too long to wait."

"It feels like forever."

It was Kevin's turn to glare. "Are you serious, man?" John raised his eyebrows, but didn't respond verbally. "It's just that she looks so young, and she's not very pretty." John looked hurt, but Kevin went on anyway. "At first I thought it was like a charity dance. I really didn't know what you were doing. I'm sorry, man. Not meaning to offend—just sayin' it like it is. Anyway, I'll lay off Sarah; to each his own. But, either way it's six weeks. I may go through three girlfriends in six weeks," only slightly exaggerating, "who knows, maybe I'll be going out with Janice by then."

John's expression softened and he smiled a bit. Kevin was right: he had never kept a girlfriend for such an eternity as six weeks.

"Look, let's go with Amanda and Janice. It'll be fun. Sarah can't go anyway, so she can't be upset. We'll do something real cool with Sarah when she's old enough. Come on, man. Plus, Janice is awesome. You'll be impressed, I'm tellin' you. She's the kind of girl that could make you forget about anyone else. I'm just sayin'. At least she could make those six-weeks cruise on by."

John smiled. "I don' know."

"Now look who's not being cool."

"Alright, but you owe me. We're going to give Sarah the best sweet-sixteen first date a girl could have. I'm depending on your creativity."

"Deal."

John and Kevin both had reputations as players and heartbreakers. Neither of those were completely deserved. John had no interest in girlfriends. He had never actually had a girlfriend. He dated a lot, and was extraordinarily popular— desired. But, when the girl got that look in her eyes, he always backed off. It was always too late, and another heart was broken. He wasn't trying to be a player; he wasn't just dating for fun. He didn't intend to break any hearts, but if he gave a girl his attention, for even a little while, her heart was sure to be broken. John was hardly aware of the effect that he had on the girls. A smile, a dance, some friendly conversation would be all it took to have a heart primed for shattering. What John did want to do was to court the girl that he would marry. Up to this point, every girl he had known came up lacking. As soon as she was serious, he no longer saw the point. What was the point of holding the hand, writing love letters, whispering sweet nothings, or kissing just any girl? No, he only wanted to share those things with the girl that would be his girl forever.

Kevin, on the other hand, couldn't have been more on the other extreme. He saw no point in looking for love with the girls he went out with. The thought of marrying any of them wouldn't cross his mind. He was dating for the pure pleasure of the experience. He wanted girlfriends. Lots of girlfriends. Girlfriends brought many pleasantries with them. They were soft, warm, nice smelling, and great to look at. Hugs and kisses were an extraordinary delicacy, and each girl brought something different and special to the experience. Kevin was a player, but he had never broken a heart. Like Kevin, the girls that he was attracted to wanted the same thing. They were not looking for lasting love, but rather the pleasure of the present. Once they had both experienced what they would from each other, they were both ready to move on. Lots of past girlfriends, but none angry or jealous.

John, the unwitting heartbreaker, and Kevin the non-heartbreaking player, were quite the team. No wonder their reputation. Still, they were the cream of the crop and all the girls knew that someone would nab them one day. Janice and Amanda thought that they had the stuff.

Janice was a gorgeous, platinum blond. With blue eyes, long dark lashes, full lips, a great figure, and exquisite long legs, she could have made a Barbie doll jealous. Amanda was not her equal, but wasn't bad in her own right. Black, mid-length full bodied hair, dark chocolate colored eyes, and a perfect smile adorned her pretty face. She was a little shorter than Janice, but otherwise was nicely shaped. Janice was more subdued than Amanda, but they both had very engaging personalities.

"I told you. Sometimes in the dark dance hall you meet a girl and think she's great. Then you see her in the daylight and you think, 'man, it must have been dark in there.' But, not those two. Wow, seriously sweet. Tomorrow will be awesome."

"They're pretty all right." John smiled and looked over at Kevin. He was starting to feel defensive, and was regretting agreeing to go out with Janice. There wasn't technically any understanding between him and Sarah, but somehow he still didn't feel right about it. What would she say? What would she think if she saw him with her? He felt like he was betraying her. Still, he rationalized that there was nothing wrong with it. Plus, he and Kevin would show her a great time in just a few weeks. Did she expect him to just sit around and wait—watch the grass grow—while he waited for her to turn sixteen? Of course, that would be what she was doing—waiting, patiently waiting.

The next afternoon Kevin and Amanda walked hand in hand up the trail chatting pleasantly. John and Janice beside them, hands apart, also were having a nice conversation. She really was cool. She was more confident than the other girls that he'd dated. She was more mature, and carried herself so naturally. The thing that impressed him the most was how polite she was. The longer they were together the less defensive John felt. In fact, he was really enjoying himself. Unlike most of their double dates, where it was more like a foursome hanging out and having a good time together, this was more like a single date with another couple happening to be in the vicinity. Kevin and Amanda were in their own world, as were John and Janice.

Soon John was smiling comfortably as he talked, and as he listened. She got his humor—she was no silly, giggly girl, but she laughed naturally when he was clever. She also could bring a smile to his face, and a chuckle from time to time. They had similar interests: they both loved reading, even some of the same books. They were both into fitness, and loved the outdoors. IQ wise, they were on the same level, and it was high.

When they reached the top of the trail the waterfalls were in full view. It was a warm sunny fall day in the early afternoon. The couples were about fifteen feet apart, and in no time Amanda was in Kevin's arms. After staring at the lovely falls for a few minutes John saw them plant a kiss on each other. It may have been their first kiss together, but it was clearly not either of their first kisses.

"You'd never know it's their first date would you," Janice whispered to John as she put her hand on his muscular triceps and led him in a way to turn his attention from them.

Very discreet, he thought. She helped him get the blanket set on some flat grassy ground with a perfect view of the falls. They opened up the picnic basket and started divvying up the lunch. Kevin and Amanda joined them and lunch was underway. Janice sat with her back to the falls. She wore a just-above-the-knee length yellow dress. Her perfectly shaped legs were positioned in front of her and to the side, giving John an excellent view. She looked absolutely radiant with her blond hair, yellow dress, and flawless skin positioned in front of the magnificent falls. Her fingernails were painted red, and matched perfectly her lipstick. Even the way she ate was charming to him as she ate the small, white, crust-less sandwiches that he and Kevin had prepared.

Amanda couldn't stop talking, and a few times part of her food came shooting out of her mouth, to which Kevin teased her relentlessly. She would laugh right along with him; no blushing from this girl. Kevin and Amanda were quite the pair. They seemed like they had known each other all of their lives. John had been with Kevin along with nearly all of his girlfriends, but he had never seen him with a girl that he seemed so compatible with. Although in front of him was a scene of loveliness unparalleled, he couldn't help but stare at Amanda. She was so animated, and seemed so well matched to his best friend. He looked back at Janice, and she gave him a wink. She seemed to know the meaning of his stare.

After finishing tasty strawberry shortcake, Kevin and Amanda weren't shy about helping to remove the whipped cream around each other's lips. After chatting pleasantly all together for a quarter of an hour Kevin announced, "I'm ready to hit the water."

The girls nodded in agreement and everyone started shifting to a standing position. John had grown rather fond of the beauty in front of him. But then the uncomfortable feeling came over him again. She was so beautiful as she was, the idea of seeing her in a swimsuit felt indulgent, and he thought of Sarah again. Would she want him swimming with this beautiful girl? They were all standing, and John stared at Janice awkwardly. Janice smiled sweetly and motioned with her fingers for the boys to turn around. The girls wore their suits underneath their outfits, and Amanda had begun to remove her outer clothes with the boys looking on. Both Kevin and John turned around and removed their shirts, leaving their shorts as their swimming trunks.

When they turned around both girls were wearing modest one-piece bathing suits, but no bathing suit could hide their exquisite feminine charm. John could feel his heart rate increase as he looked on.

"Let's go," exclaimed Kevin as he took off and ran to the side of the fifteen-foot cliff, diving in head first. Amanda took off gleefully and jump gracefully, performing a perfect jack-knife dive.

John's eyes were wide open, and he looked over at Janice who was standing beside him facing the cliff. She reached for his hand and the two walked to the cliffs edge. Their hands felt like a perfect match together. At the cliffs edge they could see Kevin and Amanda splashing each other playfully, giving plenty of room for their friends to dive in. Janice let go of Johns hand and after giving him a quick smile, dived in gracefully. Once the coast was clear John jumped in. He went feet first, bending his right leg and grabbing around it with his arms so as to create an enormous splash. All three had ganged up on him and were splashing him when he resurfaced. The water was very cool and the air outside was warm but certainly not hot. Swimming, playing, and diving had gone on for half an hour when John noticed Janice shiver.

"Cold?" he asked her.

She hesitated, not wanting to ruin the fun. Then she shivered again and nodded. "A little."

Amanda was then on top of Kevin's shoulders. "Janice, hop on John. Let's play chicken," shouted Amanda.

"I think we've got this one, they clearly are chicken," said Kevin good-naturedly.

John and Janice exchanged a look. "Let's get 'em," he said with a wink.

Janice smiled and made her way over to John as he turned around and went under. In a moment, she was on his shoulders and he stood up confidently. John was taller, stronger, and more athletic than Kevin. Kevin didn't like losing at anything, so he usually wouldn't challenge John to a game of this nature. But the boys had both spent enough time with these girls to know that Kevin had a tiger on his shoulders compared to the kitten on Johns. This would be an interesting challenge and John thought it would be fun.

Kevin looked at John with the look of a champion. Amanda looked like she was ready to take on the world. John could only image the look on Janice's face, and he wasn't expecting much. The battle was fierce. John used his strength and leverage as best he could to balance and bring Kevin off balance. Kevin fought with everything he had, fully trusting his partner on top to carry the day. But even beautiful, soft kittens have claws, and Janice was no exception. She was stronger and taller than Amanda. She also wasn't about to lose, and while everyone was thinking of her as the weak link she was thinking of John as an invincible anchor. It took just under a minute, but soon Amanda was toppling over backwards and Kevin fighting to the end was being taken with her. Amanda and Kevin came up to a scene of John beating his chest standing tall with Janice fully out of the water and her arms in the air shouting, "Champions!"

They looked like a team: both extraordinarily beautiful, strong, tall, and fit. Kevin was not about to challenge them again. Losing once was bad enough, but to lose twice would put him in a bad mood. He didn't want to be in a bad mood. This had been his best date of all time.

"Race ya," said Amanda as she took a head start. Kevin raced forward grabbing her foot and pulling her back, then darting into the lead. They were back in their own world.

John didn't crouch down to let Janice off of his shoulders. Instead he walked over to the bank and let her off on land.

"Let's get you warm," he said.

"I need to dry off, but I don't want to get my dress wet. I'd rather wait until I'm dry."

"I should've brought towels. It's not as warm as it was a few weeks ago. Here, you can put my shirt on."

John brought his shirt and put it around Janice. They sat on the ground in the sun both facing the water. John put his arm around Janice, and she snuggled in comfortably. He gently ran his hand up and down her arm as her shivering increased.

Janice looked up into his eyes and smiled. "Thank you, that feels nice."

She really was beautiful and sweet. She felt so perfect in his arms. John's heart rate had been up from the chicken fight and carrying Janice around. But the primary reason his heart was beating hard and fast was because of the beauty in his arms. He knew that she was his if he wanted her to be. Just one week before he had never met a girl that he saw any future in. During this week, he had met two. Janice was everything that he could have imagined a girl could be, before he had met Sarah.

Chapter 6

"Sounds like Sarah's home," said her mother to her father—both were waiting in the living room illuminated by a roaring fire. Sarah's father sat reading to the lamp light on his end table. Her mother sat with a cross stitch, but was really just anticipating Sarah's arrival. Mr. Peningham was anxious to get to bed. Mrs. Peningham was anxious to find out all about Sarah's night.

The door opened and shut, and Sarah was in the room a moment later, absolutely beaming.

"Hi, Sarah, how was the dance?" asked her mother.

"Wonderful!"

Her mother began to beam as well. Her father had not yet put down his book.

"Did you get asked to dance by many boys?"

"No, just one."

"Oh." Mrs. Peningham was a little disappointed.

"Who asked you?"

"John Bennett."

"*Oh.*" Mrs. Peningham was no longer disappointed. The smile and beam returned to her face. "That must have been nice. Was he kind?"

"Oh, yes. He was wonderful!"

Mr. Peningham was no longer looking at his book. Mrs. Peningham gave him a look of excitement. Mr. Peningham just looked confused.

"But you only got to dance one dance all night?"

"Oh, no—I danced the night away."

"You did? But...you danced the whole night with John Bennett?"

"Yes, it was amazing!"

"Who's John Bennett?" Mr. Peningham was becoming very interested, and a bit perplexed.

"Oh, Daddy, he's just a guy." The look on Sarah's face told him that this was far from the truth.

"I'm glad that you had a nice time. Get to bed, it's late. Goodnight." Sarah kissed her father's cheek, and then hugged her mother before she glided towards her room.

"Honey, he's not just *a* guy, he's *the* guy. All of the girls want to dance with John Bennett."

"Have you seen him?"

"Oh, yes, and he's very handsome." Mrs. Peningham was really beaming then.

"And this John Bennett, who's *the* guy, danced the night away with *our* little Sarah?" The look on his face was beyond perplexed.

"Apparently," she replied. She was no longer looking at her husband, but was staring wistfully in the distance.

⌘⌘⌘

Sarah was not the type to have a sleepless night. But, on this night sleep could not be found. Perhaps a nocturnal dream is not so requisite when one is living and then re-living a beautiful dream while fully awake—more than awake, alive— more alive than she had ever been. The synaptic furry going on in her head caused such a pleasant confusion. Feelings came before thoughts; thoughts then searched for memories to match up with the feelings. Neither thoughts nor feelings could completely corroborate, which only allowed for another opportunity to remember, to image, to create, to re-live the excitement, the wonder, the infatuation, and most especially the peace that Sarah felt in Johns arms.

As the illumination from the waxing rays of the sun entered her room and the early morning sounds broke the silence, Sarah realized that she had not slept for a moment. Half of her longed to arise and continue to live still in her dream state. Half of her longed to slumber the day away. Perhaps her subconscious could put the pieces together better than her conscious self could. Changing her thought process to this deliberation allowed her body's need for sleep just the foothold it needed, and moments later she was out.

"Dear, she had a late night. Let her sleep. I can manage without her help this morning."

"This is not like our little Sarah to sleep in so late. Is she not well?" Mr. Peningham had not slept well either. He did not appreciate the changes he saw in his daughter since her return the previous night.

Mrs. Peningham gently felt Sarah's forehead. Sarah did not budge. "It's cool. I think she's fine. Let her be, she'll be with us soon enough."

At 11:00 AM Sarah awoke with her heart pounding. She felt over-indulged in every way—sluggish, groggy, upset stomach, slight headache, and stiff. She aroused to a sitting position, brought her legs up—still under the covers, and wrapped her arms around them. She turned her head and rested it on her knees for a few moments before trying to hold it up. Once John Bennett re-entered her consciousness every ounce of discomfort fled. *I wonder what he is doing now?* In fact, he was sitting under an apple tree having a mild argument with his friend Kevin who was strumming a guitar. But Sarah would have never thought of that.

Fatigue soon overtook her and she allowed herself to fall back abruptly on her pillow with her arms outstretched and she smiled brightly. Mrs. Peningham was walking down the hall near the bedroom door and peaked in.

"I see you're awake."

Sarah looked over startled and blushed deeply.

"Are you feeling well?"

"Yes...no, well yes. I...I just didn't sleep."

"You've been sleeping all morning, honey."

"No...well, yes, but not last night. I fell asleep as the light came up. I was...I...it was such a nice night last night, at the dance...I couldn't sleep."

Mrs. Peningham smiled. "You'd better be up now. You still have chores...if you're able."

Sarah nodded.

After dressing and eating what she could tolerate she took to watering some autumn flowers—the only chore left undone by her mother. It was a lovely day and Sarah's physical strength had returned, if not her mental strength. *I shall go for a walk*. Which she did.

Some distance from her home was a place—a special place, where she liked to think. Though it was not consciously planned, this is the destination that her feet took her. The half hour walk passed as had the previous night, with no appreciation of time. It seemed as though she had just set off and then she was there. *Breathtaking*, she thought upon arrival. Her senses were super-heightened and the beauty was dazzling. A gentle waterfall fell seemingly through the wall of the towering mountain. The pool—this magical, mystical pool, of which so much folklore centered, was Sarah's special place; where she turned for contemplation, for reflection, and for solace. She approached the crystal-clear water's edge and dived in, clothes, shoes, and all. The crispness bit in pleasantly and she swam gracefully underwater until she reached the mountains edge. She climbed the edge, ten feet or so up, and then pulled herself up on the ledge immediately behind the waterfall. She sat sideways with her feet towards the edge she had just climbed. She removed her soaking shoes and began to play with her feet as she looked through the broken part of the waterfall in front of her. She could see clearly the pool in front of her through this section. Unlike a month ago, the air was much cooler and Sarah, still soaking in her clothes, shivered lightly at a chill. She pulled her hands up to her hair and began to squeeze the water out.

Neither her sleepless night nor her slumbering morning had brought her any peace. Here, then, she was at peace. The sight, the sound, the mist of the waterfall just inches in front of her, had the power to soothe and calm her completely. Pleasant thoughtlessness engulfed her soul. The monotonous stimulation of the fall brought her into a near hypnotic state. She sat motionless, barely blinking, as she looked out though the falls. And in this state she stayed for a good hour. It was the discomfort that she felt in her backside from sitting still on the rocky edge that caused her to shift and consequently aroused her.

In her shifted position she felt some relief and then John entered her mind. Excitement began in her chest and then spread throughout her being. This time it did not overpower her. She enjoyed every bit of it and allowed it to run its course. She felt it and understood it both deeply and on the surface—she was John Bennett's and he was hers. Warmth, peace, and excitement interplayed harmoniously within Sarah Peningham. Everything was as it should be, until two realizations hit her. First, no degree of shifting would relieve her bottom's discomfort; it was time to go. As she slid to the edge and began to climb down the second realization hit her. She would not be sixteen for six more weeks—she would not see John again until she was of age.

Six weeks, I can't make it. Turbulence began to dissipate her tranquility. Here was a girl who had never asked, never expected, never hoped for anything beyond her simple station in life. She was peripherally aware that others had more than her, but she was also aware of all of the sorrows that others had which she did not. Hers was not a bad life, but neither was it an exciting life. Until last night she was okay with this. Suddenly, at this moment, she wanted something, hoped for something, expected something, and all she could do was wait. She was both the master of patience and longsuffering, and completely unprepared to deal with this desire that filled her heart.

Most of our daily actions and events have no significant effect upon the world. We arise, we shower, we eat meals, we brush our teeth, we say, "Hello, how are you?" to passers-by, and this is all as it should be. The world goes on; these actions are expected and anticipated. Perhaps the absence of these actions may cause a mild ripple, but they are unlikely to change any course. Sarah had lived a life full of actions and events that never caused any change in the course of the world. She was the proverbial tree that had fallen in the forest and no one was there to hear it. She did not feel that she had made a sound. She was a part of this world but this world was no different because she was here.

She had come to the place where she accepted that the previous night's events had changed the course of her world. If pressed, she may even have admitted that the course of John Bennett's life was then changed, though this would be more difficult for her to comprehend. But, in no way did she—could she—see, believe, or comprehend that her actions, her dancing the night away with John Bennett, had changed everything for everyone in her social structure. It was no subtle adjustment either, it was a seismic shift! No one saw the world this morning as they had seen it the day before. Something had happened that did not fit anyone's worldview. Whether consciously or not, everyone was at some stage in a paradigm shift this morning to enable them to continue to deal with the world as it had become.

Everyone, that is, except for John Bennett. His world had changed, and in a huge way, but not the course of his world. The night before fit perfectly in his worldview. He would one day meet the girl of his dreams—finally it had happened. This would not require any paradigm shift for him, it was rather a next stage—an exciting and highly anticipated next stage at that. Even though at this moment he was on his way with Kevin to meet Janice and to get a date with her, his mind was on Sarah.

As Sarah meandered back home, soaking wet again, she ran into Maryanne, the perky red-head that she had been passed by on for a dance with Jimmy Smithy the night before. Maryanne was a friend—as casual friends go. They sometimes interacted, but never unnecessarily. Most of the time Maryanne seemed to just look through Sarah. This never bothered Sarah particularly, as she was very used to this treatment. It seemed proper to her for others to hardly notice her. For Sarah's part, she admired Maryanne. Maryanne was fun, full of life, and fun to watch from a distance. She was a magnet of sorts. Her looks were above average to be certain, but this was not her prime attraction. It was her personality that brought people to her.

"Sarah!"

Maryanne's countenance became brighter and she began to run towards Sarah. Maryanne was made up beautifully in a pretty blue dress, almost as nicely as she was at the dance. Still, she was in flats so that she could run.

Sarah stopped in her course. Something must be wrong for Maryanne to be acting this way towards her. Her heart began to beat rapidly.

"I've been looking for you. You're all wet? Why is your dress all wet?"

"I...um...I was just swimming."

"Swimming? Who with?"

Sarah blushed in shame. "No one."

"Swimming all by yourself with your clothes on? That sounds cool. I've never done that before. Anyway, we're having a little get-together at my place. I want you to come. Let's get you ready so we can get back before the girls arrive. I didn't figure that I would have to go looking for you." Maryanne smiled sweetly and stared Sarah in the eyes.

"A party..."

Sarah had no idea what to think. It was weird being visible. She couldn't comprehend why she was visible and she felt much like when John first asked her to dance—awkward, embarrassed, and highly suspicious.

"Yes, you've got to come. Please." And Maryanne hopped up and down in anticipation.

"Okay. I'll ask and..."

"I've already asked your mom. She said it was fine, I just had to find you."

"Oh...really?"

"Yeah, come on. We've got to go. You're a mess and we have to hurry."

Maryanne grabbed Sarah's hand and the two girls ran off together, Sarah's feet sloshing with each step.

Chapter 7

Sparks flew and a loud clink rang as Jashion barely blocked the blow with his sword. Sweat dripped in his eyes and he began to fall backwards just catching himself as he stepped back. But the relentless blows kept coming. His muscles ached and his heart pounded. Only adrenaline and will-power allowed him to continue to block the fierce strikes.

"Fight back!" yelled Daxton.

"Stand your ground!" hollered Marcus.

Aiden's dark eyes were fixed upon Jashion. He was barely perspiring in the noontime sun. Again, he lifted his sword and again he struck. This time Jashion's sword did not make it up for the block. Aiden's sword stopped millimeters from Jashion's neck. Jashion closed his eyes accepting his fate.

"Nice round. Get some water and cool yourself." Aiden looked over at the trio cheering Jashion on. "Who's next?"

Marcus and Terence looked at each other dumbly. Daxton got up slowly with fear in his eyes. "Take it easy, alright. You could have killed him."

Aiden was amused on the inside but he did not dare even a hint of a smile in his expression. Jashion, who was sitting on the ground and wiping the sweat from his forehead, handed Daxton the sword. Jashion was in the way but was lightheaded and didn't want to get up just yet.

"Get him some water," Aiden said toward Marcus and Terence. Both boys got up and fetched a cool cup full together while Daxton hacked away at the breeze.

"We need to build your endurance. Your skills are improving."

Jashion nodded lightly. Compliments from Aiden did not come often. Terence handed Jashion the cup and Jashion drank it up quickly. He still wasn't ready to arise but did so anyway. He filled his own cup and sat his back against a tall tree such that it's shade engulfed him while he watched the training.

Daxton was more aggressive than Jashion, preferring offense to defense. Aiden allowed him a few moments of attack before taking advantage of Daxton's overreach. Moments later Daxton was on his knee's blocking blows and trying to verbally surrender—Aiden, unaffected by his pleas. Marcus and Terence sheepishly looked on. Jashion, partially recovered, allowed a slight smile. Aiden took aim for Daxton's sword, held up above him from his kneeling position. Aiden swung for the fences, as it were, knocking the sword out of Daxton's hands and flinging it toward the brothers. It landed with the handle next to Terence's foot.

"Looks like it's your turn."

Terrence swallowed hard and reached down slowly for the sword.

"Marcus, fetch me a cup of water, will you?" Daxton had not fought long enough to be exhausted, but Marcus complied anyway. Taking his cue from Jashion he sat in place and drunk his cup, then joined Jashion by the tree.

Terence had not taken any practice swings. He just stood there eyeing Aiden with his sword in blocking position. Terence, though the youngest and the shyest of the trio, was the tallest and the strongest. Daxton was confident beyond his qualifications while Terence was more self-conscious than his skill set should have caused him to be. During the training sessions Terence had shown more promise than his brother and cousin, yet he was the most insecure. Since it was time to spare, Aiden was anxious to see him at work.

As expected Terence did not go at Aiden. Rather, he eyed him cautiously keeping his sword ready for a block. Aiden slowly circled him and began to shrink the distance between them. Still, Terence did not shift for an attack. Aiden sent his sword toward him and Terence easily blocked the blow and put himself back on the defense. Aiden went for his leg, then side, then his neck, and finally his trunk. Each blow was blocked as Terence stood his ground and readied himself for another blow. Aiden saw no point in bringing him down quickly and having Terence hide deeper within himself. No, Aiden wanted to build his confidence and allow Terence to come out of his shell. There might be a tiger rather than a turtle within that shell.

Slowly Terence's confidence did increase. Aiden began to leave his defensive position weaker. He wanted to entice a blow from Terence. It took some time but eventually it came. Terence swung at Aiden and Aiden blocked it sending sparks flying. Daxton began to cheer Terence on, Marcus smiled. Marcus too was growing in confidence.

Aiden continued to leave himself open for Terence's blows which became more rapid. Terence's blows were strong but never so much that he left himself wildly out of defensive position. Aiden was pleased with his potential. It was time to defeat him. Terence's next blow was met with a new force from Aiden. Terence's sword was then badly out of position and Aiden counter attacked. Terence did all that he could to defend the blow. He was being driven back as Aiden sent him blow after blow. Terence was not yet fatigued and he was past his self-consciousness. He found his legs and began to counter the attack without losing position. The spare had become a fight. Aiden did not let up but Terence held his own. Terence even found room to enact blows of his own. Inside, Aiden was thrilled. Terence had what it takes. For several minutes the fight looked even. Then Aiden drew him off balance again and fought him to his knees. Still, Terence defended himself and sought opportunity to arise. Aiden did not allow it, but neither did he seek to discourage him. The fight lingered for a minute or two before he had Terence on his back.

"I am ready for a drink and a rest," said Aiden. Terence took this as a great compliment. Aiden reached down and help Terence to his feet.

"I'm ready to go again," said Daxton getting to his feet.

"It's my turn!" shouted Marcus. "You've had your turn, it's my turn."

Terence chucked his sword toward his brother who beamed from the justice. Aiden looked at Daxton. When Daxton made eye contact, Aiden tossed him his sword.

"Why do I have to fight Daxton? Everyone else had a turn at Aiden."

"Aiden knows I'll school you as well as he would."

"Are you kidding me? You didn't even last a minute before you were screaming like a baby."

"Ha! I had him on the run before I tripped. He hadn't taught us how to fight from our knees yet. I'd have had him if I hadn't tripped."

Aiden and Terence, cups in hand, made their way over to Jashion who was still sitting by the tree.

"Do ye think they'll hurt themselves," said Jashion.

Aiden didn't say a word.

"It might do them some good," said Terence. Aiden just looked on.

After some back and forth Marcus had Daxton down. Daxton was complaining about being tripped again while Marcus was smiling and shaking his head in reply. Jashion and Aiden had been sparing for over an hour before the Tengeer boys had shown up.

The three blond haired, blue eyed look-a-likes were eager to continue.

"You'll spar amongst yourselves now. Time for a brothers' duel." Aiden nodded at Terence who took the sword from Daxton. Daxton was about to protest as Aiden looked him in the eye. He stopped and looked back. Go fetch more cool water. Daxton did as he was asked, leaving Aiden and Jashion alone.

Jashion and Aiden watched the fighting for a time.

"I shall not stay amongst the Tengeer much longer," said Aiden.

"What did ye learn?"

Aiden was silent for a time—a rather long time. Jashion waited patiently. Aiden had left for ten days. He returned with meat from a hunt. The meat was fresh, killed the morning that Aiden had returned. Where he had been the previous nine days he had not yet mentioned.

"There may be war," Aiden finally replied.

They watched the sparing for some time. Daxton had returned and was taking his turn sparing with the brothers.

"I shall not stay here either, I shan't."

"Jemma will be kept well. This is a good home for her."

"Aye, that it is...that it is."

"Will you continue with me?"

It was Jashion's turn to pause. Both of the young men looked out in front of them towards the sparing and not at each other.

"I...I seek the promise land, I do," and he looked up at Aiden, searching his face. Aiden's face could never be read.

"You believe in it then?"

"Don't ye?"

After a few moments, "I'm still coming to terms with your Dromreign. I haven't seen it, or its charred effects. I have had enough witnesses though, including yours, that I believe. The promise land sounds like a beautiful, wonderful myth. A story to calm frightened children. An idea that brings hope to those who are hopeless. Something must be on the other side of those mountains—why not make it a promise land. A place of beauty, peace, security, love, and all things grand. Take everything that you don't want here and not let it be there. Take everything that you do want and put it there. Then, make it so difficult to obtain that most people will never try for it. Those that make it, of course, never come back to tell the tale. Some say that they have come from there but what real proof do they have? I don't say that there is no promise land. What I say is that we really don't know, and there is something mighty suspicious about it. We could risk our life and waste our days in search of it, or we could spend our days and energy in a world we do know of, and do much good."

"Aiden, ye would consider joining me on this quest, wouldn't ye?"

"I would. Would you consider joining me on another quest? One where we hunt, fight the bad, and seek the good things in this world. This world we know."

"Aye. I'm not ready to seek the promise land just yet. I don't think that I'm able to do it on me own. I will join ye and become more powerful—more capable like ye are. Then we'll seek the promise land together. If there ain't nothin' there then we'll keep fightin' the good fight in this here world, together."

"We'll need to leave soon. We'll need time to prepare for the winter. You don't suppose we'll go anywhere without these boys here?" Aiden asked, indicating Daxton, Marcus, and Terence.

"I believe we are stuck with them for life, I do."

At this moment Terence was waiving his sword in the air and yelling, "I'm the champ!"

Marcus lay flat on his back, sword still in hand. Daxton was yapping about something ceaselessly. Aiden afforded a smile and they both laughed heartily.

As the gang arrived back to their homes Jashion's attention turned to a little scene taking place near Tollybrit's hut. Tollybrit's sister, Linda, was giving Tora, the little dark skinned woman, an earful. Jemma was near Tora with her head down. Jashion could tell that Jemma was very upset. Linda was a very domineering woman. No one stood up to Linda, except sometimes Tollybrit. Most of the time Tollybrit just smiled and let Linda do her thing. Tora was no match for Linda. Jashion had seen Tora cower obediently to Linda many a time. This time Tora was trying to stand her ground as best as she could and Linda was more intense than ever. It was clear that Jemma somehow was at the center of it all.

Jemma had become friends with Tora and her children right from the time that they had arrived in Tengeer. Tora was clearly not a Tengeer, though Jashion did not know where she was from. He had never seen evidence of the father of Tora's children. Perhaps he was away or was dead. Tora may have sought refuge among the Tengeer. Jashion could not think of a better people to live among. It was safe here, at least relatively safe. There was food and shelter, and the people were kind— sometimes Linda could be a bit bossy, but overall Jashion thought they were the best of people.

At first, Linda didn't seem to bother with Jemma. Once they had been here for a few weeks and it became clear that Jemma was here for good, Linda became very interested in Jemma. From what Jashion could tell Linda was not pleased with Jemma's education, or lack thereof. She did not seem too pleased with the progress or the potential with Tora's children either. It was becoming obvious that Linda considered it her duty to see to the care and education of Jemma, despite how Jemma, Tora, or anyone else felt about it.

Jashion was thrilled that she would be taken care of so well. He was very fond of the little lass, seeing what all they had been through together. She and he were the last of his people, and he wanted her life to be good. But he really couldn't care for her, and she was happy here. Still, he suspected that her upbringing thus far had not been very happy, that she was domineered and raised in fear and strict obedience. She cowered in this environment but she flourished when given love and freedom. Jemma was happy with Tora and her children and Jashion longed for her to be raised in that loving environment.

Jashion made his way toward Jemma. Jemma looked up at him with a fearful expression in her eyes.

"I need to talk with the little lass, here."

"We are conversing about her just now. You will need to wait," said Linda tersely.

"It can't be waiting, ma'am." He took Jemma by the hand and walked off without awaiting a further reply.

"Humph," Linda sighed before turning her attention back to Tora.

Meanwhile, Aiden had made his way to Tollybrit and the other boys had wandered off. Tollybrit sat back smoking and listening carefully to Aiden. Tollybrit and Aiden had developed a deep respect for one another. Occasionally Tollybrit nodded, but other than that he seemed to focused on listening.

Jashion and Jemma walked until they were away from anyone. He held her hand. Jemma and Jashion had not spent much time together since arriving at Tengeer. This was a special treat to have some time with Jashion and she appreciated this bit of affection.

"Jemma, we need to talk some, we do."

Jemma's countenance dropped again. This did not sound good to her.

"Me isn't staying here much more. I'm gonna go with Aiden, see. And we might not be back. I don't know, maybe we will be back but maybe we won't. So, this is a good home for ye here. There is children and good people and lots to eat and the stinkin' dragon doesn't come 'round these parts. So ye will be taken good care of, ye will."

Jemma looked Jashion in the eyes. Jashion could see tears beginning to form.

"Ye's got friends here, now. Me seen ye play all the day with 'em. Ye even sleep at Ms. Tora's with her children, ye do. Ye is safe here, see."

Tears were then streaming down little Jemma's face and she began to sniffle. Jashion opened up his arms and Jemma embraced him tenderly.

"Jashion, I love ye," followed by sniffle, sniffle, sniffle. "Ye saved me...and Aiden saved us both, he did." "I'll miss ye...so much, I will."

"Now there...I will miss ye too, Jemma. Ye is a fine little lass. Ye saved me, too. We helped each other, we did. We's a good team, we is. But, ye is little and me's leavin', me is. And ye needs a mother and all. So, Aiden's found ye a good home, and Tora will be a good mother to ye and..."

"Nay, but Linda is a gonna take me, she is. She's a tellin' Tora just now that I ain't a being raised proper and me play's too much, and me needs more learnin', me do. So, she's a gonna take me and then sometimes I can play with me friends."

"Do ye wants to be with Linda and learnin' and bein' raised proper and all?"

Jemma stood there frozen with red eyes and tear stains. Slowly she shook her head. "I want to be with Tora and me friends, I do."

"Well, then, I'm gonna see to that, I will. Will that make ye feel better, eh?"

She stood still again. "Aye, but I'll still miss ye."

"And I'll miss ye too."

⌘⌘⌘

"Those boys have imprinted on you two," explained Tollybrit. "Their families will worry and fuss some but it will be better if they just head out with you. If you don't take them they will just follow after you, anyway." He sat back and let out a puff of smoke. "I like their survival chances better if I know they're with you. Winter'll be rough. You know that. They'll not survive a winter on their own, I dare say, if they don't catch up with you."

Aiden sat back and listened. The two men sat next to each other but did not give eye contact while they spoke—both preferring to look ahead of them at the happenings around Tengeer.

"You're not planning on taking the littl' un with you?"

"No," said Aiden. "We'd like for her to be brought up here. She has no family. I think that she is happy enough here and she will be safe."

"Tengeer does make a fine refugee camp," Tollybrit said with a wry smile and puffed out a smoke ring.

Aiden let out a laugh and the two men laughed pleasantly together. It was obvious as the men looked over the people that the Tengeer was a mongrel bred. Yet mongrels are often the strongest and the happiest.

"My sister'll take her. She'll complain of the injustice while not letting anyone else near her. She's a smart littl' un. Linda'll make sure that she is raised up good and proper. She'll educate her and teach her manners—may even let her play sometimes."

"It's settled then."

"Yes, I believe so. When do you expect to be leavin'?"

"Waiting won't help us survive the winter. We'll leave first thing in the morning."

"I don't suppose you'll want a going away party tonight? We put on quite the bash when you got here."

"I'm all for a grand welcoming. I prefer to leave early and quietly. The less fuss the better."

Tollybrit made his way over to Linda. Aiden watched as she put her hands on her hips, then shook her head, put her hands up in the air and scurried off to her hut. *Good, Jemma will be kept well.* No one watched Tora, who was huddled over a fire preparing dinner for her family. Tears welled up in her eyes as she realized what was happening. She pulled her food off of the fire and walked to her hut, head down, and didn't return to her food for a quarter of an hour.

Aiden made his way over to the blond trio. They were all lying in the grass under the shade of a large tree and sipping cool water—recovering from their severe exhaustion after thirty minutes of sword fighting.

"We're leaving early in the morning—just as the sun comes up."

Daxton sat up straight. "Where to?"

Aiden stood there for some time eyeing the boys. "Hard to say. We'll be gone for good, though."

"You're leavin' us?" asked Terence.

"We're leaving."

"I'm coming, too," said Terence assertively.

Marcus looked at Terence with his eyes wide.

"Then I'm coming," said Daxton.

"I'm going, too," said Marcus.

Aiden looked over the boys. "We may die. Winter's ahead, and we'll have to take cover in the dark forest. War may be on the horizon and we may be called to battle. If you come your boyhoods are over. Only men can make this journey."

Marcus looked a little pale.

"I'm coming," said Terence getting up.

"I'm coming," said Daxton frustrated to be beaten to the punch again.

"I'm not staying here," said Marcus.

"We leave at dawn. Only bring what you can comfortably carry. We'll be walking a very long way," and Aiden was gone.

Aiden returned to a bit of a scene. Jashion had returned with Jemma and had made his way over to Tora who was still by her fire.

"Oh boy," muttered Tollybrit aloud to himself as he watched again from his chair. He looked over towards Linda's hut and could see that she was busily preparing it for the littl' un.

Linda looked up and saw Jashion talking with Tora and Jemma by his side. She watched for a moment and then began to stomp towards them. Tollybrit looked back at Tora who had just stood up. He could see the joy on her face. She looked down and spoke something to the Jemma; then Jemma ran into her arms and they embraced.

"Oh, no, you don't!" he heard Linda screech while stomping even faster. Tollybrit almost got up to make his way over but then thought better of it.

"That littl' un is stayin' with me. It's already been decided. I've already set up the place. She's stayin' with me. I'm looking after her now that you boys are leavin'. It's already been decided." She was making a beeline for Jemma with her hand outstretched to take the child's hand.

Jashion moved assertively to block Linda's progress. "Nay, but I'm decidin' where she's stayin', me is. Jemma and me's decided she's stayin' with Ms. Tora, here. Jemma has friends here, she does. I decided and that's that.

Linda moved to get around Jashion but was blocked. "Oh, no. Tollybrit and Aiden already decided," she said with fury in her voice.

"Tollybrit," she yelled. "Get over here, Tollybrit!"

Tollybrit arouse slowly and began a slow jaunt over to where the action was.

"Where's Aiden...there you are, Aiden, get over here," she said loudly beginning to gather her strength. Coming to her senses she realized that looking like a mad woman might be unseemly, she began to take a more diplomatic approach in her loud responses.

More quietly so that just Jashion, Tora, and Jemma could hear she said, "You fool. You and the child would be dead if it wasn't for Aiden. You even speak like a fool. You have no idea what the needs of the child are."

"Jemma and me...we's the last of our people, we is. I'm gonna make sure she's fine. I want her raised by Tora, I do. If I don't have this assurance, me's takin' Jemma with me."

"You can't take that child with you. You're all likely to die as it is. You'd just be killin' her, too. And you," then addressing herself to Tora, "you can't even read or write. You don't educate your children. They're practically savages...with no manners, running around, making noise, playing all day. They'll be no good, those children of yours!"

"Now, Linda," said Tollybrit who had made his way to the group, "Tora is a fine woman. She takes good care of her children. She is a good mother and has been good and kind to everyone here, you included. You've said so yourself many a time to me. Don't you go insulting Tora just to get what you want."

"Humph," Linda expressed. "You told me yourself that it was decided, you and Aiden decided that it would be best if I kept the littl' un here. Don't you go changin' your story just to not upset folks."

Aiden had made his way to the fire. Jemma and Tora were still holding on to each other.

"Aiden," Linda began, "you and Tollybrit already decided, didn't you? Jemma is stayin' with me, not Tora."

"Jashion," said Aiden, "the choice is yours. Who do you want Jemma to say with?"

"With Tora, Jemma and me's already decided, we has."

"Tora, will you take and raise Jemma as your own," asked Aiden directly.

When Aiden asked a question directly with his presence and penetrating eyes it could freeze even the most confident man or woman. Tora had never been asked such a question by such a powerful figure as Aiden before. She trembled under the weight of his inquisition. She then looked at Linda who glared intimidatingly at her. She continued to tremble and look around, not able to answer.

"She's..." Linda began.

Aiden held up his hand, immediately silencing Linda, while continuing to bore into Tora with his gaze.

"...I...love this child," she spoke in barely a whisper. "Jemma...she has lost everything. She should be happy. I'd be pleased for any teaching she or my child should receive. I want them to read, but I can't teach that. Mostly, I want the children to be happy. I'll raise her if you let me." Her final words were nearly incomprehensible as she began to sob.

"Jemma will stay with Tora," Aiden declared.

"Aye," said Jashion.

Jemma smiled brightly and glowed as she looked up and embraced the sobbing Tora again.

Linda was befuddled, having never been overpowered by such a presence as Aiden before. She was about to bolt when Jemma made her way over to her.

"Linda, thank ye for wantin' to take care of me. I'm sorry to make ye mad." Jemma embraced Linda warmly. For a moment Linda stayed stiff. Then a single tear drop formed in her eye and she bent into the child and embraced her warmly.

"Alright; it's okay. I'm not mad; I'm just makin' sure that you are well cared for. Don't fuss now. You can stay with Ms. Tora here. But I will teach you and her children to read. You can't play all day. You have to work, and learn, and become proper, now."

Jemma looked at her in the eyes and nodded. Tora made her way over and embraced Linda.

"I'm sorry, Linda..."

"Now, now it's fine. We've got work to do. I've got some things prepared for the child. I'll just bring them over to your hut."

Tollybrit put his hand on Aiden's shoulder. "Well done," he said to which Aiden made no reply. Tollybrit made his way back to his chair and his smoke. Too much excitement for him, time to calm back down.

"Ye is gonna be just fine now, little lass, ye is." Jashion leaned down and gave Jemma a kiss on the cheek. Jemma looked at him for a moment and smiled. Tora's children had gathered outside of their hut's door watching and listening with interest. Jemma ran over to them. Within moments they were holding hands, running in a circle, and making marry.

Two hours before the crack of dawn Aiden's eyes opened. Aiden loved the dark hours prior to any departure. He visualized in his mind all that would be required while making any last-minute preparations. He always traveled light—only the clothes on his back, weapons, and minimal supplies. Everything was ready within minutes and he began to sharpen his already adequately sharpened blades. He became aware of a presence next to him and nearly jumped. Spooking Aiden was a nearly impossible task.

In the darkness Aiden had to strain to tell that it was Terence who had seated himself quietly beside him. "I'm ready when you are," Terence said quietly.

"I believe you are," said Aiden warmly. "Let me see what you've got." He inspected Terence's things removing a few items and making some mild suggestions. Aiden laid his blades aside and began to teach Terence how to sharpen his.

"Daxton will be here shortly. I'm not sure if Marcus is coming." Aiden could hear the significance in his voice. The spreading of wings and the flight from the nest is a very individual experience for each bird. Aiden was two years older and significantly more prepared when he left home than Terence was. Aiden allowed himself to feel a brief nostalgia. He loved his family and his people. It was good to be reminded from time to time.

Jashion stirred a few feet away but continued to sleep.

"Will he be ready?" asked Terence.

Aiden looked over at his sleeping friend. "Yes. He's ready; perhaps more ready than any of us. Let him be for now. I'll tell you when to wake him."

Daxton arrived twenty minutes later, not surprising at all the other two.

"We're going to need to work on your footprint," said Aiden.

"Huh?" said Daxton. "Let's go, Marcus is staying."

Terence looked over toward Daxton for a moment. He took the knife that he had been sharpening and began carving aimlessly in the dirt while looking down. Aiden made his way over to Jashion and put his hand on his shoulder. Jashion opened his eyes and looked up."

"It's time."

Jashion nodded and arose.

"Have you eaten?" Aiden asked the cousins.

"No, I'm not hungry yet," said Daxton.

"You may not eat again today. Better eat a good meal now."

"What?"

Aiden went and fixed a nice meal. Jashion gathered his limited things. Though Aiden had not supposed, Jashion's heart was heavy. He was leaving more in Tengeer than expected. He had been safe here, enjoyed pleasant associations, and was leaving the only person left of his people. Jemma had become very dear to him and he would miss her. While the other boys were departing from their home, and perhaps forever, they at least had a home they could return to. Jashion was cutting the last tie he had to any home at all.

Daylight broke and Aiden stood. The other boys followed suit and were soon walking away from the rich dark soil and bittersweet scent of Tengeer. Each heart was heavy in its own way but every face was brave. No one dared a look back. Each focused on the white peaks of the mountains in the far distance.

"Wait," they heard from behind them. Marcus ran towards them.

Aiden stared searchingly at the boy running towards them. Behind him he saw a beautiful blond woman and an equally handsome blond man. They both embraced each other and were clearly emotional. Terence waved and they echoed in response. Marcus had said his goodbye's and did not turn around again.

"Let's go," said Marcus in a quavering voice. "Why didn't you wait for me, I told you I was coming." His cheeks were stained with tears but his eyes were resolute.

"You've eaten?" Aiden asked.

"Yes."

The other four turned around taking in their final view of Tengeer.

"Where we's headin'?"

"Same as we came here."

"We's headin' to the dark forest, we is?"

No one answered for some time. After several yards Aiden explained. "There are two major strongholds in this land. We can't make it to either before the onset of winter. If we head out on this barren plain, east towards Cardsten, we will either die of starvation, the winter elements, or your friend Dromreign. The dark forest isn't exactly a picnic spot, but there is food, shelter, firewood, and we will be hidden from the dragon. We can head east through the edge of the forest. The wolves won't like it but if we hug the edge they are not likely to try anything. If they do, I like our chances together. We survived a few nights in the heart of their land with just me, an invalid, and a little child. The five of us should hold our own against them. They'll remember us. We are already legend among the wolf.

"During the day we can head deeper in and hunt and fish. At night we'll hunker down closer to the edge. It will be slow going but we should survive the winter and be much closer to Cardsten. When we reach the corner of the forest and it follows the mountains to the north we have two choices. We can head south to Cardsten or continue east towards Agedon."

"What's the difference?" asked Daxton.

"Everything."

They walked on in silence, reaching the little oasis by mid-day. A few fish were caught and fried.

"We'll stay here today. We can rest and will have food for dinner and breakfast tomorrow. Tomorrow's journey will be much longer."

The trio napped in the cool tall grass and Jashion followed Aiden a little way off.

"Where we's headin'?"

"I don't know yet. There may be war between the two capitals. Once we understand the two sides better we can decide which to give our assistance."

"Maybe neither ain't worth fightin' for."

"Perhaps."

Jashion leaned back against a large rock and tossed pebbles into the pond.

"It's all about Dromreign. He's becoming a greater menace. Towns and villages like yours have been slaughtered throughout the land. He seems to be growing in power. The destruction and the frequency are increasing. When you were a child attacks on Dargaer took out sections of the town. Now he can wipe it out entirely. Agedon believes it is time to take the dragon head on, to destroy it, and stop this menace forever. They are amassing an army to do just that."

"That must be where we's headin'."

"Perhaps. Cardsten is also amassing an army. An army to stop Agedon. They don't think that it's possible for man to defeat Dromreign. They think that it will just infuriate the dragon and bring destruction on the capitals. Thus far, the dragon has been content to attack just the towns and villages and not the major cities. Cardsten believes that all Agedon is doing is stirring up a hornets' nest. They figure that Agedon will fail and then Cardsten may receive repercussions from Dromreign. Cardsten has a lot to lose. It is a fine city. A land of opulence, of finery, and wealth. They have a great wall and high lookout towers.

"They think that they can continue to enjoy their existence at the expense of the other towns and villages who are taking a beating. It is said that some there even worship the dragon, like some kind of god."

"We should definitely go to Agedon, we should."

"Yes, perhaps. Still, not all you hear badly about a place should be believed. Those of Agedon would want others to think badly of Cardsten. Agedon needs to amass an army both large enough to ward of Cardsten and defeat the dragon. This will not be easy and they may be exaggerating Cardsten's position in order to gather mercenaries, such as us, to their side. Cardsten is very wise. They have learned much over the years. They have knowledge and power there that is unheard of in other parts of the land. The power of Dromreign is great. There may be something to building adequate defenses against it rather than aggravating in. A hunter must know that it can defeat its prey before he goes after it—otherwise he becomes the prey."

The following day they began their journey before the crack of dawn. Aiden hoped to arrive at the dark forest before nightfall. In this he was disappointed; they were still boys and not quite men.

"I'm exhausted," said Marcus.

"I'm starving," said Terence.

"Well, you should have stayed home with your mamma. This is a journey for men," said Daxton.

"Oh, shut up!" the brothers shouted at him and Terence flung his pack at Daxton hitting him in the shoulder.

"Ouch. What are you doing? Pick that up; we're not in the forest yet. Besides, you're not eating anything until we hunt. If you're too tired to hunt, you'll stay starving."

From close within the nearby forest a wolf howled stopping the travelers in their tracks. Aiden held up his hand.

"Was that the wolves?" asked Marcus.

"Hush," whispered Aiden. They listened for a while and continued to hear howls and activity nearby. "We can't enter now. Something is going on," Aiden continued to whisper. "I've never seen them behave like this. I don't think we can stay the night here in the open either."

"What are we going to do?" said Daxton too loudly.

"Hush! You may sleep here for now."

"Here, on the hard ground, right in the open?" whispered Daxton.

"You may continue to stand if you prefer," whispered Aiden. "Stay here." Aiden walked solitarily into the dark forest.

Several hours later he returned to four sleeping travelers. "Wake up," he called softly. Only Jashion stirred. "We must enter in now. The wolves are sleeping." Jashion's body ached both from the travels and the poor sleeping conditions.

"Get ye up, ye's," he said as he pushed on Marcus' shoulder.

"Huh, what?"

"Get ye up, we's goin' into the forest now, we is."

"Oh. Hey, get up Terence. Get up Daxton."

"Shh," said Aiden. "If you can't stay quiet, you'll be wolf meat soon enough."

Minutes later they entered the dark forest and headed to an area Aiden had already picked out. The four who had been sleeping easily found their way back into a slumber. Sleep would not be Aiden's companion that night. He stayed awake and listened to the silence. Finally, the light of dawn approached. Perhaps then he could venture a little sleep. He closed his eyes briefly. Then the hair on his arms and neck stood straight up. He flung his eyes open and listened carefully. Something was not right, but what was it? Then his eyes took hold and he drunk in the filthy odor. Above the trees Dromreign flew. Aiden stared as long as he could. The bloated belly told of the nights' destruction. Terror had struck again. Aiden looked at the massive beast, trying to find a weakness or a soft spot. The beast did not seem to have a scratch or a scar. Its muscles rippled with each stroke of its wings. The wings were massive and powerful.

Only the beast's fierce red eyes seemed weak. They squinted in the early dawn's sunlight. The odor began to gag Aiden. Even when Dromreign was gone its scent lingered. The sleepers muttered and coughed in their sleep. Jashion's face showed distress. What horrible nightmares that scent brought to his sleeping companions.

The following weeks went by without one day much different from another. They headed east slowly, hunting and fishing during the day. Sometimes Aiden would disappear asking them to continue on. Once he was gone for three days and the others feared the worst. Hunger on the second day forced the four to hunt on their own. They were eventually successful. Aiden arrived just in time for the meal. Jashion suspected that he had stayed nearby to watch them. They couldn't always rely on Aiden's skills. They needed to strengthen and grow if they were going to survive the dark forest in the winter.

The days were shortening and the air was cooling quickly. "We'll need winter skins to wear, soon. Tomorrows hunt will not just be for food." That evening a few flakes of snow fell.

Chapter 8

A few snowflakes had fallen the night before, but this day was beautiful. Warm, sunny, clear blue sky—a perfect late fall day. It was the day before Sarah Peningham's sixteenth birthday. Sarah had not heard from John. She had not heard anything about John for they ran in completely separate circles and did not live nearby each other. Since their dance, she had anticipated her birthday more than she had ever anticipated anything before. With it nearly upon her, she felt the pang of disappointment arising. It had been a perfect night but it was so long ago. And he was John Bennett. So many girls longed to be with him—so many girls who were so much prettier and cleverer—more talented, more popular, more fit to be in his arms than was she. It was a beautiful dream but soon, she feared, it would be over. Not only would her heart be broken but her newfound social prominence would also disappear. She had never minded being Sarah Peningham before. But that was before—before she had had a taste of the affection of John, before she had experienced being visible, before she saw herself as worth as much as anyone else. She could never be comfortable and satisfied being invisible and forgettable again

These types of thoughts and feelings had washed over her many times that day. But they were often replaced with a feeling of excitement and anticipation. Maybe he would come and ask her out. Maybe he was also waiting with anticipation for this day. He had asked and re-asked her when her sixteenth birthday was. He had asked and re-asked her to dance. Every girl was there, at the dance. He could have danced with her once or twice and then asked the others to dance. Even if he was interested in her, he didn't have to dance the night away with her. He wanted to be with her over every other girl. He couldn't ask her out before she was sixteen. If he had wanted to go out with her he couldn't have done anything up to this point, anyway. She remembered how he had looked at her and how he treated her. There was no question about how he had felt about her. In just one short day he could see her if he wanted to. She could see him. The excitement would build, until doubt set in again.

"I'll bet John will bring you flowers on your birthday!" said Maryanne the day before. "He's probably been planning everything out for weeks now."

Sarah had left her birthday open. Everyone understood— her mother, Maryanne, Natalie, Kendra, and Bernice. Everyone, except for her father.

"But our little Sarah always likes to plan her birthday, and this is her sixteenth. What are we going to do all day? She seems to have a lot of nice friends these days. Why don't we have everyone over?" Actually, Mr. Peningham knew much more than he was letting on.

Dinner was finished and the sun began to set. Sarah walked out onto her deck. She just wanted to be alone, but she didn't want to be far from the house. The tall snow-topped mountain peaks glistened as the sun fell behind them. Sarah loved those peaks. She loved their majesty and their strength. They encircled her like a warm embrace from her father. She was protected, secured, and comforted by the mountains that surrounded her. Not only were they exquisitely beautiful as she gazed upon them, but they meant so much to her. Sarah understood their value and significance. She cherished them. Nearly everything about her life, and her way of life, was possible only because they were there.

The land where she lived, the land encircled by those majestic mountains, the land known as the promise land, was a land of peace and prosperity. It was void of much sickness and disease. The people there were good. Sarah knew that there existed an entirely different world on the other side of the mountains. Many people lived on the other side, many more than lived in the promise land. In the outer land the people lived in fear. She had heard the stories of fierce creatures that sought human flesh. There was sickness, disease, famine, pestilence, war, and sorrow. Sometimes she reflected upon those people. They were just like her and yet they did not live as she lived. There was nothing to be afraid of in the promise land. How could so many people live in fear and sorrow all the days of their lives?

There was a way to get into the promise land from the outside world. Yet, it was so rare that anyone came through. Sometimes people would explain that their father or grandmother had come from the world outside. Most people she knew went back generations of being in the promise land. If she lived in that world she would stop at nothing to get into the promise land. Why live in fear when there was a land that offered complete protection? She sorrowed for those whom she did not even know. The way in was underneath her special place, deep below the waterfall. There was a deep cavernous passage that linked the water in her pool to the water in that land. Though difficult the way it was possible to reach those waters. Though a person must be healthy, strong, and well, and must leave all behind, they could immerse themselves deeply in that water and swim the passage, allowing them to surface in the promise land. The very pool she swam in regularly was the entrance—the only way in. None of the fearful creatures would attempt to enter. Only a person who knew what she was doing would go this way. The people who came did so knowing what they would find. They were happy to be a part of this glorious world. They were accepted in and helped to become established there. It was so strange to Sarah that more did not come.

Stranger still, some within the promise land actually left. Through that same opening they would simply swim back out. Why someone would leave this land to go into the other was incomprehensible to her. She did not spend much time reflecting on it. It made her shudder.

This night she was not thinking about those who came and left. She was simply admiring those immense peaks that allowed her to live just as she desired. She felt empowered and free because of them. They protected her from every danger and allowed her to experience life peacefully and without fear.

⌘ ⌘ ⌘

It must have been women's intuition how Janice knew that John would be coming by that evening. Somehow she even knew the time. She peeked out the curtain of her upstairs bedroom and sure enough there he was walking down the path. He hadn't seen her yet, so she drank in his presence a little longer. Janice's heart leaped. *He brought flowers!*

The past six weeks had been the time of her life. She and John had spent every moment possible together. He was everything that she could ask for in a young man, and more. She had worried when Kevin and Amanda had broken up that their relationship would be in jeopardy. It was not. Sometimes he and she just spent time together. Other times they were joined by Kevin and whoever he was dating or wooing at that time. At other times they were joined by Amanda and Riley, her new guy. The thing that was troubling Janice was how platonic the relationship had been. They both seemed blissful in each other's company yet John never moved toward any affection.

At first this was refreshing for her. She liked moving slowly and found that most guys she showed even a passing interest in wanted to move along way too quickly. Then, six weeks later, she was ready to be kissed—more than ready. Tonight, he had brought flowers; that meant something.

Just as she was about to turn away and head downstairs John did something strange. He put the flowers down behind a large rock in the path and continued on without them.

What's he doing, she wondered. *He must have something planned. I'll play along. Tonight will be a new beginning, the start of a deep and meaningful relationship.* This is the man that Janice was going to marry and tonight would be special. It would be sealed with a kiss.

She turned to her mirror and looked herself over. She was wearing a lovely maroon dress with her hair down straight. She was made up nicely. She wanted to look great but not so adorned that she looked like she was expecting him. *Perfect*, she thought.

The encounter at the door only lasted a few minutes. Janice closed the door and the tears that had welled up began to overflow. She didn't want to sob with him close enough to hear but she could hardly contain herself. Sickness and darkness filled her heart. She had been warned; she knew what he was like. So many a girl had been heartbroken by John Bennett. She should have known. Six weeks and not a single kiss? Anger, frustration, and bitter sorrowed filled her. Love turned sour is utterly unbearable. There was no other John Bennett and he had not left the door open, even partway. He was gone and she regretted every moment, every happiness she had ever felt in his presence.

If I'm not good enough for him, who is? He had brought flowers? There must be someone else, but who. He has been with me all of the time. All of a sudden there is somebody else and he just wants to throw all of this away? It just made it hurt that much more. Not only had she been rejected, she had been usurped. Some girl probably laughed at her misfortune this night. *Oh, she knew. She must have known who John was dating. Now, she has beat me out and is loving every moment of it. Well, enjoy your week or maybe your month. Soon he'll come dancing down on your heart and tearing it into pieces. Laugh today, cry tomorrow. My first moments with him, those glorious first hours together, must have been at the expense of some other girls' bitter tears. What is his problem? And what is wrong with me? What is so special about this girl? Does he just like variety? Will he not stop until he ruptures every girl's heart?*

Janice was bitter. She had never really felt the pang of a broken heart. Not really. She never imagined that she wouldn't win the guy of her choosing. She was not an arrogant person. She was confident—had been confident, until then. Some broken hearts mend faster than others. Janice had become inconsolable. The darkness and depression would last a very long time for her. Janice's heart would mend, and in some ways it would be for the better, but it would never be the same again.

⌘⌘⌘

John was tired. He had stayed up more than half the night deliberating the actions of this day. It was getting dark and his eyes were heavy. Saying goodbye to Janice was hard. It had never been hard to say goodbye to a girl before. He was used to the tears and the drama; that didn't bother him. He'd even had things thrown at him before. Girls could get so emotional. Janice was classy. She was always classy. Both the tears welling up and the expression on her face were fair. There was something special between them, and he felt badly too.

He tried not to lead her on too much. He didn't want her to feel so hurt if he did say goodbye. But Janice had had a chance. He had considered her—seriously considered her. He wasn't just stringing her along. It could have just as easily have been Sarah whose heart would be broken. In the last night, he could see one thing lacking with Janice, and that one thing was what he saw in Sarah: pure goodness. Janice was a good person, but he hadn't caught that glimpse of eternity that he saw when he looked into Sarah's eyes. He saw in Janice everything that he wanted in the present, but when he looked at Sarah he saw a glorious eternity.

He was having the time of his life with Janice, except that it wasn't as good as when he danced with Sarah. That experience surpassed what he had felt over the past six weeks. Janice was everything he had ever wanted, until he met Sarah, and he had to make a choice. At times when he said goodnight he was holding the girl of his dreams and all he could think about was Sarah. If at those moments his heart returned to Sarah, then that must be where his heart led. Janice was wonderful in every way, but she was not Sarah. In fact, she was nothing like Sarah at all. His mind caught the memory of the vision of his first looking at Sarah at the dance. It was the sweetest memory of his life. There was no question in his mind, he was in love with Sarah and he knew that no other girl in the world could compare to her.

Yes, another heart would be broken. Somehow he understood that that would happen this time. Perhaps it was because this time he felt something too. Still, John wasn't looking for girlfriends. He was looking to court the woman that would become his wife. If he hadn't met Sarah, Janice would have filled his heart. But he had met Sarah and he was sure that she was all he would ever need. No sense in wasting any more time with any other girl. He knew who his girl was and he couldn't wait until he could spend his time with her.

⌘⌘⌘

A beautiful warm day was getting a little cold. Sarah rubbed her upper arms with her hands. She could hardly see the mountain peaks. They were but a darker silhouette against a dark sky. She felt so good inside. She was at peace; whatever tomorrow would bring. Sarah stood in preparation to head inside.

"Sarah," she heard from the distance behind her. That voice, she knew that voice. Her heart skipped a beat and then caught up quickly beating hard and fast. It was John.

Sarah turned around seeing a figure moving towards her. She stood and watched as slowly the figure's features came into view.

"John, oh John, you came!" she said, not attempting to conceal her excitement and relief.

"Oh, Sarah," and his heart felt everything he had hoped that it would. Janice was wonderful but Sarah was special. He closed the short distance between them and opened up his arms to which Sarah entered lovingly in. The magic in its entire splendor had returned to both of them.

"These are for you," he said, indicating the flowers and presenting them to her. "Happy Birthday!"

"Oh, they're lovely," and she drank in their scent holding them close to her nose. "But, it's not my birthday yet; I'm still fifteen...not until tomorrow..."

"I know. I thought that I could at least set up a date with you. Meet your parents and such. They won't be upset?"

"No, I don't think they will. Come in...no, wait here. No, come in. Just a minute."

John smiled as Sarah moved towards her home awkwardly. Everything about her, even her awkwardness and quirkiness brought joy to his soul. But when she embraced him he felt joy unlike anything had ever prepared him for.

Sarah reappeared at the door motioning John to come closer with her arm. She was still holding the bouquet in her other hand. She didn't quite seem to know what to do with it.

John arrived at the door simultaneously with Mr. Peningham. Sarah's father extended his hand saying, "I understand you are John Bennett. I'm Mr. Peningham, Sarah's father. Now, Sarah won't be sixteen until tomor...

"Hi, John, do come in. I'm Mrs. Peningham, Sarah's mother. I'm so pleased to meet you, do come in."

John changed his gaze from the father to the mother. She was all aglow and beckoning him in. He looked back at the father who had dropped his head in resignation. John smiled and made a move towards entering, not sure who of the three individuals that were blocking the doorway would make way for him. It certainly wasn't going to be Sarah. She was staring at John's handsome features lit by her homes indoor lighting. John smiled. The family's awkwardness amused him in a pleasant way. He felt no condescension towards them. Mrs. Peningham began to back up and she grabbed her husband's elbow and helped him move back some. John entered with Sarah's gaze unbroken from his face.

John followed Mr. and Mrs. Peningham into their living room. Sarah followed John with her pretty flowers held in both hands, walking almost trance like behind them. Sarah was not capable of wiping the heartfelt smile from her face. The three sat down together and awkward silence ensued. John sat apart in a comfy chair—actually, Mr. Peningham's. Mr. and Mrs. Peningham sat on a loveseat and Sarah sat on the arm of the loveseat higher up near her mother.

The family faced him until Mr. Peningham bent over slightly and dropped his head. He fumbled with his thumbs for a few moments. Mrs. Peningham and Sarah both stared at John with bright smiling faces. John smiled back and decided that he had better begin.

"Mr. Peningham, I know that Sarah's birthday is not until tomorrow. I know that she must have plans already. I thought I might at least invite her to go horseback riding with me tomorrow. Of course, we could make it another time if tomorrow is not a good time."

Sarah's eyes widened and she looked down at her mother's exuberant countenance.

"Sarah, you didn't seem to want any plans for your birthday. You seemed to be hoping for a quiet day at home. Would you want to be away...horseback riding with..."

"Oh, yes, daddy," she said looking back at John.

John looked back at her, feeling Sarah's excitement radiate from her.

"Your father owns horses, son?"

"No, sir, my..."

"Would you be going alone, or are others going with you?"

"No, sir, my friend Kevin, his father has..."

"Sarah will be going with you and your friend?"

"Yes, sir, K..."

"Honey, do you want Sarah going horseback riding with two boys we don't even know?"

"John, is Kevin bringing anyone along with him?" asked Mrs. Peningham sweetly.

"Yes, Ma'am. I'm afraid I don't know her. I know that she'd agreed earlier today."

"Well, why didn't you say so?"

"Well, sir..."

"Sarah, dear, is that how you would like to spend your sixteenth birthday? With three people you don't know so well."

"Oh, yes, daddy!"

Then turning to her mother, "Is it okay if I go?"

Mrs. Peningham turned to Mr. Peningham gleaming. "It's okay, isn't it dear?"

"Um..."

"She'll be sixteen tomorrow, and it's such a nice offer."

Mr. Peningham felt the glare bearing down on him from all three. After a short paused he nodded tentatively.

"Thank you, daddy!" Mr. Peningham looked up and smiled at his adoring daughter. At least for the moment she was still his girl.

"John, thank you so much! That sounds just wonderful. What time shall we go?"

"Well, I'll be by at nine in the morning. Dress in layers—I don't know if it'll be warm or cold tomorrow. Wear some sturdy pants and shoes for riding. I'll take care of everything else. Eat a good breakfast. We'll lunch at noon."

Sarah nodded excitedly.

"John it's so nice to meet you. Thank you for being so kind to Sarah," said Mrs. Peningham.

John nodded and got up. "I'm sorry to have intruded upon your evening," he said pleasantly.

Everyone arose and brushed his comment aside by shaking their heads. He extended his hand to Mr. Peningham who shook it warmly. He then took Mrs. Peningham's fingers and kissed her knuckles softly. Mrs. Peningham blushed a little. He then stood across from Sarah. She beamed at him, but holding her flowers in both hands did not think to offer him her hand.

"Sarah, happy birthday. I look forward to tomorrow."

"Thank you, John."

⌘⌘⌘

A quarter of an hour late wasn't really too bad considering that they had to bring four horses with only three riders. The real problem was that Naomi wasn't the type of girl to be ready at the appointed hour. Sarah was just beside herself when she finally saw the ensemble approaching.

Mrs. Peningham had made an especially nice breakfast because it was Sarah's birthday and more especially because she wanted her well-fed for this day's adventure. As she watched Sarah's nervous excitement, and then thought about her bumping up and down on the horse, she began to worry that Sarah had eaten too much and would upset her stomach. *Oh, dear*, she fretted. Fretting can be a rather enjoyable pass-time for mothers. Especially fretting over things that nothing can be done about. Mr. Peningham was done fretting by the time he had shaken John's hand the night before. He was reading a book and ignoring everything else.

"Do you see that beautiful horse, mother." It was dark brown with white socks and a white star on its nose.

Mrs. Peningham peaked through the window. "That horse is so big. How will you ever mount it?"

"I'm sure John will help me; he is ever so strong."

Mr. Peningham was no longer ignoring everything else. He got up thinking he may want a look at what was coming.

Sarah was ready, so it should have only taken a few moments and they could have been on their way. Mr. and Mrs. Peningham both needed to fret and fuss a bit. So they both fretted and fussed until they had had their fill. John was extraordinarily patient with them. He answered any question, allayed all concerns, made any and every necessary adjustment, and re-answered every question. Kevin had had enough. He caught Naomi's eyes and rolled his own. Naomi gave an awkward partial smile in reply.

Naomi was pretty enough. She had long brown hair flowing down in large ringlet curls. She had on an olive-green top with brown pants. She had a freckly face, particularly on her nose. It worked with her light complexion and baby blue eyes. Her lips were thin and very pale; so pale that the color hardly changed from her skin tone to her lips. She had on some blush, eyeliner, and mascara, bringing out many of her nicer facial features. But she wore no lipstick giving her an unfinished appearance. Kevin was confused and a little irritated by that omission. He was even more irritated because he considered it, at least partially, his own fault. She was running late and he acted just anxious enough to rush her. Maybe she forgot, or didn't think she had time, so she left without it. *The few extra moments it would have taken to put it on would have been moments well spent*, he thought.

Naomi had been very quiet thus far on the ride from her home to Sarah's. Kevin had met her in a group of her friends.

She hadn't said much at the time either, but he figured that it was because it was a large group and she just wasn't the biggest talker. But she was pretty and seemed interested in him. He'd just broken up with a girl the night before and needed a date for John's 'big' first date with Sarah—he'd promised. He wasn't feeling that things were off to a good start.

After re-looking over Naomi, Kevin took a good look at Sarah. Unlike Naomi, Sarah was very nicely made up. Still, there was only so much to work with. *Hey, at least she tried.* Looking back at Naomi, he thought, *we've sure done better before.* Kevin remembered fondly his first date with Amanda joined by John with Janice. *We were on to something there.* He looked over at John. John was as pleasant as could be. Ordinarily the scene going on at the Peningham's would have driven John nuts. But he was patient and seemed happy. He looked back over at Sarah. *What on earth does he see in her?* Sarah looked up at Kevin and smiled pleasantly. Kevin nodded politely.

It was time for Sarah to mount. John stood beside her, giving her token assistance. Mrs. Peningham looked on with delight while Mr. Peningham looked on suspiciously. Sarah was no weakling and really had no trouble mounting at all. John took his mount and they were off.

The destination was a good three-hour ride from Sarah's home across a long prairie to a different portion of the encircling mountain range. There were some good horse-riding trails along with a gorgeous view. Kevin hoped to arrive by noon. Leaving by nine from Sarah's house would have given them a chance, if the girls were willing to go at a decent pace. Leaving nearly forty minutes late meant that Kevin was going to have a late lunch and this just added to his irritation.

Kevin was not irritable by nature. He was not destined to stay in a foul mood that day either. The girls were decent riders and the day and the ride were pleasant. An hour into the ride and Kevin had sorted himself out. What he was really frustrated about was John and Sarah. He genuinely wondered if his friend had suffered brain damage. Maybe something was wrong with his eyes. Sarah made no sense. John was not desperate, not by a long shot. He couldn't have lost his confidence—he'd just broken everything off with Janice to pursue, whatever this was with Sarah. Kevin had been irritated at the dance, frustrated the next day, and was getting this irritation and frustration out of his system.

He tried some casual conversation multiple times with Naomi. Each time resulted in her awkward half smile. She was capable of answering close ended questions, however, which he began to resort to. Most of the time she answered by nodding or shaking her head. Kevin looked back and saw John and Sarah chattering away pleasantly with each other. *Look who's talking. At least they're having a good time. So, talking isn't Naomi's thing. We'll just ride then.* A good long, looking straight ahead, silent ride and Kevin was back to himself. Naomi, who appreciated the long break from the inquisition, was in better spirits as they stopped for a break near a cool stream.

John and Kevin took care of the horses and the girls walked along the stream together. Sarah and Naomi had never met before. Sarah had picked up that Naomi was the silent type. Sarah muttered a few pleasantries without adding any questions to force Naomi to talk. This increased Naomi's comfort and soon the girls were talking. Naomi was impressed with Sarah. Not for anything in particular about Sarah, just that she was clearly the desired date of John Bennett. Whether John knew them or not, every girl knew about him. Naomi felt completely out of the league of John Bennett, but felt honored to be in the pleasant company of his date. Sarah enjoyed the way it felt to be looked up to by Naomi.

"I hear it's your sixteenth birthday today. Happy birthday!"

"Thank you."

"Have you known John for long? That's pretty great to go out on your actual sixteenth birthday."

"We met at the end of summer dance."

"Oh...was that you dancing with John that night?"

"Yes."

"I guess everyone notices who John is dancing with," said Naomi giggling softly. "I just didn't know you."

"When did you and Kevin meet?"

"Um...just a day ago. He came up to me when I was with my friends. He talked to me for a little and asked if he could come by. I said sure. Then he actually came and asked me out. I don't...get asked out a lot. I have a hard time talking with guys." Naomi shrugged.

Sarah didn't know what to say. She brought her hand up and gently rubbed Naomi on the outside of her arm. "Kevin seems nice."

"Yes. Have you never met him before?"

"Oh, we've met—when we were younger. But, I don't think I've ever really talked with him before."

"You two ready?" asked Kevin from the distance.

"Let's go," said Sarah.

After mounting, Kevin nudged his horse up to Sarah's. John, taking the cue, road up to Naomi. Naomi looked over expecting to see Kevin but rather saw John next to her. She blushed deeply. John didn't have much better luck talking to Naomi than Kevin did. John's mood, however, was not to be broken. He figured really quick that the girl riding next to him wasn't going to have much to say, but her blush told him that she didn't mind him being next to her. He began telling her stories of some of his adventures out in the mountainous areas. Naomi listened, and laughed, and gasped when appropriate. Without much effort John had this girl completely charmed.

Kevin had given in and figuring that he might be spending some time with Sarah—she being John's likely companion for some time; he decided to get to know her. Kevin was neither impressed nor disappointed. Sarah was smart. She laughed at his jokes. She kept the conversation going but didn't talk his ear off. He certainly couldn't find anything wrong with her. Sarah would be alright. She certainly seemed up for adventure.

"Are you a good diver?" Kevin asked.

"I'm okay, I guess," said Sarah.

"Have you ever been out to the farthest side falls."

"Yes. We went once when I was a child. We don't usually travel too much. How long does it take to get there on horseback?"

"You could probably get there in two days if you pushed it. We usually plan for three days each way. Summer time is the best time to go. The ride can be hot but it's the best time to be there. The lake at the base of the falls is deep. I've dived in from thirty-five or forty feet. There is a way to climb up to sixty feet. I hear that it's deep enough to make the dive from sixty feet. John's done it. He's not afraid of anything."

Sarah smiled.

Like I've got to help him out. Kevin smiled to himself.

"There's plenty of smaller dives. You can work yourself all the way up."

"It sounds nice."

"You've got to pack quite a bit. Not too many people live out that way. I guess the ground is rockier and food doesn't grow so well. But, the falls and the diving can't be beat. I like a good adventure. It's as good as it gets here in the promise land," he said putting up finger quotations around, 'the promise land.' Sarah didn't get the gesture.

Kevin felt his stomach growl. Food was important to Kevin. He'd reached the age of the endless metabolism. They were still some ways off, and he'd be less comfortable than desired.

Kevin looked back. John and Naomi were way behind them.

"Let's get this show on the road. Race you." With that Kevin started a gallop.

Sarah was game and off she went, already a few horse lengths behind Kevin. John looked over at Naomi. Whether she'd noticed Sarah and Kevin galloping off or not, she showed no sign of hurrying up. John was a gentleman. For at least the moment, he was escorting Naomi and would do so at her pace.

They arrived to the picnic lunch fully spread out, minus the portion that John was carrying. Sarah had obviously helped Kevin with the preparations. In fact, she may have done most of it. Kevin seemed to be more occupied with the horses. John felt some irritation. It was her birthday, and his special date. He wanted to take care of her. Kevin should have been more considerate. Still, Sarah beamed at him sweetly as she smoothed out a few ruffles on the blanket and watch him dismount.

"You two were in a hurry."

Sarah smiled. "Kevin wanted to race."

"Who won?"

Sarah looked over towards Kevin. "He did, but not by much. Plus, he had a head start." Sarah was obviously having the time of her life.

Naomi hadn't made a move towards dismounting. John considered helping her down. But Kevin, who was holding the rains of his horse and staring off towards the nearby mountains, hadn't even acknowledged his date upon arrival. John decided to walk both horses over to Kevin, with one carrying Kevin's date. John wanted there to be no confusion as to who was with whom from this point on.

As they got close to Kevin he looked over at John. "Not a bad rider at all," he said indicating Sarah.

John could tell that Kevin's mood had been sorted and his compliment genuine. Kevin looked up at Naomi. He smiled pleasantly.

"Here, let's get you down." His manners were back and he was very pleasant with Naomi.

Naomi was in seventh heaven herself. Kevin had long since been an afterthought. John left the horses with Kevin and Naomi, and returned to Sarah.

"Do you mind helping me, here," said Kevin. Kevin and Naomi got the horses watered and secured.

The psychology between them was different then. Naomi was no longer nervous in Kevin's presence. She was twitter pated inside and Kevin wasn't the culprit. She began to talk to Kevin about some of the adventures that John had told her about. Pretty soon, Kevin was joining in with his renditions, and modifications. Once he got Naomi to giggle, he knew the rest of the date would go much better.

"Here, I'll help you," said Sarah, getting up.

"You've done far too much already. This is your birthday lunch. Let me finish up."

"Okay," she said sweetly.

She sat close by him as he made the final preparations.

"I like how it feels having you near me," said John.

Sarah nodded. She knew exactly what he was talking about.

Lunch was nice. All four were talking. These girls aren't so bad, thought Kevin. After lunch Naomi borrowed some of Sarah's lipstick and Kevin thought she looked great. He remembered why he had asked her out to begin with. He still considered Sarah rather plain to look at, but her spunk and personality made up for that to some degree. After letting their lunch settle for a while John suggested that they take the mountainous hike.

Kevin and Naomi set off in front with John and Sarah behind. John reached his hand for Sarah's. She grasped it and interlocked the fingers. Their hands were made for each other's. Sarah's hand felt warm and so smooth to John. For all the feelings that they felt, they hardly knew each other.

John wanted to know all about Sarah's family and friends. Sarah was genuine. She saw no need to put on airs. She spoke lovingly about her family. She explained that she had not ever had close friends until recently. She talked about Maryanne and how much she enjoyed her friendship.

"When did you and Maryanne become friends?"

"Well, we've known each other since we were kids; I guess we were friends. But we weren't really friends until after the end of Summer of dance...when we met."

"But you were with me. I don't remember you hanging out with any of the girls."

"A lot has changed for me since that night. Please don't misunderstand me...but, when you're the girl that, 'John Bennett,' is interested in...people don't see you the same anymore."

John had a confused and disturbed look on his face.

"I'm not interested in you...because...you're John Bennett. I like you. I didn't really realize what would happen when you showed an interest in me. But, it has been nice...you know. It's nice having people pay attention to you...to me. I like having people care about what I think and what I feel. Still, if none of that had ever happened, I'd be just as interested in being with you. If you went away and all of that went away too, I'd miss those things...but I'd miss you more—much more.

"I can't figure out how you were ever not the most popular girl."

"I'm glad." Sarah squeezed his hand tightly momentarily. His strong hand felt invincible in hers. "I'm glad that you see me differently than anyone ever had before. It means the world to me. I doubt that there is any girl who isn't interested in you. But you are the first guy to ever be interested in me. I'm not the same girl that you first asked to dance—the girl who wanted to wither and die in your presence. I'm better because of you— because you saw something that neither I, nor anyone else had ever seen in me before. What I love most about you is how I feel when I'm in your presence. Second, I love what your attention has done for me. And third, and this is the icing on the cake, is that you are so incredibly handsome and *the* John Bennett." Sarah smiled pleasantly.

John looked at her face—not a hint of a blush. John was pleasantly stunned at her boldness. Sarah had no reason to conceal her feelings for John. She had never flirted with and ensnared him. She was entirely comfortable and relaxed in his presence. There was no doubt about his affection for her and hers for him. This could only be one thing—true love. Between a Sarah Peningham and a John Bennett only one type of relationship could exist, it would have to be genuine.

As they ascended the mountains in the early afternoon the air cooled significantly. After the long ride the crisp breeze was a breath of fresh air. A breeze blew through Sarah's short blond hair, exposing the back of her neck briefly, and the perfumed scent wafted to John. It was light and sweet and endearing to him. John could not be happier than he was at that moment.

Kevin and Naomi, having moved at a quicker pace, were at the apex of the trail. The trail itself was not very green, nor scenic. No streams nor rivers were visible. It was a hard and packed turf that was rocky with a tannish brown color. Above them stood rocky cliffs that seemed impenetrable.

"Here it is, as far as it goes," said Kevin towards John and Sarah.

Naomi had seated herself on a rock and was turned towards the mountain peaks. She had a light perspiration on her forehead and was breathing a little deeper. Kevin hadn't broken a sweat and seemed ready to attack the cliffs above.

"Do you know what this place is? It's the closest anyone can get to the top of the mountain peaks anywhere in the promise land. Nowhere else does a trail go up so high. Imagine, we're this close to freedom, yet we can't make it over the top."

"Freedom?" asked Sarah.

"...I mean, er... this close to utter and cataclysmic disaster, yet we can't get over to it," said Kevin.

Sarah could take a joke. That just didn't seem funny.

"Lots of people try to climb as high as they can from this spot. Kevin and I made it up about thirty feet last year. Still, that's a far cry from the top."

"Were you *trying* to get over the top?" Sarah was concerned

John looked at her reassuringly. Not even John Bennett could climb over the top of that towering cliff. It was mildly amusing to him when any girl, even Sarah, seemed to expect super powers out of him. Somehow, he discerned that it wasn't really about that. It wasn't whether he *could* climb over, it was that he *would* even try.

"What's the matter, Sarah? Haven't you ever wondered what was on the other side? I mean, there's got to be more on the other side than there is here. It's nice here, and all, but really this isn't the whole world," said Kevin.

"Yes, I'm sure there is a lot on the other side that we don't have here. Horrible things..."

"Maybe so, Sarah," said Naomi. "But look," and she indicated the circumference of the mountain range. "We are kind of trapped, you know."

"We're caged birds, Sarah Peningham," said Kevin. "The cage might be nice—plenty of food and water, lots of great perches, and toys to play with, even some great birds to hang out with—but it's still a cage."

"You don't think there's any danger on the other side?" asked Sarah.

"Oh, sure, I expect there is. It can't be *as safe* as it is here. But, I mean, *fire breathing dragons*, let's get real. Whenever someone doesn't want you to go somewhere they come up with some awfully scary things to keep you away."

Naomi smiled. John could tell that Sarah was feeling frustrated by the conversation, not to mention being ganged up on. This was her birthday, first date with him, and he loved her. It was time to give her support.

"As far as I'm concerned, I'm happy to stay in the cage as long as I'm here with you," said John to Sarah.

"You know, some birds prefer to stay in their cage," said Kevin. "I've seen birds that had their cage door open and it agitated them. They seemed scared because it was open and they wouldn't leave. I suppose the cage is a protection to the bird not just a prison. Whatever is lurking outside of the cage can't get in so the bird is safe. In that sense, I suppose, the cage could be appealing. And a free bird could be injured or killed at any time. There are plenty of predators out there to get them. I suppose birds die every day from these things. Still, there are a lot of birds out there free and flying each day. Most of them are fine. And they are free. They go where they want, do what they want, and aren't trapped. Even if you like your cage, Sarah, you're still caged in, pleasant though it may be."

Sarah had never heard such talk before. It didn't so much confuse her as frustrate her. She didn't agree, and she felt sorry for those who saw things that way. Her world was no cage, no trap, no prison. No, it was a paradise; a lovely and remarkable existence. What was wrong with the freedom that safety and protection provide? She was free. She felt free and those lovely endearing mountains provided her with that freedom. But, she couldn't put it into words, and she didn't feel that even if she did, that Kevin would listen anyway. Sarah was not argumentative. She remained silent and John indicated that they walk away from the other two. Pleasant conversations were had by both couples and after a time they all returned to their horses.

The ride back was uneventful and everyone was tired and mostly quiet. Kevin had decided that things with Naomi were at least somewhat promising. She didn't give the impression that she was going to be easily wooed into affection. Still, the idea of the chase intrigued him. He'd ask her out again.

It was dark and cold as they arrived at Sarah's home. Her parents were anxiously awaiting her arrival. They still had some birthday surprises in store for her. Sarah was physically, mentally, and emotionally exhausted. Still, the lingering embrace that she received from John was heavenly. It gave her an extra bounce in her step. This night, the night of her sixteenth birthday, she slept soundly and peacefully.

⌘⌘⌘

"Bernice, look at these!" said Maryanne.

"Ohh, pretty!" said Bernice as she came over to inspect the flowers olfactorily.

"I've never gotten a good look at John in the light. Does he look as good as he did at a dimly lit dance?" asked Kendra.

"Kendra?" exclaimed Natalie, with a faux expression of shock. "How rude." Then turning to Sarah, she asked, "well, does he?"

Sarah didn't blush but instead smiled and gazed momentarily at the expectant expression on her friends' faces. "Let's just say, I wasn't complaining."

"Coming from Sarah, that's sayin' something," said Maryanne and the other girls chided Sarah good-naturedly. Sarah blushed, but only a little.

"Tell us more," said Kendra.

"Ladies, you've known me long enough to know that I would never kiss and tell."

"What? He kissed you...on the first date?" asked Natalie excitedly.

Sarah really blushed. "Actually, no...no, he didn't kiss me, but..." Sarah was bright red, but she stated it more apologetically than ashamed.

"Girl, don't you get all bashful on us. Here we all are just hoping someday, some guy—any guy—will ask us out, bring us flowers, or something. And you've got the dream guy bringing you a beautiful bouquet, taking you on a perfect date, on your sixteenth no less—you've got John Bennett wrapped around your pretty little finger, and your embarrassed 'cause he hasn't kissed you already; the day after your sixteenth birthday. Girl, we've got nothin' on you. Don't you let any of us get under your skin," said Bernice.

"That's right," said Maryanne.

"But, if you've got more to say, do tell," said Bernice with a smile.

"Yes, do tell!" said Kendra.

Sarah smiled. "I don't know why I blushed. Sorry. I guess any girl would be excited to be with John. I mean, Naomi, she went with Kevin; she couldn't take her eyes off of John. She was real nice, and I wasn't mad. It's just that...I don't think I'm the prettiest—you know, the biggest catch. If I was, and I liked John just because he was so handsome, I guess I would have daggers out for any girl that he looked at or who looked at him. But, it's not like that. He likes me and it's real. He's going to see prettier girls and plenty of them will be available, but he love...likes me for me. If I had to win his attention, I never would, you know. It's not really different for me. I really like him. Not just who he is or how great he looks—and he does look great both sunlight and dark. But seriously, I really like him. He could be smaller, and plain, and forgettable to everyone else and I would still feel the way I do. So, I guess I turned red because I don't want anyone thinking that I'm just interested in him 'cause he's some kind of a trophy. I really like him. I don't want it to be perceived as something superficial and lessor. Do you know what I mean?"

"Oh, yeah, we know what you mean. He was really looking good yesterday!" said Natalie. Everyone, including Sarah, had a good laugh.

"Sarah, honey." Mrs. Peningham entered the room flush and slightly out of breath. "John's here, and he..."

Sarah was out of the room and on her way before anyone else had the time to react. Mrs. Peningham turned to follow but after a few steps thought better of it. The other girls stayed put. Each wanting to go and be introduced and none of them willing to move.

"Hey, John!"

"Hi, Sarah."

Sarah embraced him and then led him outside to sit on the porch. John wore a heavy brown coat and thick leather boots.

"Are you okay out here? It's cold and you're not dressed for it."

Sarah wore a long blue skirt and a white short-sleeved top. It was cold outside but there was no breeze blowing and Sarah was excited. It would take her a few minutes to feel the chill.

"Here, take my coat," said John as he began to remove it.

"No, I'm fine. You've been out here for a while; you're colder than I am."

"You're sure?"

She smiled and sat down on the porch, instinctively clutching her bare foot and rubbing it. John looked down at her massaging her own foot.

"You don't even have shoes and your feet are cold already."

"Oh, sorry." Sarah let her foot go and then let her feet hang down off of the porch. "I had so much fun yesterday...with you. I was just telling my friends..."

"You have company? I won't keep you then..."

"They're fine...I'm glad you're here." Sarah reached for John's hand. It was a sign of affection but it was also getting a little cold.

"I don't have an excuse for coming by. I figured I'd ask you out again, but...I just don't want to be apart from you, Sarah. Is it okay that I came by?"

Sarah smiled and leaned in close to him. The temperature and her feelings were working in conjunction with each other. John put his arm around her shoulder and felt the side of her bare arm. Goosebumps were already forming and her skin felt cold. John rubbed her arm gently as Sarah laid her head back against John's shoulder.

"Kevin comes up with all the good ideas. He's not so...preoccupied...with anyone right now. Usually, I'm tagging along with him and whoever he's chasing. It works out fine. But now I'm the one who's head over heels and can't keep my mind off of...you. I figured, I'd rather spend my day walking back and forth in the cold, if it meant that I'd spend a few minutes with you, than going stir crazy sitting at home and wishing that I was with you. But now I feel like I'm interrupting you. I just stopped by and assumed that you'd set your whole birthday aside to be with me and then figured I could just come by unannounced and you'd be just waiting for me—nothing better to do."

"So far, you've got me figured pretty well."

"Oh, Sarah."

"All I want to do is be with you, too."

Mrs. Peningham had made her way to the door. Sarah had left the door open and the chill had entered into the house.

"Honey, it's too cold to be out there without a jacket. John, if you don't have plans would you like to stay for dinner?"

Sarah, moving to get up, smiled at John and then looked at him expectantly.

"Mrs. Peningham, I've already intruded upon you. I don't want to cause you any trouble."

"Non-sense. It'll be our pleasure. Sarah, I've already invited your friends. It'll be a day late birthday dinner for you."

Sarah had grabbed John's hand and was dragging him into the house. "You're staying, right?"

"Thank you, ma'am. You're very kind."

The four girls had made their way to the living room and a light chatter could be heard emanating from that direction.

"Let me introduce you to my friends."

Maryanne was seated in Mr. Peningham's chair. The couch had been left for John and Sarah. The other girls were bringing in chairs from the kitchen.

Maryanne turned in her chair and smiled sweetly at John as they entered the room. John recognized her. He had never asked her out but he had asked her to dance a few times, in the past. He smiled back. Maryanne was a pretty girl with fiery red hair. Her smile was contagious and she exuded excitement and joy as she interacted with people—strangers as easily as friends. Maryanne was feminine; she was girly without being prissy. Her attractive figure and aptitude for adorning herself, along with her hair, made her at once noticeable and instantly recognizable. Today she had on a powder-blue dress that accentuated her figure, yet was modest and comely.

Maryanne did not have a jealous bone in her body. It simply was not a part of her makeup. She was genuinely thrilled for Sarah. John was super attractive to her but she was no flirt. It was just her personality to smile, be friendly and fun, and delight whomever she was addressing. At the end of summer dance Maryanne was quick to notice John with Sarah. She had kept an eye out for John, hoping for a dance. She was surprised at first to see John with Sarah but that quickly turned into pleasure for her acquaintance. Sarah had never been a close friend to her. Sarah had sometimes been around and she was nice enough. But Maryanne could be selective with her close friends. Everyone liked Maryanne and there were so many girls around that she simply couldn't be buddies with everyone. So Sarah fell amongst her wide group of acquaintances.

When Sarah had become the apple of John's eye she became intriguing to Maryanne. If Maryanne wanted to be close friends with someone then that took place. Maryanne was not using Sarah to get something that she wanted. Her interest in Sarah had been piqued, and as they spent time together over the past several weeks their friendship had grown such that it was approaching best-friend status. The other girls, longtime Maryanne's inner circle, were equally thrilled to have Sarah in the group. If John's interest in Sarah had been fleeting, perhaps their interest in Sarah would have waned, but not Maryanne's. This friendship had reached the threshold of long lasting.

Sarah had never had a close friend before Maryanne. She enjoyed all of the girl's company but felt a particular kinship for Maryanne. Life had never been better for Sarah Peningham and it kept getting better. Sarah was at a loss as to how to present herself. This skill had alluded her thus far. Because she found herself in a prime position, minus this skill, she started becoming interested in it. It was not because she felt insecure and she was trying to hide that. Rather it was because she felt so secure and good about herself that she desired to allow this to come to the surface. She wanted to present herself as she felt about herself. She just didn't know how to.

Maryanne's gifts were quickly brought in. Maryanne could not do for Sarah as she could for herself. Sarah's less than inspiring figure, short stringy blond hair, eyes that wouldn't pop, and overall plain facial features did not provide the canvas Maryanne was used to in painting her masterpieces. Still, there was something about Sarah. John could see it and so could Maryanne. And that something was growing, expanding, improving, perfecting. It was still subtle, to be sure, yet not so subtle as it had once been. Perhaps Sarah's inner happiness and confidence were beginning to shine through; that must have had something to do with it. But that wasn't all. Sarah was becoming more beautiful. It took some time, but Maryanne was starting to get things moving. It would be fair to say that Sarah was a pretty girl—not overtly so, but faintly. Maryanne was pleased with her progress—to what extent she could take any credit.

"It's a pleasure to see you again," said John to Maryanne. "I didn't know until just yesterday that you and Sarah were such good friends."

The other girls were edging up awaiting their introductions. Sarah complied and John addressed each of them pleasantly. Natalie appeared as though she may swoon. John had seen this look before.

"Perhaps we should all sit," he said and then, perhaps not helping the situation, grabbed Natalie by the upper arm and helped her to the chair she had just brought in.

Bernice and Maryanne exchanged a glance. Kendra took her seat near Natalie. Sarah waited for John to escort her to the loveseat.

"You okay?" Kendra asked Natalie quietly. Natalie was pale white already and the color was still fading. Bernice was up and soon brought in a glass of water. Maryanne had leaned over and was gently fanning Natalie.

"That chair must be heavier than it looks," said Bernice handing her the water.

Natalie looked up curiously as Kendra attempted, unsuccessfully, to hold back a giggle.

"Yes, I'm sure it was the chair," said Maryanne ironically.

Sarah and Bernice began to laugh and Maryanne smiled brightly. John looked uncomfortable, though only momentarily. Soon, he displayed his hearty laugh and everyone was settled. Everyone that is, except for Natalie. Her color returned and overwhelmed her leaving her deeply flushed.

The front door opened and Mr. Peningham entered in. He looked at the crowd in the living room, somewhat bewildered, and then nodded his head and moved toward the kitchen.

"Honey," shouted Mrs. Peningham.

"Yes, dear."

"Come in the kitchen," she shouted back.

The laughter and giggling had paused upon his entrance. With his departure, everyone looked back towards the still reddened Natalie and it erupted again. This time she joined in. Though unplanned for, this introduction eased everyone into comfort with each other.

After dinner, dessert, and some nice conversation back in the living room, Mr. Peningham was looking fidgety. Mrs. Peningham caught Sarah's eyes and got her to look at her father. He liked some quiet time in his chair reading each evening. Sarah could see instantly what was needed. It was agreed upon that Sarah and John would accompany each of the young ladies to their homes and then John would escort Sarah back before returning home himself.

Everyone bundled up and set off. Depending on which way they circled either Kendra or Maryanne would be the closest. Both set off in the opposite direction of their homes hoping to be brought home last. Maryanne won out and the group set off as she went, towards Kendra's. Kendra reluctantly caught up. She was disappointed when she arrived and had to leave the group.

Next they made their way to Natalie's. Natalie's mother, pretty and extraordinarily plump, invited everyone in to warm up by the fire and have some hot cocoa. John took the lead in thanking her but declining. He said that it only made everyone colder to keep warming up and then cooling off. At this point, Natalie was disappointed. The rest of the group, however, agreed. Bernice was starting to shiver, having brought the lightest coat. They all spoke at the door for a few minutes.

"Either we go in or we take off, but I'm not standing here shivering another minute!" said Bernice with a chatter in her teeth.

"You're freezing, honey," said Mrs. Maxwell, Natalie's mother. "Let's get you something warmer."

"Thank you, Mrs. Maxwell. But let's just go, the moving will warm me up."

"Bye, Natalie," said Sarah.

They picked up the pace to let off Bernice. She was a little out of the way from the other girl's homes. There was no lingering at the door at Bernice's. She hustled up to the door and opened it.

"Bye, everyone. It was nice meeting you, John. I'm freezin', see ya."

With that they headed towards Maryanne's. The remaining three were bundled up nicely, and though the temperature was cold and continuing to drop, no one felt rushed anymore. They took a leisurely pace, each enjoying the other's companionship.

Snowflakes floated by in the full moon's glow occasionally lighting on someone's cheek or nose.

Sarah was on John's right with her left arm through his right arm, cuddled up tightly. Maryanne walked alone while Bernice was with them. As soon as Bernice went inside and the three turned towards Maryanne's home, Maryanne walked up on John's left and slipped her right hand through John's left arm in typical Maryanne style.

Sarah felt blissful in the company. She loved a walk in the moonlit night and she loved a light snow. The cold night only enhanced the warmth that she felt radiating from John. She enjoyed watching his breath condensate in the night's air.

"What's your favorite color, John?" asked Maryanne.

"Favorite color of what?" he replied.

"That's a weird answer. Everyone has a favorite color," said Maryanne.

"Ah. What's yours?" he asked.

"Huh," she let out mildly irritated by his ability to turn control of the conversation. "Aqua-marine."

"I think you're teasing," said John.

"How so?"

"You're just being clever. I know what your favorite color actually is."

"You think it's red, don't you?"

"Is it?" he asked.

"I already told you—it's aqua-marine."

"Right. But is red your favorite color?"

"You said that you knew what it is. So why are you asking?"

"Just being polite."

"I see," said Maryanne. They all walked in silence a few paces. "It is red." John didn't reply. "Red is actually my favorite color."

"If you say so."

"You still don't believe me?"

"I told you, I already know what your favorite color is."

"So, what is it then?"

"Teasing is one thing. Now you're just being silly. You've got to know what your own favorite color is. Everyone knows what their favorite color is."

"Then what's your favorite color?"

"Of what?"

"You're impossible," she said as she reached over and tapped him on the arm.

"My favorite color of hair is short blond." Sarah looked up at him as he said that and smiled sweetly. John looked down and towards her. "My favorite color of eyes is baby blue. My favorite color for a bow in the hair is white."

"That's what I had on when we first met," said Sarah.

"I never had a chance, you see; short blond hair, baby blue eyes, and a white bow in your hair."

Sarah reached her right arm around and gave John a squeeze.

The glow from Maryanne's home came into view. As they arrived on the porch, Maryanne gave John a short embrace and then Sarah a longer one.

"Good night, it was lovely."

They walked silently out of view of Maryanne's home. The snow started coming down harder and was beginning to stick. There was a short space on the journey between Sarah's and Maryanne's home where they were in view of neither home. They both slowed their steps instinctively and then stopped. Sarah turned towards John and looked up at him. The moon was behind him. John had several snowflakes in his brown hair. They sparkled in the moonlight and increased his beauty—if that was even possible. Sarah melted into his embrace and held him tight for several minutes. She felt warmer than ever in her life. When she pulled back to look at his face again his glare bore into her.

John leaned in slowly towards Sarah as Sarah lifted her chin. Shortly before their lips touched their eyes closed. Sarah could feel the breath that she had been watching, it was washing over her face. The impact of his lips did not bring a swoon to Sarah but rather it charged her. Her heart beat hard and fast. She tightened her arms around him as he did around her. At first touch his lips seemed cool, but with a moment they were warm and then they felt hot. They broke the first kiss and embraced. Sarah had never felt such an exhilarating rush nor such a soothing peace as she did then. The first kiss was John's to her. She did not wait long to deliver hers to him. He sensed her movement and the second kiss began. She could hardly believe that the intensity of feeling and emotion would repeat itself, but even more so. It was warmer, stronger, and her heart beat even faster. As when they grasped hands for the first time, their lips seemed made for each other. They embraced for several minutes after the kiss and then slowly made their way back to Sarah's home. One more kiss at the doorstep shared and then a warm Sarah sent a warm John home in the freezing night air.

John knew that he had given Sarah her first kiss, he just knew it. Sarah, however, could have never guessed that she had given John his first kiss. She expected him to be an experienced kisser and nothing about the kiss gave her a reason to think otherwise. Nevertheless, it was John's first kiss and Sarah's lips would be the only lips his would ever touch.

Chapter 9

With nightfall, the snow fell faster and harder. The temperature dropped and Marcus was particularly glad for the warm pelts from within he slept. For a long time, the forest remained silent. Perhaps even the wolves lay huddled together in this blizzard rather than risk the cold.

Then he heard a twig snap. His heart leaped, but then it was silent again. *I'm surprised Aiden is up*, he thought. *I can't imagine getting out of the warmth tonight.* He began to drift off to sleep again when another twig snapped and then another. The sound drew closer and it wasn't Aiden's gait.

He felt a heavy paw on his chest and then the smell of the wolf's breath coming through the small crack through which he breathed. The wolf smelled him too and began to growl. Marcus knew Aiden was nearby; his best bet would be to lie still for a moment and let Aiden take care of the beast.

The wolf's other front paw was on his chest then, too. He felt the claws engage and realized the wolf was trying to rip through the pelts. He felt sharpness on his skin. The wolf was tearing open the pelt with its teeth. Marcus' face was exposed and he could see the face of the wolf by the light of the moon. Its teeth were bared and he could hear it growl as it looked into his eyes. Marcus tried to scream but he couldn't make the sound. He tried to move from underneath the wolf but the wolf's claws were dug into his chest and his body was frozen in paralysis. The wolf's mouth open and it was coming for Marcus' neck. He could feel the cool air, and he could smell the strong scent of the wolf. Saliva dripped from its bared teeth.

Then he felt a human hand on his shoulder.

"Marcus."

"Marcus!"

"Wake up, Marcus," said Terrence.

Marcus opened his eyes. The ground was covered in a thick blanket of snow. The scent of the wolf was intense as it emanated from the pelt with which he slept, but there was no wolf atop him. It was the breaking dawn of the first snow-covered winter morning.

"Help us get the fire going before we freeze to death," said Daxton.

"What were it ye was dreamin' of, Marcus? Ye seemed awfully disturbed," said Jashion.

Marcus didn't answer. He wrapped his pelt around him but still felt colder than he had ever felt before. The blinding white of the ground was no better than the crisp blue above. His eyes teared up briefly and he quickly wiped it away. Firewood was easy to come by on the edge of the dark forest. It wouldn't be long before they had plenty. But it was frozen through and getting it lit would be the challenge.

Aiden must have known what kind of trouble they would be in because he was nowhere to be seen. He must have left before the blizzard was over because there were no tracks nor an impression where he had laid. This was disconcerting—but not surprising to Marcus. It was unspoken between them, when Aiden left. They simply moved on, did what they had to do, and awaited his arrival. For all they knew he may be nearby and watching all that transpired.

Terrence seemed to like the challenge. Aiden's departure opened up leadership opportunities for him. Though the youngest of the group and the younger brother to Marcus, Terrence was built more stoutly and had the most adventurous spirit. Jashion, treated as second in command by Aiden, happily acquiesced his position to Terrence. Daxton and Marcus were less pleased but nonetheless non-argumentative.

Marcus returned with a bundle of wood and dropped it near Terrence, who was flinging sparks at twigs and branches with his knife.

"Thanks," said Terrence without looking up.

Daxton was hacking at some meat with his knife while Jashion sat on a fallen tree limb shivering under his pelt.

"Need a hand?" said Marcus to Terrence.

"Nah, I've got it."

Marcus made his way toward Jashion.

"What's our status with food," he asked Jashion.

"Enough for breakfast...and probably lunch," answered Terrence from behind. "We'll need to hunt today if we want to eat tonight and tomorrow morning."

Sparks were still being sent, but nothing was igniting.

"We've not hunted in the frozen snow before," said Marcus, apparently to Jashion.

"Doesn't matter," said Terrence. "We've got to eat...you've got a better idea?"

Daxton made his way towards Terrence.

"Meat's ready. Need help with the fire?"

"Na. Just be a minute. Sharpen your knife's, they must be getting dull."

"It's too cold. If you don't get this fire going, we'll freeze to death," replied Daxton.

Daxton and Marcus were under their pelts and sitting by Jashion watching Terrence struggle. His skin was looking blue and his movements were slowing. Deep body shivers came occasionally at first and then became more rapid. His breath appeared to freeze instantly, and was slowing. Jashion unwrapped himself and walked over to Terrence and put his hand on his shoulder.

"I'll take a turn, I will."

"I've g-got it." Terrence kept at it, but his strength could hardly produce a spark.

"Terrence," said Jashion still holding his shoulder. It took a few moments and Terrence looked up with fear in his eyes.

"Terrence, ye've done what ye could. It's me turn now, it is."

Terrence was defeated. His hypothermia made him numb and his mental capacity was slowed. Yet his determination was such that he would have continued to strike the stone until he was unconscious.

Jashion helped him to the pelts and got him covered. Once Terrence was covered he asked Marcus and Daxton to help. He began to rub a stick into another and asked Daxton to do the same. Marcus became the spark flinger. It was a good quarter of an hour before the first ignition. It didn't last, but the next one did, only a minute later. Within ten minutes a decent fire was roaring.

Jashion made his way back to Terrence. He appeared to be asleep. Jashion felt his skin and it was cold.

"Marcus, help me get Terrence to the fire. His body is cold, it is."

Both Daxton and Marcus helped Jashion get Terrence to the fire. Terrence needed warming more than the food needed cooking. Daxton took the fire duty and eventually got it roaring. Marcus and Jashion huddled up to Terrence. Eventually he was warmed and his mind returned. Daxton cooked up all the remaining meat and they ate.

Aiden would have never allowed such a bonfire—even in the bright morning. A fire such as this on a frozen morning in the dark forest would draw the attention of every creature, not hibernating, for miles around. Aiden sat perched under his pelt high in a nearby tree. With his keen eyes he had watched the happenings of the morning. There was only so much that could be taught by words and example. Some lessons could only be learned with the subject's proverbial back against the wall. The difficult fire had been started and Terrence's life had been saved. But at the expense of the frozen and sleeping dark forest becoming fully awake. Coming to the rescue would be problematic on many levels—but he may not have a choice. A large scout wolf was making its way towards the fire and to his companions. More than anything it was the deliberate nature with which the wolf traveled. Aiden strained in the direction from which the wolf came. Moments later he saw the pack.

A frozen morning would not ordinarily be a time for the wolves to come as they were. The wolves knew of Aiden. They had been cautious, knowing the hunter who invaded their territory. But a fire such as this was a sign of complete disrespect. They were being taunted. Allowing the humans to act as though there was no threat would be tantamount to defeat. Their individual lives were not worth this.

Aiden was on full alert. This pack was large—much larger than he had yet encountered. Warriors who fear not death are the most difficult to face. They were not coming to deliver any warning or to cherry pick off one of the humans. This was a pack coming for battle—to the death. It was also possible that this was not the only pack making its way, perhaps just the first. Time was short but he scanned for other packs making their way. None were apparent.

Aiden climbed down the tree and set up to shoot the first wolf between its eyes with the arrow he had drawn. He hoped to drop it without a sound. Yes, the sound would alert Jashion and the boys, but so would it alert the pack. The wolves were not to be intimidated this day.

Aiden watched patiently. This wolf moved in perfect silence but Aiden had triangulated its arrival. He had watched its pace and knew its preferences. Though the wolf gave no other clue it arrived just as Aiden had anticipated. Aiden let go of the string and the arrow flew. Between the wolves eyes it struck, dropping the marvelous creature instantly and silently.

Aiden listened for the pack. Whatever sound they may make was obscured by the roaring of the fire. His companions weren't even thinking. As if the fire wasn't big enough already, they were reloading and enlarging it. He couldn't leave his post, it was the best place to kill off two or three and set the pack into temporary disarray. He turned toward his companions and fired an arrow.

It struck in a tree a few feet above their heads, not far from the fire.

"It's Aiden, it is," said Jashion.

"Is he in trouble?" asked Daxton.

"I think we're in trouble," said Terrence. "Get this fire out!"

The boys sent copious amounts of snow onto the flames and in several minutes the fire was quenched. Indeed, it quieted the fire and helped Aiden hear the pack. What he heard was the pack coming much more rapidly, for they too heard the fire being extinguished. They suspected that they were no longer coming for a surprise attack. They were known, but were not going to stop the attack.

There was no time to rejoin his companions. The pack's progress would temporarily halt as they encountered their fallen companion. He would take out as many as he could as they halted. No matter the wolves resolve, this would divide them at least temporarily. This division may allow at least some advantage to he and the boys.

Twenty wolves could not move silently. Aiden heard them arrive. He could have shot one or two at this point, but he preferred to have most in view staring at their fallen brother. This would allow him to choose which to take out and to kill, perhaps, three or four of them.

Aiden watched them gather and having picked out the alpha male and alpha female, released his shots. Both went down and that disquieted the pack. Most were off in whatever direction their first reaction took them. One headed towards Aiden, unwittingly. Its body became the next carcass. Two others were slower to move and they were gone. Fifteen leaderless wolves remained; disunited, stunned, and confused. Another day, they may have left and re-banded awaiting a more opportune time. Aiden did not suspect that this would be the case that morning. The frozen air would have kept them from coming this far had their resolve not been as strong.

At least two wolves were heading toward the smoke that was once fire. He couldn't head that way. His friends could handle two, especially since they knew something was up. The howls that followed Aiden's kills left his companions without any doubt of the danger surrounding them. His friends were to his right and Aiden went left. The wolves would no doubt all head to that landmark eventually. He would pick off those he could from behind.

The howls had stopped; to some extent the wolves were regrouping. Aiden's non-silent friends confirmed the arrival of at least two of the wolves. He was left without doubt of the success of the kills. Whatever he heard, the remaining wolves heard also. Aiden's count was thirteen to go. For all he knew, those thirteen may have rejoined together.

From behind him the nearly black haired wolf watched closely. The mighty hunter was focused in front of himself and not behind. The cold may be affecting his judgment. This hunter was vulnerable and it readied itself for the pounce. The unfortunate twig made it so that that the hunter was warned. Still it mattered not, for the wolf was on him.

Aiden turned and readied his knife. It struck the attacking wolf in the heart. But the claws sunk deep into Aiden's left shoulder. Twelve wolves to go, but then Aiden was injured. He knew not the state of his friends. Blood dripped from his shoulder, warming the skin temporarily. There was no time to wait, to rest, to recover.

"That was close," said Daxton. "I hope that's it. Why didn't Aiden just get those two? Do you think he chased them to us? To test us?"

Jashion reached down and pulled his knife from the chest of the brown wolf near Daxton. If it hadn't been for Jashion's perfect throw, Daxton would have been gone. Daxton had shot the gray wolf with his arrow and was admiring his work as the brown wolf came upon him.

"If it'd been so easy to get these two, Aiden'of gotten 'em, he would. He'd not test us with this danger, he'd not. I fear there's more out there, else Aiden's in trouble himself. Let's go!"

Terrence was feeling better, but was frustrated that he hadn't got either of them. He hoped that there were more. He wanted his kill. How often does a person want something that they should never want? Terrence would get what he wanted, and soon.

The young male and female, destined to become the new alpha pair, had come together and were closing in. These humans, whom had invaded their territory and were so respected—even feared by the packs, didn't seem such a concern. They were easy enough to track; fire, smoke, loud talk, and loud march left the pair in no doubt as to their whereabouts. Still, much of the pack had been killed. They were deadly, if not discreet. They were not quite in sight, but via sound and smell it was clear that they were not far away and right where the pair were headed. The female circled left, the male circled right. They would both be upon them in no time.

Aiden approached the campsite carefully with bow drawn. As he suspected, some of the pack had gathered. Three wolves were sniffing around. Their fallen comrades had distracted them temporarily in their search. Aiden took out the one looking the opposite direction of him, hitting it squarely at the base of the skull. The she-wolf fell quietly without initially alarming the other male and female who were facing each other. It would not be possible to pick either one off without the other noticing. He strung and aimed for the larger male. The shot was good, but not perfect. It struck the body, just missing the heart. The male howled and went down but was not dead. The female ran. Aiden's shot hit the she-wolf in the hind quarters. This shot was not deadly either. It continued to limp away. The pain in his shoulder had affected those shots. The male still howled until the next shot put it out. *Ten*, Aiden calculated, *with one injured*.

Another pack of four had gathered some little ways off. They answered the howls of their fallen pack mate.

The howls disquieted the boys. The warmth of the fire had worn off. Each of their skin was frozen and numb. Still, inside a fire burned.

"There's more," said Marcus.

"Let's go back," said Terrence. "It came from that way."

They hardly felt the cold so warm was their blood being pumped rapidly through their bodies. The sun shone brightly and their adrenaline rushes took some of the chill out of the air. The boys turned around and headed back to the campfire site, ready for more battle. This time they were coming for the wolves, they were hunting rather than being hunted. This change temporarily threw off the young alpha pair.

The other young female, the one with an arrow stuck in its hind quarters lay on their return path. The wolf was unsuccessfully attempting to remove the arrow with its teeth and licking around the wound. It heard and smelled the boys returning. It got up painfully, yet ably, and crouched for a spring.

Terrence had taken the lead back, sword drawn, with keen eyes. The female bared its teeth and leaned back. The wolfs leap was weaker than it hoped; it came down near Terrence's knee. The she-wolf instinctively nipped at his knee as he brought down the hilt of his sword upon its head. It was not a strong hit, but it did minimize the effect of the bite and forced the wolf back a little. Terrence drew the sword back and swung hard. The injured and fierce creature moved and prepared to lunge at him. Daxton had his bow drawn but was afraid that he may hit Terrence as easily as the she-wolf. Jashion circled to the left with his knife drawn. The movement of the boys provided some distraction and the wolf didn't pounce. Terrence struck again, this time hitting it with a glancing blow. The angry wolf turned and Jashion saw the arrow stuck in its backside. That had to be Aiden's. It was a poor shot. Something was wrong, he feared.

The next blow from Terrence was significant—hitting it across the face and drawing blood with the gash. The wolf reeled and Daxton let his arrow go. This one struck its shoulder. The wolf turned to run but Jashion let his knife fly, striking it in the heart and putting the wolf out of its misery for good.

"That was mine," said Terrence with anger seething in his expression.

"Terrence!" said Marcus.

Terrence dropped his head and calmed down. "Let's go, there's more where these came from," Terrence said.

"I'm concerned about Aiden," said Jashion as he retrieved his knife. "See this arrow," he said indicating the arrow in the hind quarter. "That's Aiden's, it is. I've never seen a poorer shot from Aiden, has ye?"

The realization of Aiden's mortality concerned the boys. He actually could be hurt—or worse. This thought had never occurred to them before.

"Let's find him," said Marcus.

An isolated wolf had approached the campsite at the time that Aiden had killed the male with his second shot. The wolf watched, not thinking that it had been spotted. This one had seen Aiden at work before. In fact, the skin that Marcus wore was the skin of its brother. This wolf was cunning, it wanted revenge, but was patient. Aiden had sensed its presence. He shot an arrow in its direction but missed. The wolf ran.

Aiden pursued but at a slower pace. He could see the trail in the snow. It was better to let the wolf return. He heard the pack of four howl again, and another isolated wolf returned the howl. He suspected that it would join. Aiden's count was still ten, but the true count was down to nine with Jashion's kill.

Terrence walked with a limp. His knee stung and he felt the warmth from the blood streaming down his leg. This did not slow him down but rather helped to speed him up. He wanted blood, the blood of a wolf more than anything.

They heard the cry of the wolves, then closer, and headed towards them. The sound of an unfrozen river could be heard some ways off, in the direction of the pack. They walked purposefully in this direction for some time without any other sights or sounds.

The young alpha pair gathered at the site of their fallen sister. They sniffed the she-wolf for a moment and then took off at a more rapid pace in the direction of the foot tracks in the snow.

Aiden's instincts brought him back to the camp. There he saw the fallen she-wolf, and the direction of the tracks where his friends had gone. They were heading towards the pack and not away from it, a pair of wolves were clearly on their tail. Aiden followed.

Behind him he sensed danger and turned. An older and very large, majestic grey stood. He had seen this wolf before. This wolf had entered the camp when Jashion and Jemma had been attacked by the anaconda. The wolf stared him down and bobbed its head up and down. Aiden reached for his bow. The wolf did not move. Its stare was fixed and it showed no fear.

Aiden did not pull back the string. But he held it ready to do so. After a minute the wolf turned slowly and calmly and began to walk away. Something was very different about this wolf than the others. Aiden chose not to shoot. Aiden headed towards the others.

They had reached the edge of the gorge with the river fifty feet below. The view was gorgeous. Icicles lined the edge and mirrored the water with a sparkling reflection. Evergreens bent with the snow and ice. Had they come upon it at a moment of peace they would have stopped and admired. Under the circumstances they hardly noticed, their focus on the danger surrounding them. Walking along the edge meant that the wolves could only approach them from their left side, allowing them to keep a close watch.

This group of five wolves was neither the bravest nor the smartest of the pack. But together they presented a challenge. Jashion was the first to spot them ahead. He crouched and indicated that the others should crouch too. The wolves ahead did not seem to be aware of them as yet. That presented some advantage. The real problem was the pair behind them. They had spotted the boys and were approaching from behind. When Aiden arrived, and saw what lay in front of him, he drew the string of his bow, but hesitated. It was a long shot and his aim had been off since the injury. If he shot and missed, he may hit one of his friends. Quickly he decided that he had no choice. He pulled, aimed, and fired. He hit the male in the chest and it fell. The female saw and howled. This alerted the rest of the pack. It was six wolves to four young men.

Terrence turned and ran towards the female. It was ready for the attack. Terrence swung his sword as the wolf ducked and pounced. Terrence bent over but it clawed his back. He screamed in shock and pain but turned his angry eyes towards it and swung again, missing again. The female was determined to take this one out—if that was the last thing it did. Aiden ran towards him. The others stood and watched, knowing that Terrence wanted this one. Jashion changed his attention to the pack coming.

"Daxton, shoot ye arrow at them. Quick! Get ye one," said Jashion.

Daxton fired and hit a small female giving it a flesh wound that barely slowed it down.

Terrence swung again, angrily, carelessly, thoughtlessly. The wolf bit his arm and he screamed again. Marcus had had enough. He took his club and threw it at the wolf, hitting it in the ribs. The wolf howled and turned. Terrence regrouped and swung again. This time hitting the wolf. Marcus was defenseless with his club lying beside the wolf. The wolf turned to attack Marcus and Terrence struck again. The wolf was hurt. Terrence thrust his sword into its side and penetrated its heart. Marcus was going to go for his club when he heard Aiden shout.

Marcus turned where Aiden was pointing and realized that the pack was nearly upon them. All he could do was reach for his small knife. It was a poor weapon against a wolf. Marcus backed away from the group closer to the cliff's edge. He spotted a more sheltered area and walked towards it with his knife drawn.

Jashion and Terrence were back to back with their sword's drawn. The wolves circled around them. Daxton fired another shot, missing the wolves and grazing Jashion's abdomen.

"Ye'oww," he yelled and one wolf lunged, biting Jashion near his ankle.

Aiden fired a shot and dealt a fetal blow to the small she-wolf that Daxton had grazed before. Jashion delivered his dagger into the wolf at his foot. It was not sufficient to kill the wolf, but it got its jaw off of him. The dagger was stuck within the animal and blood came from it, yet the animal crouched for another attack. Daxton was afraid to fire again. Aiden's next shot struck a male, but not fatally. The male moved away from the group and Daxton shot at it. He delivered a fatal blow and turned his attention to the group. Jashion was lunged at again, and again was bitten. Jashion was able to remove the dagger from the beast and delivered another blow, this time killing it. Then Jashion dropped to his knees in agony.

Terrence moved towards one. He could sense the fear in the wolf's eye. He struck with his sword and injured the wolf. It moved back and then went forward again. Terrence's next blow brought the wolf down, but only temporarily. Terrence went for the final blow but was struck with a sharp pain in his calf. He looked down and saw an arrow through his calf. Daxton had regained his confidence and fired, missing the wolf and injuring Terrence. Terrence's anger knew no bounds. He tore into the wolf with every bit of strength he had left. The wolf was killed and minced all at once. The final wolf was baring down on Jashion. Jashion look resigned to his fate. Aiden, however, was not. He aimed and prepared to fire. As Daxton turned to watch Aiden fire he saw another wolf coming at Aiden from behind. He instinctively shot at the wolf hitting it squarely in the head and knocking it down as Aiden fired and killed the wolf attacking Jashion.

Aiden, Terrence, and Jashion were injured but alive. Daxton ran to his cousin Terrence feeling horrible about putting the arrow through his calf. Aiden approached Jashion to see about his injuries. Aiden calculated the threat. *One wolf left*, he thought. The one left was the wolf who stared him down and then walked away. He suspected that they were temporarily safe.

"I'm fine," said Terrence to Daxton with eyes still filled with rage. "We'll get it out and I'll be fine. Where's Marcus?"

Where was Marcus? They began to look around. There he was at the edge of a cliff with his back towards it and the wolf who stared down Aiden walking towards him. Marcus' knife was drawn and he was edging back towards the cliff's edge. Aiden sprung up and ran towards the cliff looking for a better shot. The wolf walked purposefully towards Marcus. The old grey was within the reach of a lunge. Aiden set up for the shot. He would only have one shot and he could not miss. The wolf began the lunge and Aiden let go of the string. The arrow fired true and hit the wolf in the stride of its lunge through the ears. The blow was fatal.

Marcus had reached the edge of the cliff. His heart beat out of his chest. The wolf showed no emotion, it simply stared as it walked towards him. Marcus couldn't go in any direction. He nearly slipped and then the wolf lunged. He edged back instinctively and lost his balance. He dropped his knife and tried to bend over to catch his balance. It was too late. Both feet slipped off and he began to fall. He caught himself briefly with his hands on the edge of the cliff, but the force tore through the skin and down he fell.

During the thirty-foot freefall time slowed. Marcus considered his short life and his circumstances. He thought on his family whom he missed, and his friends. Hopes, dreams, fears, and concerns all became one. He impacted a small ledge about thirty feet down with his face. He then tumbled the remaining twenty feet landing upon the edge of the water and lay there with his head bleeding and broken, his body torn up. He lay on his back with his eyes open—unblinking.

"No!" shouted Terrence.

Aiden took off running with Daxton not far behind. Terrence and Jashion limped and crawled towards the cliff's edge. Aiden began crawling down the icy rock edge as Daxton watched from above.

"Marcus," Daxton called. "Marcus, are you okay?"

There was no response from Marcus. His skin looked white, covered with blood. His unblinking eyes unnerved Daxton and he felt sick. He began to vomit on the cliff's edge.

Terrence arrived moments later. He looked over the edge and then promptly passed out on the side.

Jashion's thigh was bitten badly and he moved at a snail's pace towards the cliff's edge. Aiden got down the frozen and icy cliff and made his way toward Marcus. He shook him and shouted at him, checked his pulse and put his ear on his chest checking for a heartbeat. None was found. He pounded his chest with his fist twice and listened again. Then he reached down and pulled Marcus' eyes shut for the last time.

After covering the body with stones from the river, Aiden began climbing back up the treacherous cliff. He was frozen from the cold and the river water, his shoulder was in intense pain and the cliffs edge would be challenging to climb even in the best of circumstances; but what choice did he have? Nearly everyone was injured and would require treatment, including himself.

Up he climbed, slipping more than once and wincing when he had to use his left arm to catch himself. Upon reaching the ledge he had nothing left to pull himself over. Daxton came over and helped. With some effort Aiden pulled his legs over and lay on the frozen, snow covered ground. As he lay there he reflected on the wolf that took Marcus, the wolf that he could have killed twice, the wolf that he had let go both times. If ever he had the opportunity to take out a wolf he would never let it go again. No wolf of the dark forest was a friend to man.

Aiden only allowed himself a five-minute rest. He was close to succumbing to hypothermia himself. He alone had the ability to treat the wounds, his own included. The air had warmed some, but was still below freezing. Between the cold, the injuries, and the threat of further attacks they were in a precarious position. Aiden was a man of action and action was required.

He broke off the arrow tip in Terrence's calf and pulled the arrow through. Terrence passed out again in agony. He bled profusely and Daxton again looked sick. Aiden tore cloth from his shirt and held it over the wound.

"Daxton, hold this."

Daxton held it but turned his head while looking white and faint himself. Aiden had learned much about healing while with the Tengeer's. He had brought with him a pack of the best herbs for healing. He administered them skillfully to Jashion and Terrence. Once their wounds were dressed and the bleeding had stopped he got Daxton to help him dress his own shoulder wound. Daxton struggled with the wound but found it within him to continue.

"We must get to a safer place. We need our pelts. We cannot use fire today; it will be unsafe."

Neither Terrence nor Jashion were in any position to walk. They proceeded anyway. They settled down much further from the edge of the dark forest than Aiden felt best, but they clearly could not go any further. Aiden and Daxton retrieved the pelts and other supplies. It was late afternoon by the time they were settled. No fire meant no food, and minimal warmth. The pelts would have to be sufficient, but the lack of food made it harder for their bodies to warm themselves and made the healing more difficult. Still, Aiden did not think that they could risk an attack by igniting another fire. If they could survive the night, the morning would bring better opportunities; at least he hoped.

That night was the worse night each of those young men had ever faced. There was no attack on them. But between extreme hunger, freezing conditions, miserable pain, and most especially the sickening grief, what sleep each one took in felt dark and heavy. The best news that the morning brought was warmer air. It would be a few weeks before the air was this cold again. They moved slowly and cautiously through the edge of the dark forest. Aiden realized that they would not reach the corner of the woods where they would have to choose between the paths to Cardsten or Agedon by the end of winter, not with them moving so slowly. He also realized that their preparations were not yet sufficient for what may lay ahead. He decided to stay in the dark forest past the winter to allow for healing and learning. By the next winters end, they'd be ready.

⌘ ⌘ ⌘

Aiden's healing art was successful. The boys were stronger and more capable. When the next winter ended, they reached the corner of the dark forest. They had chosen Cardsten as their destination, but the vote was not unanimous.

Whether Dromreign hibernated or not they were not certain, but they had had no sight of the beast during their second winter's months. They had not met another soul during the dark of the winter and had not heard any news. On the evening of their last night in the dark forest they heard the excitement among the wolves again. Aiden recognized this activity like when they had initially entered the dark forest, and he remembered catching sight of the hideous dragon. He feared that the dragon had awoken and was hungry.

"We shall camp tonight in or near a small village called, Golopse. It is midway between here and Cardsten. I think that they will be friendly towards us. We leave at the break of dawn."

Civilization seemed like a pleasant and distant memory to the young men. Terrence, however, was still in a dark and quiet state. He had changed from the time of the battle with the wolves the winter before, the one that took his older brother's life. Marcus had been dead for over a year, and he was leaving the dark forest, his brother's final resting place. The finality of his loss sickened him.

Aiden hardly slept that evening. He watched and listened to the wolves. He searched the sky for a sighting of the great beast, but saw and heard nothing. At daybreak, they left the forest, well fed and stronger than ever. It would be an easy, and hopefully, quiet walk along flat earth. Aiden's greatest fear was sun exposure. They had been within the forest for so long that they had not acclimated their skin to hours of the rays of the sun. It was still cool, however, and he had everyone dress with long pants and shirts.

Daxton and Terrence had never experienced concern upon being exposed in the wide openness. When they entered the dark forest, it seemed more frightful to be inside than outside. But here their instincts called for being quiet and hidden. They felt naked and isolated, and fully visible. Never before would they have considered the dark forest a place of protection; nearly everything about them had changed.

The sun was setting and a beautiful sunset was on the horizon to their right. Everything was still and peaceful. Golopse was near and they were both excited and nervous to interact with other people.

Aiden stopped short and sniffed the air. Jashion turned and looked at Aiden with deep concern. They picked up their pace towards Golopse. As Aiden and Jashion feared, there was no village to be found. Rather, still smoldering remains of homes and people covered the ground. Dromreign had made this village his feast after its long winters nap.

Sickness filled the pit of Jashion's stomach. He had left Dargaer before he had seen the total demolishment of his home, his village, and his people. Upon gazing at the ruin of Golopse, he felt as though he was looking at his own people the morning after. Perhaps inside of him a small hope remained that it was not as bad as it seemed, when he left. At that moment, he saw that his escape was miraculous. Dromreign left no survivors. It ate all that it could and consumed the rest with fire. They looked for anyone whom they could help. None were found. They found nothing edible. Still they slept there on the edge of the village. They had enough provisions to get them through breakfast. On the morrow, they would complete the journey to Cardsten.

Chapter 10

Mirinda brushed her luscious, long, gently-curled, black hair as she sat at her vanity and stared contemplatively into her mirror. Mirinda was beautiful—unlike any other; perfect skin—olive and blemish free, clear black eyes with naturally long dark lashes, dark ruby lips—colored and full on their own, but always adorned with gloss or lipstick, somewhat high cheek bones, and an extraordinary figure that balanced poetically both athleticism and charm. Her three friends, finishing touches already completed, patiently looked on with some jealousy and a high dose of admiration. Miranda was good for each of them; she was, however, too perfect for her own good, so they thought. She was incomparable with no obvious flaw—keenly intelligent, eloquent social grace, more than comfortable in her financial security, confident without undue arrogance, and certainly not lazy; but, never frantic, always in control, always the center of attention, always pleasantly intimidating. When she was ready she'd be ready, in the meantime observing such beauty was impossible to tire of. With her short-sleeved top the tone of the muscles in her arms gently rippled from triceps to shoulder with each brush stroke.

Tira did not have the gift of a strong first impression. She was beautiful—quite beautiful, but with the kind of beauty that grows on the observer slowly. There was depth and mystery to her appearance. For those who knew her well, and for a long time, she was considered a top-class beauty—but she hardly garnered a gaze from strangers. Portraits were always mortifying for her. The artist could not capture on canvas the beauty that she possessed. Any portrait of her always looked like a first impression even to those who knew her well. Even when the artist showed their skill in other people's portraits they were considered a failure when attempting Tira. Tira had no intention of sitting for another session. It would be an artist indeed that could capture her beauty on canvas. With medium length brown hair, pale blue eyes, and average height, Tira sat poised and patiently. Her personality, like her looks did not attract at first but over time the attraction grew—such was the depth of her thoughts and psychology.

Myrtle could not be a greater opposite than she was to Tira. With glorious blond hair, bright blue eyes, and a face so pretty that it at times approached, but never eclipsed, Mirinda's, her beauty provided a pleasing contrast to the dark featured Mirinda. When observed as a group, Mirinda and Myrtle provided a one-two punch that left scores in their wake. A portrait of Myrtle, without exception, portrayed every ounce of her beauty. It was too easy for the artist. Everything she had was apparent upon first glance. There was, however, no depth nor mystery to uncover. She was how she was seen. Once the stunning effects of her first impression wore off there was nothing further to attract and engage the gazer. She had the rare beauty that grew tiresome. Those who hungered for something more starved and their interest withered. Those who were most acquainted with this flock of girls found Myrtle to be tiresome both in look and in personality. She, however, was too simple to ever notice, or so it seemed. The looks she garnered from her first impression left her without doubt of her own beauty. The waning interest of the guys she met never clued her further. Her initially adorable laugh always became an annoyance over time. It was so predictable and superfluous that it became background noise once the annoyance wore off. Still, Myrtle was always fun. She was impossible to dislike at first, but easy to disengage from later.

Finally, there was Myrtle's best friend, Tasha. Tasha was rich, even compared to these other girls who were all very well off. Her cloths were impeccable. Her handbag, short stylish hair, footwear, etc., were the cutting edge and the best that money could buy. What she lacked in natural beauty was made up for with attention. She left no stone unturned and everything surrounding her showed her taste and wealth. She was impressive, but would have been much less so had she been less rich. She spoiled her friends and never left anything to chance. Myrtle was her perfect companion, for Myrtle had always brought them as much attention as could be had; Tasha was always near at hand when the attention for Myrtle faded. Tasha was wise, cunning, cleaver, and witty. She may not have carried with her the unfathomable depth that Tira possessed, but she had enough to gleam the left-over attention from Myrtle. Tasha was good to Myrtle and the value that each brought made the relationship symbiotic.

The degrees of perfection for which Mirinda was elevating through were not necessarily observable to anyone else, as she completed her hair and make-up. But Mirinda knew when she had achieved her desired objective. She stopped, smiled, turned gently ensuring perfection from every angle and then stood and faced her friends. They fawned appropriately and then the girls were off.

Gorgeously blossomed trees lined the streets of Cardsten. Everywhere it was clean and manicured. The warming weather brought out the young people on that beautiful late afternoon. The streets were packed and these girl's arrival on the scene brought no less of the desired attention than expected. Besides their exquisite beauty, these girls came equipped with an additional attention grabber. They each wore shorter dresses than any of the other girls around, and with their tanned and shapely legs they were sure to be seen by all. It was only just warm enough to get away with dresses like those. For most of the others their legs had not seen the sun for the entirety of the winter and they would surely have not wanted to be seen with sickly pale skin. Tasha, as always, had the solution. A greenhouse type of sunroom, warmed as needed that allowed for winter sunbathing. Even the pool was warmed constantly by servants, allowing for winter swims. They exercised, swam, and sunbathed the winter away such that when spring had sprung, their external preparations were already piqued. Even Tira and Tasha were relative knock-outs, Tira in a white and Tasha in a black dress.

The only problem was the ever-present problem of finding those worthy of their attraction. Quantity was never a problem, quality always evaded them. Pretty boys were the worst—except to Myrtle. She liked the pretty boys. They were so simple, but Myrtle never noticed anything lacking. However, the pretty boys, who spent all of their time on their own looks, found Myrtle to be too much competition. Everyone, even the girls, would look first at Myrtle before noticing the pretty boy beside her. This got old fast, as did Myrtle.

The rich boys brought some class and could be mildly entertaining for a time. But they brought nothing substantive to offer. Money, and all that it would bring, was prepossessed by each of the girls. Once the initial charm wore off there never seemed to be anything else to offer.

The athletes brought with them some appeal—especially to Mirinda. She appreciated a tall, strong young man with great capability. Still, even these relationships left her wanting. Like the pretty boys, they were always stuck on themselves. Often, their intellectual acumen was deficient and they didn't seem to enjoy their girls giving them a run for their money in sports and games. They liked being king of their own hill which didn't have room for a queen.

Then there were the smart boys. Tira liked them, at least some of them. They were not so beautiful, rich, or athletic as the others but they were also not such easy prey. They were smart enough to know that they stood no chance with such exquisite beauties. They admired the girls distantly and did not let on to their attraction so readily. Of course, the girls were not desperate, so there was no need to throw themselves at the smart boys. They, however, were smart too. They knew how to put themselves in position such that the smart boys were smart enough to know that they shouldn't let a chance like that pass them by. These relationships could have lasted a little longer, but these guys really weren't very handsome, particularly rich, athletic at all, or even really as smart as they needed to be to make up for all of their deficiencies. In short time, it was time to move on.

All that was left were the artists and the laborers. Laborers were sometimes worth a short flirt. They weren't pretty, but occasionally they were ruggedly handsome. They were never rich but some of them were good with what money they had. They often had athletic builds, but they were more often brutes than athletes. They were certainly not educated, but some of them carried a good deal of common sense. Occasionally, flirtatious fun was had with the laborers, but Tasha was always aghast and so she ensured that additional time with the girls would be more expensive than the laborers could afford.

"Let's go eat at, 'Sydney's.'"

The Laborers would disappear and Myrtle would giggle. She enjoyed turning around while still giggling and catching them look with longing gazes at the perfect girls that they would never talk to again.

The artists did appeal to Tasha, but were dreaded by Tira. Tira would just leave and the artists weren't worth breaking up the group. Still, Tasha would commission them for a painting or poetry at some other time. Even this got old after a while.

With all the trouble that they'd had in finding suitable companionship, the girls were undaunted. There were many fish in the sea and that night they might meet someone better. It couldn't be much worse. There was an emerging new class of young men that they wanted to test out. These were the military guys. Those fools from Agedon were going to be taught a lesson soon, so the military was being ramped up. They looked good in their fancy uniforms. They were fit, with crisp short hair, and dressed in red or black from head to foot. Training took place out of the city wall near the main gate. It was as much for show as for anything else. Agedon had their spies and they would see that Cardsten was serious. About this time the exercises would end and the military boys would come in proudly donning their uniforms.

Mirinda, as always, was in the lead and made a beeline for the gate. None of the girls objected. Mirinda liked seeing the boys with some sweat beaded on their foreheads and with flush cheeks. She liked that the military guys tended to be taller and more muscular, like some athletes, yet not so stupid. There was some hope, she thought, as they circled around eventually garnering all of their attentions.

Myrtle struck first. One guy, more handsome than most, was caught gawking at her. She timed her twist perfectly with the drop of his gaze allowing the skirt of her blue dress to float up several inches and ensuring an unforgettable view of her legs. He was mesmerized and at her side momentarily. Myrtle could flirt and she saw no need to hold back. James, as he was called, had not had the chance to even notice Mirinda, so caught up was he with Myrtle. Mirinda smiled. He was cuter than most and perhaps the best catch of all among the military boys, at least from what she'd seen. It was never a problem to wean a guy off Myrtle and onto her if she so desired. *Let her have her fun. If he's worth anything, he'll be mine in no time.* Mirinda liked

Myrtle and certainly didn't covet *her* beauty. She just knew that it was only a matter of time. James would notice her and she could decide if it was time for her to move on, or her turn with James.

James' buddies were not on par with him and there were only two of them, both short, pudgy, not cute, and rather obnoxious. James clearly didn't like competition. At this point, James' friends had both noticed Mirinda—and couldn't keep their eyes off of her from the time they'd seen her. But they didn't have the courage—nor would it have done them any good if they did. Tasha and Tira were less picky, or perhaps they thought it was worth it having James around. Tasha figured if Mirinda wasn't interested she may have a shot. They struck up conversation with Tad and Blake.

"We'll teach them a lesson—they're fools; you know they are. They can hardly afford the weaponry, and we're fully equipped. I've seen how they dress up, but they aren't even real uniforms. We'll beat 'em down hard and quick. We'll whip the foolishness out of 'em before they really get into trouble—just stupid, they are." Tad was enjoying Tasha's company, but kept glancing over at Mirinda and talked tough to see if he could get her attention.

"Can't we reason with them?" Tasha asked. By reason, she meant using Cardsten's superior financial means to get them to back down. In her mind money was the most powerful force on earth.

Blake jumped in, "tried, but they...I don't know. They're different. They've got weird ideas. Think they can march into the dark forest and climb up the mountain and kill Dromreign. I don't think they could even make it through the dark forest alive to the mountain. But the worst they could do is get the dragon all riled up and angry. He's getting bigger and more powerful; bolder too. I don't think he could take down Agedon in a night, but maybe in two or three he could. They're fools; stupid, stupid fools."

"It does sound foolish," began Tira, "but they are not simply fools. Agedon is no Cardsten, but they have their own wisdom. Have we tried listening to them?"

Myrtle laughed in perfect timing to the end of Tira's question. Tira couldn't tell is she was being mocked or if Myrtle was giggling at something that James said.

"I'm sure we have," James cut in. "Our leaders are no fools. They are doing what they can. I don't think this will come to blows. I'm sure they'll back down once they get wind of our operations. They can't beat the dragon, that's for sure. They won't get past us, either. They'll back down."

Mirinda was bored. Such serious conversation for a flirtatious spring afternoon. She was feeling disgusted with being looked up and down by Tad and Blake. Women hate being objectified. She turned a little and began looking around.

Another cute one, she thought. She waited until he looked over. Oh, yes, he noticed. She smiled and shifted a little, providing an enhanced view of her figure for the onlooker. No question, but that he was drinking in the view. It felt so nice for her to be appreciated and noticed. He started to make his way over but was accosted by a group of buddies. His momentary protest went unheeded and he soon was off and out of sight. *Men; how could he be so blind? Lost his chance.*

Reluctantly she turned her attention back to her friends and their admirers. James was staring straight at her. *That didn't take long. You can't be bored with Myrtle already; it's only been ten minutes.* She looked him in the eyes. *Not as handsome as the other guy. I think I'll pass.* But he kept looking at Mirinda and Myrtle noticed. *What a jerk,* Mirinda thought. A fisherman may cast a wide net, but anything caught that was not intended is but a menace and a nuisance. Such is how Mirinda felt about James and his friends.

At this point, all three guys were checking out Mirinda without being coy at all. This was an utter and total turnoff to Mirinda as well as to every other girl. Mirinda was turning to leave knowing that the others would be behind her shortly, when something caught her eye. A young man wearing some sort of animal skin shorts and no shirt walked through the gate. He was the most gorgeous thing she had ever laid eyes upon. His chest was muscular and perfectly proportioned. He had long dark, beautifully unkempt hair. His skin was dark and glistened with a gentle perspiration. There was a scar on his left shoulder but in every other way he was flawless. She had never viewed beauty such as this except when looking into the mirror at herself. Her eyes could not drop from the scene. He was followed by three companions that she hardly noticed. The young men, getting through the gate, looked around. They were not from Cardsten, that was clear. They did not appear to be from Agedon either. If they had been, they would not have appeared as such. Anyone coming from Agedon these days were spies and tried to look as though they were of Cardsten.

Mirinda moved slowly so as to be in full view. It wasn't long and the stranger's eyes met her own. She had captured his view entirely. He looked at her without blinking or turning his attention. They both appeared to drink in a beauty they had never before seen in another human being. Neither could, nor would, turn away. Never before had a man dared to hold her stare as he did. The other young men had found the object of their friend's attention and were turned her way. Never had Mirinda felt so beautiful or angelic as she did in this man's gaze. Never before had she gazed upon beauty that rivaled her own.

Chapter 11

In all the time since Jashion had left Dargaer, he had never allowed himself to reminisce, to go over, or to contemplate all that had transpired on the night of his homes destruction. Yes, he had told the story, sure he had answered questions, and of course he had passing thoughts and images. But these thoughts, images, and scenes had receded soon after they surfaced. Jashion faced forward. He had survived, and what portion of survivor guilt that may have plagued him, he did not let overwhelm him. Perhaps he had been conditioned for this since youth. He had lost his mother to just such an incident while younger. So had most everyone from Dargaer lost a loved one. People moved on, hardly mentioning those who had passed in such unspeakable ways. Jashion was neither uncaring nor insensitive, but neither was his life swallowed up in the tragic lives that were lost around him.

The fresh and smoldering destruction of Golopse that was thrust upon him had had its effects. It was Jarem, Jashion's best friend of Dargaer, to whom his mind turned. They had passed by a scene that sickened Jashion to the core. The embers of a bon fire still shone. Mugs and kegs along with the scorched bodies of merry makers were strewn across the ground. Jashion had been there, he'd seen the before and during, finally his eyes witnessed the after. Jarem was gone and all that he had meant to him. Jashion had never thought once on Jarem since he had departed. He was not capable of doing so. But as he cast his eyes upon this scene, that was whom he saw. His pleasant and engaging life, the friend of his youth, destroyed by some wicked and ferocious being. Jashion was overcome with emotion, with sickness, with horror. His skin paled, his stomach turned, and breakfast was gone. Some few moments later, once the nausea had passed, his eyes then red, burned with bitter tears.

The sights and smells had disgusted each of the boys to varying degrees. Aiden seemed to understand and left Jashion to cope. Terrence felt anger inside. Death reminded him of Marcus. Though Marcus was not killed by the dragon, the senseless killing before him allowed hatred for Dromreign to ooze through his veins. The dragon and all the wicked creatures would pay.

Terrence, still sorting through his grief, had never understood Jashion's ease of moving on once Marcus had died. Jashion focused on healing and getting through the wintery forest. He had said nice things to Terrence, but had never been caught up with emotion. Even Aiden had taken Marcus' death with difficulty. Aiden had never lost a friend before. Aiden had never failed. Aiden cared for Marcus as he did all of his companions. Aiden also considered himself their guardian and protector. His failure, as he considered it, was humbling to him. It did not cripple him, however. Aiden, redoubled his efforts. He was stronger and more powerful than ever. The scar on his left shoulder reminded him of his need to improve and progress. Terrence appreciated what he had seen in Aiden's eyes. He did not understand all that was in Aiden's heart, but he had sensed mourning, loss, and grief.

Daxton was nearly as devastated as Terrence—at least at first. His recovery had come quicker, but for a time the cousins were equally stricken with grief. It was Jashion's quick recovery that boggled Terrence's mind. Was it the next morning or the morning after, that Jashion seemed to be completely over Marcus' death and ready to move on. At times Jashion seemed impatient with the others who were struggling with their own injuries but even more weighed down in grief and sorrow. Up until then, Terrence had pushed this frustration with Jashion away from him. Jashion was a friend and he trusted him. He trusted Jashion with his life. But that morning's grief was too much for him.

"You been here before? D'you know them?" Terrence said with some malice.

Jashion shook his head. "Nay, I've not been here before." He sniffled and looked down.

"D'you ever cry for Marcus?"

Jashion looked at him confused and hurt.

"You knew Marcus. He was your friend and companion. Did you ever cry for him, when he died?"

"Leave it be," said Aiden.

Jashion was overcome and the tears gushed. Much had been built up inside of him. Whether it was Marcus, or Jarem, or dozens of others, perhaps the sorry state that his world seemed to be in, he cried as a child—as he had when his mother had died.

"These losers here, drunk and wasted. They never saw it coming. They didn't feel a thing. Probably passed out on the ground when they died. This is who he mourns. I mourn my brother, not these worthless strangers." Terrence marched off kicking up a dust storm and any rocks in his wake.

Daxton stood there, confused. What Terrence said made some sense to Daxton, but Jashion had not done anything to Terrence. It was pretty heartbreaking and disgusting what was in front of him; he felt sick himself. He did not see what Marcus had to do with any of this and he did not appreciate the reminder of Marcus' death with all of this surrounding him.

Aiden moved somewhat closer to Jashion but maintained some distance. Finally, Daxton left to comfort Terrence.

They left the scene as soon as Jashion had recovered sufficiently. Terrence was silent throughout that day as were the other young men. By the time that the great walls of Cardsten became visible the good long walk had brought a degree of healing and settling of emotions.

Aiden, who had never actually witnessed Cardsten, had told what he knew of it. The scope and scale of his stories were pale compared to the scene before them. This city and its surrounding wall in the distance were magnificent. No wonder they feared not the dragon. Yes, the dragon could destroy a little village like Golopse with ease, but it could not touch a walled city such as Cardsten.

As they moved closer they watched the military perform their final exercises of the afternoon and slowly disappear into the wall through the gate. Jashion reflected upon his quest to the promise land. *Perhaps I've found it,* he thought. The dragon could not overcome that wall. The elusive promise land, through the dark forest and on the other side of the mountains, seemed less likely at that point since he had spent a good time in the dark forest and so near to its supposed entrance. Perhaps it was fantasy and a child's story after all. But not this. This lay before him in all of its glory. The military alone seemed larger than Dargaer, Golopse, and Tengeer combined. The walls were tall, thick, and impenetrable. If there were any promise land, this must be it.

Terrence was impressed yet a little bit irritated. He had voted, alone, for Agedon. He preferred to fight rather than cower from the dragon. Still, what lay before him made him less disappointed in their destination.

Aiden walked through the gate as though this entire, magnificent city were here just waiting upon his arrival. Jashion was next, but slower through the gate. Nothing in his experience prepared him for the level of sophistication, civilization, and sheer numbers of people before his eyes. His eyes caught upon Mirinda as had Aiden's. But unlike Aiden, Mirinda's beauty was blinding upon his eyes. Only the briefest second of her brilliance and glare were bearable. He turned his eyes and saw something unbelievable. There in front of him was Siccly Turney. She was alive and well, and as popular as ever with all the boys surrounding her. As he watched and stared dumbfounded, she turned towards him. No, that was not Siccly. The more he stared the less she looked like Siccly. But she was beautiful, and carried herself like Siccly and she was looking at him the way that Siccly had looked at him, daring him to drink in her presence and beauty.

Myrtle, getting frustrated with James, who seemed more interested in Mirinda, was happy to move on. And move on she did. The darker man was already taken, it seemed, but who was this tall boy with brown hair staring her down. He was not a pretty boy, but was he ever handsome. He looked at her with such familiarity, not like some kind of first impression. She had certainly not seen him before.

Jashion swallowed hard and looked over at Aiden. Never before had Aiden seemed transfixed. He, who was used to the ladies flocking to him, had met his match. He did not move. Jashion walked over to him as had Terrence and Daxton. All eyes were on Mirinda except Jashion's whose were back on Myrtle. The game was a draw. Mirinda, Myrtle, and Aiden who had never met their match, were each at a loss as to what to do next. Jashion, however, was used to being beaten and he dropped his eyes. Myrtle had won, and she made her way towards them. Tira and Tasha were close behind. It was these three who cut off Aiden's view, and brought him back to the present. His unblinking eyes burned as he blinked to try and hydrate them. He moved so as to see Mirinda again. He continued towards her and she stepped forward slowly, too.

"Hi, stranger. What'cha starin' at?"

Jashion smiled at Myrtle awkwardly.

"What's your name?"

"Me's Jashion, me is," he stammered.

Myrtle giggled and then laughed mercilessly.

Jashion reddened. This girl was bolder than Siccly.

Jashion would not have guessed, but he was charming to her, speech and all. Myrtle laughed at everything, and though it may insult those whom she laughed at she meant nothing mean-spirited by it. He had entertained her, his looks, his speech, his reddening face, and awkward glances, even the way he had stared at her like he had known her before. She laughed because it was fun, and she was enjoying him. Jashion felt like crawling into a hole.

"You's is not's from's around's here's, now's is you's?" she said barely getting it out before covering her mouth and giggling more than before.

"No, me...I'm not."

"Ha, ha, ha, ha, hee, hee, hee, hee, hee..."

Tasha and Tira were mortified. Terrence and Daxton were flabbergasted. Jashion was helpless and Myrtle was in ecstasy. She really liked this handsome stranger. The dumb ones never bothered her one bit. He might be a complete imbecile. But he was tall, cute, thoroughly entertaining, and his shy innocence was unlike anything she had seen before. The redder and more uncomfortable he became the more endearing he was to her. Not once had it occurred to her that he may not be feeling the same as she was.

Since Aiden had left home in search of greater game he had not been disappointed. The world he had known was far too easy, simple, and challenge-less to him. He loved his family and his people but he was made for a world far different from the one he had come into. In Dromreign he had met the ultimate challenge. The greatest hunter in the world meets the greatest hunter in the world. Aiden was not yet ready to take on the beast, and with time the beast was growing in size, strength, ferocity, and power. Even the lesser beasts, those with whom he had faced and conquered in the dark forest, were formidable—

especially in number. His match had been found and he would continue to strengthen until he was indeed matchless.

Never had it occurred to him that he would find another match in this world. The thought had not entered his mind that there was a woman in this world that was truly worthy of him. It may have been that he would marry happily, settle down, and rear a family one day. But she would be a woman to his choosing for a variety of reasons, not because she was worthy in and of herself of him. For the first time in his life he was looking at another human being for whom he had as much respect and admiration as he had for himself.

As they slowly approached each other with unblinking gaze he saw what he had always seen before, in every other girl. She was mesmerized by him, whether his looks, his presence, or whatever it was, she was caught. This did not surprise him; the opposite would have. What surprised him though, was that he, for the first time ever, felt the same feelings towards her. He had been ensnared and he knew it. What concerned him was that she, for all of her vulnerability, showed that she could see it too. She knew that he was infatuated with her, she knew that he was hers, that she had enchanted him. This he could see, and she was comfortable and confident with this knowledge, yet equally twitter patted with him.

From five feet away they began to circle each other ever so slowly still without dropping their gaze—both the perfect predator and at once the perfect prey. Aiden had stared down his prey before. At once, as soon as her eyes dropped or fluttered, once he knew he had won, he would be there. She, though defeated, would be the ultimate victor. She was worthy, and every second that she held her ground, he saw that she was even more worthy. At last her eyes broke...but wait.

She had not lost, they moved to his shoulder—his left shoulder, still showing its scars. It was but a moment and then she looked back with even more power than before. He looked at her as though no wound had ever taken place, yet the scar was there. Aiden knew not how to be defeated, but neither did Mirinda. Perhaps her scar was not showing, and perhaps it was the greater wound.

Mirinda foresaw at once the great weakness of Aiden. He had not yet learned humility and so was not yet omnipotent. She could beat him, but perhaps his pride would further weaken him. No, that would not do. His presence with her would do more to foster humility and greater strength than defeating him would. Mirinda acquiesced, but not in defeat. She dropped her eyes, but only briefly and then reset them upon Aiden's with a gorgeous blink showing nothing but her true vulnerability and admiration for him.

Aiden saw her gesture and returned it at once. He opened up his soul and allowed every vulnerability within him to be on display at once. She could look at his shoulder, could see the pain in his eyes for his lost companion, his poverty and lack of clothing. He was at her mercy and had given himself to her. He did not have to, for she had given herself to him. There was more power, even humility, in this man who stood in front of her than she had suspected. He was testing her and she passed the test in every way possible.

"I am Aiden."

"I am Mirinda."

Everything else was already known.

Daxton, Terrence, and Jashion had had enough. So had Tira and Tasha with these uncouth, uncivilized foreigners that Myrtle was berating.

"Let's go," said Terrence as he placed his hand on Jashion's shoulder. Myrtle still giggling.

Daxton backed away and into someone. It was Aiden with Mirinda at his side.

"We have accommodations," Aiden said to his friends.

Myrtle smiled.

Aiden, for all that Mirinda saw in him was in need of bathing, clothing, and grooming. His friends were in at least as bad of shape. A night on the town would have to wait for a time. Mirinda's family owned several apartment homes with two recently vacated. The girls escorted them there. Aiden walked with Mirinda and held her hand. Jashion took to Aiden's other side, trying to ignore Myrtle. He would have no such luck. She took to his other side and put her left hand through his right arm.

Myrtle talked and giggled while Jashion walked stiffly and quietly. Myrtle was none the wiser and Jashion was as confused as ever. Daxton and Terrence walked just behind Aiden and Jashion, while Tira and Tasha walked very reluctantly six or eight feet behind them.

"These skins you wear will not do, in Cardsten. We'll return in a few hours with clothes and then we shall dine."

Aiden nodded. Besides Aiden and Mirinda, only Myrtle seemed pleased with the plan.

"She likes you," said Aiden to Jashion after the girls had left.

"Nay, but she thinks me a fool, she does."

"I'm sure she does...and it seems to be working in your favor."

Jashion shook his head in frustration while Aiden smiled uncharacteristically.

"Do you believe in soul mates?" asked Aiden.

"What do ye mean?"

"You've never heard of a soul mate?"

"Nay."

"Ah. The one for you. Your perfect match. The girl you're meant for and she's meant for you. This type of thing. Do you believe in that?"

"I've never heard of that before. I figured ye married a girl if ye likes her, eh. Do you believe in that, in soul mates?"

"Yes, yes I do," said Aiden contemplatively.

"Have ye always believed in such a thing as that?"

"No. I just started believing in soul mates about an hour ago."

Jashion looked at him with confusion and irritation. Then a light bulb went off and he smiled and chuckled. Aiden smiled and laughed boisterously back.

"Perhaps she's your soul mate," said Aiden.

"Who?"

"Myrtle."

Jashion was aghast. "Nay."

Aiden's laugh became almost giddy.

"Everyone has got to have a soul mate; so why shouldn't you be hers? She latched onto you rather quickly and she's very pretty. Plus, she laughs at everything you say. Guy's like it when a girl laughs at his clever remarks."

"She thinks me not clever. Nay, she thinks me a fool. She laughs at the fool, she does."

"You shouldn't let that bother you..."

"Why?"

"...if she's your soul mate." And Aiden roared with laughter.

Servants had entered and exited numerous times in filling a small indoor bathing pool with hot water. Daxton and Terrence were excited. They had a sulfurous hot spring near Tengeer that they occasionally bathed in. Never before had they had such an experience indoors and without the smell of sulfur. They each took turns, and each took too long enjoying the delightful experience.

The girls waited below, having brought them exquisite outfits. Tasha had funded the purchases and was very disappointed in what was immediately available. The men would need to be fitted and clothes made properly. Still, the young men would have to be in better shape than they had appeared before—stinking, rugged, and without class. Tasha firmly believed that something could be purchased to make up for all deficits.

Jashion bathed last. He looked around the room. He had never seen such finery. It was surreal and made him uncomfortable. The other three were talking in the next room and were anticipating a prepared meal fit for a king. Jashion dreaded being mocked by Myrtle again. He was drawn to her briefly, but the thought of seeing her again sickened him. The concern was heightened when he saw the outfit that was to be his. It was silky blue on bottom and silky white on top. It reminded him of an outfit a doll may have worn. He put it on and looked in the mirror. He decided he would prefer hunger to this humiliation.

He left the bathing room and looked at all of his companions. They all looked foolish. Everyone was in silky clothes, but none so ridiculous as his own.

All three whistled and cat called as Jashion emerged.

"I'll stay here, I will. I shan't go out in this."

Aiden did not look so ridiculous in with his brown pants and black top. But he had fastened the back of his hair and Jashion couldn't believe his eyes.

"You're coming. This will be grand."

Tasha was pleased at what she saw. Bathed and dressed up, these boys were very handsome indeed. The blond brothers, as she thought them, would have to do as Mirinda and Myrtle were set on the others. Daxton, who had a taste already for the finery, was looking sharp and very happy. Tasha approached him as they came down and struck up a conversation. Daxton, having gotten a good look at Tasha was pleased too. He asked about everything, and she was happy to share all she knew. Daxton was in love, perhaps not yet with Tasha in particular, but with everything surrounding him. From this moment on, everything in his life that had transpired before was simply prologue. His life had just begun. This new, amazing world, that he hardly knew and could not yet comprehend, was his. The lovely woman by his side fit as perfectly as a glove into his new world and he was happy. Very happy.

Terrence had enjoyed his bath, and the surroundings had lightened him significantly. Tira looked deeply in his eyes. She saw pain. It was this that attracted him to her. With the others paired off, it would have been awkward for Tira and Terrence had they not paired up for the short journey. Tira approached cautiously and waited a moment not saying a word. Terrence, still baffled by the circumstances and surroundings took several moments to comprehend the scenario. He looked at Tira and smiled. He had not noticed her before. The two did not talk, but he offered her his arm. She took it and walked silently with him.

Myrtle had never been offered Jashion's arm, but she took it at once anyway and began to chat. Even as she asked questions, Jashion refused to speak. She filled the silence with more chatter quickly. She so much wanted to hear this silly boy speak. His speech brought such joy and laughter to her. No matter, though, she had plenty to say.

They all turned off of the main highway and onto a darker street. Three of the couples were full of conversation, but Terrence and Tira remained quiet. The silence did not bother either as they walked behind the throng. Noise was heard in the distance and Terrence realized that the fancy tavern was up on the right. The others each entered in as couples, and hardly noticed their surroundings, but Terrence saw the sign.

The Tavern was called, "The Dragon's Lair," and on the sign was a horrific portrayal of a fire breathing Dromreign. Terrence gasped and shivered.

"Are you okay," Tira asked with genuine concern.

"The Dragon's Lair!" he replied.

"Yes, you've heard of it? It's very good."

"But, that's the creature who destroys villages."

Tira continued to guide him toward the entrance. "Yes. I've heard some about that. But this is just a tavern. Every tavern has a name and a theme. That's all it is. Just a name and a theme. The food is very good. I dare say, you've never had anything like it before.

Terrence felt uncomfortable. His friends and their companions had all entered in. Tira paused at the entrance. She was not forceful. Terrence looked inside and then looked at Tira, searching her eyes. There was something in those eyes, brown, soft, intelligent, and warm.

"I *would* like to have a meal," he said awkwardly.

Tira gently nudged him forward and they met up with their friends.

Upon Terrence's arrival, the other young men had noted the restaurant's name and theme. There was a large mural of the dragon on the wall. Aiden and Daxton looked to be not much more than amused. Jashion looked like he had seen a ghost, but part of that may have been his uncomfortable companionship. Everyone in the room had noticed the group. Several men stared at Mirinda or Myrtle. Aiden's glare effectively removed all eyes from Mirinda. But Jashion was not chasing any stares away from Myrtle. He was not so much aware of it, as such. Instead, her obnoxious laugh was so penetrating that he suspected that all eyes were drawn uncomfortably to it. He felt as though the entire room knew that he was a fool and was being violently mocked by the blond beauty by his side. The restaurant's name and decor simply added to his disgust.

"What would you like," said the man approaching the table. His gaze was directed at Mirinda.

"This is Sean," she said. "He owns, 'The Dragon's Lair.'"

Of course, the owner would come out and serve Mirinda and her friends himself. Aiden turned towards Mirinda and looked at her as if to say, 'Surprise me.'

Mirinda ordered for both of them and Sean looked at her knowingly.

"Let's share the Turtle soup," said Myrtle excitedly.

Sean looked at Jashion for confirmation. He received none. Myrtle nodded the confirmation for him and Sean jotted it down.

Daxton and Tasha were pouring over the menu. Daxton asked about everything and Tasha filled in every detail. Duck was decided upon for Daxton but Tasha only took a salad.

"I like the pork tenderloin," said Tira to Terrence quietly. Terrence gaze was towards the menu but his racing mind did not allow him to take anything in. Sean continued to look at the pair. Tira spoke up. "I'll have the pork tenderloin."

"Got it. And you?"

Terrence looked up and met Sean's eyes. On Sean's shirt was an embroidered dragon with the title, 'Owner of The Dragon's Lair." Terrence was filled with enmity towards Sean. Terrence nodded slowly.

"Pork Tenderloin for you. Is that to share?"

Tira looked at Terrence who was still looking at Sean. "We'll each have a plate," she said sweetly.

Moments later a young lady brought bread and cheese, wine and goblets, for all. The goblets were filled and the bread was divided. Myrtle's goblet was the first to be refilled while Jashion's sat untouched beside him. Instead, he nibbled slowly on a slice of bread. Jashion's discomfort grew. Initially it was Myrtle who had made him feel such, but the growing feeling inside of his guts was betrayal. The dark tavern, with the smell of brew and of smoke, reminded him of home. But everywhere he looked he saw mugs held up with Dromreign's image proudly displayed. They were drinking to him...to it, to the monster who murdered all his people right before his eyes. The vicious creature was celebrated, idealized, invoked by all around him. The lives of thousands were mocked in front of him. And he, who knew better than anyone the destruction and the devastation, he who held the memory of the dragon's filthy stench in his nostrils, was participating in the midst.

His turtle soup arrived along with another refill for Myrtle. It smelled delicious. One large bowl, two spoons. Myrtle turned to him and spoke, the alcohol reeked from her breath.

"You first, take a bite," she said as she handed him his spoon.

To take a bite seemed to make him complicit with all that surrounded him. He held the spoon and looked around. Daxton was already devouring his duck. Aiden was slicing off the first bite of his bacon-wrapped filet. And then he looked a Terrence who had just had his tenderloin placed in front of him. Terrence glared at Sean. He made no motion for his knife or fork, unlike Tira who was unwrapping hers.

Jashion swallowed hard. "Me's seen ye dragon, me has," he said quietly and with a shake in his voice towards Sean.

Myrtle choked on her wine and some of it sprayed out of her nose. Her eyes began to water as she tried to laugh amidst her choking. She was laughing at what Jashion said, how he said it, and at herself for snorting the wine through her nose. She couldn't catch her breath for all that was happening simultaneously. The goblet she held in her hand was nearly full and as she choked and sputtered the wine also spilled from the goblet onto the table. This made everything even funnier to Myrtle who was red but not out of shame. Her throat finally clear, she laughed as loud as she could and slammed her goblet down in front of her spilling and spraying half of it all around. She kept her hand around it and laid her head on her arm while continuing to laugh.

No one else was laughing. Everyone looked at her dismayed.

"She's drunk," said Mirinda both for Aiden's and Sean's sake.

"Me's is not drunk, me isn't...ha ha ha ha ha. I'm just having a great time...and I snorted. He he he he he."

The ladies shook their heads while the men stared dumbfounded.

"Did you say you've seen a dragon?" asked Sean as Myrtle's display had settled. He had a look of contempt as he asked the question.

"Nay. I said I've seen ye dragon. This here dragon, Dromreign, I have."

Myrtle giggled and then exploded into another laugh.

Sean smiled slyly. "Ah, that so," he said and began to walk away.

"Aye. Me was there when it torched all me's people, those of Dargaer."

Sean stopped deliberately, pausing briefly and then turning with a new look in his eyes. "Humph. They say there's not a living soul that has seen the mighty dragon. He doesn't leave survivors."

"Aye, but me and a lass escaped, we did. I've never met another who survived. All the rest of me people died, I believe."

"Is that so," said Sean. "It's a shame..."

"Aye, 'tis a shame so many good people is dead now, and here we's celebrating and mocking their death in Dromreign's name."

"It's a shame that you and a girl escaped. Dromreign rids this world of fools. When fools escape, they bring more fools into this world. I'm looking forward to the dragon torching Agedon, a whole city of fools. If you let the fools alone long enough they'll make so many of themselves that the world will be overrun. If Dromreign doesn't take care of Agedon, Cardsten will. Now eat your soup and drink your wine. When you've drunk enough you'll think that you escaped your dragon again as you leave," he said starting to walk away irate and indicating the mural on the wall.

Terrence stood and pounded his fists on the table. Tira sat back fearfully.

"That dragon's a menace. Only half a day's journey from here he torched a whole village, just the other night. We walked by the dead men, women, and children earlier today. Not a soul survived. And you think that beast brings good to the world?"

"So you've escaped the dragon, too?" Sean asked mockingly.

"No, I've only witnessed its horrific destruction first hand. I've seen what it can do. Only a fool would celebrate Dromreign as you have done, here with your, 'Dragon's lair!'"

"Not another word, you fool, or I'll have you out on the street." He looked at Mirinda. "You've found yourself some companions tonight. Settle them down or we'll have to call it a night."

Sean walked away with Terrence still standing. Myrtle had quit laughing and was looking around like she had been transported to a different dimension. Daxton looked at Terrence and motioned for him to sit down, which he eventually did, but very reluctantly.

The scene had attracted plenty of attention. Five men approached the table. The girls became concerned. The men were large, middle-aged, with black leather coats, and they each wore a goatee. Each of their jackets had a colorful representation of Dromreign thereon. The images were not like the tavern's; they were patrons not employee's. The largest, though shortest man in the middle spoke up.

"You've taken on the master, have you, young man." His voice was gruff and he and each of his gang laughed. He looked at Jashion.

"I've come by to spook you." He lifted his hat and bent down. On the top of his head was a tattoo of the dragon and the tattoo ran down the back of his neck. He lifted his head and put his cap back on smiling. The others around him laughed.

Then the laughter and his smile ended. His face became threatening.

"You'll not escape this time. If the master wanted you dead, you will be." He leaned in close and spoke quietly to Jashion. "The master will never let any fool escape. But if you're fool enough to mock the dragon, then you also deserve to die. Eat your last meal and drink up. This will be your *last*." He grabbed Jashion's face by the chin. "Understand!" He threw his fist off of his face violently and he and his friends walked away.

Aiden began to get up as the man grabbed Jashion's face. Mirinda placed her hand on Aiden's knee and squeezed. He noticed her shake her head almost imperceptivity. Slowly she relaxed her grip as the men walked away.

Chapter 12

Tasha, who had been chatting rapidly with Daxton, spoke up. "I'll talk with them. We'll get this settled. You boys just got here and don't understand things. No one'll get hurt. Daxton, come with me. You'll explain it, too. They'll let it go this time, I'm sure. I'll give them whatever they want."

Mirinda nodded and Daxton followed Tasha reluctantly. Aiden watched as the dragon tattooed gang behaved obnoxiously towards them. After some time, Tasha opened up her purse and pulled out several bills of currency. She put them on the table but continued to talk. Daxton then talked for a few moments and then the two listened to the pudgy leader of the men. After some time, and some head nodding from Tasha and Daxton, he turned and looked at Jashion. Jashion was not paying as close attention as was the rest of the group. The leader waited for eye contact and then pointed squarely at Jashion with a menacing glare. He then slapped the table where the money was laid and snatched it up. He waved Tasha and Daxton off and began to divvy up the loot.

Tasha walked over with the air of a woman who had been once again vindicated in her life's outlook, adding to her already abundant confirmation bias— 'money can take care of or fix anything.' Yet, there was some concern on her face, Mirinda noted. This encounter ended with the desired results but not as easily as Tasha would have liked. Still, there wasn't going to be any more trouble tonight.

Jashion still had not touched anything other than the bread he had nibbled on. Myrtle had finished off most of the soup and another glass of wine. He sat there dumbfounded upon Daxton and Tasha's return. After getting situated and enjoying a few bits of her salad, Tasha looked at Jashion and said severely but quietly, "no more dragon talk in public!"

Jashion looked at her with glazed eyes.

"This isn't a joke, Jashion. Listen up. No more dragon talk, you understand."

Myrtle began to giggle. Tasha and Daxton shot her a look. This only made her giggle more. Tasha looked over to Mirinda irritated and pleadingly.

"Myrtle, button it," shot Mirinda.

Myrtle rolled her eyes and looked away disinterestedly.

"Jashion," said Daxton. "That was no empty threat. That cost Tasha a fortune to keep you safe. You'll be watched from now on."

Jashion felt sick. He nodded slightly and then just looked down at his hands. *So much for this being the promise land.*

Tasha looked irritated as she opened up her purse and put more money on the table. This had been a very expensive night out, and an expensive group of boys. There was no other way out then past the dragon gang. They tried to not make eye contact, but the men called out at them and lifted their hoods showing off their hideous tattoo's. The leader glared at Jashion all the way out boring holes into Jashion's back.

The evening had a chill. It was good for Tasha, she needed some cooling off. She led the pack outside walking quickly with her short skirt and high heels clickety-clacking away. Daxton watched as he tried to catch up. Admiration was quickly morphing into attraction within him. Eventually he caught up but kept a little distance. With time, she closed the gap between them. Daxton put his arm around her. Again, they talked. Daxton was enchanted by this beautiful, powerful companion by his side.

"Why'd you call it a fortune?"

"What?" he asked.

"You told your friend that getting him off cost me a fortune. Why'd you say that?"

"You said so..." he said with wonderment.

"I said, 'that was expensive,'" as she poked him lightly and playfully in the ribs. "Expensive is a far cry from a fortune."

"Oh."

"You were good, Daxton. You helped. If it'd been just me, it wouldn't have gone so well. They're crazy. Everyone likes money, though. Still, thanks."

"What's a fortune?"

"A fortune? That's when...that's when you have so much that you can do whatever you want, whenever you want. When you don't have to earn an income. When no matter what you spend, there is always just as much afterwards. You can't carry a fortune as bills in a purse. A fortune means you can spend through the purse and just fill it back up again as often as is needed."

"Does everyone here have a fortune?"

"No, silly. Having a fortune wouldn't do you any good if everyone had one. You can't get whatever you need if everyone has so much money that they don't care about yours. You need people to work for you; to make your clothes, your food, fill your bath. Money's only worth something if people want it and need it. If those crazy dragon worshipers had a fortune what good would my cash be to them? Why would someone put up with all they put up with running a pub if they didn't have a want or need of money? They wouldn't. Then you could have all the money in the world and you'd still have to do everything for yourself."

"Wow. Do you have a fortune?"

"You bet!"

"Do people hate you...because of it? Because they have to work hard and you don't?"

"Hardly! They love me, they love my whole family. They might be jealous. But what would Cardsten be without my family. We'd be one of those villages that your friend Dromreign likes to light up. People work hard, not just to get by here, but because they want what I have. They want power, luxury, leisure, and if they get enough money, well, then they can have a taste of that. Where you lived, did anyone have a fortune?"

"No. Not at all."

"Did people work hard? I mean really work hard?"

"No, we had sufficient. People worked, but not real hard."

"Did you ever imagine that you could have worked yourself into a fortune? To have it all?"

"No, not until now.

"You see, seeing my fortune gives you a vision of what is possible. People love that vision. Because I have it, it means that it is possible. If one person has it then it is possible for someone else to have it, or maybe a portion of it. It gives them something to work for. But it's more than that. If everyone has just enough to get by...to eat, for simple shelter, basic clothes, then there is so much that can never be. You've seen the exquisite architecture of the buildings here. You've noticed the outfits that my friends and I are wearing. I mean look at these shoes, how do they make my legs look?"

"Great..."

She smiled, "What are you doing checking out my legs?"

Daxton reddened slightly.

Tasha turned to him and reached to hold both of his hands while peering into his eyes. She leaned in and they kissed. Daxton felt his insides melt. Her red lips felt warm, soft, and perfectly moist. All that Daxton had experienced, and how much his eyes had been opened upon meeting Aiden and Jashion, paled in comparison to how meeting Tasha opened his eyes. He was a new man in every way.

"What were we talking about?" she asked, just inches from his face.

"Uh..."

"I think you were just telling me how beautiful I look in this outfit."

"Yeah, I..."

"Good, 'cause it cost me a fortune!"

"Tasha, you're the most beautiful, wonderful girl in the whole world!"

"I've been told I'm a good kisser. I must still have the touch."

"No, well yes...but, it's everything about you."

"Daxton, you're not so bad yourself...now that you've bathed and cleaned up a bit, that is." Daxton smiled. "You're worth spending on. You and your friends sure are expensive, though. Do any of you have any money, yourselves?"

"No, we don't have any."

"So, you figured you'd just walk into Cardsten and meet the prettiest, richest girls around and have them take care of you?"

"When you put it that way..."

"Thought so."

"I don't think we thought through it at all. We didn't know what we'd find when we got here. I guess Cardsten isn't so scary when you've survived a couple of winter's in the dark forest..."

"What?"

"Well, we didn't all survive. Marcus, Terrence's older brother, my cousin, he didn't make it..."

"Oh, I'm sorry. But, I mean, you aren't serious about the dark forest?"

"Yeah, we spent the last year and a half or so there. So after that, I guess, we figured Cardsten wouldn't be hard to survive in."

"But, that's not possible. People can't survive the dark forest. You're not dragon hunters are you, spies from Agedon or anything?"

"No..."

"Jashion wasn't serious about all that, was he?"

"Yes, he was..."

"Daxton, you listen to me carefully. Are you planning on staying here? With me? In Cardsten?"

"Yes, I am."

"Then listen: I don't want to hear any more about the dark forest, about dragon's, adventures, or anything else. I don't care about your past. Do you understand? Whatever it was, whatever craziness you've been up to, or your friends think they're up to. I like you. But if you're planning on being here, with me, then that's the past and it's over. Those days are over. This is your life now. I have a fortune. We won't have to want for anything. You can have a life like people only dream...imagine. But you can't have it both ways. I'm not going to sponsor any Agedon nonsense. No dragon hunts. No dark forest craziness. The good life or I'm done with you and your friends. I don't want to be embarrassed ever again in a nice establishment. I don't want gangs spying on us. I don't want any accusations, or any government officials looking in on my family's affairs. You've got to understand: this stuff you're talking about is over. It's done."

"Tasha, when I awoke this morning I didn't know what this day would bring. I've been on an adventure for a long time now, and I have experienced more than anyone could ever imagine. But, until today, I was just along for the ride. I'm home now. I didn't know what I was looking for, but I've found it. I'm happy to spend the rest of my life in this world, in your world, with you, forever. There is nothing outside of these walls that I want, need, or ever care to see again. I'm with you!"

"Good."

Tasha leaned back in and they kissed. Aiden and Mirinda walked by and Aiden tapped Daxton on the arm. Daxton broke from Tasha and looked over. Aiden just smiled and winked and then turned back around and kept walking. Daxton turned back to Tasha who was looking at him expectantly. And they began to kiss again.

For some time, Terence and Tira walked along silently. Terence had his hands in his pocket and Tira walked along nearby but without trying to directly connect to him. Emotions and thoughts ran quickly and fiery through Terence's mind.

Finally, Tira broke the silence, "Will you be leaving here soon."

"Huh, oh. I'm not sure. These guys all wanted to come here."

"Where did you want to go?"

"I better not say."

Tira looked hurt. "Why?"

"Look, I didn't know. Aiden told us that you and Agedon were at odds. None of us had been to either. I figured...I don' know, I don't want to get into trouble."

"Go on."

"I didn't want to hide from the dragon." He said dragon so quietly it was almost imperceptible. "I figured I'd rather join with those who would fight it, not hide from it."

They walked silently for several steps. Terence began to regret opening his mouth.

"You think we are trying to hide, here in Cardsten?"

"I don't know. I don't really know anything about any of it. It was just my vote. Here I am, it's fine. But I didn't like that place."

"What place?"

"Back there, where we ate, 'The Dragon's Lair,' or whatever. I hate that filthy creature."

"You mean the dragon?"

"Yeah.

"So, you have seen it?"

"No, I haven't. But I've seen what it's done. There is something evil about those filthy creatures in the dark forest and that Dromreign. I guess I like the idea of going after them. Between Aiden and I, and even Jashion, we can take on just about anything. I thought maybe we could help. I don' know, I'm sorry if I'm offending you."

Tira smiled. "I was more offended that you weren't talking to me before. At least I know what's on your mind."

"Sorry."

"Terrence, Agedon isn't going after anything. They're fools. If they really do try anything, Cardsten will stop them. If we let them they'd just get themselves killed. But, worse, they'd rile up the beast and he would just destroy more and more villages. It may seem like we aren't concerned about the death and destruction of so many villages, but it's not entirely true. Some might think like those idiots back at the pub, but most don't. The best way to stop the dragon is to protect against it with barriers; to not get it upset. We're trying to show the world how to protect itself and trying to not anger it further. All Agedon will ever do is cause its own hurt and the hurt of many others."

They walked for a while in silence again.

"Terence, I don't mean to tell you what to think. You can do as you must. It's just...I don't want you to get hurt."

Terence looked over and saw that her deep brown eyes were in earnest.

"Thank you," he said, softly and sincerely.

"Can I ask you a question?" he asked.

"Sure."

"Please don't take this the wrong way."

"Okay?"

"How do you know?"

"Know what?"

"Know all that you just said about Agedon, about the dragon, and everything. I mean, that's what people here think, but how do you know? The people in Agedon can't really all be a bunch of fools. They're a big successful people, too. They see it all differently. If you lived there, wouldn't you just see it the way that they do?"

"So, when you said 'don't take this the wrong way,' what way exactly is the wrong way to take it?"

"I'm sorry."

"Please stop saying that."

Terrence and Tira stopped and looked at each other. The moon was full and the light brushed softly off of her face. Terrence began to drink in her beauty and delicacy.

"It's a good question, Terrence. It's fair, but it is a little hurtful."

"I'm..."

"Don't say it. I don't know how I would see it if I saw everything from a different perspective. I don't tend to go against the grain. I don't tend to stand out. Maybe I see it that way because that is how I am supposed to see it."

"Fair enough. And maybe I see everything the way that I do because I've had a really rough day, and I'm tired and cranky, and everything is so new here, and I just about got killed back there except for these really pretty girls that we just met."

"Do you think I'm pretty?"

"Do I think you're pretty? That goes without saying. You're the most beautiful thing I've ever laid my eyes upon."

"Thank you," she said sweetly. "I think that I'm looking at the most beautiful thing that I have ever laid my eyes on."

"Beautiful?"

"Yes, Terrence, beautiful. Ruggedly handsome, yes, and exquisitely beautiful."

Terrence gave Tira his arm and she slipped her hand through as they walked along still mostly silent but no longer so separate.

At the front of the group, Mirinda began to question Aiden.

"Why'd you come here, Aiden?"

As was his custom, Aiden walked for a spell before attempting to answer. Mirinda, self-assured as usual, saw no reason to repeat herself. Finally, he spoke:

"If there is a Cardsten in this world, why wouldn't I come to it?"

"You don't fit in well here."

"Yes," he said and then paused for some time. "It is not in my nature to fit in. Neither is it in your nature to fit in. You are not simply a part of this world around you. This world is different because you are here. I see the gravitational pull that surrounds you. You can't be a part of what is—what is, in large measure, is because you are a part of it. Your presence is the defining aspect of wherever you are and whatever you do."

"Are we talking about me or you?"

"Yes...yes we are."

"I see. Yet, your friends have seemed the more impactful tonight."

Aiden smiled. He was pleased with the conversation thus far. Without question his friends had been the more impactful, at least quantitatively. But Aiden knew that there was much more to being impactful than the amount of impact. What he was referring to was equally important in the qualitative sense. Any fool could have impact, bring attention to himself, or cause a fuss. Neither Mirinda's nor Aiden's presence could be characterized in this way.

"Yes, I'm afraid my friends have made quite the entrance into Cardsten."

"Quite."

"Perhaps the contrast is sometimes helpful." He paused briefly. "Myrtle provides a valuable contrast for you."

It was Mirinda's turn to smile. This man was so self-aware, among all of his other qualities. But what was he doing here? He was no city boy. He was not afraid of the wild. Had he come to Cardsten to seek refuge within the walled city? *Why is he here?*

Mirinda was no hopeless romantic. Aiden had found her and was satisfied for now. Whether he had ever intended to find a mate or not when he came to Cardsten, he had found her. How long would he be satisfied with this? Here was a wild man from a distant tribe. A hunter, a warrior. *Yes, a warrior. Cardsten has a powerful military, perhaps...* But would this satisfy the mighty hunter. Keeping peace, keeping Agedon at bay, running drills, fancy uniforms, leading silly boys who knew nothing of the world at large. Here is a hunter who can walk into Cardsten and be right at home in a fancy pub, with the wealthiest and classiest women, who can be dressed in the fanciest attire and at once fit right in, and at the same time make them look like they are underwhelming compared to his presence. He would be equally majestic with nothing but his loins simply girded. The clothes did not make this man. How long could this last? A week? A month? A year?

There was no question that with Mirinda's influence and Aiden's presence and capacity, he could be given an influential position in the military. He was no businessman. He could be a general in no time. This would fit him better than anything else in Cardsten. Would it last forever? Could they settle down with him as a great Cardsten military commander and live happily ever after? Never before had Mirinda considered that the man of her choosing could ever be dissatisfied with her alone. But here she had found the only man that she could ever choose and she felt severely inadequate. But, what was he thinking? *Maybe he thinks he'll do the Cardsten thing for a while and then take me with him. As if I'd ever leave this place. There is no place in this world that would ever do. No place compares to Cardsten. If Cardsten isn't good enough for him, if I'm not sufficient for him, then so be it.* Still, what wouldn't a woman do for a man such as this?

"I'm sure that I can get you a commission in the military. Of course, you'd earn it yourself, but I could get you to the right place, to the front of the line."

Aiden nodded emotionlessly and they walked on for some time, hand in hand.

For Jashion, Myrtle's drunkenness provided some relief. At least her mirth and giddiness came across as more fitting her state and less mockingly towards Jashion. She left the establishment somewhat quiet and distant from Jashion. With every other couple paired off it didn't take her long to begin to hang all over him. She muttered, not entirely coherently, and seemed to hold onto his arm not just for form but for actual support. This softened Jashion's heart to some extent and he shifted so as to give her the needed support. He could not have retold a word she had said, until she said this:

"No boy stays with me for long..." She then belched impolitely and began giggling. Jashion was still fearful of uttering a word in her presence.

"They all look at me as though I'm the most beautiful girl in the world. Except when Mirinda's around," hee, hee, hee, hee, hee, snort. "Then they treat me as though I'm worthless. But I can always get another guy. I can have any guy I like." The giggling and the laughing stopped and she was quiet and even serious for a few moments. "You looked. You looked at me. You even looked past Mirinda and just looked at me. You liked what you saw. Now you don't even like me. We could ignore each other tonight but then it would be even worse. So, since you looked, you have to escort the poor, foolish, drunk girl home. Don't worry, I won't bother you tomorrow."

Jashion was confused but his heart was pricked. "If ye want me with ye, why do ye laugh me to scorn?"

Myrtle put her hand up and giggled. Jashion didn't redden but his heart began to harden again. Myrtle could sense the body language then.

"I don't laugh to scorn you. I laugh because it makes me happy to hear you talk. It's funny. I like it. I like it when a guy makes me laugh. You're charming."

"I hate the way I talk. I know 't'ain't right but it's how me people speak. My friends try to help me, but they don't mock me."

"Okay. You're very sensitive Jashion."

"I suppose ye's right. It's been a long day for me, it has."

"Why'd you make up that story about the great dragon back there? That was pretty foolish."

"Tasha said to not talk about that anymore."

"It's just me. I'm not going to attack you. I might giggle though."

"I didn't make it up. I did see the dragon. Dromreign destroyed me people. Just me and a littl'un made it out. A littl' lass, Jemma. We escaped by headin' into the dark forest, we did. We left her with Terence's and Daxton's people. We lost all we's family and friends to that beast that day. All those who me hadn't lost before. Why'd they want to eat and drink in that beast's name? Why'd they want to imprint him on their own heads? Why'd they want anyone who's seen the beast to die? I don't see why they'd not want the beast dead, too. If he could get through the defenses here he'd kill them too, he would."

Myrtle knew nothing of death or destruction. Serious conversation and subjects such as these made her feel down and she avoided that feeling at all cost.

"Tasha's right, you shouldn't speak of these things. You're here now. You're safe and you can have everything you could ever imagine here. Cardsten is a wonderful place. Ye not so silly as I thought ye was?" She let out just a light giggle.

Jashion even smiled.

"Friends?" she asked.

Jashion paused and looked over at the silly, drunk, blond beauty by his side. "Aye," he said as she embraced him, squeezing so tight that she kept him from breathing. When she let go, he breathed in so rapidly that she thought she'd made more of an impression than she had. It made Myrtle happy and Jashion didn't mind.

The women led the men to their apartments. Daxton, Jashion, and Terrence entered in while Aiden stayed outside still holding Mirinda's hand. Jashion looked questioningly at him.

"I'll escort the ladies home." He spoke assertively so as to make it clear that he did not want the others to come. They had become accustomed to Aiden's regular disappearing acts. It could be hours or even days before they would see him again. Cardsten was not the dark forest, but still, sometimes Aiden's best work was done alone.

Chapter 13

Though no one knew when Aiden returned the previous evening, he was up at the crack of dawn. Daxton was up early, too. Food had been brought in by the servants and it was unclear how they were supposed to occupy themselves.

"Why're you up so early, Aiden? You can't have slept much."

"Mirinda will be introducing me to the military command this morning. I don't want to keep her or them waiting."

"You're joining the Cardsten military? I thought that you wanted to just check the place out."

"I did check it out and I found it desirable."

"Oh?"

"I found Mirinda, didn't I."

"Oh."

"And you. What brings you to such an early arousal?"

"Tasha. She will be introducing me to her father. He may have a commission for me in his business. Her family is the wealthiest of those of Cardsten."

"But we just got here? Don't you want to check it out for a while first before you jump right in?"

Daxton smiled. "You've said it yourself, there is no other place quite like Cardsten."

"Is she the one, then?"

"Yes."

"Poor thing. She has no idea what it's like living with you and trying to keep you out of trouble."

Daxton's eyes narrowed briefly and then he relaxed. "She's a fortune."

"Yes."

"If her father goes along, if I get my commission then I will marry her and live here like a king for the rest of my life."

"Daxton, I wish you well."

"I'm off. And you?" said Aiden.

"Tasha will meet me here shortly. I've not been to her place."

"It's very nice."

Daxton nodded. Aiden left.

Tasha arrived shortly. They kissed for a time in the entrance way. If possible, Tasha looked even better and more made up than she had the night before. She must have been up for hours with her short blond hair done up so nicely and wearing the most exquisite blue outfit. Her skirt was longer today, nearly knee length—she had already impressed Daxton, today she was impressing her father.

"You will need more outfits than just the one," she said looking over him. "I know a place. This was fine for last night but it won't do for today."

Once Tasha was satisfied with the preparations they made their way to see Mr. Cards. His office was in a majestic stone building, taller than the rest. The streets were paved with tiles and wider than in other parts of the city. The men and women who made their ways up and down the streets walked at a fast pace. They looked fine in their dress and were single minded in their demeanor. This was the heart of Cardsten both in geography, being located in the city center, and in practice. The seat of government was located elsewhere but that was not the power center of Cardsten. It was here, the business district.

Reaching the fourth floor, Tasha walked into the reception area. The woman at the desk looked up and smiled kindly upon seeing Tasha.

"I'll be right back, Miss Cards."

Only a minute later she returned and said, "Go ahead," gesturing to her right.

Daxton took a deep breath.

The office was large with a beautiful desk and several filled bookshelves. The rug was bright and the workmanship superb. Mr. Cards came to Tasha and embraced her warmly. He seemed to have not noticed Daxton or was just utterly uninterested in him. Tasha talked pleasantly with her father and made no reference to her companion. Daxton felt awkward like he was a fly on the wall. He stared at Tasha and her father for some time but then felt uncomfortable and began to look around. It must have been a quarter of an hour before his presence was acknowledged.

Mr. Cards broke from his daughter and walked directly toward Daxton. "Max Cards," he said directly and held his hand out for Daxton to shake.

Daxton accepted his hand and shook it rapidly. "I'm Daxton."

"You're from away?"

"Yes sir, I'm of Tengeer."

"Medicine people."

"Yes."

"Are you skilled?"

"No, I've never learned. I don't think that I was ever meant for such a life."

"Ninety-nine percent of everyone does not think that they were meant for the life that they are leading."

Daxton did not answer, though there was a pause. This man had a presence not unlike Aiden's. Daxton had learned to listen when a man such as this spoke.

"You are tall, strong, and handsome. You and my daughter will make fine children."

Tasha smiled, her father was satisfied.

"You look the part—now you must be the part. The Cards are not to be trifled with—by anyone. No one is to feel equal to us. We are good, and kind, and fair to everyone but they are not equal to us."

"Yes, I understand that your wealth and fortune is beyond anyone else's fortune," Daxton ventured.

"Wealth, yes. We could live comfortably with the wealth and be worthless and unknown. We are more than our wealth, young man. Our wealth is fitting for our position but it is not the only defining aspect. If we were slothful, and lazy, and simply indulgent then we would be hated, used, and destroyed. But we are not. We are the visionaries. I awake before anyone and put in more hours in than anyone else. I eat well, I sleep well, and I have any and all comforts needed. But I push for a better place. The secret of Cardsten is that those who have wealth are visionaries. We push for art, for beauty, for security and protection, for science, for knowledge, for wealth. We are the keystone of this great society. Without us as we are, the whole thing falls apart. There is no Cardsten without the Cards.

"I suspect that the average man lives better here than a great man most anywhere else. We may have more, much more, than anyone else. But we live as we do so that even the poor do not go to bed hungry at night. Everyone has hope. There is work to do and work makes people happy. I am happy because I work, not because I have so much."

"So you give to the poor?"

"I give to everyone, but I never give a penny away. I employ directly, or indirectly, forty percent of Cardsten. The beautiful, quality homes, lived in by nearly everyone, were built by me. The great wall that protects this grand place is here because of my father and I. The government is financed by taxes provided by me, my employee's, and my industries. We push for what is needed and practically finance the entire operation. We grow and raise the quality foods, or make sure that they are done right.

"I don't want to be better than everyone else, for its own sake. It's necessary. I want to be in the best place possible and it requires someone that I trust at the top. Someone who will ensure that the right conditions are met for a people and a society to thrive. I'm that man. It is essential for me to succeed that I'm wealthier than everyone else. It requires that no one thinks themselves better, smarter, or more capable than I. So, I am, and I must be, or else the greatness will turn to laziness and we will implode and become useless in only a few generations. It is easier to have a society like Tengeer, endure. It is not a bad way, I'm sure. But it is not great; it is sufficient. Greatness requires continual greatness.

"A society requires a solid top, but it also requires a strong bottom. If those who have the least are fed and cared for by the wealthy, rather than working hard for their needs, then the society collapses. The poor must work hard just as the wealthy must. And there must be every stage in between, and everyone must work. But, if at the top, if the wealthy are at work, are visionaries, are willing to continue to push for greatness, then the poor will be satisfied as they work and hope for better than they now have. The poor in my world are not poor. They are just the poorest; they are merely the relative poor. The poor are wealthy as are the rich. You've looked around, we've no beggars, have we?"

"No, I've seen none. But what of the infirm, the insane, the blind, those without mental capacity."

"There are not many who are so infirm, so insane, so blind, or so mentally incapacitated that they cannot do something for themselves and for society. Those who are, are cared for by someone. It would not do to have institutions dedicated to providing comfort and sustenance to those who are not living, really living at all. When those who do nothing are simply provided for, then the society will quickly fall apart."

Tasha, who had sat quietly aside, entered into the conversation briefly. "Father ensures that those who provide for such, are given employment that will satisfy their ability to care for those."

"Yes, my dear, but they are not given anything. They work for what they require. I never turn a blind eye to anyone and I never give anyone anything—not without the opportunity for earning it."

"I've not been here long," said Daxton. "But I see many who are at leisure, who are comfortable, who seem to be doing well."

"Many? Everyone is doing well. Everyone is comfortable. There is wealth here. There is opportunity for leisure. But most do work. There are some of the wealthy who do not see as I see, perhaps some of the middle class, too. There is always more work to be done. This society will never be able to run flawlessly on its own. There will always be correction, effort, and leadership needed. But, why would we all work so hard if it wasn't to have a good and enjoyable life. The poorest can have and enjoy as can the rich. They just can't have as much. They must be willing to do that which is not desirable. A society cannot function without having those who are willing to do that which is least desirable. We cannot feel sorry for them. They work, they have, and they are happy. We are not happier than they. Some say that we could not do the jobs that they do. Perhaps they are right. Perhaps they can do those things which we cannot. But, they are certainly not capable of doing what we do. It is the rare man indeed that can do what I do. If we reversed roles, society would collapse on itself.

"If I gave to the poor without allowing them to earn it, society would indeed collapse on itself. If we all tried to be equal to each other, then society would collapse on itself. We are not equal; nor can we be. I am not equal to the poor and what they do, in many ways they have a hard life and I am not equal to it. In many ways, I have a harder life than they and they are not equal to it. We do not force anyone down. Those that are meant for something different, perhaps something better, may work to achieve that; and many do achieve it. Many who might have had more were not sufficient to the task and now have less. There are many complications and it cannot be a perfect system. But it is very fair, in its way. It is never equal, however. Equality would ruin it and turn it into something different, worse I dare say.

"But, equality also seems a worthy goal."

"Yes, in a way of looking at things it does. But, you see, equality is not possible. Goodness, even greatness, is possible but equality is not. A society would have to force equality in order to achieve any semblance of equality. Someone has to do the forcing. Those who force and those who are forced are not equal to each other. So, in this way only the forced are equal. Yet, are even they equal? I think not. Everything cannot be forced. People are different and even when they appear to be forced into equality they are not really equal, at least in most ways. And those in power are as unequal to them as possible. Equality is the great antithesis to goodness and greatness. I make no attempt for equality; this is so that everyone can be happy, can enjoy a good, hard-working life.

"A great society, a truly great society, makes no attempt to force the bottom up or the top down. Once you see a striated society as unfair and try to make it different, then you are setting up for its collapse, or for it to be made up of those who are thoroughly unhappy and without hope. Hope requires that there is something better possible. Equality is the destroyer of hope. Hopelessness is a life with no joy, happiness, or satisfaction. Pleasures are a poor substitute for hope."

"So, you force inequality?"

"No! My boy, are you not listening? You neither force equality nor inequality. Forcing inequality is just as destructive. If you force inequality, then you are hated and someday the pendulum will swing and those on bottom will be on top and vice versa. You cannot judge a person because of any external characteristic as belonging to one class or another. These prejudices are foolish and will lead to problems. Any society that forces inequality at any level will one day be forcing equality. It makes everyone look at it from the wrong angle. Force will always be resisted.

"No, accepting the necessity and inevitability of inequality is completely different from forcing inequality. If you are to be on top then you must accept the privilege and responsibility of such and never feel guilt, sorrow, or that somehow it is unfair that you are in the position that you are in. You must never think that it is unfair that that person must work as they do so that they may eat and enjoy the comforts and privileges that they do. No, they must—someone must work as they do, and if they were privileged more than they are, then they would not do such work. Relatively speaking, they may have less privilege than anyone else, and they may do the least desirable work, but they are happy and they have hope because they know that something better is out there. They have hope. They are not forced to be in the position that they are in. They choose that position. They want to eat, they want shelter, they want what they must work for and the work is absolutely needed. So, we appreciate the work that they do and we do not treat them in a bad way.

"I get up every morning and work hard so that they may have this position and they may have food and shelter. Their capacity may be much weaker than mine, certainly much different, but they are each valued as a human being, they have a good life, they have happiness and hope, they do not starve or go without shelter and clothing, and they have all of this because I provide the opportunity in the way that I can. I do not devalue these people; not at all. I work hard so that they may have what they do. I am grateful to them for they are necessary for me to have what I have. And, you know, they too are grateful to me. They may not understand it all, but they know at some level that they have what they do because of what I do for them. We are all important and necessary.

"Daxton, do you see? I cannot give to you a position so that you may be wealthy and marry my daughter. I can, however, place you in a position. A position where you may work—work hard—and enjoy a wonderful life. Where you may lead, and help to keep this great society, Cardsten, continually on the track for greatness. You cannot slack in your position. A poor man may slack and the society will not be weakened, at least not perceptively. But if the wealthy and powerful slack then the society will fall apart. Not in a day, a week, a month, or a year, but it will be destroyed eventually, either from within or from without. You cannot hold an honorary title and play a charade. No, you must be that man. And you must lead your children, my grandchildren, to be that person who will continue this legacy on.

"Tasha, my lovely child—she knows all of this. She has been taught from birth. She is wise and is filled with power. She knew that it was not in her heart to lead in this way. But she sees the value and she has always known that when she found a man that could be a great husband to her and would fill this role, that she would bring that man to me. This is that day, and you are that man. Will you lead with me? I do not offer you a simple and formal position. I offer you the hardest position in Cardsten. To lead beside me and to never falter. To be that great man that will stand in my position when I no longer have the capacity."

He looked Daxton in the eyes as he had never been looked at before.

"Daxton, I cannot make you that man. Only you know if you are that man. Can you and will you be that man?"

Daxton had been a bit of a fool when he first left Tengeer. But he had endured the crucible of the dark forest. He had trained under Aiden for many months. He was not the boy that had left Tengeer. He looked over at Tasha who smiled serenely. She knew what she was looking for and knew that she had found that man in Daxton. Aiden somehow knew what Daxton was heading towards this day, and he had wished him well. If Aiden felt him incapable, then he would not have teased him. Yes, he felt his capacity within him and it was confirmed by those who surrounded him. This place appealed to him on every level from the moment that he set foot within its walls. Tasha was everything that a woman could be and he wanted what was being offered to him. Yes, he was that man, and he had everything he ever wanted.

"Mr. Cards, I am that man."

"Yes, Daxton, you are that man.

Chapter 14

Though Terrence did not sleep particularly late in the morning he did sleep longer than he was used to. He lay in his comfortable bed reflecting on how different it was than sleeping on the ground. He had no idea what this day would bring and wasn't particularly interested in finding out any time soon. He assumed that with the apartment so quiet that Daxton must still be sleeping. If he was needed, Aiden would be by. Half an hour later he arose. The breakfast that had been laid out was not so warm as it had been earlier but it was sumptuous none the less. He then wandered around and saw that Daxton and Aiden were gone. Jashion still slept.

Terrence felt restless. He had not felt so in his life. He felt worthless and useless sitting in a comfortable home with food placed before him. He did not entirely dislike the luxury, but on the whole, he was miserable. Perhaps if he had company to talk to it would have helped. But, Aiden and Daxton were gone and doing something, and he was not.

It was nearly noon before Jashion awoke. More food had been brought for lunch and Jashion breakfasted upon that. Terrence ate his lunch while Jashion ate his breakfast. There was some silence between them. The outburst on the way to

Cardsten from Terrence and the strange uncomfortable evening, the night before, had left them both still out of sorts.

Finally, Jashion broke the silence, "Where is they?"

Terrence shrugged.

"Did Aiden return last night?"

"I don't know," said Terrence, not looking at him.

"When did Daxton leave?"

"I don't know. They were both gone when I awoke."

"Did ye just awake?"

"No, I've been up for some time. Sitting here in silence is all I've done today."

A gentle knock came at the door.

Terrence and Jashion looked at each other. Terrence got up and opened the door. Tira stood there, alone. Terrence stood there and stared at her strangely. It was daylight, Tira's long brown hair was braided and her outfit made her look different enough that Terrence didn't immediately place her. Something about her eyes were so familiar though. He stared at them until Tira smiled.

"May I come in?"

"Oh, yes." Terrence's heart began to beat a little faster.

Terrence did not leave room for her to walk by him and into the apartment. She took a small step forward and looked up at Terrence, smiling slightly again.

"Tira."

"Yes."

"You...look different...today."

"Oh..."

"Come in."

"...okay."

"Hi, Jashion."

"Hello, Tira. Good morning, it is."

"Yes, it was. It's not morning anymore. Did you just get up?"

"I did, not long before, and now I'm just eating me breakfast, I am." Jashion smiled awkwardly.

"I've been up a while, but I wasn't sure what to do. Jashion was sleeping and the others are gone."

"Yes, I think that Mirinda and Tasha were anxious. I thought that I'd give you some time to rest from your journey. Was the rest nice?"

"Very," said Jashion.

"Good," said Tira. "When you're ready, I thought I'd take you for a fitting for more clothing."

"I'm ready," said Terrence.

"Thank ye, I'll be ready soon."

Jashion disappeared to his room and Tira and Terrence looked at each other silently for a few moments.

"How do you like it here?" asked Tira pleasantly.

Terrence looked sullen. He shrugged. "I don't know. I don't think that we will be staying long, though."

Tira looked at him curiously.

"I mean, we're hunters. It's nice to rest up a bit, and you and your friends have been great, but this isn't our kind of life here. For all I know, Aiden may come back and say, 'let's go.' And we'll be off. There is nothing holding us here."

"Oh," said Tira. "But..."

"No, I mean it is nice here. I like it, in its way, and I wouldn't mind staying for a little while. I guess, we're getting some new clothes so maybe we'll stay for a few weeks, I don't know."

Jashion came in the room. "I'm ready."

The threesome left and Jashion and Terrence learned how to be fitted with clothing. Neither of them appreciated the violation of their personal space. Both were happy to return back home. Mirinda and Aiden were sitting in the living room when they entered.

Mirinda looked stunning. She was in a very short red dress. So short, in fact, that all Terrence saw were legs as he walked into the room, with her right leg neatly crossed over her left. The effect was unpleasant for Terrence. His light blush and looking away did not go unnoticed by Tira.

"How'd it go?" Mirinda asked Tira.

"Fairly well," she answered with a smile.

"You must've had your hands full," said Aiden.

"Where've you been?" asked Terrence looking straight at Aiden and trying to ignore Mirinda.

"I've joined the military."

"What?" said Terrence.

Jashion looked over and narrowed his eyes.

"You sound like you enlisted as some kind of a scrub, dear," interjected Mirinda. "He has a post under General Malright. He is his understudy. It won't be long and Aiden will be a general himself. Frankly, I think Malright will get you promoted and away from him as soon as possible. He knows the better man when he sees him, and I'm sure he doesn't want you to be commanding more attention than himself."

Terrence looked at Mirinda as she spoke. Her eyes were so much like Aiden's—they commanded so much attention and respect. He began to understand the way that women looked at Aiden; they were all so in awe of this perfect masculine specimen. For Terrence, he struggled to get past Mirinda's feminine perfection. Her black hair was curled and hanging on her shoulder. This perfect black on perfect red gave such a powerful impression. Then, those eyes with such a pretty face, and lipstick that matched her dress. He unconsciously dropped his eyes from her presence and once again they met with her legs. Again, it was too much for him. He looked back at Aiden as she finished.

"Aiden?" Jashion said, but couldn't complete any further question.

"So, that's it," said Terrence, "one minute we are coming to see Cardsten and the next we're joining up; we're all in. I guess we should go back to, 'The Dragon's Lair,' and celebrate. Might as well sing up to the dragon; if Aiden's on Cardsten's team then the dragon has won."

Aiden stared at Terrence but showed no emotion. Mirinda looked disgusted.

"What's your problem?" asked Mirinda.

Terrence was steaming up inside. He didn't have additional words at this time.

Jashion stammered, "We've never spoken on this, we haven't. Why'd you not wake us an' speak with us this morning. We've thought our time here short, we did."

"Where's Daxton?" asked Terrence, looking at Mirinda.

"Did he not get your permission, either?" she said sarcastically.

"Terrence," said Tira from behind. Terrence turned. "I'm afraid that Daxton will not be returning. He and Tasha have agreed to wed, and he has been given a very powerful position by Tasha's father. I'm sure that we will get together soon with them and he can tell you all about it. I'm sorry that I didn't tell you before."

Terrence felt the ground slipping from beneath him. Marcus was dead and Daxton was gone; gone to this place that was becoming revolting to him. Aiden was his friend and mentor and here he was ensnared by this...she-devil, dressed in fiery red. He thought that he was on a quest, in part to fight off the evil creatures of this world. His friends were joining the dragon's team; they were joining the enemy and it hadn't taken even a day. *A couple of pretty faces, and that's it, games over, new plan now.*

Tira watched Terrence's face. She could sense the pain.

"Give me a day or two and I'm sure that I can secure posts for both of you. We can't just free load on these kind ladies who have been taking care of us. Daxton has work and so do I. You'll need positions soon, too."

"Aiden," said Jashion, "do ye want me to join the military with ye. Is this what ye would ask of me?"

"Yes, it is, my friend."

"Then I will."

"Good. Thank you."

"I will not!" said Terrence defiantly. This is not the right course of action. I will not be a part of defending Dromreign.

"There are other options, Terrence," said Tira.

"You are not obligated to stay with us, Terrence," said Aiden. "I would *not* have left you in the wilderness without protection. But you are a man now. I could use your strength and skill with me in the military, but that is up to you. If you choose a different path, then so be it. I will always respect you and consider you a great friend."

Reality was beating upon him but he was not able to absorb it. Tira walked up close to him and put her arm around his. He was mostly numb, but he looked at her and waited for what would come next.

"Would you walk me home, Terrence?"

He nodded his assent and they left together without saying another word. It would be a block or two before either would speak.

"There are many positions that a man of your strength and understanding could acquire. Daxton will be very powerful here in his new position. He could get you involved with Tasha's family business. They are very powerful and have many options available. I could use my influence with my family to help you also. You don't have to directly fight against those who fight the dragon. We are more than that, here. You could do anything and be anything that you like. I don't want you to do anything that makes you unhappy."

"But stay here I must?"

"No. I didn't say that."

There was a significant pause.

"But, I hope that you stay."

"Why?"

There was a look of pain in her eyes.

"That hurt's, Terrence."

"I feel trapped. I feel alone in the world. We were a band of brothers, even when I lost my true brother. Now, they have all taken their own paths, and I want another. I don't believe that I can be home here. I'm not happy here, and I don't want to be happy here. I don't want it to grow on me. I don't want to be okay with what is okay here. And I don't want to help that dragon, or even to act like I'm helping it. I want out of here. I think that you are beautiful and kind. You have been a friend when every other friend has deserted me. But you are of Cardsten and I find everything repulsive about this place."

He looked over and tears were lightly rolling down her cheeks.

"What did I say?"

She shook her head and said, "nothing."

"Would you leave with me, then?"

Tira looked up, confused.

"Go away with me?"

"Where?"

"To Agedon."

"To Agedon?" she said, hardly believing her ears. "Who else would go?

"Perhaps, no one."

"The two of us alone, but..."

"We would wed before we leave. I'll stay for two more weeks as we plan and carry out the wedding. Then we'll go. If Agedon is filled with fools as you suppose, then we will return and I will make this our home, and I will be happy. But, if they are not fools and there is truth to what they say, then would you stay with me there?"

Tira's arm was around Terrence's arm as they walked. She had initially squeezed a little tighter, but at this point her arm hung looser.

"You don't know what you ask. Agedon is hated by my people, by my family. I don't think that they would let me leave.

They hunt down and imprison those that defect. I...I don't know if it would be possible, even if I wanted to..."

"You don't have to go Tira. I am leaving, and I may return but only if Agedon is as Cardsten describes it. I will not stay here, at least not until I have seen Agedon for myself."

"I don't understand. One minute you would marry me, and the next you would leave me forever to see if you like Agedon better. And if I am to marry you, then I must leave with you and say goodbye to all of my family, friends, and the great life that I have here. And go to a place which I have hated since birth, to become my own sworn enemy. I do not even know if you love me. I see no evidence that you do. You seem to only see the world through your own eyes. You've abandoned your own family to leave on a quest. Then, when your friends find a place and women that they love and choose to settle down, you are ready to abandon them forthwith. You tell a girl, who loves you, that you will marry her but only if she too will leave everything and do what you want. Do you not see that there are others in this world? That people care for you, but may not see all things as you do? The world does not revolve around you."

"I'm sorry Tira, but I must do what I feel is right. My conscious will not allow me to join in when I feel it to be wrong. You are right, though; I am too rash. I have spoken of wedding you and I have not even kissed you. I do not know you and your world, and then I ask you to leave it all. I will take a few days to consider everything more fully. But, I do not take back my proposal. If you would have me, then I would marry you and I would care for you and protect you forever. I can't say if I could do this in Cardsten at this time."

"Kiss me once then Terrence. If this is what is best, then may we both come to terms with it together. I will be your friend and you may count on that. I don't know if I can be your wife, if I must leave all else."

Terrence kissed Tira softly. Inside of him a passion ignited. He had locked his heart thus far and was only thinking. He began to feel and understand the way that his friends felt. The world was different when one felt that way for a woman. His perspective expanded in that instant. He could leave all else, but could he leave her? Agedon may indeed be a bunch of fools. And this place wasn't so bad. Tira walked up to her front door. He could hear soft sobs as he walked away.

Chapter 15

Two weeks had passed since the young men had entered Cardsten. As anticipated by Mirinda, Aiden had been successful in the military. General Malright had given him his own troop to command and Jashion was his lieutenant. The real-world experience stood head and shoulders over the drills that the military of Cardsten only knew. Only men with a genuine fire in their belly were drawn to his troop. It was quickly becoming clear that Aiden was the most powerful military man in Cardsten. Many considered him a blessing bestowed upon Cardsten and a sign of their preeminence in the world. Some questioned his motives and loyalty. None stood ready to challenge or defeat him.

Among those who trusted implicitly in him was Jashion. He neither understood why they were in the military nor questioned it. It was as Aiden saw fit and that was good enough for him. He had never seen Aiden's influence go toward anything but good and could not imagine this being an exception. The underlying political motives of the military being primarily ramped to stop Agedon from taking on the dragon, and that being counter to his general feelings about the beast, Jashion was only vaguely aware of. He spent his days practicing his craft with the sword alongside Aiden, while being well fed, well clothed, and sleeping comfortably. He was happy, respected by his peers including the various men in the troop, and generally got along fine in life.

On that evening a feast was being held by the Cards family on behalf of Tasha and Daxton. He and Aiden were in full formal military attire and began to walk together towards Mirinda's home. The past two weeks had been busy and Aiden had spent less time with Mirinda than he would have desired. There was a spring in Aiden's step that Jashion noticed. Mirinda was sure to be more stunning than ever for a night such as this, and for this even Aiden could not conceal some emotion. Aiden wore the Black Uniform of the general, and Jashion wore the scarlet uniform of a lieutenant. Mirinda was a few minutes coming when they arrived at her home. Aiden, the picture of calmness and coolness, paced slightly as they waited. Perhaps very few would have noticed this simple anxiousness, but to Jashion it was profound. She, and only she, could elicit this hint of vulnerability in Aiden.

A grand staircase of white marble stood before them as they waited, without sitting, in the entrance way. The home was quiet and seemed empty—the servants were as ghosts in performing their labors. Nothing was out of place or left wanting. Jashion had stopped by with Aiden before, but had never had a quarter of an hour to look around. It was Jashion who saw Mirinda first beginning to descend the staircase. She too was in black. A dress no doubt designed and fabricated just for this evening. If possible, it seemed to accentuate Mirinda's physique more than anything she had worn before. She was at once beautiful, sensual, and stunning. She smiled at Jashion as he looked up at her, enjoying his drinking in of her presence. Jashion swallowed hard and then opened up his mouth a bit. His nostrils no longer were sufficient in supplying him with the necessary oxygen.

Aiden's keen senses were aware of his friend's changes and he too turned and beheld this beauty. Aiden smiled broadly in genuine appreciation. Mirinda's expression seemed to imply both an appreciation of her man in uniform and his obvious appreciation of her. Both men followed her with their eyes until she was next to them and held Aiden's hands. They kissed briefly and then walked. Mirinda walked between them and placed a hand around each of their arms.

Jashion had not been to Tasha's home before. He could not have imagined it eclipsing Mirinda's, but it did. Both in size and luxury, it had no equal. Tasha was as beautiful as she could be in a cream-colored dress with royal blue trim. Daxton with black pants and a white, princely looking top met the threesome. Jashion thought he detected a look from Tasha when she beheld Mirinda. This was Tasha's evening and Mirinda had upstaged her. That was inevitable, however, and she quickly moved past it. Daxton, to his credit, was oblivious to Mirinda. He kissed her hand upon arrival but seemed no more affected than if she had been a homely stranger. Daxton had been absorbed entirely in his new world, in Tasha's world, and in his love of her and all things about her. Mirinda, to her credit, was pleased with the slight.

They were shown to one of the top tables nearest to the stage where Tasha, Daxton, and the Cards family were seated. Jashion, feeling uncomfortable enough in the environment, did not feel more uncomfortable due to the honor received, perhaps because he was not aware of it. If he had been and had understood the ranking of those around him, he would have shrunk even deeper. A lieutenant in scarlet looked absurd next to a General in that environment. As it was, his ignorance was bliss. Aiden and Mirinda were both pleased when they saw how highly they were honored, and in such society. There were not many single men present, he observed, the odd number of place settings at the table stood out to Jashion. He had not been asked by anyone to come with a date and so he decided to not fret over it. At least not immediately.

On his left was Mirinda who was seated next to Aiden. On his right was an older couple who turned out to be Tasha's maternal grandparents. Jashion sat next to her grandfather. This was how he knew that his being dateless put him out of place. Nearly everywhere he looked two men did not sit next to each other. The Cards, for all of their qualities, were not particularly beautiful people. Tasha was fortunate to have gotten her looks from her mother's side. It was clear that though the Cards side were not beautiful, they had an eye for it. Tasha's mother was more beautiful than Tasha, and her maternal grandparents were lovely even in their age.

After introductions and pleasantries expressed around the table, Jashion found himself without conversation. In such an environment, he preferred to listen rather than to speak. No one had his ear just yet and so he looked around. Upon turning to the right his eye caught hold of Myrtle. He had not seen her since their first night coming to Cardsten. At first he saw only her profile and it again reminded him of Siccly. She laughed at something said at her table and knew her for Myrtle thereafter. A sickness entered upon his breast when he recognized her. It was at that moment that she turned towards him. She recognized him instantly and smiled sweetly while giving him a slight nod of the head. She then turned her head back towards her company and was again engaged in the local conversation. The young man on her left next attracted Jashion's attention. This must be her date, her companion. Perhaps they were together. He had very light brown hair, though not quite blond. It was short and comely. His nose was a little narrow and a little long, but not overly so. His eyes were grey and inset deeply. He had a light complexion with some freckles. He reddened easily and often as he laughed. Though he knew not why, Jashion found himself provoked by this young gentleman. He irritated him and Jashion found himself wondering why Myrtle would be with him. Jashion was unaware of the length of time that he sat staring in their direction until Myrtle turned towards him again, and once more smiled in his direction. This made Jashion redden and he turned away awkwardly back towards the table at which he was seated.

Jashion hadn't caught a glimpse of Terrence and Tira that evening. They had been given seats at a table far behind and over to the side. Terrence was not immediately conscious of the slight, but Tira was. Terrence the cousin—almost brother of Daxton—and Tira the close friend of Tasha, were seated amongst those who were more distantly connected with the Cards family—those who were honored simply by being invited at all. When Tira saw that Jashion was seated with Aiden and Mirinda, rather than seated with her and Terrence, she saw how things were.

Recently Terrence had been invited by Aiden to come for military drills. Reluctantly he had attended and had impressed everyone tremendously with his skills. But, unlike Jashion who did not connect his being in the military with his hatred of the dragon, at least not consciously, Terrence could not, and indeed would not disconnect the two. His pleasure in wielding the sword and the respect that would so easily be granted by those around him were not enough to induce him to join. He respectfully declined.

Daxton had come to him, with his new-found position, and had offered him employment—leadership within the Cards kingdom, as it were. Daxton and he had conversed, and Daxton had explained how it was, the philosophies of Mr. Cards and all that would be required. Terrence did not buy into it, though he saw some merits. But, he did not see how this philosophy translated into a pious and honorable city. Rather, he saw a people that were selfish, ignorant of those around them, and even evil. Advancing the position of Cardsten, whether militarily or economically was to him advancing the cause of the dragon. He declined Daxton and found himself in limbo.

Tira and he were not engaged. They were, however, together and growing quickly in fondness and respect toward one another. Terrence began to love Tira and his devotion and desire towards her perfectly balanced his hatred and disgust for Cardsten. He would not leave her, yet he would not become connected with Cardsten. So there he was, unemployed—useless as seen by those of Cardsten, but not willing to leave and seek his fortunes or adventure elsewhere. This was not a position that he could stay in much longer. He wasn't merely subconsciously aware of this reality; he just didn't know what to do.

Tira understood perfectly well how it was before the evening, but then she saw that even she was slighted because of her connection to him. Something would have to give. She understood instinctively that he stayed in Cardsten only for her. She saw in every way how unhappy he was, how disgusted he was. He stayed because he loved her and because he saw how unfair it was to force her away from her world. Yet, he could not be a part of her world, so distasteful it was to him.

Terrence was respected by Tira entirely. He was handsome and strong, he lived with conviction and was unapologetic, yet in her influence he had softened, at least externally. He was gentle with Tira and seemed to see in her all that she was. They were, in so many ways, made for each other and yet in other ways so entirely incompatible. Quietly, in her thoughts only, she had begun to consider leaving her home and setting out for a new life with Terrence. Every time that he rejected a new offer of employment it became clearer that this could not be their home.

At this event, she saw that everyone else saw this too. A freeloader was not welcome in Cardsten. Terrence had overstayed his welcome and it was time for him to become one of Cardsten or to go. Tira had to choose between Cardsten and Terrence; she felt that Cardsten had made their decision already. She was only one step away from being forced out.

"Does it seem strange to you that everyone else is up at the front and we're back here? I can hardly see what's going on," said Terrence as he became more conscious of his circumstances.

Tira smiled sweetly but did not answer. Inside it cut her like a knife.

Mr. Cards had stood up from his seat. He, with Daxton and Tasha, and the closest family members sat at a table facing the crowd from the stage. He motioned for Tasha and then Daxton to rise. This event served both as an engagement announcement and as an introduction of Daxton as heir to his company and fortune. Perhaps the two should have been separated, but they were inseparable in Mr. Cards mind. Tasha was to marry the heir of the kingdom and the heir of the kingdom was to marry Tasha. The fact that Tasha, in this sense, was to pick the heir as opposed to Mr. Cards only showed how much he loved and trusted his daughter. Mr. Cards was entirely pleased with her selection.

The fact that he was not entirely prepared and educated, indeed a foreigner, did cause some pause for Mr. Cards. Quickly he found that Daxton was a clean slate and a quick learner. Whatever preconceived notions he had brought with him were not closely tied to either Cardsten or a world such as this. Not only was Daxton not prejudiced but he had a natural desire and inclination towards the world of Cardsten. Mr. Cards and he were entirely compatible in thought and purpose. What Daxton didn't know, he learned. What he didn't understand he was quickly shown. Nothing was incompatible nor incomprehensible to him.

It was not his love for Tasha that drew him to Cardsten and to Mr. Cards' empire. For Daxton, these were completely separate. He would have loved Cardsten whether or not Tasha was there. And Tasha was perfectly attractive to him on her own. The reality of this convergence was fantastic to him, but not essential. Daxton never questioned his circumstances. He did not find everything fitting like a glove to be unbelievable. It had all happened so fast and so easily that it just seemed as though all was as it should be. Daxton was happy; completely and utterly happy.

As Mr. Cards introduced him he smiled widely. This beautiful, confident, and strapping young man was thoroughly and enthusiastically approved of by the crowd. He and Tasha were beautiful together and so clearly in love. Daxton ate it up. He was not swallowed up by all around him, but rather drank it in. He felt equal to the task. He had spent most of his life, among his cousins and friends, on the bottom rung of the latter. He never felt comfortable in that position. In his mind, he belonged on top. Here, on top of the world, and in front of the best people in his new world, receiving applause and looking out over approving faces, he was comfortable. The larger the crowd, the more eyes focused on him, the more he was in the spotlight, the more comfortable he was. Daxton was in his element as he had never been before. He had everything that he had ever desired and was ready for even all of this to expand.

Aiden nodded at him when their eyes met. This approval gave Daxton whatever final comfort he could have asked for. Whatever would happen with his cousin and friends, Daxton had finally arrived home.

With a final introduction of the happy couple everyone arose and cheered. Upon sitting, Jashion glanced over towards Myrtle again. She was so beautiful. He felt annoyed at the pathetic young man who was next to her. He looked so far below her that it was embarrassing. Something was awakening within him that he had never experienced before. Jashion never worried when his various thoughts or feelings were incompatible. He felt for Myrtle just like he felt about being in the Cardsten military: conflicted. In some ways his world had always been conflicted. Being conflicted felt normal to him. Being jealous, now that was an entirely different feeling and one which he was not enjoying at all. This was eating him up inside. When the food arrived, he found that he had to unclench his fist to hold the utensils. His fingernails had left marks in his palm.

When the feast was over and people began to get up and mill around, Terrence spoke to Tira, "Let's go up to them and congratulate them."

"No. We should wait a bit."

"Why?"

She just looked at him with a pleading and uncomfortable expression in her eyes. For the next few minutes they sat together quietly at the table. The table emptied, besides them, and they were apparently invisible to all around them. Terrence saw as Jashion, Aiden, Mirinda, and Myrtle went to Daxton and Tasha.

"Okay, let's go."

Tasha nodded in consent but her countenance fell. Going from so far back to the front would signal to everyone just how slighted the two were. Terrence did not comprehend but he was irritated sitting back away from his friends and the action. Upon arrival Terrence ignored Daxton's outstretched hand and instead embraced him. Daxton embraced him back warmly. Neither of them noticed the look that Mr. Cards gave to them, but Tira did. Tonight had been no accidental slight, it was deliberate and meaningful. Terrence and Daxton began to converse but Mr. Cards cut them off, placing himself between them and with his back towards Terrence.

"Let me introduce you to some of our honored guests," said Cards.

Daxton smiled delightedly and they were off. Tasha gave Tira her hand and curtsied as she may have done politely to a distant acquaintance. Mirinda gave Terrence an unkind look and then, taking Aiden by the arm, walked away.

"I've got to go," said Tasha as she too left.

Jashion stayed and talked with the couple. He seemed genuinely happy to see them. Myrtle and her companion were conversing with Mrs. Cards. Jashion seemed reluctant to leave the area near to her. Their proximity to each other may have opened up a chance to talk. Maybe he wanted her to have a good look at him in uniform. Still, he was glad to see Tira and Terrence.

"Will ye be working with Daxton?" he asked, not knowing that Terrence had already turned down the offer.

"No, it doesn't suit me, I'm afraid."

"Oh. Then what shall ye do? Ye isn't employed at all, is ye?"

"No, I'm afraid not."

Jashion look confusedly at Tira. She did not betray her thoughts or feelings.

"Does ye like it here better, now? Here's in Cardsten?"

"Well..."

"I'd like to think that you like something about it here," said Tira as she leaned in and took his arm.

Terrence looked at her and then smiled and nodded.

"Yes...there is *something* about Cardsten that I am rather fond of."

"Jashion, tell me plainly: what keeps you here?"

"I like it here, I do. I like the military and the food, and the beds. It's nice here, it is. The people's nice too. It's good here and," he lowered his voice tremendously, "Dromreign don't comes here. Me thinks the walls keep the dragon away."

"Do you think that this is the promise land that you speak of? Is this the safest and most protected place in the world? Have you given up on your quest to find the land of safety on the other side of the mountain?"

"Nay."

"Well, what then?"

"When Aiden's ready, we'll go there together."

"Aiden seems happy here, though. He's a general and he's found Mirinda. Cardsten suits him well. Will you stay with Aiden forever?"

Jashion paused. "Yay, Aiden is happy, he is. He was happy before he'd ever left his home land, too. He led all the men of his people, though still a young man at home. He could have married whomever he'd have wanted to, he could've. When he'd conquered all where he was, he needed to do something more. When he has conquered Cardsten, he will be ready for something new."

Tira looked concerned. "What will become of Mirinda? Will he leave her when he tires of her?"

Jashion had not considered that before. He did not answer her question.

Terrence glanced at Mirinda. "He'll not find another like Mirinda if he searches the whole world over."

That comment did not please Tira.

"What of Daxton, and Tasha," she asked. "Will Daxton leave too?"

"Nay, I think not. Not Daxton. I think that he is home, he is. I don't think Daxton has ever been, nor couldest ever be happier than he is here. Daxton has found his home, he has."

Terrence nodded assent but not in a pleased manner.

Myrtle walked by and said hello to the trio. Jashion followed her with his eyes as she passed. Tira looked at Terrence and gave him an expression noting Jashion's attention on her. Her expression indicated some confusion and a question as to why Jashion would do that. Terrence shrugged and his expression seemed to ask, 'search me?'

Jashion was oblivious to them then, he was lost in other thoughts.

"Let's go," she said to Terrence.

"Okay?"

They left the home and walked out into a beautiful spring evening with a luscious pink sunset on the horizon. Neither Terrence nor Tira was ever quick to speak. The evening walk was pleasant and Terrence was glad to be away from the discomfort of the evening inside.

"Terrence," she finally said. "What shall we do?"

"I'm enjoying the walk."

"Yes. It is nice. But, I don't mean tonight. I mean more generally, what shall we do? I know that Cardsten is not right for you. You stay just to appease me. I am pleased that you do. You may, that is, I hope that you may never tire of me. But you will tire of this place. I believe that you have already tired of it."

"Tire?"

"That's putting it nicely. You could never be happy here, my companionship notwithstanding. You will either leave or be forever unhappy. This weighs heavily on me tonight. If we stay, unhappily you must do something. But you will not do anything here, that is clear. I see that you must leave."

"I will not leave you, Tira. I feel..."

"I see that, too." They walked for some time again, slowly.

"I am ready to go with you, Terrence. I was not prepared to leave before, but I am now."

They stopped and looked at each other. Terrence held her hands and looked into her deep brown eyes. She was in earnest and though he saw some trepidation, he also saw conviction.

"But...can we?"

Tira dropped her eyes.

"Our friends are of such influence. Can they just let us go? I think that they will make this difficult for us."

Tira shook her head. "They can't know."

"What?"

"Terrence, they can't know. None of them can know. We have to go it alone. And quickly. If they suspect...any of them, they will not allow it."

"No one can leave Cardsten?"

"Anyone can come and go from Cardsten, but not to Agedon. Once we had free intercourse with Agedon, but no longer. We are at war, if not in reality, in our hearts. We must leave secretly and quickly. Perhaps tonight. They will be occupied late and we will not be missed. We weren't even wanted, really, it seemed. If we go now we can get far enough along before they notice and we will not be overtaken."

"Tira?"

"Terrence. I am giving myself to you."

They embraced and kissed for some time. Terence felt powerful, complete, and whole. A small part of him wanted to protest because he felt that he should. Could he take all that she offered him? But he did not protest. He accepted her offer as he kissed her. She was his and he loved her. He could leave everyone else behind as long as she was with him.

Terrence did not fear the journey of several days in the wilderness. Nor did he fear being uprooted and making a new home. But, though brave, he knew that she would find this extraordinarily difficult. In fact, it was only possible for her because he was there and she trusted in and loved him.

"We must marry," he said to her concerned.

"We cannot marry tonight. We will have to marry when we arrive in Agedon."

Terrence considered this briefly. He breathed deeply and nodded his consent.

There would be no better evening to start the journey. It was not late and it was comfortable. There was no moon and it would be dark. This, he considered advantageous. They should be able to disappear easily out of the city gate and then their direction would be undiscoverable. They could head north first and then turn northwest when they were out of range. There was a seldom used highway between the two great peoples that they would cross soon enough. Getting to Agedon would be easy enough once they were on their way.

Tira arrived at his home in changed apparel but with too much baggage. Terrence carried only the minimal essentials. He suspected that she would take too much and then he could help. Even with his minimal belongings they would be too weighed down.

"Tira, my dear. We must leave some things."

She was not prepared, her eyes welled up and she was about to protest.

"If we leave with so much we will be noticed and perhaps watched."

Tira sniffled, looked down and nodded. Terrence began to go through her things. It was embarrassing to her for him to see everything. He took out too much as though she could travel and live as a man.

"One more bag, I must have these things."

Terrence assented, suspecting that in a day or two she would understand and leave them behind. He hid the remainder of her things deep in his dresser drawer and they set off.

She was not dressed as before. She was dressed in what she considered rugged attire. It would have to do. She wore a thin coat with a hood. She put on the hood as they left the apartment. Who would have noticed her? All of her friends and those of her kind were at the party. Still, she felt a foreboding. Walking in and out of the gate was never a big deal. But then at this point, it was. Her heart beat faster; she looked around nervously and felt cold inside. A crow's cry in the late dusk made her jump.

"Tira," said Terrence as he put his arms around her. "Tira, it is not too late to turn back. I can reconsider Cardsten. There is good here, I see it. I have judged it so harshly because of what I dislike. But there is much here that is good and right. I would not take you from your home, to a sworn enemy, and perhaps a foolish people. The price of your love should not be your departure."

"No, Terrence. You may feel so earnestly now. You may put in a great deal of effort because of your love for me. But the price of your love should not be to live in a place you loath, and with a people who are so opposed to your sense of right and wrong; who celebrate a being that is so vial and your sworn enemy. I see it too, Terrence. My eyes have been open. I do love my home and my friends. I love my people and there is much good here. But you are right in what you have said and in what you feel. There is, at best, contempt for those who have been killed and had their homes destroyed by Dromreign. We are a people who have much in all things desirable. We have safety, food, comfortable homes, and many of us live with such luxury. Perhaps this is not wrong. But we care nothing for those who have less—much less. We care not if they live or die, if they suffer, if they are left wanting. We care nothing about anyone outside of these walls, unless they affect our world in a way that would be undesirable. If Agedon riles up that beast such that it would, in its rage, come here and attack us, then we care about them. But only with the care that would make us build up an army to stop them from annoying us. We care enough to kill them if they are a bother to us. If they do not cause us any distress, then we simply do not care about their existence at all. So little do we love those outside of these walls that we have come to celebrate, even worship that being who bears down on all those who are weak. We sing, we dance, we drink to its health, and make light Dromreign's terror. We are safe and so we mock those who are not. Some even hate all those who are not of Cardsten. They think that the dragon is our ally. That it rids the world of our enemies. That it cares for us as we care for it. That it would protect us against our enemies. That if we stick up for Dromreign, this will somehow endear the dragon to us. That somehow there could be love or devotion between us and that vial creature."

Tira had worked herself up in a frenzy, but as she spoke something inside of her brought more peace and confidence. These thoughts had not been expressed by her out loud until this moment. They had not been so clearly put together even in her own mind until they were just spoken. They were vague and disparate until then. But as she spoke the words, she was convincing herself of the truth of them. Her mind was finally clear and she felt her path forward with conviction.

"No, Terrence. You are right. You've always been right. I can forgive myself for being blind before. I had never seen what you had seen. My world has been so comfortable and happy and those outside of it were distant, and though I did not hate them, I never saw any concern when others did. But now I love a man who comes from the world outside of these walls. Others, your friends, also from without, are good, noble, beautiful, and strong. Those outside of here are not to be hated, treated with contempt, and celebrated in death and destruction. I know what that creature is. It would consume Cardsten as quickly as it would consume Agedon, or Dargaer, or Tengeer. We may not be such easy prey, but we are nothing more than food to its belly. When Dromreign has consumed the rest of the world it will consume us, too. Are these walls so strong that they are impenetrable? Do we battle so fiercely that no people or creature, even Dromreign, would not stand up to us? Have we so perfected ourselves that we can stand apart while the rest of the world burns; and sing, and laugh, and mock them in their sorrows? Is Cardsten so grand? I have come to believe that you are again right, that we cannot simply hide from this beast. Dromreign must be faced. If it can be defeated, then it must be defeated. Agedon is where we must head. Not for protection from the beast but rather to help those who understand so well that it must be defeated. They are not fools, at least insofar as they know what must be done. I do not know if it can be done, but I know that building walls and shutting out the rest of world is not the answer."

She paused. But there was fire in her eyes. She shook no longer.

"Then we must go. We must hurry. If we wait much longer we may cause suspicion, and we may be overtaken on our way."

They set off again and this time more quickly. The tree lined path was lit only by the street lamps. A slight chill was in the air. The gate came into view and they quickened their pace. They would not have to answer to anyone. There was no need to explain themselves. No one would even take notice of them. They would simply head north and not immediately get onto the old Agedon road, and then no one would care. When they were sufficiently far away they would head west and then take the easy path, on the old Agedon road, to their new home. Yet, they both glanced around them and considered how they would each answer if asked what they were doing.

One streetlamp was out along the street. Terrence noticed, but it did not alarm him. An alleyway beside it was completely darkened. They began to pass the alleyway and Terrence noticed movement in his peripheral vision.

"You," he heard a harsh but quiet voice say. "I say you two, stop. STOP NOW! I want a word with you."

They both stopped and peered into the alleyway. Their hearts beat quickly and they breathed rapidly. A figure was coming into view. Then they noticed the shadows of others, five more in all moving towards them.

"Ah, yes. I thought it would be you."

"Who are you?" whispered Tira.

"We have met," said the figure.

He walked a little closer and the dim light revealed the face of a man wearing a hood. He paused and looked at them menacingly. Then he bowed his head and removed his hood revealing his shaved head and a dragon tattoo.

Chapter 16

"Where to?" the dragon worshiper asked. His companions continued to walk closer, encircling Terrence and Tira. "You are dressed very strangely for an evening stroll. See, no one is about except perhaps an occasional person, here or there. I suppose those who can afford an evening stroll are being served at the grand banquet tonight."

The six men encircled them completely. Tira moved close to Terrence.

"But why are you not there? Are you not the friends of the betrothed? Surely you were invited? And this hood you wear, m' lady—what strange apparel for a woman of your stature. I do believe that something is amiss tonight."

All of the men began to laugh along with their leader and spokesman. There was a pause as he glared at Terrence.

"I told you that I would watch you." He reached into his pocket and pulled out brass knuckles.

As he began to put them on his hand Terrence yelled to Tira, "Run!"

She started to but did not get far. A man from behind grabbed her and put his hand over her mouth. She proceeded to kick at his shins and bite his finger. He screeched in pain, let her go and then swung his arm backwards hitting Tira in the face hard with the back of his hand. She fell to the ground and two others took hold of her making sure that she could not use her arms, legs, or teeth against them.

"Let her go, it's me you want," said Terrence tensing up with anger. "Why do you bother us? We have left you alone and have not caused you any trouble. You seem to know who we are. Do you not understand the power of our friends and family? You cannot think you can get away with any of this."

"Friends? Family?" said the tattooed man. "Perhaps it is you who misjudges your position. Are you not on your way out of our great city tonight? See how you are dressed. See how you are packed. You are leaving us. Do those who you call your friends know of this departure?"

He paused staring Terrence in the eye.

"Your silence betrays you. You leave those, whom you have now just invoked, in the hour of their celebration, to steal away in the night from them. And for how long? An hour? No. A day? A month? No, you leave them forever!"

The bitten man made his way to Tira who was still being held tightly by the two men. He punched her in the stomach and she doubled to the degree she could.

Terrence reached behind his back and pulled out his sword, it having been concealed underneath his shirt. Some of the men moved with the revelation but their leader stood fast.

"If she is harmed I'll run each of you through! And if any escape I'll ensure that they are imprisoned for this treachery!"

"If you make a move she will be harmed. Of that I can assure you. You speak of treachery, but I speak of treason. You speak of prison, yes, that is where those who would defect to Agedon are put. That is what you are attempting, isn't it? You intend to leave and join forces with those fools and our enemies. You, who speak of treachery, prison, justice for those who would do wrong. Yes, you who are caught in the very act of treason should speak of such things. What of your friends, now? Will they defend one who commits treason against those who are loyal—fiercely loyal to Cardsten. Will a great leader of our Cardsten military, and those who hold such economic power—those who have the ears of our political leaders and control the purse strings, choose to side with those who would defect and empower our enemy. You think on their loyalty to you, as you cowardly depart from them in silence."

Terrence held his sword, moving his head around and watching for signs of movement. Tira was in pain, he wondered if she was hurt badly. He eyed each man and searched out their weakness.

"You make no argument against what I have said. You see the truth with which I speak. You are caught and found out. Falling from grace socially is the least of your concerns. You are now enemies of the state, of the city of Cardsten. I see no hope for you, young man. You are lost. You should never have come here. But for the lady, I see a different story. She is of us. You've blinded her, it's true, with your lies and deceits. But she will see the light. And when she, as a witness, describes all you've planned to do this night, she will be given mercy, I am sure. How easy it is to fool a young woman when she is attracted by your looks, your strength, your experience in the world. You can even make her leave her friends and country and turn her into a traitor. This is wrong of her, but it may be forgivable; especially when she is brought to an understanding of her actions, and to an understanding of how diabolical you are. But you, we will have no mercy upon you. It is your carcass that will be brought to the rulers. You, who have pulled a weapon upon us—a weapon forbidden in the city by those not of the military. You have threatened each of us with death. You, who would attempt to bring all of Cardsten down by your traitorous acts. Everyone will rejoice that for your crimes you will have already paid the price. And she, to save her life, will tell all about you and all you have done. Do not be a fool. All you have the power to do now is to ensure pain and harm for this foolish girl, whom you claim to love!"

He and two of the men stepped forward towards Terrence. The men held clubs that he had not yet seen. Terrence held his position but did not act. With the first swing of a club Terrence blocked it with his sword and kicked the man in the gut. He doubled and went down. The other raised his club above his head but before dropping it found steel in his chest, puncturing his heart. There was not even time to make a sound such was the speed of Terrence's sword."

"Kill her!" shouted the leader.

The bitten man lifted a club and prepared to crush Tira's skull. Terrence moved swiftly and this time punctured a heart through the back. The two men holding Tira let her go.

Tira screamed violently.

Terrence moved towards the two men who'd been holding Tira, as they got to their feet.

"Get up, man!" said the leader to the man who'd been kicked. He arose, club in hand. Terrence turned and faced him again. This time the man held his position and did not strike. "Get him!" he yelled to the other two. They looked at each other and then ran off, leaving Terrence and Tira with just the leader and one man with a club. Tira sat where she was left, petrified, in agony.

"To go with all else you are a murderer!" yelled the leader roughly. "Your acts will be known by all soon enough. See, they are gone. If you place down your sword I will be merciful to you. If not, I will kill you or you will be hunted down and killed by your friend—the general! There is no hope for you, now. You cannot kill the citizens of Cardsten on your way out of the city to join with Agedon and think that you will get away. It is death that awaits you and nothing more!"

The man with the club held his position until Terrence stepped towards him and then he stepped back. Terrence stepped again and the leader made his way towards Tira.

Terrence moved to get between them and the man with the club swung. With agility Terrence made him miss and continued to move towards Tira. The man swung again and this time it was blocked with the sword. The leader picked up a loose cobble stone and threw it at Terrence hitting him in the upper lip. It stung badly and forced him to drop his sword down, though he still held onto it. The club came at Terrence again but he blocked it and this time, with the man out of position, Terrence ran him through. Only the leader of this pack of dragon worshipers remained. Blood ran down Terrence's lip and a stream ran down his neck. His lip swelled and felt hot and three times its normal size. Terrence's blood boiled towards this man.

"Fools!" yelled the man looking around him.

Terrence stepped towards him, ensuring that Tira was behind him.

"You know not what you do! Are you going to kill me now, in cold blood? I am unarmed. Will you just run me through? Leave, take your victim with you. You will be found, but if you hurry you may get away for a time."

Terrence felt a rage inside. To him, this man was Dromreign, or one of the wolves that killed Marcus. They were all the same. Their eyes were the identical: bitter and evil. He knew that he had to leave, and leave quickly. They would be pursued. Only, this man was dangerous—to them yes, but perhaps even more so to his friends. He could not let him go.

"No, I shall not run you through, you vial creature. You do not deserve such kindness. You will pay—slow enough to think on all you've done."

"No Terrence," yelled Tira. "Leave him, let's go."

Terrence did not look around to acknowledge her. Instead he kept his gaze upon the short stocky man with the shaved head and the dragon tattoo. He continued to move forward towards him.

"I give up," said the man. "You have bested me this day. Let me go, and I'll buy you some time for escape. If you kill me, you will bring down more wrath than you know. I swear, you do not want to do this thing."

"Terrence, he speaks the truth; do not harm him!"

Terrence swung his sword towards his neck and sliced through his right carotid artery. The man fell to his knees grabbing his neck with blood spilling through his hands. He looked up at Terrence with a pleading expression, hoping to be killed quickly. Terrence stood, watching him. In a matter of moments, the man's face became paler with the loss of blood, bringing on severe weakness. When Terrence was convinced of his ultimate demise he headed towards Tira.

Tira sobbed uncontrollably.

"Tira, my love. We must leave now, if we are going. Otherwise we will be taken."

"Why didn't you listen?" she pleaded. "You do not know all, Terrence. You should not have killed him. You don't understand what you do!"

"Tira, we must go."

Tira got to her feet. She was nauseous and felt each step and each breath she took. Terrence put his sword in his hidden sheath and then put his arm around Tira. They made their way to the gate leaving four bleeding bodies in the street. Darkness encompassed them as soon as they were without the walls. Only the stars would light their path that night. Some distance from the city gate they began to hear noises from within the city. They had not traveled as far as he had hoped yet. They moved too slowly, but Tira could not go faster. Her choked sobs tore at his heart. Whether physical, mental, or emotional her pain, she was hurting deeply. Her words echoed in his mind. He had cooled to some degree. The images of bodies run through by his own sword tortured him. He had killed many a beast before, but never a human. Even in self-defense the act tortured him.

It would be hours before Tira spoke. She walked along mechanically, not questioning the way that Terrence led. There were times when Terrence thought that they were being followed. At other times, he felt that they were very alone. If they had left Cardsten cleanly he would have stopped for the night sooner, but he felt no safety in stopping yet.

"Terrence, must we walk all night?" Tira said after some time. There was a pleading in her voice that tore at Terrence.

"Are you hurting?"

"Yes," she said softly.

"We haven't made it to the road to Agedon. It may be safer to stop now, before we get to the road."

The ground was stony and had been for some time. Even sitting would have been uncomfortable for any length of time. They carried on for another quarter of an hour before Terrence felt that the ground would provide at least a minimum of comfort. Terrence made ready a makeshift bed for Tira out of clothes and baggage. As Tira lay she looked up at Terrence.

"I'm afraid."

Terrence nodded. "Try to sleep. I'll keep watch."

"You must rest, too."

"I will, but for now I'll keep watch. In the morning when you awake I may rest some."

Tira had never slept upon the ground. Her body felt as though she slept upon the most jagged of stones. Were it not for the extreme fatigue that she felt, she could not have slept. In the earliest moments of dawn, she awoke. Her abdomen ached. Between needing to urinate, sleeping on a rocky ground, and the blow that she had taken there the night before, it was no wonder that it ached. Before opening her eyes, she considered which seemed to be the cause. Getting up and urinating would be her only immediate solution.

"You seemed sound as you slept." Terrence said in a calm demeanor.

"Good morning, Terrence. Did you sleep at all?"

"No, my love. I've watched you sleep. You are more dear to me now even than before. So sweet your face is as you sleep. I've always loved your eyes. It is what I love the most about you. And yet, as I watched you sleep, with your eyes closed, I felt as though I got to know you better."

As she moved to a sitting position she betrayed her discomfort with a groan, putting her hand over her belly.

"You're hurting," he said with concern.

"Yes, the ground was so hard and I must relieve myself."

"You were struck there also. You might be injured."

Tira said nothing but got to her feet with more pain. She knew that something was wrong, then. She eyed the terrain. It was flat without a tree or a boulder in sight.

"I could turn my back or we could walk until we find a suitable location. I'm afraid that I don't know how long that may be."

"Turn please."

It was at this moment that the reality of how much she had given up, how much she had left behind, really hit her. Tira had never known anything other than sleeping in the most comfortable bed, bathing comfortably, a luxurious toilet, and food at her side. Here, she was hurting, hungry, dirty, tired, and squatting upon the ground in a barren open area. Her condescension was unbearable. She removed a pretty scarf to clean herself and then realized that she must not toss it, but rather, she would need to use it again, later. Brave as she had been the night before, she felt she was nothing but a fool. After doing herself up she looked at Terrence, his back towards her. Even with his clothes on she could see the muscular form that he had. He appeared to be staring off into the distance but his slight slouch gave away the overwhelming fatigue that he felt. He had saved her life—both of their lives, against a foe she had thought unconquerable. He was powerful and strong and held deep convictions. She loved him and he was worthy of her love. She walked slowly toward him and placed her hand upon his shoulder.

He turned and smiled slightly towards her, even the little movement of his bloodstained lips brought discomfort to him.

"Any better?"

She smiled and nodded.

"Good."

In reality, she did not feel much relief at all.

"Your lip is very swollen. Did they club you to the face? Will you rest now?"

"It is nothing and we are in a bad place. We could be seen for miles, there is no water or food. We must try and reach the road this morning. If we find a place of shelter or water, we will stop."

"But you must rest."

"Yes, but I don't think that I could. If I lay down my heart would race and I would only feel worse."

They walked until mid-morning. Tira felt somewhat better once she had walked for some time. The blood flow seemed to help. She felt tenderer towards Terrence at that time than she had the night before. She put her hand around his upper arm and at times leaned in towards him. Terrence spoke softly about his adventures in the dark forest. This talk had been forbidden in Cardsten and he had been careful. At this point his stories were the least of his concern. Tira listened with much interest. The time passed more quickly and it helped to take her mind off of her discomfort.

After telling of Marcus' death Terrence became quiet. Tira did not know if she should speak. Terrence was either in deep contemplation or his fatigue had bested him. Off in the distance they saw a team of horses riding southeast, towards Cardsten.

"This must be the road. Lie down."

The two lay and watched in the distance. It appeared as though the riders had stopped and were resting. Terrence and Tira continued to lie upon the ground, watching and waiting. They were too far away for whispers to be heard and so Terrence began to talk with Tira.

"It has been bothering me since last night what you said about the man who attacked us. You said that I should not kill him; that I knew not everything and that I should not do this. I knew that there was much to be frightful for after all that occurred. But, my killing him seemed to distress you the most. What is it that I do not know?"

"Oh, Terrence. Let us go to Agedon. We'll marry and be happy. We will fight for the right cause. We will live as people should live and be able to hold our head up high. We will not have to be deceptive and two-faced. You were never made for Cardsten. You are blessed to see the world so clearly, as that which is good and that which is evil. You see all as black or white. In Cardsten, perhaps more than all else, you despised the subtleties. You saw the good and you saw the evil but you could never see how they intermingled and worked in a sort of harmony. Cardsten is not a world of black and white, put rather a world of every shade of gray. When, in a world such as Cardsten, you try and define all as black or white you are hated. Cardsten was never meant for you. Let us turn our back to the world of shaded grays and let us go to Agedon where they are not fools, but they see the world as you, and now I, as black and white, good and evil. We have no need to delve into the subtleties of Cardsten."

Terrence pondered for a time. His sleepless mind, however, did not have the faculties of comprehension.

"You have lost me, my dear. I still do not understand about this man who has attacked us. Why should his death, in particular, concern you?"

"It is in the past, my dear Terrence. Cardsten, and all its foolishness is in our past. Let us get to Agedon. Everything will be clear in Agedon. Do not make me speak of Cardsten, of its subtleties, and of our past."

"Tira," he said pleadingly. "I am stubborn. I must know, and then I will not bother you again."

Tira placed her hand on her stomach and winced. Her lying position did not help the pain.

"We can speak on it later. You are hurting and my mind is so tired."

"Yes, but you must know and so I will explain. Then, when I have spoken, let us leave this subject for good."

The men on horses began to mount and continued their ride southeast towards Cardsten. Terrence and Tira continued to lay while they spoke and while the horsemen were still in sight.

"You know of the military in Cardsten," Tira began.

"Yes."

"We brag on them and their might and power. We speak of them and their awesome strength—in numbers, arms, understanding, and conditioning. And it may be that the military of Cardsten is the most powerful in the world. And yet, they are not powerful in Cardsten. They have no authority whatsoever. They wear their cute uniforms and parade with their swords. But they are of no use unless Cardsten and Agedon do truly battle. They are under complete control of the politicians. The government controls the military. They are a pet, a puppet, a show for the people. Cardsten loves to feel safe and secure. They desire to believe that they are beyond any danger. So, we have a great wall to protect us from the dragon. We have a great military to protect us from all other peoples of the world. We have an economic engine to protect us from any wants. Cardsten thinks that it is untouchable from the world. Perhaps we don't truly think this. Perhaps we do all of this because of our fears and insecurities. But, outwardly this is what we portray."

"I still don't understand about the dragon worshipers?"

"Patients, my dear. I will explain all, at least so far as I have come to understand it myself."

"Go on."

"The government is supposed to be the supreme authority of Cardsten. This is how it is spoken of by all. Everyone speaks of it as such; it could not be spoken of differently. Yet, no one believes it, for it is not true. Beyond the power of the government are those who control the economy of Cardsten, Mr. Cards and those like him. The government is, and does, as is dictated by those who control the business and economy of Cardsten. The government and the military are financed by the wealthy. If the money were removed the government and military would be impotent. The people are employed by the businessmen and the life and comforts that they enjoy are brought to them by the businesses of Cardsten. The government gives them nothing other than the farce of freedom. They elect the political leaders and therefore they are free, you see. And the political leaders are powerless themselves, so they are flattered into believing that they are now something. They carry great titles and are given wealth. They live in great places and give great speeches. Those who are in power applaud, and bow, and provide feasts for them, and butter them up. If some foolish politician begins to act as though he has real power and authority—that he is autonomous and supreme, then he is quickly put out of power. When the businessmen turn their backs on a politician and remove all of their resources, and slander him, then the people see him as rouge, or useless, or dangerous and he is quickly put out. This rarely happens and normalcy is soon restored. The military is at the bidding of the politicians who are at the bidding and mercy of the economic powers of Cardsten. The powerful leaders that are paraded in front of the people are nothing more than a front. There is no substance behind them. The people are not ignorant of this, yet no one speaks of it. It is understood, accepted, and even appreciated by the people of Cardsten. We like our front, we like the image that we portray of ourselves to each other and to the world. It is pleasing to the eyes to have a powerful military and a powerful government that is at the bidding of the people who elect them. But we all know who holds the cards. It is the Cards."

Terrence smiled and Tira planted a kiss on him. Terrence winced in pain and Tira apologized.

"You still haven't told me about the man I killed."

Tira smiled.

"Ideals are powerful things, my dear. The Cards family and others like him carry with them a most powerful ideal of how the world should be. They have such a strong sense of the world and they have the resources to move forward with their ideals. It has many benefits to the rest of society that they have been most successful in carrying it out. They have built Cardsten, both the structure itself, but most especially the function. When a man such as Mr. Cards speaks of it, it makes so much sense that it would seem as though a city such as Cardsten could be made with such ideals and a willingness of those in power to carry them forth. The success of Cardsten would seem a testimony to that. And yet, as you have seen, there is a darker side to Cardsten, one in which the ideals of Mr. Cards do not address. It is there, its presence is ever felt, and yet it would seem to have no place.

"Within human nature there is a love of the ideal and a love of the counter to the ideal. It is my opinion that if Cardsten had forced the natural evolution of the counter ideal out from its presence, then it would have fallen under the weight of the ideal itself. But whether in their wisdom, foolishness, ignorance, or weakness, the economic power players of Cardsten did not squash those who were of the darker ideal out of existence, but rather allowed them to grow alongside such that they have allowed ideal Cardsten to carry its full front, while the darkness of Cardsten thrives in the background, in the nooks, the cracks, the empty places of the ideal. Where the ideal does not fill space a vacuum is created. The ideal of Cardsten is not so powerful as to withstand the pressures of the vacuum. So, darkness and the counter ideals fill the voids. The voids being filled, now the pressure is released and the ideal can stand up, put on its full front and portray its strength and glory to all the world; all the while being held up and supported by darkness and the counter ideals. This Terrence, you saw, whether or not you understood it, and it was revolting to you. Whatever the appearance, goodness held up and supported by evil, is no longer goodness. When what appears is so entirely different from what it really is, then one lives in deception. It does not bring internal peace. This along with material comforts does not bring true happiness and joy. Appearance and pleasure, while not bad in and of themselves, when not combined with goodness and joy, are very unsatisfying indeed."

"I think that I agree with you, but I still don't think that I understand."

"I warned you, you know."

Terrence smiled and winced again. The horses were nearly out of sight, but Terrence was in no hurry to move positions. His bodily fatigue was about to overtake him and he still hadn't had his questions answered.

"Among the voids left by Mr. Cards and his ancestors' ideals, was worship. Though the need may vary from individual to individual, a large society has many among them that desire worship. The legend of Dromreign and its acts have been known for generations. These legends propelled the building of the walls which allowed for greater protection. But they also provided a fuel for dragon worship. I suspect that it simply evolved slowly until it was accepted as part of the society of Cardsten. Most in Cardsten do not worship this beast, not in any meaningful way. Yet, they accept its worship, its image, its likeness, and its name invoked in reference to Cardsten. We built the walls to keep it out, yet we have let it in entirely. Dromreign is everywhere in Cardsten. Even the capital building hoists a great green banner with the image of the fierce black beast breathing out its fiery destruction. No, the walls have not keep Dromreign out of Cardsten.

"Now, the government controls the military, at least in so far as I have explained. But the government has no means of policing the people. Cardsten, as you may have observed is not filled with crime. On the surface, this is explained by the powerful ideals on which it was built. The people are self-reliant, they work hard, they have the means to better themselves. Crime has no place in such a society. Yet, crime *is* a part of society. The ideal does not provide for everyone's satisfaction, as I've already said. People are not so happy and internally peaceful as they try and appear. There is plenty of impendence for criminal activity. But the economic leaders, the employers, the idealists, do not want a military marching forth upon the common people. This could lead to revolution, to revolt, to greater dissatisfaction among the people to their circumstances and inequalities. So, these things are taken care of quietly. The man you killed leads the dragon worshipers, as you call them. They have no name among us, they are simply a part of the fabric of Cardsten, the dark side of the fabric. I don't know how much they truly worship the beast, though it is tattooed upon their heads, but it is at least their pious front. What they really do is discipline the 'criminal element' in the name of the dragon. Those who break the laws, whether written or not, are in opposition to the omnipotent beast. Those who stand against the societal ideals are the enemies of Dromreign and therefore must be punished.

"There is no legal jurisdiction for such behavior, for such an entity. Yet, it is not questioned. They do not threaten those who conform to the ideals of the city. They eat and drink, mix and mingle among them. They are not the economic force of the city but they are provided for somehow and this is not spoken of. They are not members of the government nor do they attempt to be, and they are not arms of the government. But they do the governments bidding. They fill the voids left by our ideal system and they make it work, at least they make it appear to work. The man you killed leads this force of darkness within Cardsten. He is at least as powerful as Mr. Cards, Aiden and the other generals, our governor and other political leaders. He may spend much of his time in the shadows, and may not be a part of the pretty front that Cardsten portrays, but he was a critical part of the fabric of Cardsten. You have created a void when you put him to death. That void will be, must be, filled. But, in the meantime it will create chaos and trouble within the city. Its infrastructure has been weakened by this act and there will be shifting and power struggles that must run their course. For us and our friends, those who were once our friends at least, I felt it better to leave him be. There is no certainty that whoever replaces him will be better than he. A greater suspicion and a greater watch will be upon those with whom we have loved and been acquainted. I had hoped that we would leave at a point that we had fallen to such little importance, that our absence would be largely forgotten. Now, I fear that our leaving Cardsten has put Cardsten in a horrible state."

Tira's eyes again filled with tears and she wept silently. Terrence was also silent as he considered all this revelation entailed. In a quarter of an hour his eyes had fallen shut and he slept. Tira, afraid to arise still, put her arms around him and fell asleep, too. It was several hours past noon before they awoke.

Terrence felt better and his mind was clearer. Tira's condition had worsened. Staying put, however, meant death for sure. She moved on slowly, if not bravely. They worked their way to the place that the horses had stopped. Though they saw nothing to indicate water, food, or shelter from the distance, there was within them both a faint hope. They were not disappointed. Though it was only a small stream, well hidden from the distance, they were able to refresh themselves with water and wash their faces. The water and sleep strengthened both of them physically and emotionally. They rested in some shade for another hour and then set off. Terrence believed that they would be safer on the main road with darkness in the sky.

The air was cool but not cold and their exertion kept them comfortable until a wind picked up. The late afternoon wind was loud and at times blew dirt into their eyes. It was becoming cold and they worried about a storm approaching, though the sky was clear. They did not have enough clothing to keep them warm in these conditions. Terrence kept his eye out for some type of shelter for the night. He was frustrated, among other things, that they had made such little progress on their journey that day. His focus was in front of him and the wind disguised the sound. But overtaking them quickly were the riders that they had seen earlier in the day.

The riders were upon them and surrounding them before they were aware of their presence. Terrence put his hand back to retrieve his sword.

"Hold there!" said a middle-aged dark bearded man riding directly to Terrence. Terrence froze.

"What do we have here? I don't recognize ye, now do I? No, well, I don't know ye, do I?"

The two remained silent. Tira recognized the accent as from Agedon.

"Are ye spies of Cardsten, heh? Ye are coming from that a way, now aren't ye?"

"No," said Terrence.

"No? Well, ye are not of Agedon, but ye are heading that way, no?"

"We are toward Agedon," said Tira meekly. "And I am of Cardsten, though he is not."

"Then ye know that Cardsten and Agedon do not intermingle, do ye not? If I was of Cardsten and I met some travelers of Agedon, then I'd run them through forthright, would I not? What do ye say, fella's, should we run 'em through?"

A cheer arose from the seven other riders. Terrence pulled out his sword.

"Well, men, I think we've found the Cardsten army! But do ye think he knows how to use the blade?"

The riders laughed mercilessly.

"He can't be the military, sir," said a younger, beardless, freckled faced rider. "He's not wearing red or black pajamas." And they all enjoyed a hearty laugh. The bearded man pulled his own sword.

"So, if we were taken by Cardsten and they would run us through. Should we not run ye through now?"

"Sir," said Tira, "we are defecting to Agedon."

"Ah, so ye say. But why would ye do that? Agedon does not have the comforts of Cardsten. We do not have a giant wall, a pajama-clad military, such soft beds, such sweet wine, nor such wild entertainment. Plus, everyone of Cardsten knows what fools we of Agedon are. Cardsten does not defect to Agedon."

"We want none of those things," said Terrence forcefully.

"No, well, apparently not. For ye have none of those things now. Nor do ye look or smell as though ye've bathed in quite some time." Again, a roaring laughter.

"Now, this women ye have here with ye. It's hard to say, so dirty and unkempt. But maybe with a bath, some fresh clothing, and perfume," he pinched his nose and held it in the air to a chorus of laughter, "perhaps then she might be something. Let's take her back and just run him through."

The chorus applauded cheerfully and shouted, "Here, here!"

Terrence prepared himself. Tira began to speak.

"Silence, ye wench!" said the bearded man forcefully, upon which Tira hushed up. "I said that if we were of Cardsten and ye were of Agedon, then we'd run ye through. But..." He paused for some time and the other men were silent. He stared Terrence down. "...we are not of Cardsten; we are of Agedon. And Agedon doesn't just run people through!"

He and all the other men laughed heartily. He dismounted his horse after sheathing his sword and began to walk towards Terrence who held his position strong.

"Sheath ye sword, young man. We are not upon ye. I'm Daron Drake, King of Agedon," and he held out his hand in a friendly manner. "Though I may not look so kingly in this shabby attire." The men laughed, but more cautiously this time. Terrence looked at his hand for a moment before pressing it, sword still in his left hand.

"We've been to look upon Cardsten today and see what the pajama military is up to. They're up to something, we didn't know what. Looked like they were hunting for a lost coin, all looking around the walls. They like their money there. I figure if ye lose a coin then everything stops and the hunt begins? They were probably looking for the defectors—ye here. They'll not find ye, though. No, not how closely they hug their walls. I don't think a man got a hundred yards away from the wall. They talk big, they do. They'll come out and stop Agedon from taking on the dragon with their pretty pajama's, but when the military is called to action they leave their precious walls, but only so far that they can dash back in, in a moment. I don't think there is a general among them that isn't afraid of his own shadow; that even knows how to wield a sword."

Terrence began to speak up but Tira grabbed and squeezed his hand. Terrence was silent again.

"Ah, ye are defecting to Agedon, but ye carry with ye secrets from us. From me ye're new king, if ye'll have me. Well, keep ye ye're secrets for now, we've only just met. I suspect that ye carry even more secrets from Cardsten. Come ye, ye must have names now?"

Terrence looked at Tira. "I am Terrence," he said looking back.

"Pleasure to meet ye, Terrence. And this pretty one with ye, she must have a name, too."

They were both silent.

"Come now, young lady. I was just teasing with ye earlier. Yes, we'll get ye bathed, and dressed, and perfumed, but it's not ye that stink. It's the silly sap here next to ye!" They laughed again.

"She is Tira," said Terrence.

"Ah, well ye parents must have liked the sound of that together, Terrence and Tira. She is ye sister, right?"

"No, she is my..."

"Yes?"

"...she is my, betrothed."

An, "oooh," sounded from the chorus.

"Ye betrothed is she...ye've run off with ye betrothed."

"Did ye steal her from someone? Is that why ye are off on this crazy adventure? I noticed that ye blade is stained, and not from carving an animal. Ye have run a man through, haven't ye? Was it this ladies father, or brother, or lover? Would I be taking defectors to Agedon who flee Cardsten because they are criminals, murderers?"

"I have run a man through, even more than one. But they were not kin or friends to Tira. I am no murderer, for it was in self-defense and in her protection, though I may be considered a criminal if I returned to Cardsten."

"Well," said Daron Drake, King of Agedon, "let me see this sword."

Terrence paused, but the King, as he called himself, stood with his sword sheathed next to him with a very congenial visage. Reluctantly, he handed over the sword. The king spent some time admiring both the sword and its handy work but also its apparent use.

"Ye are the original owner of this sword? Or has it been purchased or perhaps stolen from the original owner? Did ye run the owner of this sword through and then take it as ye own?"

Terrence reached to retrieve his sword but Daron feigned not seeing the gesture. "It was not mine originally but has been mine now for nearly two years. It had not been used much before I had it. It has seen much action since I have been the owner.

The king tossed the sword to one of his men as Terrence looked on, aghast.

"So, ye are a criminal of Cardsten and have excited the entire military this day. Perhaps the military was looking for money; perhaps there is a ransom upon ye head. Me thinks, perhaps that ye are of much value to us. Ye're ransom alone could bring me much wealth. We of Agedon are not so rich as is Cardsten. The money alone would do Agedon much good. But, even more, we do not hate or desire to fight Cardsten as they do us. There was once great trade amongst us. Perhaps I may be able to broker a treaty. Return an infamous criminal, even a murderer, in return for goodwill and a handsome sum of money. We want Cardsten to fight with us against Dromreign. But at least, we would have them not fight against us. I thought for a moment that ye, being young and strong, and good with a sword, that ye may be of value to Agedon. But, as I see how easy it is to remove ye sword from ye, that ye are not worth the sword ye carry. But as a reward ye may be worth much. I'll just make up how hard it was to capture ye, the great escaped convict of Cardsten." His men laughed again.

Tira began to speak again. The king shot her a glance and she shushed.

"Now, m' lady, I have been rude to ye. Speak, I say. I think that I may learn much from ye."

"My King, I do not think that returning us to Cardsten will bring to you all that you desire or hope for. Perhaps, if they let you approach at all, they may give you some money in return for us, but I do not know. We are of little importance in Cardsten. We may have left with hardly anyone knowing, except for a villainous gang of dragon worshipers who put us in danger. Terrence defended us both and we made our way out. We were coming to defect before we were attacked. I see little more than harm coming to you or us if we return to Cardsten."

"But, ye were defecting and ye were attacked, this tells me that there is much more to the story than we have heard so far. Will ye tell me all, withhold no secrets from me, that I may trust ye? Will ye do that in exchange for us not returning ye to Cardsten."

"Yes," said Tira with a tremble.

"I do not want to discover more details over the coming days and weeks. I want to know all tonight."

Terrence and Tira agreed. The other men dismounted and though Terrence's sword was not returned, the overall disposition of the company changed. A fire was built and food was placed thereon. Water was brought for the couple and bedding was laid out for all ten. They ate together and were treated hospitably. Yet, they were watched carefully and always surrounded, and their things were gone through leaving nothing that could be used as a weapon. After the time for rest and dinner Daron indicated that he was ready to hear all.

Terrence told him the story of his life, primarily beginning with the arrival of Aiden and Jashion in Tengeer. Much interest was laid upon every detail of these past two years, in particular the time spent in the dark forest. When the story came to the time that he arrived in Cardsten the King asked Tira to tell her story up to this point. She did, explaining all about her family, friends, and connections in Cardsten. When the time came that they met, they both shared, interrupting each other throughout the telling. The king and other men laughed joyfully as they both corrected, and misinterpreted, and misunderstood the details of their short love affair. Still, he questioned both of them about the details of Aiden and Jashion, of Daxton, Tasha, and Mr. Cards. He spent much time gaining an understanding of exactly why the dragon gang was interested in them.

When he was satisfied, he assigned the evenings guard shift and sent everyone to bed.

"May I ask," said Terrence, "does anyone here have healing knowledge? Tira is still hurting from her blow. I fear that she may be more seriously injured."

The king looked over at the lady preparing to lie down with her hand over her stomach. He nodded his head knowingly.

"My man, these men know how to wrap a wound, and other such things, but none know enough to treat that type of injury. They have been gone with me for several weeks. I fear that giving them the opportunity to inspect the young lady in such an intimate way would be opening her up to trouble. Let us get her to Agedon. On horseback, we should arrive in Agedon by tomorrow night. There we can turn her over to those who will know more and give her the assistance she requires. For now, sleep close to her and be her protector this night. She does not look as though it is bad enough that she will not make it. She may even feel better in the morning."

Terrence nodded and retired near Tira. She slept peacefully again and he nodded off, in and out, throughout the night. Terrence did not feel at peace. There was good reason. For two pairs of watchful eyes were upon he and Tira throughout the night. Two pairs of watchful eyes attached to shaved heads with the image of Dromreign tattooed upon them. Were it not for the guards of Agedon, Terrence's and Tira's throats would have been slit that night.

Morning came and they breakfasted. They were given a horse to share as two of the smallest men, though they were not small, shared another horse. They rode with a horse in front of them, one on each side and the other four behind. They were not prisoners, perhaps, but neither were they fully trusted. Still, the King had been generous and had fulfilled his promises thus far. Whatever lay in front of them seemed more promising than what lay behind them in Cardsten.

Chapter 17

Just before dusk they arrived in Agedon. Here was a large city without a wall. The buildings were built of wood and not of stone and concrete, as was Cardsten. The architecture was more primitive and certainly not as fine, yet there was a certain charm that it possessed. As they rode in the people stopped and saluted their king. They seemed happy on the whole and did not appear to salute out of fear or with only mock obeisance. The king in his turn smiled warmly and familiarly. The rugged charm of the architecture seemed to emanate from a people who also had a rugged charm about them. Compared to Tengeer this city would have looked wealthy and modern. But they had arrived from Cardsten and not Tengeer, so their perspective made it feel much humbler. Most people had never traveled from Cardsten to Agedon. Those who had, in the past, would have been traders primarily. They would have easily contrasted the appearance of the two great cities and with their descriptions made Agedon seem primitive, impoverished, and the land of fools. Especially if that was the way that they were expected to portray it.

They were brought directly to the city center where the Royal accommodations were. The palace was beautiful on the outside—a carved wooden building, taller than the rest, and beautifully landscaped. The dress near the palace may have even rivaled some in Cardsten, unlike the dress of those who lived farther from the palace and were much more simply attired.

Tira's discomfort had reached the threshold where at times she thought the pain may cause her to faint. In some respects, the riding helped, both in duration and energy expenditure, but the bouncing and the jolting only caused her more and more discomfort. All of the men dismounted and were quickly attended to by men and women from around the palace. Terrence and Tira did not dismount, not knowing what was expected of them. Within moments all of the men were gone, all except the king. He stood communicating with some men who looked to be of importance. He did not look around towards Terrence and Tira but occasionally the other men did. Those men nodded obediently and then the king was off.

Terrence watched but Tira bowed her head in agony. She was glad for the journeys end. Those other men left but the two were not alone. Many people from around the palace were scurrying around nearby. Still they waited. After ten long minutes an aged man came up and addressed them. He took the horses reign and led the horse with the riders several buildings away.

"Ye may dismount," said the elderly man.

Terrence dismounted and then carefully helped Tira do the same. She winced with every movement and pressure. When she reached the ground, she could hardly stand. Terrence helped her from falling but she was extraordinarily discomforted being upon her feet.

"It's not far, if ye can walk m' lady. Ye may carry her if ye can instead."

Terrence attempted to pick her up but the movement caused a sharp stroke of pain.

"I'll walk, it's better," she said. "Slowly. Give me support."

Inside, the large triangular domed hall was cool and shaded. Some torches lit the hall but it was rather dark after spending the entirety of the day outside.

"Lay on the table here, m' lady."

It was a short wooden table but still she winced and groaned as she positioned herself thereon. Terrence tried to help but everything he did seemed useless in relieving her symptoms. Though it was cool inside Tira had significant perspiration upon her forehead. She lay with her feet up, attempting to find the most comfortable position, though it was still very painful. Another ten minutes passed with no one entering. Terrence tried to speak with Tira but even trying to speak brought on too much pain. They remained silent and he held her hand.

Two middle aged men entered with shaved heads and simple cream colored gowns. They sought eye contact from Tira and when they got it, one put his hand very softly on her abdomen. He pushed down softly and she winced. He moved his hands around her abdomen both examining and trying to ascertain the level and origin of her pain. She squeezed Terrence's hand tightly. Terrence beheld that they worked cautiously and tenderly. Though neither man seemed to acknowledge Terrence he felt an instant trust with them. They treated Tira with kindness. They spoke so low to one another that Terrence understood nothing of their communications.

The next thing he knew they were removing her clothing to the point that he felt ashamed to look in the direction of their examinations. Tira continued to grip his hand tightly. He reddened some and then turned his body so that he could see only her face and not much more. For many minutes the men worked. Tira kept her eyes shut and from time to time squeezed them tight and winced. For a while both men walked away and the two were alone. Terrence was afraid to look back to see if she was covered. Tira opened her eyes and stared at Terrence. He searched her face and her deep mysterious eyes. The pain in them was obvious but there was so much more.

"I love you," she mouthed inaudibly.

Terrence smiled slightly and Tira returned as much of a smile as she could muster.

Terrence could hear the men had returned. He looked at her face. He could see by her expressions that she was being touched by them again. Tira kept her eyes open and stared at Terrence. She tried to be brave. He felt in the pressure in his hand and the expression on her face that she was in extreme discomfort. She breathed heavily then and looked at him earnestly. He heard a brief communication behind him from the men, and then, after a moment of silence, Tira's entire countenance changed and she let out a horrible scream. She grabbed his hand so hard that he felt that she may disintegrate every bone. Her head arched back and she panted between yells, tears rushed down her cheeks as she sobbed and sobbed. The gripe on his hand loosened some. Tira's cries almost muffled the sound of the men speaking, but not entirely. Terrence held her and occasionally wiped the tears from her cheeks. Slowly the sobs themselves muffled but her eyes remained shut. The men still worked behind him but she no longer winced with their actions.

A prolonged silence indicated to Terrence that the men had left them again. They returned shortly and soon Terrence realized that they were covering Tira with a blanket of animal skins. He moved to look her over then. She was completely covered in a brown bear skin, except for her face and arm which hand he held. Tira was not sleeping but she was calm. Her face was turned away from his, though she still gripped his hand. She breathed more slowly and regularly. Slowly the grip loosened and he sensed her slumber. He let go of her hand slowly and helped her arm underneath the blanket. He desired a pillow for her head that was resting upon the hard table but could not see anything suitable. He looked for anyone but no one was there. Looking back at Tira he wished that he knew more but saw a peacefulness in her sleep that encouraged him. He bent down and after wiping away tear soaked strands of hair from her face he kissed her cheek.

This gentle kiss was interrupted by sounds from without. A moment later King Daron entered with an entourage. He walked briskly and assertively towards Terrence and the sleeping girl.

"Good. She sleeps," he said inspecting her quickly. "I am told that all will be well with her soon."

Terrence breathed a sigh of relief.

"Ye may stay by her tonight. There will be those who will attend to her throughout the night. Ye're supper will be brought shortly."

"Thank you."

The King looked Terrence in the eye and shook his hand. Then he and his entourage left. The large hall was silent and empty again until Terrence's dinner was brought. He ate alone with his eye on Tira. Bedding was brought for him, though it was not yet late, and he and the sleeping Tira were generally alone for the night. He was aware occasionally of the men, or others like them, returning to examine and treat her.

In the morning, when he awoke, Tira was still sleeping.

He thought that they were alone but a man behind him spoke. Terrence turned around somewhat startled.

The man, bald and dressed like the others had been, was alone.

"She is doing fine. She will be okay. She needs nourishment, though. Would ye awaken her and let her know? I do not wish to startle her," he said with a smile.

Terrence nodded and moved towards Tira. He reached under the skin for her hand and held it for a moment. She did not stir but continued to breath slowly and rhythmically. With his other hand, he brushed her damp hair from her face and slowly stroked her cheek. Still, no movement.

"Tira," he said softly. She did not budge.

"Tira," he said a little louder and he saw some facial movements.

"Tira, how do you feel?" Tira's face showed some effort on her part to arouse but she fell back into her slumber.

"Tira, my love, it's morning."

One eye flickered momentarily and then the other. A gentle smile transformed her face.

"How do you feel?"

She nodded slowly. "Better. A little better. No, I feel much better. But, I feel so tired and so weak. I do still hurt, though. Some."

"Can you eat? You haven't eaten in nearly a day. You need nourishment for strength."

"Yes, I'll try."

Terrence began to lift her to a sitting position. The skin fell off of her shoulder and revealed it bare. Terrence caught the edge and moved to cover her.

"Where are my clothes?"

"I...I don't know," he said reddening.

He took extra care ensuring that she was covered with the skin also from behind once she reached her sitting position. All but her face was then covered. The man across the way smiled at the scene. He stood up and brought over a broth and some bread.

"This will help ye, m' lady," he said kindly.

"Thank you," said Tira.

Terrence brought the bowl to her lips and she took a short sip. She swallowed and licked her lips. Then he dipped a small piece of bread in the broth and gave her the bite. When half of the bread and broth were gone, her appetite was satisfied.

"I'm tired," she said to Terrence.

Terrence looked over at the man and he nodded his assent. Terrence helped her back to a lying position taking great care to ensure her modesty.

"May we provide her with a pillow."

The man nodded and looked at Terrence's bedding on the floor next to her. He reached for a pillow and gently propped it underneath her head. Tira appeared to slumber already.

Two young women entered the room with more food. This time it was Terrence's breakfast. The girls, about fourteen each stole a glance at Terrence and then giggled as they made their way out. The exchange was curious to Terrence but not enough for him to reflect on it. He devoured his breakfast and then stood up. Again, the hall was empty until the King returned.

"Terrence, I trust ye are well and rested."

"Yes, I..."

"And the girl, she is in good hands?"

"I do belie..."

"Good. Here's ye weapon. Let's put it to use."

"What?"

"Show us what ye've got, my man."

"But Tira..."

"She'll be fine. She's resting and the men are taking great care. Don't worry over the lass now, come and show us ye handiwork."

Terrence left the large hall reluctantly.

The Bright morning dazzled his eyes after spending so much time in the dim hall. The king walked briskly and Terrence followed a few paces behind. As they left the confines near the palace, Terrence noted the people. They were busy at work. The smell in the air was that of blacksmiths at work. More than once he saw into the open workshops of blacksmiths at their grills. *How many horseshoes do they need?* Terrence pondered ironically. Passing the fourth workshop, thus far, he saw what looked to be an iron man inside. Terrence stopped and looked. The king, not hearing Terrence's footsteps turned around. Terrence just stared at the iron man. The man was faceless but had two horns bent upwards. He looked fierce and cold at the same time.

"Terrence, ye're king awaits ye."

Terrence turned, not entirely taking in the king's gentle rebuke. He looked blankly at the king for a moment.

"Armor. A suit of Armor. We are preparing for battle. Now come along." The king turned and walked briskly in the direction that he was heading.

Terrence stole one more look at the armor and then jogged up to his king's side. In the distance was the familiar sound of swords clashing. In time, Terrence was in a large clearing and could see that many men fought with their swords in mock battles.

"Jack," yelled the king. A large athletic man with rippling muscles made his way towards them. "Are ye rested and ready for battle."

"I am, m' king," he answered assertively.

"Good. I bring ye a new recruit. He's used a sword before. Has shed blood, and more than one man. Test his skills."

Jack nodded and smiled slightly still looking at his king. Terrence and Jack moved several paces away and drew their swords. The king looked on eagerly. Terrence was not as large or as muscular as Jack but he was a fairly good match. They stood looking at each other and offered a few practice swings.

"Are ye waiting for an invitation? Begin," said the king.

Jack took a step forward but Terrence held his ground. He watched this man carefully. He was strong and confident to be sure, but he was no Aiden. His moves betrayed a carelessness. He was brash and he was strong. Yet, nothing about his moves or his attitude betrayed superior intelligence. Terrence stood ready for Jack to offer the first swing. He did not have to wait long.

Jack stood within striking distance and after eyeing Terrence momentarily, swung with full force overhead at Terrence's head. Terrence saw how exposed his opponent left himself. If it was blood that he was after, Terrence could have run him through before the blade was even dropped towards him. But this was not the purpose of this event. Instead, he coolly blocked the blow making it diverge several inches to the side of his body. Jack was then badly out of position with his back exposed for any attack that Terrence may render. The king noticed this positioning at once and cringed.

Jack, who was not attacked, quickly readied himself for the next stage of the battle. Terrence stood, undeterred, awaiting the next blow. This time Jack was more cautious. He swung towards Terrence's body but kept himself in position. This allowed for their swords to cling back and forth several times. Terrence held and blocked, keeping his feet planted and his position stable. He offered a few thrusts himself but just to test Jack defensively. The king could tell that Agedon's champion was being trifled with. He felt some anger but it was mixed with pleasure and admiration.

Jack's patience began to wear. Nothing he did deterred Terrence. He soon forgot what his last big mistake cost him, and came at Terrence with another hard blow. Again, he was put out of position, and again it was clear that the man could have been done for. Terrence again allowed Jack to ready himself. There was much less clinging around them. The men had stopped and were watching Jack, feared by everyone, struggling to gain anything against this stranger.

After some controlled fighting, Jack again swung himself out of position and this time Terrence reacted. He kicked Jack in the backside and knocked him to the ground. Jack rolled to a kneeling and then standing position quickly. Terrence was on the move. Terrence swung hard and Jack barely had time to block, in doing so he took two steps back and was in poor position. Terrence continued at him. Jack blocked but could not stabilize himself. He continued to walk backwards and struggled with his defense. Terrence showed no emotion on his face. He simply carried on. The men were hushed as they watched Jack getting devoured. With the next stroke Jack's sword sailed away. He looked at Terrence with fear in his eyes. Terrence swung at him and Jack fell backwards just being missed by the blow.

Terrence lunged at him and lifting his sword began his descent for the deathblow. Everyone, including the king were awestruck. Did Terrence not know that this was training? Would Jack be killed before their eyes? Jack, with fear filled eyes, lifted his hands in hopes of offering himself some protection. The sword fell with the tip pointed towards Jacks heart. And then it ran through. It was lodged several inches into the ground, less than an inch from Jacks side. Terrence had deviated the course of the sword at the last second missing his opponent entirely but leaving the potential in question to no one. From a distance, most of the other men thought that the sword was run through Jack. The king narrowed his eyes and looked closely. Jack, who had stopped breathing looked Terrence in the eye. Terrence offered Jack his hand and lifted him up. When the men saw Jack on his feet and the sword still lodged into the ground, a cheer rose up.

Jack looked at Terrence with awe. Terrence smiled and shook his hand.

"Nice match," Terrence said.

Jack looked at him blankly and then asked, "where are ye from?"

"Tengeer," said Terrence.

"Tengeer?" Jack muttered to himself and shook his head.

Terrence was already making his way back to the king. Jack followed sheepishly.

All of the men left their places of battle to gather round their new champion and their king.

"Terrence," barked the king. "Well done! Can ye teach this skill ye possess to the men."

"Yes, king."

"Men," said Daron. "Here is ye general! Terrence, the general of the armies of Agedon. Will ye fight with Terrence!"

"Hurrah!" yelled the men and they lifted their swords in the air. Jack looked around and nodded towards the king. He was still catching his breath.

The king put his hand on Terrence's shoulder and looked him in the eyes. "Will ye accept this position?"

"I will," said Terrence triumphantly.

The men shouted and then hoisted Terrence upon their shoulders and paraded him around. When things had calmed, Jack came up to him.

"Congratulations, sir. I will fight with ye. I will be ye're right hand man. Show me what to do and I will do it. Ye have earned my upmost respect."

Terrence smiled. Things were as they should be in Agedon.

The men milled around not knowing what was expected of them.

"What would ye have me tell the men to do?"

"Tell them to carry on. I would speak to my king."

Jack turned around and shouted to the troops. They began to fight and the clinging of swords was once more heard.

"My king, this is a great honor. I have not even been here yet a day. I have told to you all about me. What is it that we are preparing for? What is it that I am to lead the men to do? I must know if I am to lead them."

"Sit with me here."

Terrence joined the king upon the ground.

Chapter 18

"Terrence," King Daron began, "ye have lived for over a year in and around the dark forest, have ye not?"

"I have, my king."

"Ye may bear witness to the evil creatures that indeed inhabit this place."

"Yes, my king. They are the vilest of creatures. I loathe every last one of them."

"But ye have not seen Dromreign, have ye?"

"No, my king, I have not. Yet, among my companions at the time were those who have witnessed the dragon themselves. And, as I have said before, I have witnessed a village laid waste by it only hours after it departed. No other creature could have done the type of destruction that I saw. Dromreign is no creature of fiction, my king. I have seen enough to know of its existence and of its destructive and vial nature."

"Legend has it that this ferocious dragon has been around, in one form or another, since the beginning of time. At least as far back as we have legends and history."

"In one form or another?" asked Terrence.

"Yes. The earliest legend speaks of him as like a man, when all the living creatures were aligned. He was described as superior in many aspects—a little bigger, stronger, intellectually keen, extraordinarily influential, loved, adored, perhaps feared, but highly respected."

"A man?"

"Well, perhaps not a man, but like a man; in the form of a man at least. It is said that he has always had the heart of a dragon.

"The time had come to choose a leader; one who would lead all living creatures. Many suspected, including Dromreign himself, that he would be selected as the leader. When the day came and the selected leader was named, it was not he. It is said that his entire countenance changed and that the anger in his eyes caused them to glow red with that anger, malice, and vengeance.

"He was not the only one who was angry. When it was clear that he was not in support of the leader, or the majority, many others stood by his side. Though those who stood with him were only half as numerous as those who did not, still his pride brought him to think that he could triumph over the others. A great battle ensued. Though they were fewer in number, Dromreign and his legions were strong and battled fiercely. They did not, however, prevail. They were forced to retreat and they retreated towards the great mountains to the region now known as the dark forest. To this day they continue to dwell there."

Terrence looked at the king ironically. "But..."

"This is but the earliest legend, Terrence. There are many further legends to tell.

"The first great battle was over and the people had won, but the war still rages on. There have been many battles since. It is said that Dromreign and his forces primarily attacked at night. The legends speak of him and his followers eating the flesh and drinking the blood of those who they conquered. This taste for human blood and his hatred to all of humankind caused many changes. The legends speak of them being more powerful at night—in the darkness. Later legends speak of Dromreign as a vampire, literally drinking the blood of living humans during the night. They speak of the mark of fangs in the victim's carotid artery with their bodies drained of blood. It is around this time that they speak of him transforming into a bat at night and flying. This is when he is first spoken of as a flying creature. Many of the other men that were with him were said to transform into wolves at night. So they battled as men during the day but as a bat and as wolves at night. Others were said to have become serpents—both day and night.

"As the history and legends progress we stop hearing of men at all. But, day and night, the forest crawls with anacondas and wolves, and the flying bat had grown to the size of a small dragon. In these legends, the dragon is only a little larger than a man and can only consume one man or woman at a time. Stories, like these, from even centuries ago are not so unfamiliar from what we experience now. They speak of Dromreign leaving his lair at night and attacking small groups of nomads, and occasionally attacking a small village. The wolves and the snakes staying in the forest region for the most part.

"Even in my younger years, though the dragon was feared and horror stories were told of his conquests and destructions, he was not as powerful as he is now. He did not take out entire towns and cities as he does now. But in my lifetime, and over the most recent years, he has grown in greater strength and power. At one time, all the people were united against this great beast. With time, the people separated out into various groups. But we were still united, at least in so far as we were against him. We helped each other, we traded with each other; we were always one against this beast.

"Now, the people have divided apart from each other. We are no longer unified but are at odds with each other. Some, especially those in Cardsten, would even worship this wicked beast. They, though human, would align themselves with him and attack those who are at enmity with the beast. As the people divide and lose their unity, so does the beast grown in strength and power. We, the humans, seem to be helping this dragon. He begins to win the war and not just the occasional battle. Humans now are aligning with him in the destruction of their fellowman. And still he grows in strength, power, and ferocity. He is becoming bolder, too. He sets out more in the day, or returns after the cloak of darkness has passed. He attacks larger and stronger peoples with great success. He comes closer to the great cities of Cardsten and Agedon than in decades' past. While all this happens, the people become weaker, disunified, and apathetic—even sympathetic to the beast."

"This, I have seen firsthand in Cardsten," said Terrence.

"Yes, and this is why ye are here with us. Ye are not to be united with that filthy beast. Ye would rather die ridding the world of Dromreign than live protecting him."

"This is true, my king. A question remains, my king, from these legends that you have told."

"What is it?"

"Why, after all these millennia, do Dromreign and his ilk stay in the dark forest, except for hunts? Why did they not spread out and build cities and do as humans do?"

"Terrence, they left the human race long ago. They are the sworn enemy of the humans and will stop at nothing in order to destroy human kind. It is total and complete destruction that they are after. I suppose that they prefer the darkness to the light. The forest and the mountainous lair provide this for them. But, legend provides still another answer to your question.

"Perhaps ye have heard the legends of the promise land?"

Terrence chuckled. "Yes, king, of this great land beyond the mountains I have heard. A land with no wicked creatures; where people live safely and peaceably and fear nothing. I have heard these legends spoken of since childhood. But, I have lived in and around the dark forest. I have never seen an entrance to such a land. I think that this is nothing more than a children's fable."

"Aw. Well, at least let me answer ye're question by referencing this legend."

"Of course, my king."

"It is said that there is such a land and that the entrance is difficult to obtain. That one must shed nearly everything in order to enter. That one must be healthy and strong in order to enter. It is said that it takes preparation to enter, and that when one goes in that they leave the world behind.

"If such a land does exist, and if it is impenetrable by Dromreign and his forces, then it would truly be a promise land. This land would also foil all of Dromreign's plans. For he wants to destroy mankind fully and completely. But, if in this land, all the people are beyond his grasp, then he would fail. Some say that they do not stay in the dark forest for their own comfort and protection, but rather to guard the entrance to the promise land. That as long as they keep the people from entering therein, that they can eventually overpower the human race. I cannot verify all that I have told to ye this day, but this much I can confirm. Dromreign and his beasts are growing such that they may be able to destroy the people of this world."

"My king, do you believe all of these legends?"

The king smiled as he looked upon Terrence. "Terrence, these ancient legends contain truth. I cannot speak to the literal accuracy of every fact therein. This much I do know: there is a great evil in this world. And I, Daron Drake, king of Agedon do take it upon myself to rid the world of it.

"Terrence, I ask you to lead my forces against this hideous and terrible beast, the dragon Dromreign. Though it has lived for millennia, and grows stronger and more powerful rather than feeble with age and time, I do not believe it to be immortal, to be indestructible, to be able to withstand a powerful force against it. I believe we can prevail against it; it has lost battles before. If we defeat it for good, then our whole world would be the promise land."

"My king, I intend to do just that."

"That is as I have hoped."

"May I ask some questions, in regards to tactics and strategy?"

"By all means."

"Are we to go to it, to the dark forest, or are we preparing for when the dragon comes to us?"

"Terrence, we prepare for an attack on us daily. We have always prepared for this possibility. But I hope to meet the dragon on its turf before it ever attempts to come to ours."

"But, my king, the dragon is not on foot, at least not upon the ground. It is said to live mid-way up the mountain, in a lair unreachable by humans. Are we to attempt to climb to its lair?"

"I agree with you, Terrence. We will not catch him in his lair. But perhaps we can fight him on his turf, within the dark forest, without him traveling to Agedon. When a large contingent of humans invades his forest, it is hard to image the dragon not coming in for the attack. He will smell the human flesh and will savor the taste. Dromreign will come to us as we go to him."

"Now, this armor that I have seen today, is this for protection against the dragon?"

"Terrence, this battle has been considered for many years. We have consulted everyone we could consult, including the military of Cardsten some years ago. This armor may help us to get to the battle with Dromreign. We think that it will protect us from the serpents and wolves. It will also protect us, if it becomes necessary, from the arrows and swords of Cardsten. There will be no great battle with the filthy beast unless we can make it through these obstacles."

"Yes, my king, I see the wisdom in this. But, I fear that this means of getting to the beast may prove our weakness for the battle with the dragon itself. The flames that emanate from it are of such consuming force that, though the armor may provide brief shield and protection from the heat and power, ultimately the armor will heat to such a degree that the men will literally fry therein. The hot metal would increase the speed of their destruction. In addition to this concern, what of our fighting ability? Would we not be slower and weaker? Can we wield a sword, or throw a spear, or fire an arrow when we are so weighed down by such armor? Would not our march be exhausting such that when we make it to the great battle we are but weakened and easy prey for the dragon? Would we not be quickly and utterly destroyed as soon as the battle begins?

"My king, I have lived within the dark forest and have battled the wolves. They are fierce and lives may be lost to them. But, it is not beyond our abilities to be trained to not only survive, but to fight and prevail against the wolves and the serpents of the forest."

The king considered thoughtfully for a few moments. "Yea, Terrence these concerns have all been considered. But ye must also consider that ye were but a small number of able young men within the forest. Ye were not there to attack the wolves nor the dragon. Ye were not making any attempt to enter upon the promise land. Ye were there for ye're own protection alone. To find food and shelter and clothing. Ye stayed at the edge and did not show a sign of attack. Ye fought bravely and defended yerselves well. Still, we would be marching in number to the heart of the forest—towards Dromreign himself. We would attract the full furry of the beasts throughout the land. It would be a full battle. Though the men may be able to kill a number of wolves, yet we would lose a great many also and possibly lose the battle before even awakening the beast. Even if we did prevail, how many of our forces would be in battle condition when the dragon arrived. Though the armor may not be able to stop the consuming fire, are our bare skins really any better? Would not our flesh be consumed in the flame as easily as it would be scorched within the armor. What ye say is true, yet I think that the armor would prove useful.

"Terrence, it will not be long before the armor is ready. The men will learn to battle therein. They will be conditioned for the weight and the heat. They will grow stronger under the force of opposition. When we march, we will be ready to march. We will learn to throw the spear, to wield the sword, to fire an arrow with these protecting suits of armor. At the very least we may surprise or confuse the beast. The dragon may not immediately recognize the armored men as human. He will see that they have penetrated his forces unharmed. Even a brief hesitation on his part could open up the path. Dromreign, though powerful, cunning, and strong, is but the most selfish and proudest of creatures. The dragon may see harm to himself and that may prove his undoing. I speak hopefully, you understand. I do not discredit your valuable concerns. But Terrence, we will lead an armored battalion of warriors to defeat the monster and bring peace to our world."

"My king, it shall be as you have spoken. I am satisfied as to your wisdom and your preparation. My concerns have not abated, but it would not be possible to undertake this course in any way without much to be concerned about. With this understanding I do hereby join you and the army of Agedon in the quest to destroy Dromreign and bring peace back to the earth. I thank you again my king for your trust and understanding. Let us prevail!"

Chapter 19

"Tira," called one of the women attending to her. "We have a surprise for ye!" The sounds and the voices indicated pleasure and delight from the other room. Tira arose to join them.

It had been a full week since Tira had arrived and last seen Terrence. She had been given assurances as to his wellbeing and that he was leading the Agedon military. It was both for the sake of her full recovery and to allow Terrence to stay focused that she was told that they were to be kept apart. While certainly feasible, and equally bought into by both Terrence and Tira, this was not the reason that they were kept apart.

"She's coming," whispered one of the women. Tira heard her and smiled.

Tira was indeed back to full strength. Since the day of her procedure she had progressed comfortably and nicely. She had been moved from the hall that she had first stayed to a beautiful home. No longer were monk-like bald men, in cream gowns, her caregivers. No, she was looked after by a group of women from the ages of fourteen to forty. Tira was treated as a celebrity by all of the women. She assumed that it was because of Terrence's position in the military that she had been given such exquisite care and kindness. Again, she was not entirely correct. The reality was that Tira was strikingly beautiful. It may be true that in relation to the women with whom Tira associated within Cardsten that she was the least of the beauties. However, on the whole, Tira was among the most beautiful women in the world. Cardsten stood out, and indeed was well known for the beauty of their women. Tira, being among the top tier of those in Cardsten, was a sight nearly unimaginable to the people of Agedon. In fact, never had a portrait, a sculpture, or even the imagination of the people, compared to the actual beauty who was before them. Agedon, for all of its attributes, beauty was not among them. The people were good and kind, friendly and genuine, and generally as homely as could be.

Terrence, for his part, was equally as striking compared to the men. But the men were much more impressed with his combat skills. The women of Agedon, well, they were impressed all around. The men of Agedon had not had a look at Tira, other than the medical monks, and the men in the king's brigade. Tira being at her worst during this time had not fully impressed, just yet.

So, Terrence and Tira were adored by all that knew them. There was both beauty and majesty about them. They were both celebrities within their circles and were destined to remain as such.

"Close ye eyes," they whispered. "Grab her arm, and bring her this way. Okay, open ye eyes!"

Tira opened her eyes and beheld the most beautiful white wedding dress she could imagine. Each of the five women beamed as they moved their glance from the dress to Tira and back again.

"Oh, my! Is it mine? For my wedding?"

The women just laughed and cheered and then Tira hugged each of them lovingly. They all just stared at her with stars in their eyes, imagining how a beauty such as her could be made even more beautiful through adornment.

"May I..."

"Yes, do, please try it on!"

Tira, who had become used to being cared for by these women allowed two of them to remove her clothing while the other three made ready the dress. In no time it was done up. The fit was perfection and there was not a dry eye amongst the women. Tira looked around for a mirror.

"Let us do ye hair," said one.

"And make-up," said another.

"I'll fetch a flower for her hairdo," said a third.

Another fetched a stool and soon Tira was being completely done up. Hair, make-up, and adornments had been done daily since she had arrived and each day enthusiastically, but never quite like today. An hour and a half passed and each of the women pronounced their blessing upon their accomplishment. Tira was taken to a full body mirror. Tira blushed with joy.

It is true that in Cardsten she had been lavishly attired and attended to throughout her life. But she was always joined by Mirinda, or later Tasha and Myrtle. In comparison, something was always lacking. Though she was pronounced beautiful, she had always been looked past by others as they looked upon the four women. As she gazed at herself in the mirror, the reflections of the other women, good, kind, and loving as they were, provided such a stark contrast in beauty, with their simple attires and unmade-up homely faces, that Tira thought that she was more beautiful than ever. Her thoughts turned to Terrence.

"This is not ye're only surprise," said a woman of about forty.

"Oh." Tira thought of Terrence and that perhaps he would be just outside awaiting her. Her heart began to beat faster. *Perhaps*, she thought, *the wedding will take place presently!*

"Wait here." Four of the women left, leaving Tira with a girl of sixteen. The girl stood there glowing and then grabbed Tira's hand and held it.

After a few minutes passed Tira turned to the girl, "you can't tell me, can you?" The girl blushed and shook her head smiling with delight.

Ten minutes passed and Tira's heart continued to beat hard and fast. The downstairs door to the outside opened and she heard the sound of the women returning. A man's voice was also there, but it was not that of Terrence's. The group entered the room and a short man of fifty, with short grey hair and a goatee, entered the room. He had on a dark suit with a cravat. He looked at Tira's face and then looked her up and down.

"My dear," he said softly. He took her hand and kissed it. "You are as beautiful...no, more beautiful than imaginable. I am Victor Crown, and am at your service." He bowed gracefully towards Tira.

Each of the women smiled and some bounced a little with delight. Tira looked at the man and then at each of the joyful faces around the room. Whatever the surprise was, she was still in the dark.

"M' lady, may I have the great honor of capturing your personage?"

"What?" said Tira with a dreadful look on her face.

"He wants to paint ye portrait," said a woman of about twenty-eight.

"No!" said Tira, horrified and directed towards the woman.

Victor stepped back and the look on everyone's faces was changed instantly.

"My dear," began Victor unsure how he would finish the statement. "My...dear, I would cause ye no discomfort at all. We may do the portrait sitting, inside or outside. Ye will be as comfortable as can be. It does not have to be now...or today even."

"I'm sorry," Tira began. "I can't...I...do...not...like my portrait made. I never...I just cannot. I'm sorry, I don't mean to offend you," and looking around. "or any of you." Every face in the room was crestfallen.

The excitement and anticipation that she had felt, followed by the horror of the surprise, evoked tortuous emotions from within. She began to sob. She tried to stifle the cry and it only forced it out with greater urgency.

"My dear, I am so sorry to have distur..." Tira ran from the room to where she had sat upon the stool to be made up. "Go to her, I shall escort myself out." The women looked at him, horrified themselves. "Go!" he commanded, betraying the emotion he felt inside. And he left the room abruptly.

The women looked at each other and then slowly walked into the room to join Tira.

"I'm so sorry..." sob, sob, sob.

The love that the women had for her overcame their frustration. They each patted her lovingly and offered, "Shh," and "now dear," as they tried to console her.

"But what shall ye give to your betrothed?" asked the girl who had held her hand.

"What?" sob, sob, sob.

Tira was handed a handkerchief that was sorely needed.

The sixteen-year-old girl was shushed.

"I don't understand. I...I just can't sit for a portrait. They always turn out so horrible. They can't paint me. No one can paint me. I never want another portrait painted of me."

"My dear, not Victor Crown. He is a master. It is a great honor to have a portrait done by him. The king commissioned it himself. Victor would capture yer beauty entirely."

Tira shook her head vigorously. "No one can. I've tried. Everyone has tried. I always look so...horrid!"

The women looked at each other, stunned.

"What did she mean, give to Terrence? I want to see Terrence. I am better, where is he? Let me see Terrence."

"Ye can't."

"Why?" sob, sob, sob.

"Ye are betrothed. Ye can't see yer betrothed. Ye must have a gift for yer betrothed and ye have nothing to give. Ye can't give a gift from another, ye have to give a gift from just yerself."

"But the portrait would be drawn by Victor, and paid for by the king. It wouldn't be from me?"

"My dear, it is not so. Ye are not giving yer betrothed the canvas, paint, and time paid for by the king. Nor are ye giving to Terrence the paint strokes and expertise provided for by Victor Crown. Ye are giving to Terrence an image of yer beauty; and that can only be given by yerself. The king's, and the artist's part are but small and minor. It is the part ye play, yer extraordinary beauty that ye provide to yer betrothed."

Sob, sob, sob, sob, sob. "That's just it. They never capture my beauty. I look ugly in portraits and I just can't..."

⌘⌘⌘

The servant approached the king and Daron Drake removed his helmet. The king shook his head and threw his helmet, shield, and sword upon the ground. "Where is Terrence?" he yelled.

Terrence removed his helmet and shouted back, "Here, king."

The two joined up and then walked off the practice field away from the earshot of the others.

"Terrence, can ye talk some since into Tira?"

"Tira? What's wrong with Tira? Is she okay?"

The king looked at Terrence with a very serious and annoyed expression. Terrence looked like he had just seen a ghost. After a moment, the king broke into a laugh.

"There's nothing wrong with Tira; nothing that any man could understand."

"Huh?"

"Look, Terrence, ye're not supposed to see yer betrothed until she's all dolled up and ye're wedding her."

"What? why?"

"It's just how it is, here in Agedon. I can't have ye and yer betrothed frolicking around together before ye're married. Everyone would be ashamed, and it would make a scene. I know it's done differently elsewhere, but that's how it is here and I can't make it different just for ye and she."

"Okay..."

"But, ye got to speak with her before ye're wed."

"Oh. What's the matter?"

"She's got to give ye a gift, to wed ye. And ye, being refugees, ye know what I mean, didn't really come with much, ye see. So, she, being so pretty and all, I figured that a portrait of her all dolled up would give ye a forever picture of her in her prime; forever an image of her beauty for ye to look at, even when ye're old and, eh hum, not so beautiful anymore."

"Oh, that sounds nice. So what's wrong?"

"Who knows?"

Terrence looked at him funny.

"She practically threw our best portraitist out of her home. He's never been so offended in his life. Touchy, those artist types are anyway. I'm not sure I can pay him enough to try again. But she's unmovable. She won't budge. No portrait of her will she allow to be made."

"Why?"

"She's yer betrothed. How should I know? So, if I sneak ye a visit with her, will ye talk some sense into her, eh?

Terrence didn't answer. There was a lot bothering him before the conversation and even more bothering him then. He couldn't see Tira until they wed, that was news to him. He'd been lied to thus far. Was she feeling better? When were they to wed? The king expected him to battle every moment of the day, there was no time. The men, they were horrible at battle. Things weren't going well at the first, but here, in full battle armor, they were useless. They couldn't move, they couldn't fight, they could hardly lift their feet and arms. The king was undeterred. All practice was to be done in full armor. Terrence couldn't even see the men's faces to know who needed the most help and the most work. Worst of all, Terrence couldn't fight any better in the armor than the other men. If the king wanted an equalizer, he had found it. Terrence had wanted to discuss with the king the idea of letting them practice for half the day out of the armor.

At this point, with the new revelations about Tira, Agedon culture, his wedding, every other concern was just a jumbled soup in his mind.

"Well, what do ye say?"

"My king, I have uprooted Tira from her people; I have taken her from her home, I have removed everything from her that she had previously enjoyed, and now you are asking me to tell her that she must do something else that she doesn't want to do. I have not even seen her in health since we left Cardsten. I am to see her to tell her to do something that she doesn't want to do? I fear the consequences of such action."

"Very good, my boy, ye shall have a long and happy life together! But this doesn't solve the problem ye see."

"Perhaps I could see her first just to see how she is. I may have a greater power of persuasion were she to feel loved and cared for, and not controlled."

"Yes, Terrence, ye are a negotiator. But see, I am not even to allow ye to be together. Once is trouble enough for me. See what ye can do, my boy!" He slapped Terrence's' armor on the back and made an awful clanging sound. "Let's get out of the armor and see what we can do."

⌘⌘⌘

"Oh Tira, how are you, my dear?"

"Terrence," she said, and moved towards him. She was sitting on her bed with her feet up and had soft tears running down her cheeks.

"I am told that you are well, but I fear that this is not true. You are still hurting?"

Tira shook her head and stood up to embrace him. Her soft tears turned to soft sobs as they tenderly embraced for a long while.

"Oh, Terrence, I have missed you so much."

"Tira, please tell me how you feel?"

"I am better, perhaps a little tender at times, but getting stronger every day. Really, I am nearly at full strength."

"Oh, I am happy. But why do you look so pale and so distraught?"

"I was told that we could not see each other until the moment of our wedding. But I see that this is not true, for here you are."

"Yes, the king has made...an exception."

"I fear that it is because I am distraught—because I do not cooperate and am upset that he has sent you here. The king has told you of my refusal?"

"He has."

"Then you know why I am upset. I am told that we cannot wed until I am able to provide a gift worthy of you. The only solution that I have been given is to allow a portrait to be made of me. But, I will not do it! I will not, Terrence. I loathe every portrait that has ever been painted of me before. No artist has ever pleased me. My parents either never hung the portraits or they put them in the least conspicuous places, while they admired the portraits of every other girl. It is bitterness to me. Tell me, Terrence, am I beautiful enough for you?"

"Yes, without question, my love."

"They tell me that my beauty is the gift that I am to give to you. Am I not giving this to you as we wed? I am happy to give everything to you. But, I think that you will think me less beautiful once you see how the artist would portray me. You would see me in a lesser light. If you hung it in our home it would annoy you and bother you. You would look away from it until you could not stand it anymore and then you would stare at it for hours. You would then come to think that I am as the artist portrays and you would think me ugly and hideous. You would regret having ever known me. You would think, this is how I look. 'When I see her in person she deceives me with her smile and her expression, but she is really very ugly.' This is what would happen. I want you to see me only with your eyes and never through the eyes of an artist—a stranger, who looks at me with no compassion, but as a specimen only.

"Artists find the flaws and they accentuate it. They scrunch their nose and they struggle. They grunt as they paint me. They ask me to smile differently, to change my expression; 'perhaps if you sit, no standing would be better—hold yourself this way, no that way. Let us change the attire, it is the wrong color, the wrong cut, it is out of fashion, it is too fashionable. Let us move it out of doors to let there be more light; no, indoors it is too bright, we must subdue the light. The scenery is all wrong, let us change that.' There must be something that can be done to make me less hideous. But no, they give up and then paint with a scowl. And then apologetically they present their portrait and take their pay and get as far away as they can, as quickly as possible. You see, Terrence, I have sat for portraits before and I can never do it again!"

Terrence smiled unconsciously. Tira looked at him with anger. "You exaggerate, my dear," he said playfully.

"Perhaps we shall not wed," she said in exasperation and turned away from him. "If I must sit for a portrait to wed you then we may never see each other again."

"Tira..."

"I will not, Terrence!"

"May I..." she turned towards him after some pause, "offer a simple solution?"

"What?"

"May I ask first, is it the sitting for the portrait that is most horrific, or is it my seeing the finished work?"

"Both."

"Yes, but which is worse?"

"It is you ever seeing it, even for a moment. I could endure the anguish of the artist struggling to paint me. But, I could never endure you laying eyes upon it. Never."

"Well, then my solution would work."

"How so?"

"I'm afraid that it would require you to sit for the portrait and I dare say that I am not telling you that you must. But, if you would be willing to go thus far, then I would be willing to keep myself from ever beholding it."

"But, it must be a gift. It will be unveiled and presented to you. I am sure that everyone will be around and will watch you as you gaze upon it. They will look for your expression; they will listen to your words as you lay praise upon it. This gift is no trifling thing here. You will look upon it, and even if you burn it thereafter, you will have seen me as I never want you to."

"True, my dear Tira, I believe that you are right. But, I still offer the same solution. You sit for it, but I never look at it."

"You are confusing me."

"Have you never defocused your eyes such that you appear to look at something, yet it is unclear? I have even gone so far as to defocus my eyes while another looked upon me and asked if there was any change in the expression on my eyes. I was told no. I have listened to an individual and when the conversation wearied me, blurred the individuals face in order to be distanced from it. The individual never knew that I was keeping them out of focus. I will simply defocus my eyes while the portrait is unveiled. I will fain my approbation and complement you, and the artist, and the king. I will have my speech ahead of time prepared. To you and to all else I will appear to be gazing and admiring. But, in reality I will see a blurry rectangular color only. I will see nothing of the image of you there upon. Of course, you will have to trust me."

Tira looked at him, yet distantly.

"You are looking at me out of focus, are you not?"

Tira laughed. "Yes. But see, you could tell. They will all know."

"No, you are out of practice. You were trying too hard. I am very practiced and will not be known. Do you trust me to do it as I have said?"

Tira paused.

"When they were healing you, you lay uncovered before me. Though I love you, and look forward to seeing you as such when we wed, and even though because of your delirium, caused by pain, you may have never known if I did look, I did not. I never allowed my eyes to gaze upon you as I will after we are wed. You trusted me then. I assure you, this will be a thousand times easier than that was then."

Tira came to him and embraced him. They kissed for some time. Such a feeling of love and attraction overcame Tira that she was ready to do as was required. She could wait no longer for them to be together—to be wed.

"I shall sit for it. And I will blur my eyes so that I can imagine that I am doing anything but this horrid thing."

"I am sorry to have to ask. Since you have known me, and in order for us to be together, you have had to change or give-up everything that you have ever known. I do not intend for our marriage to be about you doing or being something other than you are."

"There is truth in what you say. Yet, I have never been manipulated by you. I have chosen freely with a full knowledge always. It was not what you said that convinced me, but rather your kiss. For that kiss and how you make me feel, I would sit for a thousand portraits. I love you, Terrence. I want to wed and to be with you. It is worth what little sacrifice has been necessary for me to be with you!"

⌘⌘⌘

Another long and dreadfully painful ten days passed for Terrence. He had not been allowed to see Tira, though he petitioned the king unceasingly. The battling had hardly improved and the king was unmoved in his willingness to remove the armor.

"If they must battle the beasts and the dragon with it on, then they must learn to use it. They must strengthen themselves." The king himself wore the armor and knew of how hot, heavy, slow, and inflexible it made him. Yet, he believed that he and everyone else could learn to master it.

Terrence was informed, only the night before, that the next day was to be his wedding. He would be given his wedding day and the two following, to be with his companion. Then it was back to the field of battle. That evening he was fitted in another suit, not of armor, but of fine material. He looked in the mirror and felt proud.

It reminded him of how Daxton had looked at his feast, the evening when they had left Agedon. Terrence thought about his cousin and wondered if he was married yet. What about Aiden, had he been married. He felt bad that he had deserted his friends, though not regretful. He wished that Daxton could stand by his side, in place of Marcus, to comfort him in this celebratory hour. He suspected that somewhere Tira was also being fitted in her dress and was missing her family and Mirinda. There was something melancholy in being wed amidst strangers only.

The next day, at the appointed hour, the sun stood directly overhead. Terrence entered the outdoor arena where the feast, festival, and wedding were to take place. He was pleased to see that he was not amidst strangers. It is true that the women were unfamiliar to him. But he was no stranger to the men. The king and the warriors smiled, and congratulated, and cheered him on. He had been fully accepted and was loved by the people. He loved them, too. It did not take away all of the emptiness he felt from his family not being there, but it took enough away. The women, though strange to him, could not take their eyes from off of him. He had seen this look before, though it was always directed towards Aiden in the past. Well, for the moment he was a bachelor, he might as well soak it in.

He was brought before the veiled portrait. The artist and king stood on either side. He had not seen Tira yet, and wondered where she would be when her gift was given.

Jack came up to Terrence carrying a large cloth. "Are ye ready to see her?" he whispered to him and laughed jovially. "I must blindfold ye now."

"Blindfold?"

"Yes, it is she that shall remove it."

Terrence bent down slightly and Jack blindfolded him. He stood in the dark for a few minutes. He knew when Tira had entered the premises. A noise went about him. The women chattered and the men intemperately unleashed their praises. Terrence reddened a bit. He did not mind the women gazing upon him. Yet, he did not appreciate his men gazing upon Tira as they did then, while he, blindfolded, could not behold her.

In a moment, he sensed her presence near him and then felt her hands about his face, feeling for the knot of the cloth. Terrence smiled and bent forward. She removed the blindfold and he gazed upon her. She was radiant. No earthly beauty had ever penetrated to him as she did then. She smiled with a tender blush and allowed him to look her over. Her dress was a magnificent white, she glowed as though light radiated from within her. Her eyes, those marvelous eyes, were more tender and beautiful than ever. He wanted to take her in his arms and embrace her and kiss her tenderly but did not know the protocol.

Tira took his hand and led him closer to the veiled portrait.

"I take you to receive my gift," she said formally and squeezed his hand.

In the squeeze, Terrence felt the significance. She seemed to say, 'I have done my part in sitting for this dreadful portrait, now you do yours and blur your eyes so that you see nothing of it. Let us get through this hateful necessity so that we can enjoy each other fully, forever after.'

Terrence squeezed her hand back and could see that she smiled.

Victor Crown smiled proudly, standing by the veiled portraits' side as did King Daron Drake. Terrence nodded and smiled at the king and then bowed to the artist, who returned his bow. Terrence felt tension in Tira's grip as the portrait began to be unveiled. Terrence blurred his eyes as the cloth began to be removed such that he would have no appreciation of the portrait itself.

When the cloth was removed, a gasp could be heard throughout the arena. Tira's grip loosened and then she let go. She put her hands to her face and gasped. He could hear her breathing heavily and then she began to cry.

"It is so beautiful," said Terrence deceitfully.

"Terrence," said Tira, overcome. "Terrence, look at it! I mean really look at it." Then turning to Victor, "Oh, it is so beautiful. How did you do it?" Then turning back to Terrence, "Look at how beautiful it is. We shall hang it where all can see."

Terrence did not think that this was an act, but he felt uncomfortable breaking the promise that he had made to her.

"Oh, king Drake, thank you for this marvelous gift. My congratulations to the artist and to your exquisite skills."

"Terrence, look at it! Focus on it! See what he has done with my portrait!"

Terrence obeyed, hoping that he was doing the right thing. Tears began to well up in his eyes. He whipped them away hurriedly. But he had never seen anything so beautiful, other than Tira herself, in his life. The artist had captured her in her wedding gown with all the radiance that she possessed in person. Her face was that of an angel, and somehow he had even captured the majesty of her eyes.

"Oh," said he, "no verbal praise could bring this justice. You have, in truth, presented me with the gift of her beauty. I shall never forget how she looks this day."

Terrence embraced Tira and moved in for the kiss.

"Wait!" said the king. "We must wed thee first."

The crowd laughed and the king began the ceremony. Upon completion, the couple kissed and the crowd rejoiced. In Agedon it was as though they had witnessed the union of angels.

Chapter 20

"Show them in," said Mr. Cards who was seated in his office with Daxton.

Two men entered wearing hoods with their heads bowed. Neither Daxton nor Mr. Cards got up from their seats. The two men stopped behind the desk standing and waited upon further orders. Cards assistant shut the door leaving the four men alone. The men removed their hoods showing their shaved heads and dragon tattoos.

"Well..." said Mr. Cards.

"Sir," said the one on Cards left. "They've defected to Agedon."

"Of this you are certain?"

"Yes...Sir."

"And Agedon accepts them...as citizens? Or as a bargaining chip of sorts?"

"As citizens...Sir."

"And you're certain that they are responsible for...the deaths?

"Sir...there can be no question as to their motives, now. And...there are witnesses."

"Reliable, these witnesses?"

"Yes...Sir."

"Very well." Mr. Cards reached for a leathern bag that was bulging with metallic currency. He dropped it on the table offhandedly. "Thank you, we'll be in touch," he said, not looking at them. The man on the left took the bag as both put on their hoods and left without another word.

"Satisfied?"

Daxton paused for a moment. "I don't trust them. Why do we fund them?"

"They fulfill a purpose, as you know. Their actions can be ascertained—they are predictable."

"I don't like them."

"There is no need to like them; you have no reason to like them. Nobody likes them. They've never lied to me nor shown ulterior motives. They are what they are, nothing more and nothing less."

"Well..."

"Now, your friend and our new General, Aiden...some question his loyalty on this account. Not everyone thinks that he did all within his power to catch these two before they got to Agedon."

"Of course he didn't. If Aiden wanted to catch Terrence he'd have had him in no time. Terrence is good, but he's no match for Aiden."

"So, I hear. But, it looks suspicious. If I hear of him being questioned, then you and perhaps I will be questioned, too."

"You will not be questioned. No one would question your loyalty. As to me..."

"You are with me. We cannot be questioned, and so we will not be."

"When you told me to ask Aiden to lead his troop in search for him, neither he nor I ever thought you intended for him to find Terrance."

"Quite so. But did he do enough? Wandering the walls with his men for half a day. Why would anyone leave to just hang around the outer wall of Cardsten?"

"It was as we understood that you wanted it."

"Yes."

"If he'd led his troops toward Agedon, it would have been a provocation. We do not want a provocation, we want to keep them at bay with our military powers, not battle them directly."

"Yes, but our motives cannot be questioned."

"It was not his technique; I do not believe. If we had sent another General and he had done the same, then it would be left unquestioned. It is because of his association with Terrence that it is questioned, nothing more," said Daxton.

"Perhaps..."

"And it was for this purpose that we sent Aiden, in the first place. It was an opportunity to prove his loyalty to Cardsten."

"Yes, and that is just it. His loyalty was not proven, and now, at least by some, it is questioned."

"Could it be otherwise, no matter his skill and value to the city? He is a new arrival. There will always be those questions, by some."

"Yes, but I would have liked it to go better."

"So would I."

"You know that you will never see Terrence again, don't you?"

"I do."

"He and Tira can never return."

"I know."

"This must weigh heavily upon you."

"Yes, it does."

"Let Aiden know."

"Know what?"

"That Terrence is in Agedon...and that his loyalty is questioned in some circles. He will have to be even more...perfect."

"Daxton, it's good to sees ye my friend, it is!"

"How've you been, Jashion?"

"Great. Ye got word on Terrence?"

"Yeah, where's Aiden?"

"He'll be along, soon."

"Daxton," said Aiden entering the back of the tent.

Daxton turned and stood.

"They said that you needed to see me."

"Yes, Cards sent me."

"Well?"

"Terrence and Tira are in Agedon, they've defected." Aiden nodded. "Some talk is going around that you let them escape, that your loyalties are not entirely with Cardsten."

Aiden nodded again and sat down next to Jashion. Daxton sat again across the table from his friends.

"And?"

"That's it, that's the message. You've got to be more careful."

"Cards sent you, risking improprieties, just to state the obvious?

"No big deal. We're friends; I can come and go as I please without arousing suspicions. There's no impropriety in me being here."

"You can't just come, ask for me, deliver a message and take off then. You'll have to stay for lunch. Mirinda's coming."

"Now you're talking. What're you going to do then?"

"Lead my men. What are you going to do? Grow your business?"

"Exactly. Are the men giving you any trouble?"

"Of course not," said Jashion. "They love their general, they do. They'd do anything for Aiden, they would."

"Daxton," said Aiden after some pause. "The people are always on the lookout for someone else, someone better than they have. Whatever you have is never as good as it could be.

They know what they have and they're looking for something that they don't have. What's on the inside is never good enough—they want something on the outside. The funny thing is that when someone or something from the outside comes along that is better than they have, they embrace it quickly and with enthusiasm. It is, after all, what they have been looking for. It's a gift; it's providence. Then, once placed on the inside they feel suspicious—vulnerable. They feel as though it should not be on the inside because it is from the outside, it is foreign—alien. How can you ever trust anything that is not a part of you, that is outside of you? Now, what you had before is—was—preferable and superior. What you have now is dangerous. But it's on the inside and they put it there. They can't just say, 'never mind,' that would show all of their vulnerabilities and insecurities. So, they must watch and look for the mistake, for the moment so they can bring out all of the rage and extricate it—me, with full internal and superficial justification. This is the place that we are in, and have been since receiving our positions and commissions. It has always been a matter of time, and that time was short with Terrence's quick and messy departure," said Aiden.

"I'm under Cards, still, and will be for some time. Cards is as inside as it gets. Maybe, at some future time I will face this scrutiny. But you...you are under no one militarily. You, as always, face the world face forward and with your chest bare. You are, and have always been, your own protection. So, should I let Cards know that you want out?"

"Out? What are you talking about?"

"Haven't had enough fun yet? Seen what you came here to see?

"What about you? Have you seen enough, yet?"

"I'm not here to see Cardsten. I'm here; I'm a part of this place, it is a part of me. I'm home, I'm marrying Tasha and taking my place amongst the elite here. I'm not here to see, I'm here to become."

"Very well," said Aiden. "But you misunderstand me. I am not here to *see* the place, either. As if you can look in from the outside and have any knowledge—any understanding. I never go anywhere to just see it; I am here to become, too. I only see, truly see, if I become. There is much that I am seeing, but it is only because I am becoming.

"Terrence did not want to see this place any longer because he would not become a part of it. What you reject, you do not want to see."

"What of Tengeer? You and Jashion came and saw for such a short while and when you had seen enough you left. You never became of Tengeer."

"On the contrary, my friend. I came to Tengeer precisely to become of Tengeer. I did not possess the knowledge of Tengeer sufficiently in order to heal Jashion. I came and became one with the healing arts of Tengeer. This has served me well, and always will. Tengeer has been with me ever since that time. You, and your cousins have been with me upon leaving. I will always be a part of Tengeer, as I am a part of my home land. This will never leave me. Becoming of Cardsten is not so simple. Cardsten dwarfs my past homes in sophistication, in intricacy, in power, in knowledge, and in many other ways. One does not simply go to and become a part of Cardsten and then move on to bigger and better things. Perhaps it will take a lifetime to fully become of Cardsten."

"Now that's music to my ear," said Mirinda entering the tent dressed to the nines for a lunch date with the general. "Daxton, what a pleasure. How is Tasha?"

"Wonderful!" he said rising and smiling.

They all shifted seats so that Mirinda sat by Aiden and Jashion and Daxton sat across.

"We haven't had a good night on the town since the day you arrived," said Mirinda. "It's been eventful since you've all been here, to be sure. We need to go out and relax and enjoy some time together. Daxton, are you and Tasha available tomorrow night?"

"Yes, I believe so. I think that sounds grand."

"Jashion, don't you drop your eyes and pretend that you're not here. You can come, too."

"Nay, but I'd be in the way with ye couples, I would."

"Nonsense. But you could bring someone, if you'd prefer."

"Nay. I've no one to bring."

"Is that so, lieutenant? I've heard enough whispers about you to know that you'd have the pick of the city."

Jashion reddened and dropped his eyes while shaking his head. Mirinda's eyes did not move from him.

"Jashion," he looked up slowly and Mirinda waited for eye contact. "Myrtle's available."

Then he really reddened. "Nay."

"What do you mean, 'nay.' She is available, and she'd enjoy it too. She's tried to be nice to you since that first night. You've hardly had a word to say to her. You're always stiff around her, but then when she's away I see your eyes—I've seen you stare. Why don't you ask her to come? I know she would."

"Nay, but I'll relax at home. Ye all go out and enjoy the night. I'll stay home."

"Jashion, we want you with us. And we want Myrtle there too. There is more to Myrtle than you know. I know that she hurt you that night, but she didn't mean to. Don't you want to give her another chance?"

"Nay."

"Don't you like her?"

"Aye, I like her fine. But I don't want to go out with her."

"But, Jashion, don't you think that Myrtle is pretty?"

"Aye, Myrtle is very pretty."

"Well..."

"Well, what?"

"She's pretty, you've said so yourself. She likes you. Are you just shy?"

"Nay, me isn't too shy, me isn't. I just don't want to go out with Myrtle."

"'I just don't want to,' isn't a reason. It doesn't mean anything. She's pretty, she's attractive to you, and she's attracted to you. 'I just don't want to,' isn't fair—it isn't right. If a girl is pretty and she likes you, you don't just ignore her."

"Aye, she's pretty but I don't see what that has to do with anything. What if she was homely? Then it wouldn't matter if I ignored her or not?"

"Well..."

"Well, what?"

"Well, it's not the same, now is it?"

"Her feelings matter more if she's pretty, than if she isn't?"

"No, it's not about her feelings. I suppose a homely girl has feelings just like a beautiful one. But it's still not the same. A homely girl and a pretty girl aren't the same. The pretty girl possesses a power, an attribute, a value that the homely girl does not. They aren't the same. Beauty is real, it matters. Beauty leaves an impact; it makes the world a better place. A girl who is possessed of it, possesses something meaningful and of great value."

"Aye, it matters, it does. Everyone appreciates a beautiful woman, they do. And ye are very beautiful, Mirinda, ye is. And Myrtle, she is too. But, as I've been told, it's really the beauty inside that matters, now isn't it?"

"Of course that matters, Jashion. No one questions that, do they? But, the word 'beauty,' is metaphorical when we speak of inner beauty. There are clearly many attributes that a person may possess and most of them have little to do with appearance. Each is important, is real, and is of great worth. But, beauty, true beauty isn't an inward possession, but instead, is a physical attribute—it is outward. Beauty requires vision to perceive. Other qualities may bring out wonderful, perhaps even similar feelings, but if it isn't outward and visually perceived, then they are merely metaphorically beautiful. Maybe we just don't have the right words to describe them. But they are not actually beauty.

Jashion, beauty matters. It is its own quality; it is what so many other qualities are compared to because of its exquisiteness—its power. If Myrtle is pretty—a great possessor of beauty—then she contains a great deal of worth just for that attribute alone. You can't just ignore that and pretend that it is somehow inconsequential when the whole world responds to it and knows that it is vastly important. Because it is so clear, so easy to perceive, so incontrovertible, some people want to devalue it by calling it superficial. So, don't pretend that the obvious somehow doesn't exist—really exist. You can't compare so many things metaphorically to something that isn't real."

"Aye, its true what ye says, Mirinda. Still, isn't beauty in the eye of the beholder?"

"Is it? Really?"

"So, I've heard, hasn't ye?"

"Jashion, is that your experience; you who has seen so much of this world? Do some think Aiden is extraordinarily handsome and beautiful, and others not? Have you met a man, or a woman for that matter, that would look at Tasha, Myrtle, and I and not think us beautiful?"

"Nay."

"Beauty is not in the eyes of the beholder. Beauty is as real as any attribute could be. You confuse degrees of beauty. Not everyone is equally possessed of beauty. Some are more beautiful than others. What differs from person to person is where they draw the line. Some girls may be considered beautiful by some and not so by others. She possesses beauty, to be sure, but she may not possess much—or she may have distracting features that take too much away. To one man she possesses enough, and the distractions are not such that they take too much away; he says that she is beautiful. To another, her beauty is not sufficient, or her distractions are too distracting from her beauty. To him she is not beautiful. Those who are in the middle may be variously assessed by everyone. This is no counter to the reality of beauty. This simply explains that not everyone judges the sufficiency of beauty the same. Do you think that you and Tasha would judge the sufficiency of an amount of money the same? I suspect that a sum of money that would seem very large and sufficient to you would be judged as small and insufficient by Tasha. The amount is easily ascertainable by everyone, and there is no disagreement, but the quality of that quantity could be variously perceived by everyone differently. The same amount of money would have different meanings for different people just as the same degree of beauty would be judged qualitatively differently by everyone. Still, a great beauty is seen as a great beauty by all just as a great fortune is seen as a great fortune by all."

"You're making an effective, yet awkward comparison between those two, Mirinda," said Aiden. "Comparing a qualitative value to a quantitative value is difficult."

"Fair. But, it gets the point across. Degree and amount aren't exactly the same, but qualities that are judged by degrees are ultimately considered in a similar vein to quantities that are judged by amounts. Are they really so different, at least in regards to making judgments?"

Aiden smiled. Mirinda wasn't finished.

"Jashion, have I convinced you? A girl, possessed with the gift of great beauty should not be ignored."

"Aye, she certainly will not be. But isn't that just it? Beauty is a gift, it is. Does a pretty girl deserve to be treated better because of a gift which she does possess?"

"Jashion," said Aiden. "Every attribute, every quality that a person possesses is part gift and part earned. Those with high intelligence have both been given it and have worked for it. It can't be entirely earned nor entirely given. Physical skills, great personality, political power, financial acumen, and even beauty require both parts. Would you begrudge anyone what they are gifted with? Would you begrudge anyone for that which they earned? It is without question that Mirinda, and her friends, Myrtle and Tasha, have been gifted with great beauty. Still, I suspect that to be as beautiful as they are, they spend much effort each day on their physical appearance."

"You have no idea," said Mirinda. "Myrtle has earned her beauty to be sure. She works so hard, lately just to impress you. She knows that she hurt you. She wants you to look at her as you first did. Not just sneaking looks from her, but look at her and let her see you do it. What do you say, Jashion?"

"Alright, I'll ask her out. It can't hurt, can it?"

"Good man, Jashion," said Daxton. "That'll make Tasha's day!"

Chapter 21

The early cool spring had slowly transformed into a warmer mid-spring; blossoms began to fall on the tree lined streets as green shoots dominated the tree color making a sickly green and pink palate on the trees. Daxton had his own quarters at the Cards residence where he was preparing for the evening. Tasha, Mirinda, and Myrtle were all making ready in the main residence of the Cards mansion. Aiden and Jashion had cleaned up after their days drills and then put on fresh uniforms before heading to the Cards. Evening wear did not require the military attire, yet the alternatives were so much less appealing to both Jashion and Aiden; the women loved the uniforms.

Jashion walked with a spring in his step. Being a third wheel had been extraordinarily tiresome. Myrtle had been pleasant when he approached her the night before, putting her hand up and stifling a giggle only when Jashion first began to speak. When she had controlled her silliness, a significant effort on her part, she had a presence about her. She gazed into Jashion's eyes searching, he thought, to see if he had been compelled or was genuinely hoping for her company. Jashion wasn't sure what she saw in his eyes for he didn't know the answer himself, at the time. But those blue eyes, full lips, and pretty face had haunted his previous night and this full day. If she gazed into his eyes this evening she would see that he was fully in earnest.

Arriving at the Cards was always breathtaking. Size and luxuriousness only introduced the impression; the hustle and purpose of the servants was unmistakable. How so many people could have so much to do and with such urgency stood out. Those who worked for Cards, worked; if they were on, then they were on. Still, they were pleasant and professional, and immediately attentive to the men as they arrived, showing forth all appropriate deference to the men in uniform. It contrasted wildly to the indifferent and nearly invisible servants at Mirinda's.

Daxton and Mr. Cards entered after some time, Daxton's attention riveted in Cards' instruction. Aiden and Jashion arose as the men walked towards them.

"Yes, I'll see to it," said Daxton

"Gentlemen," said Cards, extending his hand to Aiden and then, after nodding magnanimously to Jashion, he exited.

A servant made eye contact with Daxton, as Daxton nodded. The servant made his way upstairs towards the main living area. A quarter of an hour later the lady's voices began to echo from the upstairs landing and the gentlemen stood, Aiden and Jashion erect in nearly military stance with Daxton more casual, yet still confident. Tasha rummaged through Daxton's hair and messed with his collar, for she already owned him, after receiving her kiss and complements. Mirinda and Myrtle primed their own hair and twisted and turned effortlessly to enhance their own appearance and to show both their confidence and interest in the men next to them. Jashion dared a kiss on Myrtle's cheek which she accepted with genuine pleasure.

Only Myrtle couldn't understand why their destination wasn't, 'The Dragon's Lair,' having the best food and being the most popular. She alone had been back, several times, and had long forgotten the events of her own embarrassment. Tasha was

Dane Bagley

in the mood for more elegant, even quieter dining. 'The State Room,' was a bit stiff and boring for Myrtle's taste.

"We'll look like kids there," Myrtle said in gentle protest. "I think grey hair is required for the gentlemen."

The others ignored her prattle but Jashion suggested that they could consider other places.

"No, silly, that's where Tasha wants to go," said Myrtle. "I'm just scolding her, that's all."

Tasha smiled.

Silly, that brought back memories—and feeling. Jashion looked at her. Myrtle turned and smiled, then noticing that it was not a glance but that Jashion continued to gaze.

"What?" she said.

Jashion smiled. "Nay, I'm jus' happy to be with ye, me is." Myrtle smiled, but only kindly. She turned her head forward and perfume from her hair wafted to Jashion. It was sweet and tangy and Jashion was enchanted.

The food was wonderful; the place was elegant; and it was stiff, boring, and way too old for the couples. Overall, they had a marvelous time. Myrtle drank too much, but not so much as before. Afterwards, they walked as couples in the pleasant night air. It was a thin mooned night, the street lamps providing the bulk of illumination.

Mirinda and Aiden held back the farthest, hand in hand.

"They seem happy. She's trying hard and Jashion has come around. Let's leave them be, I want to talk with you," Mirinda said.

Aiden continued along for a street or two and then led Mirinda towards a park with benches.

"I'm happy, Aiden. I feel complete with you. My only sorrow is losing Tira. But, perhaps she and Terrence can find happiness in their own way." She stopped and searched his dark eyes in the darkness, switching back and forth between the left and right eye. "Are you happy, my love?"

Of course, there was no answer for some time, but she thought she saw him gleam.

"I am happy, Mirinda."

She smiled and gazed expectantly, hoping that he might say more. He did not. But, she leaned her head on his shoulder and chest and he embraced her warmly. Aiden's eyes watched the starry sky overhead. The evening was pleasant and his companionship was perfect. Aiden was happy. The word on his mind was, 'complete.' She had said that she felt complete. Aiden felt content, he felt full, but did he feel complete? Was that what was required to propose to Mirinda? Did she require his completeness? Did she complete him? Was not happiness and contentment sufficient? Did he have to be complete?

The night was dark and quiet. The park was empty. Aiden looked down at the dark-haired beauty in his arms. She, unlike any woman he had ever held before, did not seem vulnerable and in need of his exquisite protection and power. He completed her, perhaps, but not because of any lacking on her part. She was the complete and perfect woman, nothing lacking. The completion was not of her but of something beyond her, beyond any individual; no matter how powerful, there is a completeness that requires another. In this way, he could complete her, and she could complete him, perhaps.

But that was the difference—she was complete and full in and of herself. Nothing was lacking, except what only another could fill. But Aiden did not yet feel complete; Mirinda filled everything that another could fill for him, but Aiden wasn't complete yet, in and of himself. There was still a hunger and a drive that no woman could fulfill, even the perfect woman. Did this have to be satisfied first? Was his own completion required before they could be intertwined together?

This great man continued to look at this great woman. She knew that he gazed at her and she loved the attention, yet she looked out and made no effort at eye contact. Aiden's arms wrapped around Mirinda's. She was as free and as liberated a woman as could possibly be, and in this state she had sought out first a man's companionship, and then this man's companionship. She had nuzzled up to him with the great hope that he would wrap his arms around her and hold her—binding, if only for the moment, him to her and her to him. But more than that, for his arms encircled her; liberty sacrificed freely—knowingly, and hopefully—expectantly, that a bond might be formed—a bond more desirable than liberty. *Is being bound better than being free?*

Some excited and distant voices broke the silence. Mirinda sat up and looked at Aiden. Aiden listened attentively.

"Something isn't right. Let's go." He grabbed her hand and walked as quickly as her high heels would allow her. Fiery arrows were seen leaving the top of the wall. Jashion and Daxton were running quickly toward them.

"It's been spotted. Dromreign is without the city walls," said Daxton. Myrtle and Tasha made their way up behind them, fear in their eyes. More excitement began to fill the air. Arrows continued to light up the sky.

"Daxton, escort the ladies home, to Cards. Stay with them and protect them, no matter what. Jashion come with me."

"I've no weapon." Jashion threw Daxton his sword.

Aiden and Jashion made their way to the gate of the city. "Hurry," said Aiden.

They exited the city and followed the trail of fiery arrows. "I see nothing," said Aiden, surveying the air.

"Nay, but I smell the foulness, I do. It's faint, but I smell it."

"Yes, you're right. Come on." They ran further, watching the sky. A faint shadow crossed the sky. The beast was returning. Aiden and Jashion watched as Dromreign flew near the city wall sailing upwards. The beast climbed to three quarters of the height of the wall, and Aiden feared that Dromreign may overtake it. The fiery darts seeming to have no impact on the dragon.

"We must hide," said Jashion.

Aiden crouched down low to the ground. He wore black and was nearly invisible. His companion, in bright red was more apparent. The dragon's focus was on the wall of the city and was not looking for stragglers without the wall.

"Let's go now!"

They ran toward the gate and entered therein. Fear and pandemonium met them as they entered. Still, the dragon had not overtaken the wall. Aiden and Jashion made their way to the top of the wall and took their archers gear.

"General, it's flown the circumference of the city but it couldn't reach the height of the wall. It has turned and left. I think that it will not be back."

"Keep watch," said Aiden.

Aiden and Jashion walked the walls and gathered reports. The dragon was gone and did not return. The remainder of the night was pleasant and peaceful except for the anxiety and rapidly pounding hearts of the people of Cardsten.

Daxton arrived in the early dawn, in the capacity of the messenger of Cards.

"How're the women?"

"Nervous. Exhausted."

Aiden nodded.

"Did you see it?"

"Yes."

"So, they weren't just spooked."

"No, it was here."

"To attack?"

"I suspect, if it could. The wall was too tall. Not by much, I'm afraid."

"So, we're safe. The wall worked. Cardsten is impenetrable."

"So it appears...for now."

Below a crowd gathered. The stealth and silent enforcers were in force—fifty plus men with shaved heads and dragon tattoos. The people gathered around to listen. Aiden, Jashion, and Daxton made their way down the wall to see the happenings.

"Do not fear...fellow citizens of Cardsten. Our great master has visited his city...this has been prophesied and was expected. There is nothing to be afraid of. He has no interest in causing us harm. We are his and he is ours. We are one with the great dragon. He was here because of the recent atrocities which have been committed by villainous traitors. It angers him that the blood of his worshipers has been shed. He comes to show his solidarity with us and his anger towards those who would stand against him. Let there be no mistake, we must not let those who would attempt an attack on him be allowed to do so. They must be stopped at all cost. He protects us at great cost to himself and we must show our willingness to protect him, as though he could need or require that."

The people nodded and some shouted their ascent.

"I ask you, was there one citizen of our great city who was hurt or killed during this visit? Did the dragon unleash any of his fiery breath towards us or even our great wall? It was a visit; there was no attack on us. This is a great day, and should be forever celebrated. Our union is complete. Now, in union we must attack our great enemy and the only creatures who could disrupt the great peace of our land: the fools of Agedon!"

Great shouts roared with this battle cry. Men put their fists in the air and the women nodded feverishly. Daxton and Jashion looked at Aiden to see if he would counter the madness that surrounded them. Aiden watched and listened unaffected. Soon the message repeated as more people came to the opening near the city gate, and the tattooed men broke into smaller groups to shout their message to all of Cardsten.

"Daxton, you must let Cards know all that has been spoken."

"Yes, of course. But what are we to do?"

"We need to know the current state of Agedon. It is critical that this is found out quickly."

"Shall we go?" asked Jashion.

"No, we must attend to our posts, Jashion. We must be on high alert, if we are called upon to go to war. Daxton, some of these dragon worshipers will easily be commissioned to go. They want the information as much as anyone."

"Would you attack Agedon? Would you attack Terrence?" said Daxton

"I will prepare my armies to go, and will leave as soon as it becomes necessary. A continuous flow of reports will be needed to know how best to respond. Tell Cards. Go!"

The fiery-red, unslept eyes of Daxton glared at Aiden incredulously. In his exhausted fog, Daxton left and delivered his report as Aiden had asked.

"Hmmm," said Cards. "This is disturbing. He's right, though."

Cards called an attendant and whispered instructions to him. The man left quickly to fulfill the orders.

"Daxton, we can't have them acting independently as they did today. They need to know who is calling the shots. By getting them out of the city in large numbers, and under my commission as spy's, it will set in order the appropriate powers. I appreciate Aiden's insight. I think he is loyal to us."

Chapter 22

Sarah and John lay in the meadow looking up at the blue sky and the pillowing white clouds meandering effortless and lazily. The silence had lasted a long time, though it flew by. Sarah could have laid there much longer just absorbed in the moment, its beauty and peace, her mind clear and calm. John's mind was active and he slowly became restless. He did not, however, know how to begin. He turned to Sarah and looked at her pretty—truly pretty—face. She had blossomed over the previous year and a half. She was pretty. Some was via effort, Maryanne had taught her well; she was fit, she took good care of her hair, her complexion, her make-up. Most, was just nature's way of expressing the value of patience. She was growing into a natural beauty. On the outside, she was as John had first seen her on the inside. He appreciated her external beauty, never surprised as it blossomed.

Sarah turned toward his face and smiled, then turned back to her sky and clouds.

"Sarah, it won't be long until the fall...when you turn eighteen."

Sarah nodded, still looking at the sky.

"We've been planning our marriage...our wedding, that is, for such a long time."

Sarah turned and gazed in his eyes.

"We've..."

Sarah waited patiently.

"...never...really made plans."

"For our wedding?"

"No, for after that."

"Plans?"

"Yes."

"Oh, where we should live, and such."

"Well, yes, and such."

"I want to live near my waterfall, at least so near that I can walk comfortably back and forth and spend some time there in a day. It'll be close to my family, but we don't have to live right by them. Just near the waterfall."

"So, that is ultimately where you want to be?"

"Yes, I've mentioned this before. You know how I love it there, so..."

"I do Sarah. I'll build there."

"Sarah, would you consider some other places before we ultimately settle?"

Sarah narrowed her eyes and looked at John searchingly.

"I'm feeling a little restless, Sarah."

"John, I know. I don't mind you going and doing. Didn't you enjoy your trip to the far end falls with Kevin."

"Of course, I've told you all about it. I don't want or need to get away from you. I'm not interested in space, from you. I want to spend every moment with you. I enjoyed the falls and being with Kevin, but I longed for you. I can't be away from you, but I need to be away from here...sometimes...for a little while. I thought that we could live elsewhere, for a time. Have some space, an adventure, a little freedom, make our own way in the world. We'd come back, settle down, live near the falls, raise a family and have everything we've both talked about. I'd just like something different, for a while."

Sarah looked at him, her eyes dancing back and forth between his one eye and the other. Her peace and calm had been disturbed and her mind raced.

"We're young, Sarah. We've nothing holding us down; no children, no responsibilities. If we settle down now, we'll never know anything else. I can see our life, from beginning to end. I can see it in the lives of everyone around us. I know it, and you know it. It's here before us. It's good, and I want to share it with you. I will share it with you. But maybe we could share something else, first. Try something different and then when we are ready for a family, come back and pick up where we left off and have the good life that we both want, ultimately."

"John, people settle these parts because the land is richest here. The crops grow, the livestock thrives and there is support and community around. Are you talking about settling out by far end falls?"

"I don't know, maybe. I don't have a plan; I want to make a plan with you. Far end falls could be nice. Or closer in, where we could make a settlement that would make it easier for people to travel. Maybe the settlements on this land would stretched farther. The land may not be barren; it may just not have been worked. That might be interesting, I don't know. I don't know what I want, exactly. I've just got an itch that I need to scratch. I don't want to be apart from you, I just don't want to be here, for a while."

"Okay."

"Yeah?"

"Sure. We've got some months to figure things out. I'm okay with trying something. I'm not afraid. I'll be with you. If it can be done, you can do it. You are the strongest, most capable man in the world. I trust you, and I would help. I want our life so much. I'll just have to get used to thinking about it. Thinking about what we could do and where we could go. It seems...kind of exciting."

John smiled and then they kissed for some time.

"Sarah tells me that you two are going on an adventure," said Maryanne.

"An adventure?" said Kevin. "When are you doing that? Where are you going?"

"It's not really an adventure. We're just going to live away from here, for a while," said Sarah. "I guess, it's an adventure of sorts. We'll try something different before we come back here and settle down. John wants to try something and he should get to. I'm excited to do something different."

"How're your parents taking it?" said Maryanne.

"Mom's good."

"And your dad?"

"Mom's good."

"I see," said Maryanne.

"John, we've been all over these parts. I'm not sure there is an adventure in the promise land, unless you consider trying to grow corn in rocky soil an adventure. If you're just trying to get away from Maryanne here, you could just tell her to scram."

Maryanne took a lemon peel on the rim of her glass of lemonade and threw it at Kevin. Kevin swatted it away, looking pleased with the reaction he got.

"How's Megan?" asked Sarah.

"Ah, Megan, what a magnificent firework she was. One minute she lit up my world with a bang, with the richest and brightest colors, then she was gone, without leaving a trace. Nice memories, though."

"You've already broken up with her?" ask Maryanne.

"Well..."

"I believe this time it went the other way," said John.

"You win some, you lose some," said Kevin unaffected. "And what about the gorgeous Maryanne? Who do you have wrapped around your finger?"

"I'm not sure you've earned the right to ask me such personal questions."

"Alright, I'll just ask John later."

This time she threw a piece of ice and hit him in the chest.

"I want to go for a walk—down by the falls," said Sarah, looking at John.

Maryanne took the hint. "I need to get home."

"If you promise to stop throwing things, I'd be happy to escort you," said Kevin.

Maryanne rolled her eyes playfully. "Will you promise to be a gentleman?" The four got up from their lawn chairs. "Have fun," Maryanne said to Sarah and John.

Kevin offered Maryanne his arm trying to look as gentlemanly as possible. Maryanne screwed her eyes and looked at him without moving.

"Are you playing hard to get?" he asked.

"Yes, and I'm not playing." With that she took his arm and they walked away.

⌘⌘⌘

"Kevin, and Maryanne, *together*?" said Sarah.

"We do stuff with them all the time."

"Yes, but they are not *together*."

"I didn't say that they were dating. I said they're going on *a date*, with us."

"I know, but Maryanne..."

"You don't want her going out with Kevin? I thought you liked Kevin?"

"I do, but...it's okay. It's just a date. But see, Maryanne...isn't fickle. The way Kevin treats a girl...the kind of girls that go for Kevin...I just don't see Maryanne...like that.

She's not in it for the moment, she want's something deeper, you know, lasting."

"Maybe."

"What do you mean, *maybe*?"

"You've seen how she's been flirting with him lately."

"That's just Maryanne, she even acts like that with you...with me right there. She's just fun, and comfortable around guys."

"So she's a flirt...but not Kevin's type?"

"She's not *a flirt*."

"Oh? What then?"

"Maryanne is...a beautiful woman. A beautiful, confident...womanly woman. She's attractive, you known that. That's what she is. She's not putting on a show...or trying to get something. She's comfortable with guys and she likes guys. They like her. She'll always be this way, even when she's married. She's not flirting...she's not a flirt. She's Maryanne, and the way she is, is very attractive."

"Fair enough. But hasn't she been more confident, more womanly with Kevin lately?"

"I don't know."

"Well, that's true. We don't really know even what's in our best friend's heads. Maybe she does like him, and maybe she does want to just test it to see where it goes. In some ways Kevin isn't much of a threat. If it doesn't go well, or she doesn't like him, there's not much worry about breaking up with him. The only thing a girl has to fear with him is falling in love and then losing him."

"Well, that's something."

"So, should we warn every girl to stay away from him?"

"No."

"Just Maryanne?"

"Well..."

"I think Maryanne has a good head on her shoulders. She knows Kevin well enough. She knows the risk."

"What happens then?" she asked.

"What do you mean?"

"Well, suppose they do date for a bit, and then break up. It will be weird. We won't be able to hang out with all of us together anymore. He's your best man and she's my bridesmaid. That could be awkward."

"Alright. I'll tell them to call off the date. They can both come but it can't be a date. She can be beautiful, confident, and womanly to him, but no more. If after the wedding, after we've moved away—gone on our adventure—they still want to try this thing out, then they're welcome to, but not while it might mess stuff up for us."

"John..."

"Okay, I'm being a little severe. I'm sorry, Sarah."

"I know you're right. I'm don't want to tell them what to do. I don't want to be selfish, but I'm concerned."

"I know. I get it. I'm surprised too."

"Why?"

"I'm surprised that Kevin would be interested in Maryanne."

"What do you mean, she's beautiful."

"Well, I get that. But she is not likely to make things easy for him. She's not just going to be his girlfriend and kiss him and then go away without any fuss. Kevin doesn't tend to go for girls that are going to take some work, and patience."

"That's what I've been saying."

"Have you?"

"Hush, they're here," said Sarah.

Maryanne held Kevin's arm as they walked up the path. John basted the chicken that was dripping on the spit.

"Ah, smells good, my man," said Kevin, and gave John a quick man hug.

Sarah took Maryanne by the hands and looked in her eyes. Maryanne just smiled coyly. They all sat down and watched the fire awkwardly for a few moments. The chicken was soon ready and John carved it up expertly.

"Perfect night for a long walk," said Kevin.

"I agree," said John.

Sarah looked at Maryanne and Maryanne nodded.

The evening was calm and comfortable and the four set off after eating. Sarah and John led the way, giving each couple some comfortable distance for conversation.

"John, if you are really thinking about far end falls, we'll need some horses. I don't want to be without transportation. What if something happens or we just want to make a visit? How will we make a house out there? It'll take some work to get the lumber and other supplies. I'm getting excited about our adventure but I don't really see how we're going to do it. Maybe we should stay here for a while and take trips out there. It may take a while to get something built, but, really, that could be part of our adventure. We don't have to just head out there and start from scratch, do we?"

"Sarah, why do you think that I want to build a house out by far end falls?"

"I thought that was what you wanted...we wanted."

"I want an adventure, Sarah. I guess that's an idea. I don't know, it sounds more like a lot more work than an adventure. I do want to try something new, something different. I really don't know just what, though. Is that what you want?"

"Well, if that's what you want. We could just live on the outskirts of our people. I don't see how that would be much of an adventure for you, though. It would be about the same as here, just with different people—away from our families and friends. I didn't think that you just wanted to get away from the people we love."

"No, you're right. I don't know what I want—not exactly what I want. I do know one thing for sure. I want to be with you. I don't want to be apart. You are my world, Sarah. I love you and I want to be with you every moment."

Sarah held his arm tighter and leaned her head on his arm. He felt dreamy to her.

As the later evening approached the couples separated and Kevin took Maryanne home. He'd been a gentleman as he promised and was very proud of himself. Maryanne was spectacular and seemed to be enjoying herself thoroughly in his company. The timing was perfect and he leaned in for the kiss. Maryanne backed away.

"Uh-uh," said Maryanne.

"So, that's it?"

"What's it?"

"I haven't even lit the firework and it's already out."

"Excuse me, I'm not a firework, I'm not a toy."

"Sorry, I thought you...we we're having a nice time."

"I had a very nice time with you, Kevin," she said with a sweet smile.

"But, it's over."

"What's over?"

"Us...this...you're done with me."

"Crazy guy, how can it be over, it hasn't even started. I'm not going to let you kiss me. That doesn't mean I didn't have a nice time. We can go out again, if you want to. I had a nice time with you, Kevin. But going out and having a nice time doesn't mean you've earned my kiss."

"How do I *earn* your kiss?" he said, somewhat sarcastically.

"Oh, Kevin, have you never earned a kiss? All those kisses, all those girls, and everyone's been stolen? You won't steal a kiss from me, but I'll give you a chance to earn one."

"I feel like you're playing games with me."

"Games? I've had fun tonight, and I'm having fun right now. But, I'm not playing a game with you. Just because you're having a nice time doesn't mean it's a game. I like you, Kevin; I hope you ask me out again sometime. Goodnight." Maryanne walked into her home waving as she shut the door.

Kevin walked home feeling very empty—and yet very full. Something, however, was unfulfilled and he couldn't just let it be. Maryanne stayed on his mind.

Maryanne agreed to another date and Kevin began to feel something in his heart that he had never felt before. He liked it, sort of. This time they went alone. They had a wonderful time and Maryanne seemed very relaxed in his company. Kevin felt very attracted to her. He took her home and at the appropriate time leaned in for the kiss. This time Maryanne did not back away. She held her ground. But she lifted up her hand to her face and Kevin kissed her fingertips. Kevin opened his eyes and looked at her.

"That was sweet," she said and then gave him a warm embrace. Maryanne knew how to embrace. Kevin felt very nice after that.

Kevin asked Maryanne out again. This time they went with John and Sarah.

"Are you two dating," asked John, seeing that they walked holding hands.

"Um..." said Kevin.

Maryanne smiled. "This is our third date together. Kevin is being the perfect gentleman."

"Really?" said John. Sarah punched John in the arm. Maryanne smiled.

When they were separated enough to talk privately, Kevin asked, "When will I be able to kiss you?"

"You'll just know," she said softly.

"I thought that I knew before, but I didn't."

"Have you learned anything?"

"Um..."

"I'm really enjoying your companionship. You should give yourself more credit. Besides, a girl doesn't like to be asked, '*when can I kiss you?*' She wants him to figure out that *she* wants to be kissed, and kiss her then. The man leads, but it's merely an illusion that he's in charge. The man leads and the woman's in charge—that is the natural order of things. When the woman wants to be kissed, then the man kisses her. When the woman wants to marry him, then he proposes."

"I see," he said, sarcastically.

"Kevin, whether anything happens with us or not, I'm doing you a favor. I'm teaching you the most important lesson in this world between men and women. Whether it's me or another woman, this is how it works. If the man tries to lead in a way counter to the woman's feelings, then things will go very badly. If the woman wants things and the man doesn't see, doesn't understand, or simply ignores, then things go badly. The great secret is to observe the woman who is giving you signals and communication all of the time. When she signals, and then the man leads, there is a beautiful harmony between them."

"So, the man really is tied around her finger. He does what she wants and doesn't think for himself, doesn't really lead, doesn't actually have any power."

"No, that isn't true at all. The man has great power, and is empowered even further by the woman. The woman watches and sees. She sees all of his signals and communications. She isn't selfish and controlling. She wants harmony; she wants a powerful man; she wants him to lead. So, she observes him and learns his desires. With time, she makes them her own, or gently helps to shape his. Then, when they are her own she lets him know, and if he is watching carefully he then verbalizes them, and she happily follows in his leadership. It is very beautiful."

"It sounds complicated."

"It is. And very simple. When I want you to kiss me, you kiss me. You'll know."

"I want to kiss you right now," he said.

"Yes, I know. But that's not when you kiss me. Watch me, you'll know."

"You two coming," said John.

"Leave 'em be," said Sarah. "They seem to be having an important talk."

"Got it. Sarah, we need to talk, too."

"Okay, what's on your mind?"

"Our plan."

"You seemed frustrated the last time we talked about our plan. I've been waiting until you were ready to talk about it."

"I know. Thank you, Sarah. You have been so completely understanding in my indecision and my allusiveness. I appreciate it."

"I love you, John. We'll be together always and we will have to be there for each other during each of our struggles. Someday it may be me who is trying to figure things out. I'm sure that you will give me the same respect and help."

"I will, Sarah. I'm going to give you everything you have ever wanted or ever will want. I need this, so that I can give that to you."

"I understand."

"Well, you've been very understanding but I haven't really been clear with you. I haven't really explained myself to you."

"Okay."

"Kevin explained it the other day. There isn't really any place here to go that would provide what I need. I don't need to take you away from our settlement and away from our family and friends. I don't need or want some kind of isolation or some kind of a domestic challenge. Far end falls is the farthest place that we could go in the promise land but it's nowhere near far enough. I can't stay here, in the promise land anymore. Sarah, I have to leave. I feel so confined and so restricted. I like it here, I really do. But there is a wide world out there and I need to get out there. I need to see it and experience it. It's been on my mind for so long. I know how you feel about that and how happy and satisfied you are here. I wish that I could be as happy and satisfied here as you are. I've been racking my brain trying to figure out how I could satisfy my feeling and stay here with you. I know that I can't. I have to leave this place—not forever—for a time. Once we've seen it, experienced it, then we'll return. We'll settle in, raise our family and enjoy everything just as we've talked. But I can't just stay here forever. I've got to leave, at least for a little while."

Sarah was stunned. She uttered not a word.

"Sarah, I love you. I have no interest in leaving you. Not for a moment. I want you to come with me. Will you? Will you come with me, away from the promise land, for a little while?"

"John," she said as her eyes welled up and thick heavy drops began to fall.

"Oh, Sarah, I didn't know how to explain it."

John tried to embrace her but she backed away.

"You've explained yourself fine. I'm not upset by *how* you said it. It's *what* you said. John, you want to leave our promise land. This place is a gift to us. It's a gift from our parents, grandparents, and on back. They achieved this land so that we could live and prosper in peace, and safety, and protection. Look at what we have. You want to leave so that you can see the evil, the hatred, the destruction. You may die. You may never be able to return to settle down, to have children of your own that would enjoy all that this land has to offer. And what of your children, of our children? Would we just let them go to explore as they see fit? 'Sure, leave this land of safety and peace; that's fine, we did it. Go explore and have your adventure, we'll be here whenever you want to return.' Is that the message we'd give them and to everyone else here? 'Come and go as you please, it doesn't make any difference?' Oh, John," she said and buried her face in her hands.

"Sarah, I know how you feel. I've always known how you feel. I've tried so hard to talk myself out of this. I've tried a thousand times. I wish that I could just make it go away and never enter my mind again. But Sarah, it won't leave. I couldn't marry you and then be miserable, or eventually leave you so that I could experience it later. I want to go with you. I don't want to leave you. We'll go together, for a short time. I will protect you. I was not born with this strength, and these powers, to just sit here in peace and silence. I was born to do, and here I have done all that I can."

"What about us, John? Raising a family is no trifling matter. We can serve others and build a better place, *here*. I do not aim to hold you back. I want you to do, and to be all that you can. We've not even started our journey yet. You may likely throw all that away; and here it is, right in front of you."

"Sarah, I understand how you feel. I expected you to be upset. Let's leave this subject tonight. I have made no final decision and I've had months to consider this, while I'm asking you to join me after only hearing of it for a few moments. No, we'll leave this be, for now. I feel better simply clearing my mind. It has weighed on me, Sarah, for so long. I cannot be deceptive with you. I don't want you to *not* know what is in my mind and heart. I love you and have no desire to hurt you. But, if you love me, you must know who it is that you love. This is me. I am a man who desires to leave the promise land *with his wife* and explore the wide world. I want to ultimately settle right here with you and raise a family. But I can't do that, yet. I want to marry you, now, and settle here with you, later."

"Take me home, John."

⌘⌘⌘

"Are you serious? Whoa," said Kevin.

"She won't come. I thought that with some time she'd come around—at least consider it. Instead, she's becoming more and more adamant and angry about it."

"John, what's it been, two weeks? Giving a girl time, is a lot more than giving her a couple of weeks. You've still got months until the wedding. Change the subject, talk about the wedding. Build her house by the falls. It'll still bounce around in her mind and once she knows that you'll give her what she wants, maybe she'll reconsider. She just feels vulnerable, like she's never going to get what she wants. Help her know and then she may change her mind."

"I don't know. I don't think so. It's hurting our relationship. Sometimes she looks at me like I'm a foreigner, she's so distant with me."

"Well, what do you want?"

"What do you mean?"

"Do you want Sarah, or an adventure?"

"Both."

"Yeah, but if you can't have both, what do you want?"

"Kevin, I want both. I want Sarah more than anything in this world. But, I can't have her and live happily with her, unless I do this. If I don't leave, I have neither."

"Man, I'm sorry. I feel like it's all my fault. I've been putting these ideas about leaving in your head ever since we were kids. I always thought that it would be fun, but that I'd never be able to talk you into it. Now, you've got everything you've ever wanted and your about to risk it, for this."

"Kevin, this is me. It's not you, it's me. I want this. Some of what you've said has made a lot of sense to me. But I've thought through it, and I'm going."

"And what about Sarah?"

"I'll ask her again. I really want her to come with me. But, I don't think she will."

"So, you're going to marry her and then leave her?"

"No, no, no. I'm going first. Then, I'll return with a full knowledge of things. If it's dangerous, like she thinks, I'll just marry her, settle down, and have a family. I'll be preaching what she believes in, with a full knowledge. Everyone will know that it is a dangerous world and how valuable our protection is here. But, if it isn't. If it is a wonderful place and a great place to settle. Then I'll come with that message. If she loves me and I want to settle there, then maybe she'll come. If she really still won't, then I'll settle here with her. I'm going to have both. I will not stay here forever. But I will return and I will be with her."

"So, when are you going?"

"Soon, as soon as you're ready."

"What? Me? What are you talking about?"

"You're coming with me, man. We've been talking about this for years. If Sarah won't come, and I'm sure she won't, we'll go together. I don't want to go alone. I want to go with you, if Sarah won't come. We'll have the greatest adventure of all time. We'll see everything for ourselves and will no longer have to live wondering what is on the other side."

"I don't know, John. It sounds good, but..."

"Well."

"Maryanne and I have been..."

"Maryanne? I'm talking about leaving Sarah. What do you care about Maryanne? She's just your girl for now. We'll wait until you break up and then we'll go. I don't care if we wait a week or two, or even a month."

"Dude, watch it. Maryanne's special. You know that. She's not some girl, she's a great girl. I'm not planning on breaking up with her."

"She's the one? You've been going out for three weeks and she's the one."

"I don't know that for sure, but maybe. Besides, you knew Sarah was the one in seconds. How long does it have to take? She's special and I don't want to leave her. I don't have her like you have Sarah. If I up and leave at this point I've got no guarantee that she'll be there for me afterwards. Besides, this whole, 'leaving the promise land,' talk is teenage talk. It's hormones and immaturity and adolescents. We're men now, John. We don't need to be playing these games. The real world is in front of us. Beautiful women, children, homes, grown up stuff. That's where I'm at. I'm ready for that stuff. I think I'm passed the whole, 'jolt out of the promise land,' thing."

"You're that hung up over Maryanne, huh. That's okay, I'll wait it out. I'm not in a hurry, I've been holding this back forever. I just thought we could take off and be back by Sarah's birthday. Once I'm back we'll sort it all out and then be good. Maybe Maryanne doesn't feel like Sarah feels. Maybe she's up for an adventure, or maybe she'll like you even more when you've proven yourself and come back."

"I don't know, John. I don't think there is anything on the other side of those mountains that compares with what I've got here. It's my fault that you're like this. I'll talk to Sarah and tell her that I've corrupted you. She can take it out on me. I know that she loves you, whatever craziness you do. She'll be there for you."

"Think about it, Kevin."

"I will. I will, but I don' know."

Chapter 23

"It's as I expected."

"Sir?"

"They're on the move, or will be soon."

"Terrence...," said Daxton.

"I've made sure that Aiden is in command. I want them on the move in no less than three days," said Mr. Cards.

"He'll have them ready to go by morning," said Daxton, looking away and out a window.

"Yes, but I said no less than three days. If I wanted them marching in the morning I would've said so. Aiden will leave when the time is right. He knows Terrence."

Daxton looked down.

"I think you should trust Aiden."

Daxton looked up.

⌘⌘⌘

"I'm ready."

"You should say goodbye," said Aiden.

"To Myrtle? Are we to die?"

"I'm not planning on it—are you?"

"Nay, but…"

"If you want to return to a, 'Hello,' you'll need to leave her with a, 'Goodbye.'"

"Aye."

⌘⌘⌘

Myrtle wore a frown. A frown didn't suit her well. She lifted her beautiful eyes when Jashion entered. The eyes smiled a bit but the frown on her lips remained. Dromreign's appearance and the reality that Jashion and others were leaving forced her to think about the world in a way that she generally avoided. Nothing made sense. Myrtle wasn't stupid, but she'd always been shallow. Depth forced feelings that weren't easily washed away—unresolved and vague emotions tugged and pulled, hurt and confused her, stirred anger, regret, sorrow, and pain. A good cry would have helped but Myrtle didn't understand that. She thought that crying made things worse. She hated tears.

Mirinda had cried and that is what partially evoked Myrtle's feelings. *Mirinda isn't as perfect as everyone thinks*, she thought. *She should be stronger*. Myrtle didn't understand that Mirinda's strength wasn't in squashing her emotions. It was in keeping her emotions and her various mental selves in harmony and balance. Crying was the right thing to do, and so Mirinda cried. She cried hard. Then, she was prepared to be strong for Aiden. Myrtle wasn't prepared for anything.

Jashion felt worried when he saw the expression on Myrtle's face. "I'm open, this night. Would ye like to spend some time, with me?"

Myrtle's expression didn't change. She was looking in his direction, but seemed to be looking through him.

"We'll be preparing and I won't see ye after tonight until we return. Me thought we could say, goodbye. It might be some time…,"

Myrtle's frowned disappeared and she forced a smile. But, his voice wasn't funny to her, not right then.

"That will be nice...I don't...I don't want you to go. It doesn't make any sense..."

Jashion sat beside her and took her hand.

"The dragon either couldn't or wouldn't penetrate our walls. It's gone. Why do we need to send our military? Let Agedon do what they want. If they get themselves killed, so what. What does that have to do with us?"

Myrtle looked away and shook her head. Jashion was silent. Myrtle began to weep.

⌘⌘⌘

"Terrence won't back down."

"I expect you are right," said Aiden.

"What is wrong with him?" said Daxton.

Aiden didn't answer.

"Daxton," said Jashion, entering the tent. Daxton turned and nodded his head, wanting to continue to converse with Aiden.

"What do you know?" said Daxton.

"You should talk to Cards," said Aiden.

"I have. He said to trust you." Aiden nodded. "I do trust you. But, I don't trust Terrence—not anymore."

"Friend," said Aiden, "you've found your place in this world. Perhaps, I have found mine. Terrence's place was not here. That is no rebuke of us. He has no quarrel with us. He will avenge his brother."

Daxton shook his head and muttered, "...he'll die trying."

"Death surrounds us," said Aiden. "We are not immortal. We all die trying—except those who don't try." Daxton looked into Aiden's fierce and kind eyes. "Until again, my friend."

"Until again," said Daxton and the friends embraced.

"I regret that we'll miss your wedding."

Daxton nodded. "Jashion, until again."

"Aye, until again, it is." Jashion embraced Daxton warmly.

Daxton left the tent only a tad bit comforted. *Death does surround us, but within these walls we are protected. They'll all get themselves killed.* Daxton was glad he was no fool.

⌘ ⌘ ⌘

The late spring began to feel like an early summer. The days were warm and the evening comfortable. Jashion and Myrtle walked along a tree lined path along the back wall of Cardsten. There were many couples frolicking along the path, playing in the gardens, or soaking their feet in the fountains. Jashion was not in uniform. He had no interest in garnering attention.

The fright from the dragon had subdued, and the people of Cardsten, at least those who's son's and lovers weren't heading to war, had settled back into life as usual. Myrtle looked lovely in red, both her lips and her dress. Her eyes were no longer red, but a perfect blue and white, fluffy clouds surrounding a clear blue sky.

"I'm in red, until you return. I'm glad you're not wearing black; it would be so mournful. I wear the color of your conquests," she had told him when he came by. A pair of cardinals landed on a tree nearby. Their stunning red against the luscious green leaves was breathtaking. Jashion was glad that he wasn't in his red uniform. They'd have stood out like a couple of birds amongst the crowd.

Myrtle hadn't drunk any. She was perfectly sober, and she was composed. Jashion had never spent time with a young lady who wasn't drinking. It was nice. She no longer laughed at his speech. He tried hard to suppress his accent and imperfections. Sometimes she smiled at his efforts. He smiled back.

For the first time, he became aware of how all eyes lighted upon Myrtle as they strolled along. She, of course, was aware, but tonight she was unaffected. Jashion wasn't jealous or irritated, he felt proud. Jashion had felt proud before. He'd had the sole attention of the great beauty of Dargaer, Siccly Turner. He'd felt proud then. He'd also felt something else. Something warm, and agitating, and exciting, and humbling. He'd begun to have feelings for Siccly, as she turned and swayed, smiled and stared. Those feelings emerged again tonight. It reminded him of... He quickly put that out of his mind. But it emerged again, a bit later. She, like Siccly, was so exquisitely lovely, so completely vulnerable and yet had no idea. Dromreign was just as alive and just as big of a threat as before. No, a bigger threat. Dargaer also had protection. They had kept the dragon away. But, the dragon found a way in, and all was lost.

A thought began to develop in Jashion's mind. It started vaguely, and it wasn't coherent. Somewhere inside of him he knew that he was readying to fight Agedon, to stop them from attacking Dromreign. But, it didn't seem that way in his mind. He'd spent years with Aiden. Somehow he knew that he was on his way to kill the dragon. He looked at Myrtle, she looked back and smiled. He would protect this beauty by his side. He'd avenge the first beauty who was taken. Jashion felt proud again. A different pride. Not for what he had, but for what he would do. His thoughts didn't make sense, except somehow to him.

Myrtle had never gotten a second look, a second chance before. She'd spent some time with Jashion, and then he was gone. This had happened to her numerous times before. But, here he was again. She had not grown tiresome to him; instead he was more pleased with her the second time around. She noticed that he was staring at her, his walking had slowed. She stopped and looked at him. He looked at her as he had looked at her the first time—like he knew her, like he was looking for something, some memory, something more than just appreciating her appearance.

"You're looking at me funny," she said.

"Oh, I'm sorry. I'm sorry."

She laughed. "It's okay. I don't mind you looking at me. I just want to know why you're looking at me the way that you are. Is it good, or is it bad?"

"It's...well, you...um...I can't explain."

"It's okay. You've got a lot on your mind."

Jashion snapped out of it, and was back with Myrtle again. She could tell he was back and she began to feel happy. They laughed and talked, and an hour after the sun had gone down Jashion walked her home.

Jashion didn't know how to say goodbye. Neither did Myrtle. Jashion was looking at her again. He hadn't tired of her. She liked that. She leaned up and gave him a soft kiss on the cheek. "You be careful," she said. Jashion reddened a little. She liked that, too.

⌘⌘⌘

Aiden kissed Mirinda as neither of them had kissed before. Neither of them wanted to let go. For Mirinda, the weeping had long been over. Aiden never saw her weep. In her kisses she communicated everything. Words are such low resolution, so choppy and imprecise. In his arms, in his eyes, in his touch, and in his kiss, she shared everything with him, her entire soul. Aiden took everything in, but could not let everything out. Part of him wanted to, but he knew that he was, as yet, incomplete. When they met again, perhaps he would be complete and then he would share his entire soul with her. Mirinda understood. She longed for their reunion. Aiden held her for a moment longer on the porch and then watched her as she disappeared inside the door. She didn't look back. He was glad. Aiden was ready to leave. It wasn't yet time. This quest he couldn't take on his own. He needed to prepare his troops. There was more uncertainty than he liked. There would be risk, and loss. He wouldn't blame himself for the loss; not if he prepared his men and himself as best he could. Aiden wasn't complete, but he longed to be.

⌘⌘⌘

Terrence arose from the bed leaving Tira neither sleeping nor fully awake. The days since their matrimony had been glorious and unbearably short. Nothing about leaving her then was right. And yet, it could not be any other way. The dragon's power grew daily, as did the destruction in its wake. It was only a matter of time before it came and destroyed Agedon. All indications were that it would be soon. The only way that he could be with Tira was if he left her then. He looked over and saw the soft skin on her back with her brown hair curled over it. She had trusted him with her life. He would do what he must.

He was ready before the sun had caused the birds to chirp. He walked towards the bed but Tira was already up. She embraced him and they kissed. He started to pull away and she held him closer. He held her tighter and they kissed some more. Then a sob. They continued to kiss and he could taste the salt from her tears. He sat on the bed and held her in his lap. She cried. He caressed. It broke his heart. He had removed her from everything—so they could be together. But, he was leaving her and she had nothing. She didn't complain. But she cried, and bitter were her tears. Just a little light entered the room. Terrance stood, still holding Tira and then he laid her gently on the bed. The crying had stopped. He stooped to kiss her and they each whispered, 'I love you.' Terrance stood above her and looked over her as only he could. Her beauty and everything about her was majestic. He would do anything for her. It was time to go.

⌘⌘⌘

The sun came up over the mountain top, but John was not rested. It has been a sleepless night; his mind had raced. He readied himself and went to the Peningham's.

"I'm sorry, John," said Mrs. Peningham. "She won't come. This quarrel between you two has Sarah all worked up."

"Please, I need to see her," said John.

"I've already told her. I've pleaded for you, John. Her mind's made up. You'll have to give her time. I'm sorry, try back in a few days."

"Please tell her, I love her."

"John, I can't tell her that for you..."

"Please tell her that I'll miss her, and I'll come back as soon as I return."

"Return? Return from where? John..."

John Bennett had begun his way towards Sarah's pool.

Mrs. Peningham shook her head as she shut the door. "Lovers quarrel," she said out loud, but quietly.

"Sarah, honey, are you sure you don't want to talk with him? That look in his eye...something's not right."

Sarah lay on her bed, face down in the pillow. Mrs. Peningham sat on the bed.

"He's talking funny, too. Says he'll come back when he returns—whatever that means?"

Sarah turned over with a look of terror on her face.

"What is it, honey?"

"I need to get dressed. I've got to go."

"Okay, honey," Mrs. Peningham said shaking her head while leaving the room and shutting the door.

Sarah felt both an adrenaline rush and numb at the same time. She struggled to get her night gown off and her clothes on. She walked around aimlessly in the room. Grabbing one shoe, but forgetting the other. She started to brush her hair and then lost interest.

"You've got to eat something," yelled Mrs. Peningham as she rushed out the door.

"I've got to go," said Sarah, running hurriedly down the path.

⌘ ⌘ ⌘

John stood at the water's edge. Word was that it was much easier going out than coming back in. John was a strong swimmer; he wasn't worried about being able to do it.

He hated to leave without saying goodbye, without seeing her one last time, without pressing his lips against hers and beholding her eyes.

John carried a knife. He knew that he couldn't take much, but he would need something. He secured it against his chest. He leaned down and felt the crisp coolness of the water in his hands. He stood again and leaped.

⌘ ⌘ ⌘

Sarah's heart raced and she was breathless. "John," she yelled just before the pool was visible. As she beheld the pool she saw his feet enter and saw the splash. She ran and jumped in after him. She swam down some and saw his legs go through the crevice. John had left the promise land.

Sarah swam up to the surface. She gasped for air. She started to sob and a splash of water went into her mouth. She choked on the water as some entered her trachea. She swam underneath the waterfall and then held herself on the ledge. She didn't have the strength, at least emotionally, to climb up. She hung there for some time. Eventually she climbed up and sat on her perch above the falls, ever watching the waters deep below.

Chapter 24

John's lungs burned as he swam through the dark narrow crevice. He thought he would bang his head several times, but as he fought against the current and used every ounce of his strength, agility, and instinct, he narrowly missed either a painful gash or a fatal blow. As he swam just a little further the current pushed him out. He was grateful for that current and then worried about it working against him as he headed back for the promise land, sometime later. It would be much harder swimming against that last current, the one which pushed him out.

John surfaced and looked around. *Not so different*, he thought. The mountains hung above him, but in the distant horizon there were no mountain tops. A thick forest surrounded the pool. John glided slowly to the water's edge, listening carefully and keeping a watchful eye. He held the edge for some time, catching his breath while listening, watching. For all the trees he hadn't heard the sound of a bird. He'd heard no sound at all.

A twig snapped and he heard footsteps. He held his breath and looked in that direction. A large, grey, ferocious creature ran through the woods. John caught fleeting glimpses of it through the trees. His hand moved subconsciously to the knife on his breast. He dipped down further so that his eyes were barely looking over the edge. He stayed there, hardly breathing, for some minutes; no other sound, no other movements, everything was eerily quiet. Then a cry unlike anything he had heard before, a wolf howl, pierced the silence. John's heart raced. He considered returning to the promise land immediately. He evaluated his strength and decided that it hadn't been sufficiently gained. He looked around the area for cover. The water moved behind a bend and he couldn't see what was there because of the shadows cast. John dropped below the water's surface and swam towards the shadows. When he resurfaced, he found that he could see just as well from there, but, perhaps from this spot he wasn't so visible, so vulnerable. There he waited, but not for long. Another creature, in fact the wolf who's howl he'd just heard, came into view. This creature, black, large, fierce, was not running past the water, but rather walking directly towards it. Its eyes seemed pointed toward John. John trusted that the shadow in which he concealed himself would obscure its view.

The creature stopped at the edge of the water, the very edge where John had been holding on just moments before. It bent down to drink. It then rose and began to move away. The wind blew a little and the creature stopped dead in its tracks. The creature sniffed the air and then turned back towards the pool so that it appeared to be looking again at John. John held fast, afraid to breath, to move, or make the tiniest of splash.

The wolf bared its teeth and began to growl, a menacing growl that caused the hair on Johns neck stand up. The wolf lifted its head up high and howled loud and long. Then, it looked towards John while bobbing its head up and down. More than once the creature put its paws in the water, testing it before jumping in. John calculated his course to the crevice while keeping a watchful eye. Before long, several of the creature's companions came into view and began to surround the water's edge. They growled and bared their teeth and pawed at the water. Some paced the edge back and forth. The chorus grew louder.

In the distance John heard another howl and then another. Soon the forest was alive with the haunting sound of these creatures. John wondered how mankind had ever survived long enough to make it to the promise land from this land without. The wolves along the bank grew restless. Each looked at the large black wolf for a cue, for direction. The original wolf did not break his stare towards John. Several wolves left and began to run towards the distant howls. Three stayed and then two. Finally, only the original remained. It's body language made it look angrier than before. Saliva dripped from its bared teeth and it jumped into the water. John watched as it awkwardly paddled towards his shadowy hiding.

John removed the knife from his chest and considered diving down, but feared losing sight of the creature who's powers he did not know. John drew closer to the shadows edge. Perhaps he'd been smelled but not seen. The creature seemed vulnerable in the water. *Maybe a quick thrust of the knife to its chest* and then he would dive down. As the wolf swam closer it caught sight of John, and let out a growl. Anger showed in its eyes. John jumped out towards it and swung his knife. The creature batted it away and sent claw marks down Johns arm. The knife dropped down and began to sink to the bottom. John dived down to retrieve the knife. The wolf sent its claws into Johns leg. The pain in his arm and leg was intense. He couldn't make it to the crevice. He swam hard for the edge.

John was a strong swimmer and he outpaced the wolf. As he climbed over the edge the pain in his arm and leg stung deeply. He pushed himself over and rolled a few paces away. The wolf was near the edge. John feared that he wouldn't be able to out run the wolf, especially in his current condition. He walked to the edge and kicked the wolf in the face hard. The wolf lost its footing and plopped briefly under water. It resurfaced with gnashed teeth and a growl. John sighted a small boulder. He struggled to pick it up. The wolf was at the edge again and John hurled the rock. It landed on a paw and the momentum landed a blow to the wolf's head. The wolf was dazed, but not out. It whimpered and then howled. John picked up the rock again and dropped it square on the wolfs head. He watched the boulder and the wolf sink deep into the water, and then he ran.

John was delirious with fear and pain. It never occurred to him to pay attention so that he could find his way back. The forest was thick and completely unfamiliar. He heard howls in the distance but over time they appeared to be further away. He knew not if he ran away or towards them.

Eventually his strength gave way, and he stumbled to the ground. He hit his knee hard against a stone and scrapped both elbows badly. He lay upon the ground gently nursing his wounds, panting yet unable to recover from his oxygen debt. Drool dripped from his mouth, yet it felt dry and he thirsted. He tried to stay alert and listen for the creatures, yet he couldn't have moved if he had to. John felt hopeless and wished that he had never done what he did. He regretted everything. He feared for his life.

His life...

Sarah.

Sarah had been his life. He had pleaded with her to come with him. If she'd come, she might be dead. She was still alive and safe. If he could make it back, maybe she would have him back. It was his one glimmer of light.

⌘ ⌘ ⌘

An hour before light, Aiden's troops were ready to go. Not a man, except Jashion, understood this. Aiden always left before dawn. Perhaps the sunrise game him strength. It was not long before Jashion was sent to quiet the grumblings. These men were soft. They had never done anything other than drills. A real march, in the real heat, with real blisters and thirst, was not what they'd ever expected. Jashion returned to Aiden's side.

"I'd take Terrence, Daxton, and Marcus over this lot, I would," said Jashion.

"We've only gone a mile," said Aiden. Up to this point they had followed the easy road towards Agedon. Aiden began to move east off the road and into the wilderness.

Another Lieutenant, a large burly man of twenty-four, came up to Aiden and spoke out of line.

"This isn't the way to Agedon, sir. We need to get back on the road."

Aiden was quiet and kept walking resolutely.

"Sir, did you hear me?"

"Back in line, steady your troops," said Jashion.

"You don't outrank me," he said to Jashion. "Sir, what are you doing? Where are you taking us? I'll report this and get you fired."

"Lieutenant, what are you afraid of?" said Aiden.

"Nothing..."

"Good."

"But..."

"Listen up, before I have you court marshalled. If you want to take the road, it will lead us to Agedon. We'll arrive to find the town occupied by women, children, and the elderly. I suppose you can show your bravery towards them, while the armies of Agedon enter the dark forest and begin the battle against Dromreign! So, by all means, Lieutenant, should we get back on the highway?" said Aiden.

"What? How'd you know that?"

"We've received word. Agedon already marches on Dromreign. If we head as we are, we'll reach the edge of the dark forest about the time that Agedon does. That is, if you can keep your men moving along."

Fear shown in the man's eyes. Aiden marched along. The man fell back. Jashion was pleased.

⌘⌘⌘

Despite the battle armor, Terrence's troops moved at a quick pace. King Darron Drake felt satisfied with their strength and endurance. The edge of the dark forest was just in view. Terrence held up his hand and the men stopped. Dusk was just beginning to settle.

"My king, a night's rest here would be ideal. The men will be rested and strong. If we start before sunrise, we will enter the dark forest at dawn and will be at them with our strength and their weakness."

"And if they should see us? If the beast leaves its snare and comes this way, we will be unprotected."

"Yes," said Terrence, "then it is good that we're still marching strong because the battle will be tonight. The dark forest doesn't truly provide much protection. Our protection is our armor, or strength, and our steel. I'd prefer to fight in the day, but we will fight with our fury at night if they come to us."

"Good," said the king.

As night fell, Terrence watched the men. They turned and looked when they heard a distant howl. Terrence gave them eye contact when they showed fear. Slowly he calmed his men and slowly they drifted to sleep. He heard the howls increase as the night went on. The wolves knew that the men were at their doorstep. The wolves were assembling. The mornings battle would be fierce and that was just the wolves. Terrence knew not how they would conquer the dragon.

In the predawn hours Terrence woke the troops. He'd slept just enough that he felt strong. The men awoke with both an excitement and a foreboding. They nervously and excitedly grabbed their shields, and their swords, and completed their armor.

"I've survived two winters in the dark forest and I've killed many a wolf. They are deadly and fierce, but so are we. Today is not a battle, but rather a fight to the finish. If we do not prevail, there will be no home to return to. Our wives and our children depend upon us, as do all the inhabitants of this land. Fight for your life. Fight for each other. Fight for your king. Fight for your liberty. Fight for Agedon!"

Cheers erupted and King Drake nodded. Terrence placed his helmet on and so did all the men. Terrence began the march with his King flanking him on his right and Jack flanking him on his left. Terrence and his men were ready. More than ready.

⌘⌘⌘

Aiden's troops grew slower and more fearful the closer they got to the forests edge. He let them stop early and sleep early the night before, but he woke them in the pre-morning hours that day again. The men were groggy, and hurting, and sore. They knew that they were going to reach the edge of the dark forest that day and had no motivation to move. Still, Aiden and Jashion had withstood the dark forest, and in some ways the men were more intimidated by them than by the wolves.

Lieutenant Janks joined Aiden and Jashion as the dark forest came into view. They watched as the armored armies of Agedon entered the dark forest. The men of Cardsten stood in awe as Aiden held up his hand.

"We're too late, General," said Janks. Aiden stood in silence and Jashion hushed him. Janks shot Jashion a look.

"General..,"

"Silence," whispered Aiden.

They watched a moment longer and then the sounds of shouts and of metal clanging and of howling were heard. Wolves came into view and attacked the men still entering the forest. An audible, 'awe,' could be heard from the men of Cardsten.

"We must retreat," said Janks, "all is lost."

"Not by a long shot," said Aiden. "We enter the forest further east, behind the wolves."

"What?!" said Janks.

"We're providing reinforcements; we are" said Jashion.

Janks didn't understand why the wolves needed reinforcements.

They began to march, and in half an hour the armies of Cardsten, behind Aiden and Jashion, entered the dark forest with trepidation.

⌘⌘⌘

Terrence was unconvinced of the utility of the armor against the wolves. He felt his agility was halved by the armor and his thrusts with his sword were slower and weaker. Still, the men were fighting strong and avoiding some claw and teeth marks. But, the wolves were learning as they fought. In packs they'd knock a soldier down and then tear at the armor until flesh was revealed. Then they would tear at the flesh. Many a man lay dead in their wake. But the wolves' forces were depleting also. However, as the men gained ground on the wolves, more wolves joined the battle. The wolves were enjoying an endless supply of reinforcement.

Drake, Jack, and Terrence held strong. The men did not surrender and hope still hung tight.

⌘⌘⌘

Aiden drew his arrow. A wolf pack was entering the area and ready to fight. The alpha male was soon down. The wolves turned to the armies of Cardsten and some men took flight. Most, however, held their ground and the pack was defeated promptly. They marched on towards the battle. Janks and the troops were beginning to understand.

Aiden caught Jashion's eye and motioned for him to take his troops deeper into the forest. Aiden stayed with Janks and his men. They moved more swiftly towards the battlefront.

⌘⌘⌘

Terrence and his men began to make gains on the wolves. The wolves' reinforcements began to slow; though he didn't know it, he could thank the armies of Cardsten for this.

As the battle raged and as the heat of the day rose, some of the men began to drop through heat exhaustion. These the wolves pounced on and quickly annihilated. King Drake's anger grew as he saw his brave and weakened men get slaughtered before his eyes. There had been no sign of Dromreign and the king's thirst for its blood increased. A brave soldier who had cut down many a wolf dropped to his knees after a kill. Drake, who didn't have a wolf at him then, saw the man drop. He saw a small pack descend upon the man. The king ran and yelled with all his might. They wouldn't get this soldier! The wolves turned on the king as he slashed at one of them, only mildly injuring the wolf. The king was out of position and the wolves pounced, knocking him over. The king held onto his sword and fought from the ground. The soldier crawled towards the king willing to sacrifice himself for his beloved monarch. The wolves ignored the soldier, barely able to move and of no threat to them.

Drake rolled and blocked, swung and thrust. The snarls, the growls, the claws, and the teeth were upon him. He was able to thrust and slice through the throat of one of the wolves, killing it instantly. But the others pulled at the armor on his arm, the one brandishing the sword. In no time flesh was exposed. As a wolf's teeth sunk deep into his flesh, King Darron Drake screamed out. Jack heard the cry and ran to his king. He began to slice at and through the wolves. Two wolves stayed at Drake while the others went at Jack. Jack tore through the small pack but when he knelt at his king's side he saw that the wolves had removed the kings helmet and bitten through his throat. The king lay dead with blood oozing from his throat and his eyes wide open.

⌘⌘⌘

Jashion was amazed at the sheer number of wolves that continued to come. It seemed that every wolf, from every corner of the dark forest, was descending upon them. As more of the men of Cardsten were taken, the remaining men became fiercer in their attacks. They finally perceived the wolves as their enemies and acted accordingly. Though some of the packs made their way past the armies of Cardsten and towards the armies of Agedon, most fought the armies of Cardsten directly. The longer the battle raged, the more wolves were upon them and the armies of Cardsten continued to deplete.

⌘⌘⌘

Aiden saw that Cardsten was losing ground. Slowly he backed up the troops, backing them in the direction of the armies of Agedon, until the sounds of that battle were heard. Then he pressed forward again. Jashion and his men were just visible and to his left. Their depletion was much greater than his and Janks, and more wolves were on the attack against them. Aiden began to make his way towards Jashion.

Within moments, Jashion's men were giving way, though Jashion was fighting strong. Aiden's arrows sailed and he provided a little relief. But, it wasn't enough. An enormous pack made their way to the front and overtook many of Jashion's men, running past them and directly for the leader.

Aiden took down three wolves and then started to sprint. Those of Jashion's men who remained fled from the battle. The wolves quickly overtook Jashion and he was down. A wolf took his leg in his mouth and began to drag him away. Jashion, still conscious, flailed at the beasts. Aiden was on them in no time. He carved them up as the master hunter that he was. When the last wolf was deserted or dead, he beheld his friend. Jashion wasn't conscious anymore, but he was breathing. The wounds weren't mortal, but he'd have to act quickly to keep him from losing too much blood.

With Aiden gone, Janks troops were in disarray, some fleeing, some fighting, and some retreating towards Agedon's army. With Cardsten nearly overcome, the last wave of wolves hurled themselves towards Agedon.

⌘⌘⌘

Though Agedon's troops were less than half of what they were at the battle's start, the armor had held strong and they had withstood the onslaught of wolves better than had Cardsten. The remaining men were the strength of Agedon. Though their king was down, the glue that held them together were their beliefs and the people of Agedon itself. These men fought with exceeding valor.

This wave of wolves had run long and hard, they'd already fought with Cardsten, and they hadn't familiarized themselves with armor. The men of Cardsten that had not fled joined themselves with Agedon and fought too, with their might. Slowly, the wolves were destroyed and a small battalion of men remained.

Terrence looked over the men and the carnage. He had never imagined in his years of living on the edge of the dark forest that this magnitude of force was here. The great army of Agedon and the large portion of the army of Cardsten that was led by Aiden, had lost all but a small portion of their men in defeating the wolves, and Dromreign remained. What force would it take to defeat that foe? It wouldn't take long to have that question confronted. A deafening screech filled the air. Terrance looked up and beheld his ultimate foe.

A final pack of wolves became apparent. They were heading directly towards Terrence. This separated Terrence from his men as he had to turn his attention to, and attack, the wolves. The men, in complete shellshock, gathered together, swords and spears drawn looking at the sky.

Terrence, filled with anger and annoyance, for he wanted to look upon his arch enemy, slaughtered the wolves with ease. They were no match for him. Ten wolves slaughtered, his mind hardly aware of the movements of his arms and his feet. He looked up and it was too late.

Jack was standing firm with the men, and they began to throw their spears and swords at the beast. To a weapon, they all bounced off the armored black scales of the beast, Dromreign completely unaffected. The men gathered together in a cluster made the dragon's work simple and efficient. Dromreign excelled his magnificent and horrific fire and the men were consumed in their armor. Terrence could feel the heat. The smell of burning flesh and of the forest full of carnage still could not eclipse the awful stench of the dragon.

Terrence braced for the dragon to come upon him. He did not fear the beast and he felt ready to avenge all. But the beast did not turn to him. Instead, it began to make its way out of the forest and toward the land of Agedon.

Terror entered into Terrence's heart.

Tira, he thought. His mind immediately caught hold of his last moments with her, as he looked upon her. She lay on the bed gorgeous and glorious, naked and vulnerable, completely at the mercy of Terrence's protection. He would do anything to protect her!

He mustered every last bit of strength he could find. Love, hatred, vengeance, and anger filled him. He hurled his sword with everything he had. It sailed true and struck the dragon in the breast. That sword made the improbable entry in-between two scales and struck within the dragon's flesh. Dromreign let out a horrendous scream and doubled up in the air. Its flight was not long interrupted and the dragon recovered. It turned its red eyes upon the hurler of the sword and saw Terrence.

Terrence stood weaponless and in short range. The dragon flew directly upon him and with every ounce of fury unleased such a powerful and furious fire that Terrence must have felt no pain as he was consumed.

⌘⌘⌘

Aiden stole his eyes from Jashion and his wounds. He could just make out the sword imbedded in the dragon. He watched closely with his keen eyes, too far away to sail an arrow. As the dragon turned again the sword, not embedded deeply in its flesh, dropped to the ground along with a single of its scales, revealing a small portion of its exposed flesh. Aiden's heart took courage. The dragon could be hurt; it could be made to bleed. Indeed, blood dripped from the dragon's wound as it flew towards Agedon.

⌘⌘⌘

Tira hung clothes in the early afternoon. She, like everyone of Agedon, kept herself busy and occupied. It helped to keep her mind off of Terrence and what he was going through. Her house had been swept and re-swept a dozen times.

In the clear blue sky, a dark spot became visible. She studied it, wonderingly, subconsciously perplexed. It grew in size. Her expression changed.

"Dromreign!" she yelled.

Everyone's eyes turned in the direction she pointed. In short order, the screams and the yells brought everyone to awareness of their impending doom.

A few of the people fled to escape the confines of the city. Most ran into their wooden homes, providing nothing more than a psychological protection. Tira also ran into her home. But, she quickly returned brandishing a shield and some spears. Others followed her lead and brought out what weapons they could find, those not carried off by their army.

The twenty or so brave young women clustered together with their shields and weapons drawn, not unlike the last group of men from Agedon, so recently incinerated.

The dragon's eyes were drawn to the shimmering weapons and the small group gathered together and flew directly towards them. They hurled their weapons unskillfully and far too quickly. None even scratched a scale. The women hid behind their shields and the dragon blew flame, not powerfully like he'd done to the men and to Terrence, but rather weakly. His strength was not at stake, but he desired to gently roast and then consume the women, which it did.

This further emboldened Dromreign for the great task at hand. Never before had it tried such a great conquest, and in the middle of the day, no less. Agedon was a dozen times larger than the largest village the dragon had consumed in a night. Dromreign started out slowly, methodically, pacing itself, as it set every building to blaze. Hours would transpire, and periodically, a small group would leave a building to flee. These brought additional nourishment to its dark soul. It killed and consumed when possible. At length, the black dragon flew higher to witness its destruction. It circled the city and torched anything left unburned. Whether anyone survived the destruction of Agedon that day, no one survived long. No survivor of Agedon was ever heard of in the land, thereafter.

Chapter 25

Not until the next evening did Jashion regain consciousness. All other survivors of the armies of Cardsten had long since deserted the dark forest. Aiden had heard the occasional howl of a lone wolf, but he did not sense any reason to feel threated in the heart of the dark forest. Its dangers had been massively depleted. Dromreign had returned, late the night before, flying much too high for Aiden to take aim with his bow.

"Aiden," said Jashion weakly.

"Aiden..."

Aiden returned to his companion's side.

"Aiden, take me..."

"You are not well. You cannot move."

"Take me to...the promise land."

Aiden was silent. Contemplative. Jashion was silent then, too. In fact, he'd fallen back asleep.

The next morning Aiden had food and herbs for Jashion. Jashion had lost much blood and many of his wounds oozed with infection.

"Eat slow, my friend," said Aiden.

Jashion did eat slow, and groaned in pain as his wounds were dressed.

"Aiden, do ye know the way? Have ye found the entrance to the promise land?"

"Yes," said Aiden without hesitation.

"Will ye go with me?"

"I will," said Aiden

Two days later they arrived at the pool. Jashion collapsed at the edge. Aiden scouted around and returned a half hour later. Aiden looked over Jashion. He was pale. The travel was too soon and his friend was unwell.

"I'm ready, let's go."

Aiden looked over him for a moment.

"Let me test the way."

Aiden dived into the pool and swam down to the crevice. The current was powerful at the crevice and the narrow entrance was jagged and foreboding. He emerged and sat next to his friend, dripping.

"Is it there?" said Jashion.

"Yes," said Aiden.

"Aye. Me's ready, let's goes."

"Jashion, it's not possible."

Jashion looked at him strangely.

"I cannot help you through. You must have the strength to do it alone."

"Ye isn't coming?"

"Jashion, it is simply not possible to help you through. I could go it on my own, but you don't have strength. You're not well. You will have to be healed and fully ready before you can go."

"We'll stay here until me's ready."

Aiden was scanning the area and listening intensely. Jashion had seen this look before. What wolves were left were clustered and drawn to this area.

"This is the one place we can't wait," said Aiden. "We must go now." Aiden helped him up and they made their way slowly back through the forest.

⌘⌘⌘

Sarah held vigil at the pool during the day and would have held vigil at night if her family and friends had let her. Nearly a fortnight had passed, but the pool was silent.

Sometimes Maryanne and Kevin would stop by. They'd hang out for an hour or so and then gently try and coax Sarah away. Sarah, however, was resolute.

"I think it'll be a few weeks before John's back," said Kevin. "He wouldn't have gone just to get a quick peek and then scurry back. I'm sure he'll want to get it all out of his system before he returns. John's a big boy. He'll be fine."

Sarah nodded sullenly.

"We're going on a horseback ride tomorrow," said Maryanne. "Come with us."

Sarah gave a halfhearted smile. "It's okay. I'll stay here."

Maryanne glanced at Kevin with a look of concern. Kevin shrugged. Maryanne took Sarah's hand and squeezed it. They sat in silence for a quarter of an hour and then the couple left. Sarah was glad. Solitude felt better.

⌘⌘⌘

Jashion had been strong, before the battle. Aiden was gifted as a healer. It didn't take long and Jashion was well, again.

"Aiden, I'm ready."

"Yes, I think you are."

The two made their way towards the pool. As Aiden had expected, the remaining wolves in the dark forest were pacing in front of the water's edge. Thirty plus wolves he counted from the top of a tree they'd climbed. Jashion looked concerned. Aiden contemplated.

After some time, Aiden said, "I'll take out a few with my bow and then draw off the rest. You head for the pool and I'll circle around and meet you. We won't have much time. You'll have to go immediately.

"Listen, Jashion. This is no frolicking swim. You'll have to dive and go down deep. There's a crevice and the current comes right at you. It's narrow and it'll be hard to pass and swim through. Don't hit your head on the rocks, if you pass out, you'll not make it."

"I'm ready. I know."

"Good."

Aiden studied the wolves and picked those that he'd take out. He and Jashion silently descended down the tree. Aiden took aim and shot three wolves who were separated from the others. They each fell silently and were not seen by the remaining wolves. Next Aiden shot a wolf in the center, the largest of the group. This death did not go unnoticed. He had time to hit one other large one and then he took off running as noisily as possible. The twenty-five other wolves shot after him.

Jashion waited a few moments and then ran to the pools edge. He could hear the wolves growling and knew that they were running in the opposite direction of the water. He didn't have much with him to begin with. He dropped his sword, knowing he couldn't swim with it. He removed a small sack, his shoes, and a belt. He had nothing else but his clothes.

It had been about five minutes. He could still hear the wolves, their cries farther away. He looked around, ensuring that none had stealthily returned. Everything was silent around the pool. He thought about what he would do if one arrived. Would he dive in immediately and head there, before Aiden arrived? Or, would he fight it off and wait for his friend. He elected to retrieve the sword.

The ten minutes that followed felt much longer. His heart was racing. He began to hear the wolves from different directions. They had spread out. Jashion never worried about Aiden, he'd never had reason to worry over Aiden before. But then he began to worry. He looked around, wondering what was taking him so long. Suddenly, Aiden appeared through the trees.

"Remove your shirt, too," said Aiden quietly. "You won't want it getting caught on the crevice."

"Aye, are ye ready?" said Jashion. "Who's to jump first?"

Aiden was at his side.

"You go to the promise land," said Aiden.

"Aye, but are not ye coming, too?"

"Perhaps, one day. Today it is not peace and protection that I seek. One day that may be my desire. It is time, Jashion. It is not safe for me to stay much longer."

Jashion wanted to protest, to tell him he'd wait until he was ready. But the words didn't form. Jashion was ready then and did not want to wait another day. Aiden would not be ready for a very long time, perhaps ever; this Jashion could read on his face.

"Until again," said Aiden with his hand on Jashion's shoulder.

Jashion nodded and looked his friend in the eye. Jashion had lost or said goodbye to everyone he had ever known. It hurt this time more than ever.

A rustling of the leaves made them each turn their head. A wolf had returned.

"Go!" said Aiden

Jashion dived in. He didn't get as deep of a breath as he should have. He swam down, his lungs already burned. He reached the crevice and felt the water rush at him. He groped for the opening and was pushed back. He pushed out a large portion of his breath. He wasn't going to make it. He thought of resurfacing and taking another breath, but realized that that option did not likely exist. The wolves may be on him and he was already exhausted. Something inside of him provided the nudge. He lunged forward and fought, with every stroke, the current. It seemed to get more difficult the farther he went. Darkness engulfed him and he swam on. The current started to abate and he perceived a glimmer of light ahead. He pushed ahead and came through the crevice.

⌘ ⌘ ⌘

Sarah couldn't believe her eyes. *John*, she thought. She blinked, she shook her head. It was real, she wasn't dreaming. *He's returned*. Sarah nearly dived into the water herself, but something held her back. A sick feeling like a pit in her stomach stopped her. All the anger she had felt for John came rushing back. While he was out of the promise land every unpleasant thought, feeling, and emotion towards John had been suppressed by Sarah. But he was back, safe and sound, and she felt them all again. This, however, only lasted for a moment.

She watched him glide up to the surface and heard him gasp for air. The feelings of love for John then erupted to the surface again and she felt a tremendous joy.

But wait. He'd changed. No. Was that John? She saw the figures back of the head. He was similar, but not quite right. He swam to the far end and pulled himself out of the water. She, concealed behind the waterfall and the shadows, looked out to see him, without her being found. She looked carefully. The body wasn't right. It was a big strong man, but it wasn't John.

The man looked around, staring at the encircling mountain range. He looked back in Sarah's direction, but she wasn't spotted.

Who is this?

The man didn't seem to be in a hurry to go anywhere. He looked around, lost. He looked back at the water, expectantly. *Is someone else coming? Is it John? Has John helped this man find the promise land? Oh, John, maybe it was a good idea to leave. Maybe you have saved others!*

After a few minutes the man walked off.

Slowly.

Aimlessly.

He clearly didn't know where anything was. He didn't even take the path. Perhaps, Sarah should have gone down to help him. The thought, however, never occurred to her. She sat for several hours longer watching the water, expectantly. That night she returned home more distraught than ever.

⌘ ⌘ ⌘

With Jashion in, Aiden turned his attention to the wolves. He'd hoped to watch Jashion and ensure his friends success, but he was in a precarious position himself. Too many wolves surrounded him and not enough distance to take many down with his arrows. He scanned the surroundings. He had three choices. Fight, run, or dive in and swim himself to safety. More than once, he considered a backwards dive in and a trip to the promise land. He'd come so far. Dromreign was wounded. Mirinda was in Cardsten. But this pack of wolves had him in the most dangerous position he'd ever been in, before.

Jashion's sword lay at his feet. He retrieved it. The first wolf sprang and Aiden laid it to rest. A second and a third then met the same fate. More wolves arrived. They each packed tighter and slowly came closer. The water may be his only escape. He looked the wolves in the eye. One at a time. He saw fear, not in all of them, but a few. Two of the most fearful were side by side. Without further wait Aiden charged towards them brandishing the sword. They flinched and he made it through. Aiden, who'd been running near sprint speed for nearly a quarter of an hour just moments before, ran even faster. His lungs burned. The pack was not far behind him. They'd been fooled more easily a few minutes before, but they knew his moves this time. They followed him more closely. His legs ached and he worried about a cramp. Still, his body had never failed him before. Aiden found a second, perhaps third-wind, and ran with his might. The pack had lost some ground, just enough; he would have to out maneuver them.

Slowly he lost the pack. He stopped by a tree and listened carefully, panting for air as quietly as he could. He'd lost them, for the moment. He'd circled back to the pond before. It sounded as though they expected the same and were heading that way. Soon they'd discover their mistake and would be back on the hunt. Aiden walked. The ground and the terrain were unfamiliar. He'd explore later. At this point, he just wanted distance, time to think, time to rest, and time to recover.

Something caught his eye. *A fallen soldier*, he thought. Reconsidering, he realized the battle and the men were nowhere near here. He came up carefully. Sure enough, a man lay on the ground and he looked dead. Aiden approached to make sure. The man breathed, though barely. He'd been attacked by wolves, some time ago by the looks of it. His body was warm with infection and the wounds were horribly infested. Only a very strong man could survive this. His face, sickly as it was, was entirely unfamiliar.

Chapter 26

Aiden felt little hope of reviving the man. Another day, perhaps hours, perhaps minutes, and the man would have been dead. Still, Aiden took his pouch and began to prepare a dressing. It may be wasted, but until the man stopped breathing there was some hope. Fortune had already smiled on him. If the dark forest hadn't been nearly cleared of wolves from the battle, the wolves would have taken him already. But, with so few wolves left this man hadn't been discovered by them.

Three days had transpired. The man had been coxed to drink some water. His breathing had improved and the wounds were starting to heal. But, the fever was high and he'd not regained consciousness. Aiden hardly slept. He was too close to the wolves. He would have ventured miles beyond this area, had he been alone. Aiden was back to full strength and could fight and out run the wolves, but this man would become wolf meat if he was found. At night, Aiden had gotten the wolves to chase him away from the man. At that point, it was working, but he couldn't keep it up forever.

On the fourth day, the man showed some sign that consciousness was returning. He mumbled a bit, incoherently, and tossed around some. Aiden took the occasion to try and help him take some meat. The man choked, but got some down. Later that night, as the howl of the wolves grew louder, the man awoke. He shivered, and spoke irrationally, and looked fearfully at Aiden. Aiden sat quietly, peering into his eyes, hoping to calm him. He worried that he may make enough noise to attract the wolves. Eventually the man settled and Aiden offered food and water. The man took several bites but then collapsed with lack of strength. He lay on the ground conscious but weak.

Aiden whispered, "you've been attacked by wolves. I found you nearly dead. You are still very sick, and weak from hunger and thirst."

The man listened but could barely nod.

"When you feel a bit stronger take some more water. Eat if you feel up to it, but don't make yourself sick."

Both men were quiet for a while.

"The wolves are circling nearer to here. I may have to leave to draw them away. Don't make a sound or try to move. You'll be safest here."

Whether or not the man wanted to protest, he didn't have the strength. Aiden listened for a long while. Then, he silently got up and left.

The next morning the man awoke, normally, as if from a typical night's sleep. Aiden's eyes were open only by sheer force of will. His exhaustion had reached the climax. Still, he dressed the man's wounds, and provided him with food, medicine, and drink. The man was very weak, but he was no longer incoherent. He looked as though he wanted to talk. That was a good sign, but Aiden required rest. Aiden crashed while the man ate. Aiden rarely allowed himself to delve so deeply into his subconscious, especially when in danger. But, his body could keep back the sleep no more. He slept the entire daylight away. The other man went in and out of consciousness throughout the day.

Aiden awoke suddenly and looked around. He felt stiff and groggy. He looked over at the man whose eyes were shut. He watched his breathing for a time and realized that he was not asleep.

"Hello," said Aiden.

The man feigned sleep.

"How are you feeling?"

The man feigned arousal.

"You're awake," the man said.

Aiden didn't answer. He went to taking care of the necessities.

"Who are you?" asked the man.

"Aiden," he said, not looking over.

After dressing his wounds and providing food and water. Aiden was ready to talk.

"Who are you?" said Aiden.

"John...John Bennett."

"What brings you into the dark forest?" said Aiden.

"Insanity," said John. "What brings you here?"

"I've lived here for most of the past several years."

"Are you alone," asked John.

"Yes. Besides you, I am now."

The men sat in silence. The wolves were far distant this night and Aiden sat vigil while John slept. They would trade sleeping morning and nights for two more days. John's strength was slowly returning and they began to travel slowly away from the wolves—away from the entrance to the promise land.

John did not bring up his history. Neither did Aiden. They spoke little and primarily about the practicalities of their circumstances.

Aiden saw that John possessed great qualities. As his health, and strength, and vigor returned Aiden included him on the hunts. Hunting was relatively easy with so few wolves to compete with. John had a knack—more than a knack; he was a natural. For leisure and for hunting Aiden taught John archery and sword fighting. In a matter of weeks John was competent;

his health was strong and Aiden couldn't be more pleased with his companion.

For John's part, he thought often on Sarah. He often considered telling Aiden where he was from, that he wanted—needed to return to his girl. The longer they went without him telling, the more foolish it seemed to bring it up. John deduced that he could find his way back to the pool by heading back to the wolves. This brought a certain sense of comfort and terror to him. The truth is, if John had really wanted to go back, he could have. But, John was happy. He was enjoying his adventure in the wide open world. He loved the hunt, the howl of the wolves at night, the archery, the rock climbing, the chase, and especially the sword fighting. He'd left the promise land for a reason and he was very happy here. If he left, he'd be itching to return, and there is no way he'd bring Sarah here. When he was done with the wide open world, he'd return to Sarah and have no regrets.

Slowly the weeks turned into months. Dromreign had not been spotted since its return to its lair after Agedon; clearly it had taken a lot out of the beast. John was a powerful companion, more so than Terrance. Aiden had been formulating his plan. He was ready to bring John in on it.

⌘ ⌘ ⌘

Sarah's vigil became more periodic and not daily. Still, she spent much time on her perch. This place was no longer a place of peace and comfort—Sarah's heart ached.

Kevin and Maryanne had become very close. They still spent time with Sarah, but she was not able to reciprocate their kindness. Truly, they preferred to be alone together, anyway. Still, they were there for Sarah.

One day, uncharacteristically, Kevin came to visit Sarah alone at her pool. He jumped in, swam to the other side and climbed the short cliff and sat beside her, just like he'd done dozens of times before, except in the past he'd always had Maryanne beside him.

"Hi, Kevin," said Sarah.

"Anymore big strapping lads come in lately? Jashion has worked out really well on the ranch. I'll take a few more, if you've got them."

Sarah smiled. Kevin was good at making her smile. Kevin was like a big brother to Sarah.

"Listen, Sarah. Can we talk?"

Sarah nodded.

"John and I have been best friends since before I can remember. I miss him terribly."

Sarah nodded slowly. "I'm sorry..."

"You and I know John better than anyone. I don't know how to say this..."

Sarah looked up at him, searching his eyes. Kevin dropped his eyes and looked at the ground.

"I don't think..." Kevin paused.

"Sarah...I don't think he's coming back."

Sarah shuddered and looked down.

The two were silent for some time.

"Kevin, I can't think like that..."

"I know...it's hard. I've been thinking a lot about this. I've been trying to find a way to tell you, for weeks..."

Sarah looked at him with tears starting to well up in her eyes.

"John left to check the place out, a little adventure. A few weeks, a month at the most and he'd be back. Either he'd got enough of it or he was going to come back to convince us to join him there. Something has happened..."

Sarah looked away.

"I've been talking to Jashion a bunch. It's crazy through there," indicating the pool. "Almost everyone he knows—towns, villages, cities—destroyed and ruined. John's awesome, you know. But, he had no idea what was there. I mean *no idea*. Even the stories we hear, they're nothing compared to what Jashion has told me."

Sarah sat, looking away quietly. Kevin wondered if he'd said too much, too soon, too indelicately.

After a while Sarah looked at him. Her eyes pleading to hear the rest.

"How long after John left did Jashion come in?" asked Kevin.

Sarah thought about it. "At the time, it seemed like forever. But now, I don't know, maybe a week or two."

"John had been over there for a while. They'd had a terrible war. The forest is infested with beasts that seek out and kill humans. Jashion hadn't heard or seen John. They'd been around that area for a while so that he could recover from his injuries and pass through to here. I just don't see how John made it. And, if he did. Why hasn't he come back? I'm really sorry, Sarah. It really hurts. I feel it's so much my fault. I was just a foolish kid. I felt so confined and wanted a bigger adventure. I filled his head with this madness. He was the one that always kept me grounded. I wished I'd done more to keep him here."

Sarah gave Kevin a hug. Kevin had worn a brave face for so long. The look on his face conveyed his sorrow and guilt.

"Kevin, thank you for talking with me. I've had thoughts like that, but I couldn't put them into words. Somehow, I feel like me being here is helping him. It's silly. It's all I can do..."

Kevin looked like he wanted to say more, but hesitated to do so. Sarah was perceptive. Sarah looked at him, tilting her head to the side.

Kevin looked away and said, "If John does ever come back he is going to KILL me."

Sarah looked at him astounded.

"There's talk, Sarah. People are starting to wonder..."

"What?"

"When you're...um..."

She looked at him strangely.

"Um...when you're going to be ready to...um...be back on the market."

Sarah sat back. "What? What are you talking about? Back on the market? What are you saying?"

"Sorry," Kevin said sheepishly.

"I don't understand," she said, but she was starting to.

"You're a cute little chickadee. You've been off the market since you've been on it, 'cause John locked you up right from the get-go. But guys are wonderin', is Sarah off limits? I've been getting queried."

"Who?"

"Woah, I can't reveal my sources."

Sarah gave him a smirk and jabbed him in the ribs.

"You're a trouble maker," she said, allowing herself a little chuckle. "Thanks for being cool."

"It's true, I am cool. But I'm not just messin' with ya."

Sarah shook her head.

"I'll tell you one, 'cause I don't really like him."

Sarah tilted her head.

"Jimmy."

"Jimmy Smithy?"

"Yep."

"He talked to you?"

"Na. Jimmy wouldn't talk to me. He talked to Maryanne. He's always had a thing for Maryanne. But I'm not going anywhere, so she's definitely NOT on the market."

Sarah smiled. "Oh, is that so...I'll have to..."

"You won't say a word," said Kevin seriously.

"Are you going to make it official?" said Sarah slyly.

Kevin hummed, feigning disinterest.

"I see. I'm glad. So if Jimmy's got a thing for Maryanne..."

"He's got to move on, and he is."

"Jimmy Smithy," she said and rolled her eyes. "I don't think John would kill you, I think he would laugh hysterically."

"Yeah, he would. But he'd also kill me."

"You'd deserve it."

"True, many times over."

"What does Maryanne say?"

"Not bad, good way to break the ice. Let the more eligible bachelors know you're back on the market."

"Sounds like her. Why's she not here?"

"I came on my own. I knew I'd stick my foot in my mouth and preferred that she not be there when I did it. I don't want her to stop kissing me."

Sarah chuckled.

"I don't know," she said and her sad countenance returned.

"We want you back, Sarah. We've lost John and it's horrible. But, we're ready to have you back."

Sarah nodded and smiled. "Okay."

"Jimmy Smithy..." said Kevin shaking his head.

Sarah pushed him off the ledge. He went through the waterfall and with agility turned his drop into a dive, swam to the other side, hopped out and waved to Sarah. She waved back. She wasn't ready to leave just yet.

⌘⌘⌘

A little hike and a picnic, Kevin, Maryanne, Sarah, and Jimmy started off in the early afternoon. Sarah felt very awkward. Jimmy was nice and gentle. He'd grown up and was attractive in his own way. Sarah didn't mind his company. When they sat down to eat, Kevin kept giving Sarah teasing looks. Sarah did her best to ignore them. Maryanne kept rolling her eyes at Kevin. Jimmy was none the wiser, until Sarah couldn't hold back any longer; she started to chuckle right after Jimmy made a comment, a comment that wasn't funny. Jimmy looked at her awkwardly.

"Sorry," said Sarah.

Maryanne punched Kevin and Kevin doubled over laughing. Jimmy turned red and looked away.

Maryanne saved the day. "Let's get dessert out. Jimmy what do you want, apple or pumpkin pie."

"Which did Sarah make," said Jimmy, after a moments consideration.

"Apple," said Maryanne.

"Okay, then I'll take apple," he said.

"Bad choice," said Maryanne. "Sarah knows nothing about making pies."

Sarah looked up and opened her mouth wide. She tossed an acorn that she'd been fiddling with in her hands. Maryanne had looked down at the pies and didn't see it coming. It hit her square on the forehead and bounced off. Sarah's eyes widened. Maryanne looked up with an evil eye. The next moment, Maryanne got up and so did Sarah. Maryanne chased Sarah into a nearby prairie. She caught up and started tickling Sarah.

"Let's get 'em," said Kevin.

Jimmy looked shocked.

But off they ran towards the women. Kevin began tickling Maryanne mercilessly and Maryanne shrieked in delight. Jimmy tickled Sarah gently and Sarah gave him a nudge in the gut. Then they sat down to watch the show. Maryanne wasn't going to give up without a fight. Soon she was tickling Kevin. Kevin was happy to let her get the better of him. Sarah and Jimmy looked on smiling and laughing. Jimmy put his arm on Sarah's shoulder. Sarah let him.

Chapter 27

Jashion had lived in the promise land for over a year. It was everything that he had hoped for. It was beautiful, peaceful, and the people were so kind. In short order, when it was discovered who he was and where he had come from, he was taken in. He soon received a live-in working opportunity with the Brown's, Kevin's family. Jashion helped look after the stables. Jashion had not spent much time around horses before. He was at first haunted by the horrible memory of his father, drunken, being trampled by a frightened horse during a thunderstorm. Compared to the other beasts he'd interacted with in his lifetime, getting settled in with horses was no big deal. He enjoyed taking them on long rides throughout the promise land. He enjoyed Kevin's company and rode out with him whenever they could.

Most of the time, however, Kevin was with his preferred companion, Maryanne. For Kevin, Jashion and his stories satisfied any lingering curiosities that he had about the world outside his mountains. Jashion's stories seemed unbelievable, but Jashion was so genuine, and his scars corroborated so perfectly with his stories. Kevin liked Jashion very much and considered him his closest friend besides Maryanne, at least his closest friend still there.

In the past, every land that Jashion had entered he had entered with Aiden. This time he came alone. The contrast couldn't be more apparent. When Aiden arrived anywhere, the place was never the same again. Here, Jashion created a tiny wave, like a pebble being dropped in a clear blue lake. The ripples carried for a short time and then it was settled back to normal, like nothing had ever happened. This was how it was in the promise land, and Jashion liked that.

Jashion was a tall, strong, and handsome man. The young ladies had certainly taken notice. Jashion enjoyed the subtle flirtations and the social invites. He had many acquaintances and found the company delightful. Nothing romantic had yet taken off, but he did have his eye on one girl. She was a subtler beauty than was Myrtle or Siccly. Still, there was something about her. The problem was, she wouldn't give him the time of day. In fact, if he ever smiled at her or tried to say, 'hello,' she would turn away from him. He would have loved to talk with her, but her body language made it clear that she was not interested. Jashion admired Sarah Peningham from a distance.

Sarah's romance with Jimmy Smithy was short lived. She enjoyed his company. Liked to walk and hold hands with him. She found his embrace pleasant and she liked kissing again. Still, she found herself, even in his company, longing for John. Sometimes when Jimmy was talking to her she found herself lost in thoughts and memories of him. Whether John was alive or not was immaterial. If, when with Jimmy, her heart was still with John, then Jimmy was not the one for her. As Jimmy began to draw closer, Sarah knew it was time to say goodbye. Things were still amicable between them. The romance, however, was over. Jimmy had moved on too.

Sarah was unaware of the indifference she showed to Jashion. She was perfectly aware of him. She often stopped by the Brown's with Maryanne and he was, of course, there. As far as she was concerned, the feelings were mutual. The most painful moment of her life, since watch John disappear, was watching Jashion emerge from the pool and realizing that it was not her love. The heartbreak was so unbearable that she became numb and suppressed the pain deeply. She couldn't completely avoid the occasional reminders of that moment, which occurred every time she laid eyes on Jashion; but something inside her pushed him away from her. It was pain avoidance and not unkindness that led her to do this. This day she would be unable to avoid him, though she had never consciously considered the reality.

Jashion had thought on it, though, many times, and today he couldn't get it off of his mind. He, like Sarah, was busily readying himself for Kevin and Maryanne's wedding, taking place in a matter of hours. Of course, Sarah was the bridesmaid. Jashion was the stand-in best man. Jashion would escort Sarah, her arm through his, just behind the bride and groom. When the honorary dancing began, she would be his partner. Other opportunities may present themselves too. He was both excited and fearful at the prospects. Sarah had suppressed any consideration of these eventualities.

⌘⌘⌘

Maryanne looked stunning, both radiant and elegant, beautiful without comparison. Kevin nudged Jashion and indicated that he should look over at her when she entered. Jashion smiled and nodded looking back over at his friend.

"Who's the man?" said Kevin to Jashion with a wink.

Jashion had his eye on Sarah, without trying to stare. Her charms were captivating him. Sarah's eyes were on Maryanne; she wore a lovely smile, but there was something deep and distant in her eyes. She had not yet looked over or acknowledged Jashion. In a matter of moments, she would be next to him. His heart beat faster.

Maryanne made her way to Kevin and primed herself a bit, swaying and tilting, drawing the attention of herself to her love, hoping to have his eyes upon her. Kevin happily obliged. She had created the effect that she hoped for and looked up at Kevin and smiled sweetly. Kevin's expression indicated more than sweetness. Maryanne narrowed her eyes and gave him the look, then showed him the appropriate expression again; this time he complied.

Jashion stood in the appropriate position, just behind Kevin. Sarah was still standing apart while looking off dreamily. Maryanne caught Sarah's eye and indicated with her head for her to come and take her place. The look in her eye showed that she'd been caught off guard. She hastened forward with her eyes averted from Jashion's. She took his arm lightly and mechanically. Sarah stared ahead, still not giving Jashion eye contact. This would not do. Jashion pressed her arm a little against his side and leaned gently, bumping into her lightly. Sarah turned to look at him with a look of wonderment in her eyes. Jashion smiled broadly and pleasantly at her.

Sarah was forced to look into his eyes.

She did not look away.

There was something in *his* eyes. Something beautiful, something kind, there was pain, there was experience, there was heartache...there was love.

Sarah began to study his face. He was remarkably handsome. But, there were scars. As she continued to look, she was reminded of John—not in an unpleasant way. Instead, it was something about holding a powerful man's arm and looking up into his beautiful and adoring face that enchanted her.

Between the ceremony and the celebration, Sarah and Jashion were again apart. Sarah could not stop thinking about him, how he looked, how he felt. Again, she was reminded of John, but when she thought on John she saw Jashion's face. *He's so like him*, she thought. And yet he wasn't. John's face,

Jashion's face, John's eyes, Jashion's eyes, John's smile, Jashion's smile, they were so similar...and yet they weren't.

Sarah gazed over at Jashion, he smiled at her. She thought to look away, yet he beckoned her to look on. She looked on and so did he.

It was time for the honorary dance. Jashion walked over and offered her his hand. She took it...that feeling. She'd felt this feeling before. His build was so powerful, she felt fully and completely protected in his arms. They danced, they smiled, they continued to study each other's face, each other's soul. Sarah felt like she had felt with John when they first danced. It was so warm, so peaceful, so wonderful. But, it wasn't that she was reminded of how she once felt. She was feeling it. It wasn't John, it wasn't a memory, or a reawakening; no, it was Jashion. She felt how she felt because of the man she was with. He brought these feelings out and joy swept over her.

They embraced after the dance. His heart was beating out of his chest.

From that point on Jashion and Sarah were together. For Sarah, it was more than the joy of being in a loving relationship. She had experienced some of this with Jimmy and it had helped to camouflage the bitter pain she felt in being away from John. With Jashion there was much more. For the first time in over a year she had been set free; free from the unrelenting torture of loving a person that she could not be with. Her love for John had been laid to rest by her love for Jashion. She loved Jashion, she was loved by Jashion, and she was complete.

⌘⌘⌘

It had been months since even a passing thought of John had entered into Sarah's mind. Jashion and Sarah spent every possible moment together.

Jashion was also busy building a home near their special pool. Oh, how they loved their pool and the lovely waterfall.

When it was completed he gave Sarah a tour. She approved and was delighted. Jashion was proud. He took her to the pool and they went for a swim, climbing to their perch. Jashion proposed, Sarah accepted and they kissed until sunset.

⌘⌘⌘

Mrs. Peningham had long been preparing for Sarah's wedding. The dress had been made, the celebration planned. Mr. and Mrs. Peningham liked Jashion very much.

Such a lovely day in the late fall was their wedding day. It had been unseasonable warm that fall. The leaves still held much of their green, but then the shades of autumn began to sprinkle in. Sarah was as lovely as could be, her blue eyes sparkled, her lips painted red, and her bright countenance shown. Mrs. Peningham smiled brightly and squeezed Mr. Peningham's hand when they kissed.

⌘⌘⌘

A ray of sunlight penetrated the curtain and settled on Jashion's closed eyes. Jashion shifted in bed and felt the warm soft body of his lovely bride next to him. A feeling of joy overtook him. Jashion gazed over at Sarah. She slept peacefully, her back was towards him. He looked at her soft blond hair over her neck that nestled gently on her back. She held her cover up to her, but her shoulder was exposed from behind. Jashion studied the white skin of her shoulder, mesmerized by her, in love with her, happy and complete. The ray of sunlight found his eyes again. Jashion moved and reached his arm over and held his wife, kissing her gently on the cheek. Even in sleep having Jashion's strong arm encircle her entirely, brought Sarah a feeling of complete peace and protection. She purred softly in his arms. Jashion had found the promise land.

Chapter 28

John was all in. The more that Aiden warned him, the more that he gave him an out, the more that John was sure he wanted to do this.

Aiden had studied the flight of the dragon back to its lair. Getting all the way to the lair was probably impossible, but they could get close. It would take months, and they would have to be prepared. There was certainly no room for error.

Rams and mountain goats were occasionally visible fairly high up the mountains. They would provide meat, and it meant that there must be some water, and some vegetation available. The climb itself would be treacherous, they'd need to nourish themselves.

When not honing their skills, hunting, or sleeping, they wound cords—long and powerful. It was not certain that they would have materials to make cords as they ascended up the mountain. They each had a sword, they each had a bow and many arrows. They made several spears. It was time to climb.

More than once they started to ascend and found themselves stuck. They would descend and try from a new location. Hunger, thirst, and fatigue were their regular companions. At times the sun baked them unrelentingly and they could find no shelter. At other times the rain would bash against them without mercy and they worried whether they could keep from slipping to their doom. Still, with the rain came water and for a time their thirst was abated.

The goats and the sheep were no fools. The conditions provided such little opportunity for concealment for the hunters and climbers. Still, Aiden was the best and John was hardly a lick behind him. They managed. As if it were somehow possible, these men became stronger and more powerful, the more they endured.

Dromreign had not left its lair in well over a year since it had annihilated Agedon. Aiden's calculation was that it must not be long before it struck out again. He wanted to be ready for the dragon. They pressed on.

Eventually they reached the highest plateau that they could. It was the spot that he'd picked out many moons before. The lair was in sight, perhaps within reach of his best flung arrow. Aiden and John settled and made ready their weapons and trap.

Another month went by before there was a stir. But Aiden's calculations were correct. The beast had recovered, awakened, and was ready to eat.

John was in awe as he watched the great dragon fly from its lair. Its darkness and ferocity mesmerized him. Then came the stench, washing down the mountainside. It was putrefying and John felt sick. He held his breath, then coughed and sputtered. Aiden indicated for him to remain silent. They watched Dromreign disappear over the tree tops below. When it was gone, they hastened to prepare for its return.

⌘⌘⌘

Myrtle had long since stopped wearing red in honor of Jashion. In fact, this custom had lasted less than a week. Within a month she had snared a new man. But Myrtle was different.

She had grown in depth and understanding, at least a little. This man did not weary of her delights. She found him equally charming and they were soon engaged and then married. Nine months later they were the proud parents of a bouncing baby boy. Oh, how Myrtle loved her son. Motherhood suited her splendidly. Myrtle was back in pre-pregnancy shape within weeks of delivery. Mirinda especially, and often times Tasha, joined with Myrtle and the baby for strolls around the gardens of Cardsten. Myrtle was always dressed to the nines as she pushed her pram and looked around, and smiled for all to see.

Myrtle also loved to look at her baby boy. He had Myrtle's eyes and Myrtle's smile. She would gaze into his eyes and smile for hours while the baby mimicked and did the same. To Myrtle, it was even better than staring into the mirror at herself. Mirinda and Tasha were nearly as mesmerized with the child as was Myrtle. The baby, like Myrtle soaked up every ounce of attention.

Mirinda had not looked at or considered another man since Aiden had left. She had given her heart completely and fully to him. She never wondered if he had died in battle. She knew him too well and did not think that possible. Why had he not returned? That was simple enough: Dromreign remained on the land. When Dromreign was dead, Aiden would return, and they would live in love and joy. How long this would take did not worry her. Mirinda was complete. And Myrtle's baby boy brought her immeasurable joy.

Tasha and Daxton had an extended honeymoon, keeping Daxton away from Cards business for some time. Cards worried that with Terrence and then Aiden behaving treacherously, that Daxton would be looked on with suspicion. Cards calculated incorrectly. With the remainder of the army of Cardsten's return and the spy's telling of the destruction of Agedon, the people understood everything very clearly. Aiden led Cardsten's army to defeat Agedon, and Agedon was defeated; in fact, completely annihilated. Dromreign, was settled because its foe in the land,

Agedon, was gone, and was living peacefully with the people. Cardsten and all others were safe. Cardsten had done it again: brought peace and prosperity to the world. What fools, those of Agedon had been. The dragon worshipers were satisfied with this reality.

The marriage of Tasha to Daxton brought peace to a troubled soul. Daxton loved Tasha, he loved Cards, he loved his business, and his life. He was heartbroken about Terrence. Tasha, too, had lost Tira and they mourned together. Still, business was business, and with time Daxton was back at Cards' side. With Daxton's youth and exuberance, and the experience and training of Mr. Cards, Cardsten was bustling like never before. Other than the sorrows in his heart, Daxton couldn't have been living in a happier time or in a happier place. He had chosen well, and smiled upon his fortune.

So strange it was hearing the horns sound and Cardsten being alerted to danger. Cards looked at Daxton across the table. Mr. and Mrs. Cards were enjoying a wonderful dinner and night out with Tasha and Daxton. Daxton peered out a nearby window.

"Go," said Cards. Tasha and Mrs. Cards followed Daxton with their eyes out of the restaurant.

Daxton checked his sources and confirmed that Dromreign was sighted and flying towards Cardsten, "...with immeasurable speed!" explained the man.

Fiery arrows sailed from the walls. The dragon had not penetrated these walls before. Daxton wondered what this could be. Shouting commenced from the men on the walls. Daxton looked up and saw men leaping to their death from the top. He watched with horror, and then a tremendous sound, and the earth under his feet trembled. Dromreign flew directly into the wall at full speed. The wall shattered and crumbled as the fierce dragon tumbled within, landing upon its belly and shaking its head. The wall to the house of Cards had fallen.

The dragon struggled to its feet and let out a bellow filled with smoke, and fire, and fury. The citizens of Cardsten ran and screamed in pandemonium. Dromreign gathered itself and took to the air within what was left of the city wall. Cardsten was no Agedon, filled with wooden buildings, just asking for an inferno. No, the walls of these buildings were of stone and concrete. Dromreign scorched the scurrying masses and then proceeded to tear open the buildings. When the dragon created an opening, it would belch its fire therein. Agedon had taken its strength some time ago. It had rested with purpose, knowing full well what it would take to bring down this city. It was a night and a day and another night before Cardsten's final destruction was accomplished. But the beast required no rest. It'd rested a long time. There was plenty of flesh to consume. Dromreign allowed itself to walk upon the grounds of the city, and slowly and methodically consumed all it could. When the dragon was satisfied that no survivors remained it took to the air. Any arrows that had grazed the beast were defended by its scales. Dromreign was exhausted but unharmed. It was careful not to allow its weak spot, the one created by Terrence, to be exposed. With tired and sun scorched eyes Dromreign took to flight and returned to its lair.

Chapter 29

Aiden was surprised that the dragon hadn't already returned. He and John had made every possible preparation. They had even killed a ram and ate it raw. They'd not had cooked meat since they began to ascend the mountain.

"Aiden," said John. "You've been preparing for this moment for a lifetime. What will you do next?"

Aiden looked out at the horizon, scanning the sky for Dromreign. "There is this woman. A woman of Cardsten. Her name is Mirinda. She is the most beautiful, most perfect woman in the world. I will return and marry her. And we will raise children and be happy."

"Tell me more of this Mirinda," said John, pleased that Aiden was opening up.

"I've explained her already," said Aiden. "She is feminine perfection in every way."

"I see," said John chuckling. "What's she look like? What color is her hair, her eyes..."

Aiden looked over the way dreamily. "Ah Mirinda, with her hair as black as night, and her dark brown eyes, and her olive skin, there is nothing more lovely in this world that eyes can behold."

John could tell that Aiden was truly affected.

"And you?" asked Aiden, after some time.

"What will you do next?"

"I shall return...to the promise land." John searched Aiden for a reaction. There was none.

"Did you know that I was from there?"

Aiden smiled and nodded.

"A man who knew nothing about this world, who was found beaten to within an inch of his life, near the pool in the dark forest—I had a hunch."

John smiled.

"Why'd you leave?"

John looked out over the forest below. "This is why. What we're doing. I had an itch that I couldn't scratch within the safety of those mountainous walls. Something called me—what we're about to do. I've had the time of my life, these past few months. When we lay that beast to rest I will return...to my Sarah."

"Sarah," Aiden said with a smile. "Let's hear of your Sarah."

"I do not claim her to be the most beautiful woman in the promise land, but she is the most extraordinarily."

"Who's the most beautiful then?"

"That would be Janice."

"What was wrong with Janice?"

"Nothing. Nothing is wrong with Janice. She is like your Mirinda, only blond with blue eyes."

"What happened with her?"

"I let her go. She was as amazing. But, Sarah was more precious to me, and I chose Sarah."

"Tell me about Sarah."

"She also is blond with blue eyes, short hair that's straight. But when you look at her face, when you look in her eyes, it's like peering into the deepest ocean—into a heavenly abyss. There is no end, like standing on the end of the world and staring into eternity. There is such light, such glory, such divinity. No one in the world is like my Sarah, not Janice, I dare say, not even your Mirinda."

Aiden smiled.

"So, why'd you leave her?"

John was silent for some time. "Why'd you leave Mirinda?"

Aiden nodded knowingly.

⌘⌘⌘

Aiden sat up strait. A black dot on the horizon emerged. It took John several minutes to see it, where Aiden pointed. They were as ready as they would ever be, the battle was about to begin.

John wrapped the array of cords around his wrist after ensuring that his weapons were ready. He sat down and made sure that Aiden was in sight.

Aiden climbed to the highest spot possible and made ready his bow. Aiden calculated and re-calculated the likely path of Dromreign's ascension to its lair.

All of the pieces were in place, just as Aiden had planned. Dromreign would be at the end of his long journey home. Its eyes would be struggling in the sun. It would be at the very end of its flight and anticipating rest and solitude in its lair. Aiden felt sure that the dragon had not rested the previous day and so its fatigue would be intense. Aiden perched where he would have a clear shot at the exposed flesh near the dragon's breast. He watched and waited.

The red of Dromreign's eyes became visible and Aiden could see the fatigue. The dragon did not search its surroundings. Rather, it looked single-mindedly towards the lair. Aiden looked at John. John was fully alert and awaiting the moment. Aiden pulled back the string slowly.

Aiden let out his breath, waited a moment and let go. The arrow sailed true and struck Dromreign in the center of its missing scale. The beast screeched, doubled up and flung its head towards the arrows direction, spotting Aiden.

John was up and pulling on the cords with all his might engaging the snare that the dragon would become trapped in. All of Aiden's calculations were correct. Dromreign, looking towards Aiden, became tangled in the cords and crashed into the mountainside. Aiden continued to shoot at its exposed flesh and continued to make impact. Blood began to ooze from Dromreign's side.

Dromreign, though dazed, struggled to right itself. The beast looked towards Aiden and let out a blast of flame. Aiden, expecting it, sheltered himself but felt the heat. The hair on his arms was singed.

After wrapping the cords around a boulder to keep them taut, John went for his spears. Hoping to do what he had learned that Terrance had done, he threw the spears at an angle trying to wedge them between scales. His throws were good, but they continued to bounce off the scales, Dromreign appearing unaffected. The stench that affected John so much when the dragon departed, filled John's nostrils anew. It sickened him, but his adrenaline rush allowed him to overcome. John rushed towards the beast, hoping that at closer range he could breach the scaly barrier. One throw had such luck. It penetrated into the dragon's flesh and the beast reeled and turned its head looking for its other foe.

Dromreign flapped its wings in hopes of freeing itself. It began to dislodge. Aiden shot at its wings. Here was another place of weakness. The arrows penetrated the wings and began to open up gaps and gashes. The beast folded its wings and let out more bellowing breath.

John continued to attack the penetrated scale. Soon another spear lodged within and the scale came off. Throwing with his all he continued to send spears into Dromreign's flesh, but they did not penetrate deeply and into the dragon's core.

Aiden saw fear in Dromreign's eyes. The beast struggled against the cords, and shuttered with each hit. Still, the great hunters were not able to deliver mortal wounds. All arrows and spears were unable to reach its insides. John continued to inch closer to the beast, sword in hand. Aiden filled the air with arrows aimed at the beast's weak spot, which kept Dromreign's focus towards Aiden, and allowed John to come upon him.

John reared back his sword overhead as he came upon Dromreign, and with all his might sunk the sword into Dromreign's flesh. The dragon screeched with all its might leaning its head back and throwing flames high into the air. The sword had sunk in much deeper, but not enough to deliver a death blow. John wriggled it out, readying himself for another lunge into the wounded flesh. As he lifted his sword above his head, Dromreign loosed its tail. The dragon swung its tail with all its might towards John and knocked John in the back and into the dragon's side—his sword still in the air. Johns back was badly lacerated and several ribs were cracked or broken.

Aiden, seeing John in trouble, left his perch and moved toward the dragon, sword in hand.

The dragons tail moved back and John was no longer pinned between the tail and the beasts bloody flesh. But he could no longer wield the sword or throw the spear. Every movement sent pain through his back. He dropped the sword and slowly backed away, each breath causing agony. John dropped to his knees. He saw the flesh exposed and the sword near it on the ground. What was he waiting for? If he didn't attack then, he might be done for.

John struggled back to his feet and held his breath. He approached the dragon and bent to retrieve his sword. The pain nearly caused him to pass out. Dromreign craned his neck, back in John's direction. John's blurred eyes focused on the wound his sword had created.

Dromreign hesitated briefly, knowing that this scorch would also scorch its own wounded flesh. Then the dragon let loose and a ball of fire engulfed John. The dragon screeched from the pain caused by its own breath upon its own exposed and wounded flesh. John was no longer, and Dromreign laid its head upon the ground in pain and agony, struggling to keep consciousness.

Aiden was upon it, sword in hand and ready to repeat what John had done to its other weak point. Dromreign shuttered with the first blow. And then trembled with the second. The sword dug deeper and neared the beasts heart.

Dromreign couldn't bring itself to inflict another fiery wound upon its own flesh. Instead, it swung its tail around to the other side in hopes of hitting Aiden. The swing was weaker, but effective, nonetheless. Aiden's arm was broken and he stumbled off balance. The ledge Aiden was on was steep and he fell over twenty feet, breaking both legs on impact.

Unable to move, Aiden looked up at Dromreign in agony. The dragon's head lay on the ground, its eyes closed. But, the beast still breathed. A quarter of an hour passed. Both warriors laying, unable to mount a further attack. This fight would end in a stalemate. Eventually, Dromreign opened its eyes and scanned the area. Its eyes caught Aiden lying broken on the rock below. For some time, these arch rivals looked at each other. Then, Dromreign raised its head and gave Aiden a nod. Aiden looked on in agony and awe.

Dromreign mustered its strength. It curled up tight and then stretched out with all its might, breaking the cords. It shook and gathered itself, trembling upon its feet. It flapped its wings and tested itself for flight. The wings were too tattered from Aiden's arrows. Slowly and painstakingly the beast clawed itself up the mountain, and into its lair.

Chapter 30

Aiden watched Dromreign disappear and then all was silent. At first Aiden was emotionless and dumbfounded, his mind unable to conjure a coherent thought. In all his wildest dreams, in all his plans, his imaginations, expectations, hopes, fears, he never once considered that both he and the dragon would be alive after they met. Yet somehow both he and Dromreign were both alive, if only hanging on to life by a thread. The beast, with belly full, would hibernate for months, even years, all the while healing and strengthening.

Aiden had no such possibilities. He was alone. He was isolated, broken, bruised, immobile, in excruciating pain, with no plan or concept of what he could or should do next. To stay on the ledge that broke his fall would mean a slow, agonizing, horrible death. But even the slightest effort at movement shot such extreme pain that he dared not attempt it.

Slowly his mind returned. He ascertained his breaks, and his gashes, and his contusions. He looked up again, towards the place of battle. There he saw the charred remains of John. Emotions began to fill Aiden. Tears welled and then spilled upon the dry and dusty ground. Aiden cried for John. He cried for Terrence. Aiden cried for Marcus, and the men of Cardsten who called him general. Such death, such destruction, such potential for life and for all things good. Those whom he loved who wanted life, were gone. Yet Dromreign, who only wanted death, lay breathing in the sweet breath of life all the while turning the surrounding air foul. Nothing about that was right; there was nothing that he could do about it.

If Aiden had known he would have wept for Mirinda, for Daxton, for all the others Dromreign had finished off just that morning. Those tears would be saved for another day, a day that would fill his breast with as much sickness as he felt then.

No mortal man should have survived the mountainside in the condition that Aiden was in. Somehow, he did. Aiden set his own bones as soon as he could muster the courage and the strength. He hit a goat with a stone and inched his way towards it. He fed upon its flesh until it was too rotting. It rained just in time for him to avoid complete dehydration. The nights became colder and at times he shivered until the break of day. There was a short phase of fever and delirium with no herbs or medicines to ease it. But this helped the time go by quicker. There was nothing he could do until his arm and legs were mended. Another goat was killed when he reached the point of starvation again. This time his arm and legs held up better as he moved towards it.

Eventually he could climb and down he went. It had taken months to ascend. He didn't have months to descend. Winter would be upon him, and he would perish from hypothermia, if nothing else. But, if he successfully harnessed gravity, it could be his friend rather than foe. He felt fortunate that the winter came late that year.

⌘⌘⌘

For several years, Aiden was a hermit and a nomad. Cardsten, or the ruins thereof, were first visited. He wandered the ruins for some days. He left with a heavy heart.

Aiden considered returning to his village. He could never quite bring himself to returning, broken and defeated. He considered many places, but each did not settle with him. Eventually, the loneliness of solitude overtook him. He'd tired of the hunt. Tengeer became his destination. He had a hunch that Dromreign had left it unharmed.

It was a lovely spring day, the morning that he set off. Some memories filled his mind. He thought on the men, then boys, who set off with him to conquer the world. He'd felt so invincible at the time. He didn't feel this way any longer. He sorrowed for those boys of Tengeer who were lost. It would be his duty to explain their fate. Some degree of survivor's guilt had plagued him for many years.

Off in the distance, from the direction of Tengeer, three figures strode towards him. Aiden eyed them as he walked. Eventually he could see three teenagers, a white girl and two black boys. Aiden continued towards them.

"Aiden, it's ye, it is!" shouted the girl and set off running towards him.

Aiden paused and watched all three run in his direction. The girl threw her arms around him and the boys stood with bright smiles on their faces.

"It's Aiden. Ye knows Aiden, don't ye?" she said.

The boys nodded affirmatively. Aiden was a legend to that day, in Tengeer.

Aiden searched his mind. The girls voice was familiar but neither her face nor the boys were.

"Me's Jemma," she said exuberantly, when he hadn't said anything yet. "These is me brothers."

A light went on in Aiden's head. "Jemma," he exclaimed and embraced her back. It hadn't seemed that long since he'd left Tengeer. "You're all grown up."

Jemma glowed.

"We're seeking the promise land, we are," she said. "Ye know the ways, don't ye? We've had refugees of late. There villages is been attacked by the wicked dragon, they's is."

A pit filled Aiden's stomach.

"For a long time, it seemed as if the dragon was gone, but it ain't. It is back and we want to go where it can't get us, we do."

Aiden looked at Jemma, searching her eyes. They had always had such life in them. Even when she'd just survived the destruction of Dargaer and the grip of the anaconda.

Aiden smiled. "Jemma, I know the way. I'd be happy to take you and your brothers there. Jemma, I think I would like to go and stay there with you, also."

Jemma smiled and grabbed his hand as they walked.

⌘⌘⌘

At the pool, in the promise land, sat a beautiful woman with her feet in the water. She had a large bouquet of wild flowers beside her. She methodically formed the wild flowers into a wreath. When it was complete, she placed the wreath into the water and watched it slowly pass to the other side.

Janice was as lovely as ever, but was lonely. She had never gotten over John Bennett. Until then, she'd hoped that he'd return. This was her final memorial to him. She was ready to move on.

She looked at the water, so clear, so blue, so peaceful. It seemed as if she could look in all the way to its depths. She sat there watching. This day would be a new day for her. *The water seems so still, so perfectly still today,* Janice thought to herself.

About the Author:

Dane Bagley studied philosophy at Brigham Young University and received his bachelor of science in physiological optics from the University of Alabama at Birmingham in 1999. He received his Doctor of Optometry degree from the University of Alabama at Birmingham School of Optometry in 2001. He is the owner and doctor at Perfect Optical Eyecare Center in Huntsville, Alabama, where he continues to practice optometry. He resides with his wife, two daughters, and two sons in Madison, Alabama. He enjoys sports, games, saltwater reef keeping, snorkeling, scuba diving, and serving in his church.

Summary:

A menacing dragon will stop at nothing until it has destroyed the human race. Some want to attack it, to destroy it, before it destroys them. Others seek the protection of walls or of armies in hopes of survival. Rumor has it that there is a land, a land where the dragon and its ilk are not able to penetrate, to spread their destruction; a land of peace, prosperity, and protection. A group sets out in hopes of adventure, romance, safety, and peace. Will they find that in their world? Or, must they seek the promise land.

Works by the Dane Bagley:

Fear and Aggression
2012

Fear and Aggression, second edition by Tate Publishing
2014